ok!

W9-CEU-708

HEARTBREAKER

JULIE GARWOOD

HEARTBREAKER

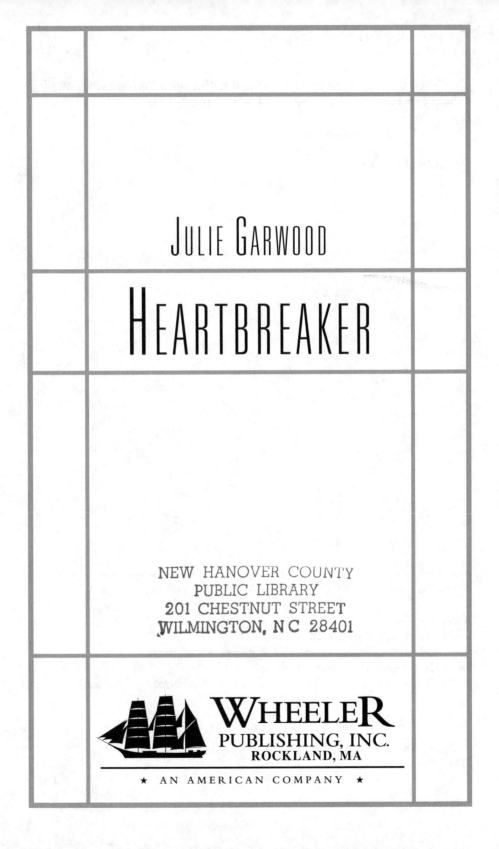

WHEELER
PUBLISHING, INC.
ROCKLAND, MA

★ AN AMERICAN COMPANY ★

Published in Large Print by arrangement with Pocket Books, a division of Simon & Schuster, Inc. in the United States and Canada.

Wheeler Large Print Book Series.

Set in 16 pt Plantin.

Library of Congress Cataloging-in-Publication Data

Garwood, Julie.
   Heartbreaker / Julie Garwood.
     p. (large print) cm.(Wheeler large print book series)
   ISBN 1-56895-918-4 (hardcover)
   1. Government investigators—Fiction. 2. Psychopaths—Fiction.
3. Clergy—Fiction.
I. Title. II. Series

[PS3557.A8427 H4   2000]
813'.54—dc21
                                          00-041674
                                                CIP

For my son, Gerry

"What lies behind us and what lies before
us
are tiny matters compared to what lies
within us."
—Ralph Waldo Emerson

May your unbounded enthusiasm bring
you great joy in your accomplishments;
May your tenacious spirit lead you
to fight the good fight;
May your heart always bring you
love in return.
Gerry, I'm so proud of you!

CHAPTER

1

It was hotter than hell inside the confessional. A thick black curtain, dusty with age and neglect, covered the narrow opening from the ceiling of the box to the scarred hardwood floor, blocking out both the daylight and the air.

It was like being inside a coffin someone had absentmindedly left propped up against the wall, and Father Thomas Madden thanked God he wasn't claustrophobic. He was rapidly becoming miserable though. The air was heavy and ripe with mildew, making his breathing as labored as when he was back at Penn State running that last yard to the goalposts with the football tucked neatly in his arm. He hadn't minded the pain in his lungs then, and he certainly didn't mind it now. It was all simply part of the job.

The old priests would tell him to offer his discomfort up to God for the poor souls in purgatory. Tom didn't see any harm in doing that, even though he wondered how his own misery was going to relieve anyone else's.

He shifted position on the hard oak chair, fidgeting like a choirboy at Sunday practice. He could feel the sweat dripping down the sides of his face and neck into his cassock. The long black robe was soaked through with perspiration, and he sincerely doubted he smelled at all like the hint of Irish Spring soap he'd used in the shower this morning.

The temperature outside hovered between ninety-four and ninety-five in the shade of the rectory porch where the thermostat was nailed to the whitewashed stone wall. The humidity made the heat so oppressive, those unfortunate souls who were forced to leave their air-conditioned homes and venture outside did so with a slow shuffle and a quick temper.

It was a lousy day for the compressor to bite the dust. There were windows in the church, of course, but the ones that could have been opened had been sealed shut long ago in a futile attempt to keep vandals out. The two others were high up in the gold, domed ceiling. They were stained glass depictions of the archangels Gabriel and Michael holding gleaming swords in their fists. Gabriel was looking up toward heaven, a beatified expression on his face, while Michael scowled at the snakes he held pinned down at his bare feet. The colored windows were considered priceless, prayer-inspiring works of art by the congregation, but they were useless in combating the heat. They had been added for decoration, not ventilation.

Tom was a big, strapping man with a seventeen-and-a-half-inch neck left over from his glory days, but he was cursed with baby sensitive skin. The heat was giving him a prickly rash. He hiked the cassock up to his thighs, revealing the yellow and black happy-face boxer shorts his sister, Laurant, had given him, kicked off his paint-splattered Wal-Mart rubber thongs, and popped a piece of Dubble Bubble into his mouth.

An act of kindness had landed him in the sweatbox. While waiting for the test results that would determine if he needed another round of chemotherapy at Kansas University Medical Center, he was a guest of Monsignor McKindry, pastor of Our Lady of Mercy Church. The parish was located in the forgotten sector of Kansas City, several hundred miles south of Holy Oaks, Iowa, where Tom was stationed. The neighborhood had been officially designated by a former mayor's task force as the gang zone. Monsignor always took Saturday afternoon confession, but because of the blistering heat, his advanced age, the broken air conditioner, and a conflict in his schedule— the pastor was busy preparing for his reunion with two friends from his seminary days at Assumption Abbey—Tom had volunteered for the duty. He had assumed he'd sit face-to-face with his penitent in a room with a couple of windows open for fresh air. McKindry, however, bowed to the preferences of his faithful parishioners, who stubbornly clung to the old-fashioned way of hearing confessions, a fact Tom learned only after he'd offered his services, and Lewis, the parish handyman, had directed him to the oven he would sit in for the next ninety minutes.

In appreciation Monsignor had loaned him a thoroughly inadequate, battery-operated fan that one of his flock had put in the collection basket. The thing was no bigger than the size of a man's hand. Tom adjusted the angle of the fan so that the air would blow directly on his face, leaned back against the wall, and began to read the *Holy Oaks Gazette* he'd brought along to Kansas City with him.

He turned to the society page on the back first, because he got such a kick out of it. He glanced over the usual club news and the smattering of announcements—two births, three engagements, and a wedding—and then he found his favorite column, called "About Town." The headline was always the same: the bingo game. The number of people who attended the community center bingo night was reported along with the names of the winners of the twenty-five-dollar jackpots. Interviews with the lucky recipients followed, telling what each of them planned to do with his or her windfall. And there was always a comment from Rabbi David Spears, who organized the weekly event, about what a good time everyone had. Tom was suspicious that the society editor, Lorna Hamburg, secretly had a crush on Rabbi Dave, a widower, and that was why the bingo game was so prominently featured in the paper. The rabbi said the same thing every week, and Tom invariably ribbed him about that when they played golf together on Wednesday afternoons. Since Dave usually beat the socks off him, he didn't mind the teasing, but he did accuse Tom of trying to divert attention from his appalling game.

The rest of the column was dedicated to letting everyone in town know who was entertaining company and what they were feeding them. If the news that week was hard to come by, Lorna filled in the space with popular recipes.

There weren't any secrets in Holy Oaks. The front page was full of news about the proposed town square development and the upcoming one-hundred-year celebration at Assumption Abbey. And there was a nice mention about his sister helping out at the abbey. The reporter called her a tireless and cheerful volunteer and went into some detail describing all the projects she had taken on. Not only was she going to organize all the clutter in the attic for a garage sale, but she was also going to transfer all the information from the old dusty files onto the newly donated computer, and when she had a few minutes to spare, she would be translating the French journals of Father Henri VanKirk, a priest who had died recently. Tom chuckled to himself as he finished reading the glowing testimonial to his sister. Laurant hadn't actually volunteered for any of the jobs. She just happened to be walking past the abbot at the moment he came up with the ideas, and gracious to a fault, she hadn't refused.

By the time Tom finished reading the rest of the *Gazette*, his soaked collar was sticking to his neck. He put the paper on the seat next to him, mopped his brow again, and contemplated closing shop fifteen minutes early.

He gave up the idea almost as soon as it entered his mind. He knew that if he left the confessional early, he'd catch hell from Monsignor, and after the hard day of manual labor he'd put in, he simply wasn't up to a lecture. On the first Wednesday of every third month— Ash Wednesday he silently called it—Tom moved in with Monsignor McKindry, an old, broken-nosed, crackled-skinned Irishman who never missed an opportunity to get as much physical labor as he could possibly squeeze out of his houseguest in seven days. McKindry was crusty and gruff, but he had a heart of gold and a compassionate nature that wasn't compromised by sentimentality. He firmly believed that idle hands were the devil's workshop, especially when the rectory was in dire need of a fresh coat of paint. Hard work, he pontificated, would cure anything, even cancer.

Some days Tom had a hard time remembering why he liked the monsignor so much or felt a kinship with him. Maybe it was because they both had a bit of Irish in them. Or maybe it was because the old man's philosophy, that only a fool cried over spilled milk, had sustained him through more hardships than Job. Tom's battle was child's play compared to McKindry's life.

He would do whatever he could to help lighten McKindry's burdens. Monsignor was looking forward to visiting with his old friends again. One of them was Abbot James

Rockhill, Tom's superior at Assumption Abbey, and the other, Vincent Moreno, was a priest Tom had never met. Neither Rockhill nor Moreno would be staying at Mercy house with McKindry and Tom, for they much preferred the luxuries provided by the staff at Holy Trinity parish, luxuries like hot water that lasted longer than five minutes and central air-conditioning. Trinity was located in the heart of a bedroom community on the other side of the state line separating Missouri from Kansas. McKindry jokingly referred to it as "Our Lady of the Lexus," and from the number of designer cars parked in the church's lot on Sunday mornings, the label was right on the mark. Most of the parishioners at Mercy didn't own cars. They walked to church.

Tom's stomach began to rumble. He was hot and sticky and thirsty. He needed another shower, and he wanted a cold Bud Light. There hadn't been a single taker in all the while he'd been sitting there roasting like a turkey. He didn't think anyone else was even inside the church now, except maybe Lewis, who liked to hide in the cloakroom behind the vestibule and sneak sips of rot whiskey from the bottle in his toolbox. Tom checked his watch, saw he only had a couple of minutes left, and decided he'd had enough. He switched off the light above the confessional and was reaching for the curtain when he heard the swoosh of air the leather kneeler expelled when weight was placed upon it. The sound was followed by a discreet cough from the confessor's cell next to him.

Tom immediately straightened in his chair, took the gum out of his mouth and put it back in the wrapper, then bowed his head in prayer and slid the wooden panel up.

"In the name of the Father and of the Son...," he began in a low voice as he made the sign of the cross.

Several seconds passed in silence. The penitent was either gathering his thoughts or his courage before he confessed his transgressions. Tom adjusted the stole around his neck and patiently continued to wait.

The scent of Calvin Klein's Obsession came floating through the grille that separated them. It was a distinct, heavy, sweet fragrance Tom recognized because his housekeeper in Rome had given him a bottle of the cologne on his last birthday. A little of the stuff went a long way, and the penitent had gone overboard. The confessional reeked. The scent, combined with the smell of mildew and sweat, made Tom feel as though he were trying to breathe through a plastic bag. His stomach lurched and he forced himself not to gag.

"Are you there, Father?"

"I'm here," Tom whispered. "When you're ready to confess your sins, you may begin."

"This is...difficult for me. My last confession was a year ago. I wasn't given absolution then. Will you absolve me now?"

There was an odd, singsong quality to the voice and a mocking tone that put Tom on his guard. Was the stranger simply nervous because it had been such a long time since his last confession, or was he being deliberately irreverent?

"You weren't given absolution?"

"No, I wasn't, Father. I angered the priest. I'll make you angry too. What I have to confess will...shock you. Then you'll become angry like the other priest."

"Nothing you say will shock or anger me," Tom assured him.

"You've heard it all before? Is that it, Father?"

Before Tom could answer, the penitent whispered, "Hate the sin, not the sinner."

The mocking had intensified. Tom stiffened. "Would you like to begin?"

"Yes," the stranger replied. "Bless me, Father, for I will sin."

Confused by what he'd heard, Tom leaned closer to the grille and asked the man to start over.

"Bless me, Father, for I will sin."

"You want to confess a sin you're going to commit?"

"I do."

"Is this some sort of a game or a—"

"No, no, not a game," the man said. "I'm deadly serious. Are you getting angry yet?"

A burst of laughter, as jarring as the sound of gunfire in the middle of the night, shot through the grille.

Tom was careful to keep his voice neutral when he answered. "No, I'm not angry, but

I am confused. Surely you realize you can't be given absolution for sins you're contemplating. Forgiveness is for those who have realized their mistakes and are truly contrite. They're willing to make restitution for their sins."

"Ah, but Father, you don't know what the sins are yet. How can you deny me absolution?"

"Naming the sins doesn't change anything."

"Oh, but it does. A year ago I told another priest exactly what I was going to do, but he didn't believe me until it was too late. Don't make the same mistake."

"How do you know the priest didn't believe you?"

"He didn't try to stop me. That's how I know."

"How long have you been a Catholic?"

"All my life."

"Then you know that a priest cannot acknowledge the sin or the sinner outside of the confessional. The seal of silence is sacred. Exactly how could this other priest have stopped you?"

"He could have found a way. I was...practicing then, and I was cautious. It would have been very easy for him to stop me, so it's his fault, not mine. It won't be easy now."

Tom was desperately trying to make sense out of what the man was saying. Practice? Practice what? And what was the sin the priest could have prevented?

"I thought I could control it," the man said.

"Control what?"

"The craving."

"What was the sin you confessed?"

"Her name was Millicent. A nice, old-fashioned name, don't you think? Her friends called her Millie, but I didn't. I much preferred Millicent. Of course, I wasn't what you would call a friend."

Another burst of laughter pierced the dead air. Tom's forehead was beaded with perspiration, but he suddenly felt cold. This wasn't a prankster. He dreaded what he was going to hear, yet he was compelled to ask.

"What happened to Millicent?"

"I broke her heart."

"I don't understand..."

"What do you think happened to her?" the man demanded, his impatience clear now. "I killed her. It was messy; there was blood everywhere, all over me. I was terribly inexperienced back then. I hadn't perfected my technique. When I went to confession, I hadn't killed her yet. I was still in the planning stage and the priest could have stopped me, but he didn't. I told him what I was going to do."

"Tell me, how could he have stopped you?"

"Prayer," he answered, a shrug in his voice. "I told him to pray for me, but he didn't pray hard enough, now did he? I still killed her. It's a pity, really. She was such a pretty little thing...much prettier than the others."

Dear God, there were other women? How many others?

"How many crimes have you—"

11

The stranger interrupted him. "Sins, Father," he said. "I committed sins, but I might have been able to resist if the priest had helped me. He wouldn't give me what I needed."

"What did you need?"

"Absolution and acceptance. I was denied both."

The stranger suddenly slammed his fist into the grille. Rage that must have been simmering just below the surface erupted full force as he spewed out in grotesque detail exactly what he had done to the poor innocent Millicent.

Tom was overwhelmed and sickened by the horror of it all. Dear God, what should he do? He had boasted he wouldn't be shocked or angered, but nothing could have prepared him for the atrocities the stranger took such delight in describing.

Hate the sin, not the sinner.

"I've gotten a real taste for it," the madman whispered.

"How many other women have you killed?"

"Millicent was the first. There were other infatuations, and when they disappointed me, I had to hurt them, but I didn't kill any of them. After I met Millicent, everything changed. I watched her for a long time and everything about her was...perfect." His voice turned into a snarl as he continued. "But she betrayed me, just like the others. She thought she could play her little games with other men and I wouldn't notice. I couldn't let her torment me that way. I wouldn't," he corrected. "I had to punish her."

He let out a loud, exaggerated sigh and then chuckled. "I killed the little bitch twelve months ago and I buried her deep, real deep. No one's ever going to find her. There's no going back now. No, sirree. I had no idea how thrilling the kill was going to be. I made Millicent beg me for mercy, and she did. By God, she did." He laughed. "She screamed like a pig, and oh, how I loved the sound. I got so excited, more excited than I could ever have imagined was possible, and so I had to make her scream more, didn't I? When I was finished with her, I was bursting with joy. Well, Father, aren't you going to ask me if I'm sorry for my sins?" he taunted.

"No, you aren't contrite."

A suffocating silence filled the confessional. And then, in a serpent's hiss, the voice returned.

"The craving's come back."

Goose bumps covered Tom's arms. "There are people who can—"

"Do you think I should be locked away? I only punish those who hurt me. So you see, I'm not culpable. But you think I'm sick, don't you? We're in confession, Father. You have to tell the truth."

"Yes, I think you're ill."

"Oh, I don't think so. I'm just dedicated."

"There are people who can help you."

"I'm brilliant, you know. It won't be easy to stop me. I study my clients before I take them on. I know everything about their families and their friends. Everything. Yes, it's going

13

to be much harder to stop me now, but this time I've decided to make it more difficult for me. Do you see? I don't want to sin. I really don't." The singsong voice was back.

"Listen to me," Tom pleaded. "Step outside the confessional with me and we'll sit down together and talk this through. I want to help you, if you'll only let me."

"No, I needed help before and I was denied, remember? Give me absolution."

"I will not."

The sigh was long and drawn out. "Very well," he said. "I'm changing the rules this time. You have my permission to tell anyone you want to tell. Do you see how accommodating I can be?"

"It doesn't matter if you give me permission to tell or not, this conversation will remain confidential. The seal of silence must be maintained to protect the integrity of the confessional."

"No matter what I confess?"

"No matter what."

"I demand that you tell."

"Demand all you want, but it won't make any difference. I cannot tell anyone what you have said to me. I won't."

A moment of silence passed and then the stranger began to chuckle. "A priest with scruples. How extraordinary. Hmmm. What a quandary. But don't you fret, Father. I'm ten steps ahead of you. Yes, sirree."

"What are you saying?"

"I've taken on a new client."

"You've already chosen your next—"

The madman cut him off. "I've already notified the authorities. They'll get my letter soon. Of course that was before I knew you were going to be such a stickler for the rules. Still, it was considerate of me, wasn't it? I sent them a polite little note explaining my intentions. Pity I forgot to sign it."

"Did you give them the name of the person you intend to harm?"

"Harm? What a quaint word that is for murder. Yes, I named her."

"Another woman, then?" Tom's voice broke on the question.

"I only take women on as clients."

"Did you explain in the note your reason for wanting to kill this woman?"

"No."

"Do you have a reason?"

"Yes."

"Would you explain it to me?"

"Practice, Father."

"I don't understand."

"Practice makes perfect," he said. "This one's even more special than Millicent. I wrap myself in her fragrance, and I love to watch her sleep. She's so beautiful. Ask me, and after I've given you her name, you can forgive me."

"I will not give you absolution."

"How's the chemotherapy going? Are you feeling sick? Did you get a good report?"

Tom's head snapped up. "What?" he demanded in a near shout.

The madman laughed. "I told you I study my clients before I take them on. You could say I stalk them," he whispered.

"How did you know—"

"Oh, Tommy, you've been such a sport. Haven't you wondered why I followed you all this way just to confess my sins to you? Think about it on your way back to the abbey. I've done my homework, haven't I?"

"Who are you?"

"Why, I'm a heartbreaker. And I do so love a challenge. Make this one difficult for me. The police will come here soon to talk to you, and then you'll be able to tell anyone you want," he mocked. "I know who you'll call first. Your hotshot friend with the FBI. You'll call Nick, won't you? I sure hope you will. And he'll come running to help. You'd better tell him to take her away and hide her from me. I might not follow, and I'll start looking for someone else. At least I'll try."

"How do you know—"

"Ask me."

"Ask you what?"

"Her name," the madman whispered. "Ask me who my client is."

"I urge you to get help," Tom began again. "What you're doing—"

"Ask me. Ask me. Ask me."

Tom closed his eyes. "Yes. Who is she?"

"She's lovely," he answered. "Such beautiful full breasts and long, dark hair. There isn't a mark on her perfect body, and her face is like an angel's, so exquisite in every way.

16

She's…breathtaking…but I plan to take her breath away."

"Tell me her name," Tom demanded, praying to God there was time to get to the poor woman to protect her.

"Laurant," the serpent whispered. "Her name is Laurant."

Panic hit Tom like a fist. "My Laurant?"

"That's right. Now you're getting it, Father. I'm going to kill your sister."

CHAPTER

2

Agent Nicholas Benjamin Buchanan was about to begin a long overdue vacation. He hadn't taken any time off in the past three years, and it was beginning to show in his attitude—or so he'd been told by his superior, Doctor Peter Morganstern, when he'd ordered him to take a month's leave. He'd also told Nick that he was becoming a little too detached and cynical, and deep down Nick worried that he might be right.

Morganstern always told it like it was. Nick admired and respected him almost as much as he did his own father, and so he rarely argued with him. His boss was as steady as a rock. He never would have lasted more than two weeks in the Bureau if he had let his emotions control his behavior. If he had any flaw at all, it was his maddening ability to remain calm to the point of being catatonic. Nothing ever fazed the man.

The twelve handpicked agents under his direct supervision called him Prozac Pete—behind his back of course—but he knew about the nickname and wasn't offended by it. Rumor had it he actually laughed the first time he heard it, and that was yet another reason he got along so well with his agents. He had been able to hold on to his sense of humor—no small feat, considering the section he ran. His idea of losing his temper was having to repeat himself, though in all honesty, his raspy, years-of-smoking-cigars voice never, ever rose a decibel. Hell, maybe the other agents were right. Maybe Morganstern really did have Prozac running through his veins.

One thing was certain. His superiors knew gold when they spotted it, and in the fourteen years that Morganstern had worked for the Bureau, he'd been promoted six times. Yet he never rested on his laurels. When he was named head of the "lost-and-found" division, he dedicated himself to building an extremely efficient task force for tracking and recovering missing persons. And once that was accomplished, he turned his efforts to a more specific objective. He wanted to create a specialized unit devoted to the most difficult cases involving lost and abducted children. He justified this new unit on paper and then spent a considerable amount of time lobbying for it. At every opportunity, he waved his 233-page thesis under the director's nose.

His dogged determination finally paid off, and he now headed this elite unit. He was allowed to recruit his own men, a motley crew at best, who came to him from all walks of life. Each man was required to go through the academy's training program at Quantico first, and then he was sent to Morganstern for special testing and training. Very few made it through the grueling program, but those who did were exceptional. Morganstern was overheard telling the director he firmly believed he had the cream of the crop working for him, and within one year he proved to all the doubting Thomases that he was right. He then handed over the reins of the "lost and found" to his assistant, Frank O'Leary, and made the lateral move within the department to devote his time and effort to this very specialized group.

His team was unique. Each man possessed unusual skills in tracking the missing children. The twelve men were hunters who constantly raced against the clock with but one sacred goal, to find and protect before it was too late. They were every child's greatest champion and the last line of defense against the bogeymen who lurked in the dark.

The stress of the job would have sent average men into cardiac arrest, but there wasn't anything average about these men. None of them fit the profile of the typical FBI agent, but then Morganstern wasn't your typical leader. He had quickly proven that he was more than capable of running such an eclectic group. The other departments called his agents the Apostles, no doubt because there were twelve of them, but Morganstern didn't like the nickname because, as their leader, it implied all sorts of things about him that he couldn't possibly live up to. His humility was yet another reason he was so respected. His agents also appreciated the fact that he wasn't a by-the-manual boss. He encouraged them to get the job done, pretty much gave them a free hand, and always backed them up whenever it was needed. In many ways he was *their* greatest champion.

Certainly no one with the Bureau was more dedicated or qualified, for Morganstern was a board certified psychiatrist, which was probably why he liked to have his little heart-to-heart talks with each of his agents every now and then. Sitting them down and getting into their heads validated all the time and expense of his Harvard education. It was the one quirk all of them had to put up with and all of them hated.

He was in the mood to talk about the Stark case now. He had flown from D.C. to Cincinnati and had asked Nick to stop over on his way back from a seminar in San Francisco. Nick didn't want to discuss the Stark case—it had happened over a month ago and he didn't

20

even want to think about it, but that didn't matter. He knew he was going to have to discuss it whether he wanted to or not.

He waited at the regional office for his superior to join him, then sat down across from him at the polished oak conference table and listened for twenty minutes while Morganstern reviewed some of the particulars of the bizarre case. Nick stayed calm until Morganstern told him he was going to get a commendation for his heroic actions. He almost lost it then and there, but he was adept at concealing his true feelings. Even his boss, with his keen eye constantly on the lookout for any telltale signs of burnout or stress overload, was fooled into thinking that once again he was taking it all in stride—or so Nick thought.

When the conference wound down, Morganstern stared into the steely blue eyes of his agent for a long, silent minute and then asked, "When you shot her, what did you feel?"

"Is this necessary, sir? It happened over a month ago. Do we really need to rehash this?"

"This isn't a formal meeting, Nick. It's just you and me. You don't have to call me sir, and yes, I think it is necessary. Now answer me, please. What did you feel?"

And still he hedged, squirming in the hard-backed chair like a little boy being forced to admit he'd done something wrong. "What the hell do you mean, what did I feel?"

Ignoring the burst of anger, his superior calmly repeated the question a third time. "You know what I'm asking you. At that precise second, what did you feel? Do you remember?"

He was giving him a way out. Nick knew he could lie and tell him no, he didn't remember, that he'd been too busy at the time to think about what he was feeling, but he and Morganstern had always had an honest rapport with each other and he didn't want to screw that up now. Besides, he was pretty sure his boss would know he was lying. Realizing how futile it was to continue the evasion, he gave it up and decided to be blunt. "Yeah, I remember. It felt good," he whispered. "Real good. Hell, Pete, I was euphoric. If I hadn't turned around and gone back inside that house, if I had hesitated even thirty seconds more, and if I hadn't had my gun drawn, it would have been all over and that little boy would be dead. I cut it too damned close this time."

"But you did get to the child in time."

"I should have figured it out sooner."

Morganstern sighed. Of all of his agents, Nick had always been the most critical of his own performance. "You were the only one who did figure it out," he reminded him. "Don't be so hard on yourself."

"Did you read the newspapers? The reporters said she was crazy, but they didn't see the look in her eyes. I did, and I'm telling you, she wasn't crazy at all. She was pure evil."

"Yes, I've read the papers and you're right, they did call her crazy. I expected they would," he added. "I understand why and I think you do too. It's the only way the public can make

22

sense out of such a heinous crime. They want to believe that only a demented man or woman could do such obscene things to another human being, and only a crazy person could derive pleasure in the killing of innocents. A good number of them are crazy, but some aren't. Evil does exist. We've both seen it. Somewhere along the way, the Stark woman made a conscious choice to cross the line."

"People are afraid of what they don't understand."

"Yes," Morganstern agreed. "And there's a large percentage of academics who don't want to believe that evil exists. If they can't reason it or explain it in their narrow minds, then it simply can't be. I think that's one of the reasons our culture is such fertile ground for depravity. Some of my colleagues believe they can fix anything with a long-winded diagnosis and a few mind-altering drugs."

"I heard that one of your colleagues believes that Stark's husband controlled her and that she was so terrified of him, her mind snapped. In other words, we should feel sorry for her."

"Yes, I heard that too. Nonsense. The Stark woman was as depraved as her husband. Her fingerprints were on those pornographic tapes along with his. She was a willing participant, but I do believe she was breaking down. They'd never gone after children before."

"Honest to God, Pete, she was smiling at me. The boy was cradled in her arms, and she held a butcher knife over him. He was unconscious, but I could see he was still breathing.

She was waiting for me. She knew I had figured it all out and I think she wanted me to watch her kill him." He paused to nod. "Yeah, it felt good to blow her away. I'm just sorry her husband wasn't there. I would have liked to have gotten him too. Any leads yet? I still think you ought to put our friend Noah on his trail."

"I've been considering doing just that, but they want to take Donald Stark alive so they can question him, and they know if Stark gives him any trouble at all, Noah won't hesitate to shoot."

"You kill a cockroach, Pete. You don't domesticate him. Noah's got the right idea." He rolled his shoulders to stretch his cramped muscles, rubbed the back of his neck with his hand, and then remarked, "I think I need to go on another retreat."

"Why do you say that?"

"I think I might be burning out. Am I?"

Morganstern shook his head. "No, you're just a little fatigued, that's all. None of this conversation is going in my report. I meant it when I said it was between you and me. You're way past due for some time off, but that's my fault, not yours. I want you to take a month off now and get your mind centered again."

A hint of a smile softened Nick's bleak expression. "Center my mind?"

"Chill out," he explained. "Or try to anyway. When was the last time you went up to Nathan's Bay to see that big family of yours?"

"It's been a while," Nick admitted. "I keep

in touch with all of them by E-mail. Everyone's as busy as I am."

"Go home," he said. "It'll be good for you. Your folks will be glad to see you again. How's the judge doing?"

"Dad's fine," Nick answered.

"What about your friend Father Madden?"

"I talk to Tommy every night."

"By E-mail?"

"Yes."

"Maybe you ought to go see him and have those talks face-to-face."

"You think I need a little spiritual guidance?" Nick asked with a grin.

"I think you need a little laughter."

"Yeah, I probably do," he agreed. He grew serious once again and said, "Pete, about my instincts. Do you think I'm losing my edge?"

Morganstern scoffed at the notion. "Your instincts couldn't be better. The Stark woman fooled everyone but you. Everyone," he repeated more forcefully. "Her relatives, her friends and neighbors, her church group. She didn't fool you, though. Oh, I'm sure the locals would have eventually figured it out, but by then that little boy would be dead and buried, and she would have snatched another one. You know as well as I do that once they start, they don't stop."

Pete tapped the thick manila folder with his knuckles. "In the interviews, I read all about how she sat next to the poor mother's side day in and day out, comforting her. She was on the church's grieving committee," he added with a shake of his head. He looked as though even he, who had seen and heard it all before, was shocked by the Stark woman's gall.

"The police talked to everyone in that church group, and they couldn't find anything," Nick said. "They weren't real thorough," he added. "But then it was a tiny little town and the sheriff didn't know what to look for."

"He was smart enough not to wait. He called us in right away," Morganstern said. "He and the other locals were convinced that a transient had taken the boy, weren't they? And that's where all of their efforts were focused."

"Yes," Nick agreed. "It's difficult to believe that one of your own could do such a thing. They had a couple of witnesses who had seen a vagrant hanging around the schoolyard, but their descriptions didn't match. The team from Cincinnati were on their way," he added. "And they would have figured her game out real quick."

"What exactly was it that tipped you off? How did you know?"

"Little things out of sync," he replied. "I can't explain what it was that bothered me about her or why I decided to follow her home."

"I can explain it. Instinct."

"I guess so," he agreed. "I knew I was going to do a real thorough check on her. Something wasn't right, but I couldn't put my finger on what it was. I got this weird, gut feeling about her, and it got stronger as soon as I walked into her house...you know what I mean?"

"Explain it. What was the house like?"

26

"Immaculate. I couldn't see a speck of dust or dirt anywhere. The living room was small—a couple of easy chairs, sofa, TV—but, you know what was odd, Pete? There weren't any pictures on the walls or family photos. Yeah, I remember I thought that was real odd. She had plastic covers on her furniture. I guess a lot of people do that. I don't know. Anyway, like I said, it was spotless, but it smelled peculiar."

"What kind of smell was it?"

"Vinegar...and ammonia. The smell was so strong it made my eyes burn. I figured she was just a compulsive housecleaner...and then I followed her into the kitchen. It was clean as a whistle. Not a thing sitting on the counters, not a towel draped on the sink, nothing. She told me to have a seat while she fixed us a cup of coffee, and then I noticed the stuff she had on the table. There were salt and pepper shakers, but in between was a huge clear plastic container of pink antacid tablets, and next to it was a ketchup-size bottle of hot sauce. I thought that was damned peculiar...and then I saw the dog. The animal tipped the scales. It was a black cocker spaniel sitting in the corner by the back door. He never took his eyes off her. She put a plate of chocolate chip cookies on the table and when she turned her back to get the coffee, I took one of the cookies and put it down by my side, to see if the dog would come and get it, but he never even looked at me. Hell, he was too afraid to blink, and he was watching her

27

every move. If the sheriff had seen the dog with her, he would have known something was real wrong, but when he interviewed her, the cocker was outside in the pen."

"He went inside her house and didn't notice anything unusual."

"I was lucky, and she was arrogant and reckless."

"What made you go back inside after you left her house?"

"I was going to get some backup and wait and see where she went, but as soon as I got outside, I knew I had to go back in, and fast. I had this feeling she knew I was on to her. And I knew that the boy was somewhere in that house."

"Your instincts couldn't be better tuned," Morganstern said. "That's why I went after you, you know."

"I know. The infamous football game."

Morganstern smiled. "I just saw it again on CNN Sports a couple of weeks ago. They must run that clip at least twice a year."

"I wish they'd give it a rest. It's old news."

The two men stood. Nick towered over his boss. Morganstern, in his tasseled black leather loafers, was five feet eight inches tall, and Nick was over six feet. His boss was slightly built, with thinning blond hair that was quickly going gray, and his thick bifocals were constantly slipping down the bridge of his narrow nose. He always wore a conservative black or navy suit with a long-sleeved, white, starched shirt and muted striped tie.

To the casual observer, Morganstern looked like a nerdy university professor, but to the agents under his supervision, he was, in every respect, a giant of a man who handled the hellacious job and the horrific pressures with unruffled ease.

"I'll see you in a month, Nick, but not a day before. Agreed?"

"Agreed."

His superior started out the door, then paused. "Are you still getting sick every time you get on a plane?"

"Is there anything you don't know about me?"

"I don't believe there is."

"Yeah? When was the last time I got laid?"

Morganstern pretended to be shocked by the question. "It's been a long while, Agent. Apparently you're going through a dry spell."

Nick laughed. "Is that right?"

"One of these days you'll meet the right woman, heaven help her."

"I'm not looking for the right woman."

Morganstern smiled a fatherly smile. "And that, you see, is exactly when you'll find her. You won't be looking, and she'll blindside you, just like my Katie blindsided me. I never had a chance, and I predict you won't either. She's out there somewhere, just waiting for you."

"Then she's going to have a hell of a long wait," he replied. "In our line of work, marriage isn't in the equation."

"Katie and I have managed for over twenty years."

"Katie's a saint."

"You didn't answer my question, Nick. Do you?"

"Get sick every time I get on a plane? Hell, yes."

Morganstern chuckled. "Good luck getting home then."

"You know, Pete, most psychiatrists would try to get to the bottom of my phobia, but you get a kick out of it, don't you?"

He laughed again. "See you in a month," he repeated as he strolled out of the office.

Nick gathered up his files, made a couple of necessary calls to his Boston office and to Frank O'Leary at Quantico, and then hitched a ride to the airport with one of the local agents. Since there was no getting out of his forced vacation, he made some tentative plans. He really was going to try to kick back and relax, maybe go sailing with his oldest brother, Theo, if he could pry him away from his job for a couple of days, and then he was going to drive halfway across the country to Holy Oaks, Iowa, to see his best friend, Tommy, and get some serious fishing done. Morganstern hadn't mentioned the promotion O'Leary had dropped on the table two weeks ago. While he was on vacation Nick planned to weigh the pros and cons of the new job. He was counting on Tommy for help with the decision. He was closer to him than he was to his own five brothers, and he trusted him implicitly. His friend would play his usual role of devil's advocate, and hopefully by the time Nick returned to his job, he would know what he was going to do.

He knew Tommy was worried about him. He'd been nagging him by E-mail for the past six months to come and see him. Like Morganstern, Tommy understood the stresses and the nightmares of Nick's work, and he also believed that Nick needed time away.

Tommy had his own battle to fight, and every three months when he checked into the Kansas Medical Center for tests, it was Nick who got the queasy feeling in the pit of his stomach that stayed there until Tommy E-mailed him with good news. So far, his friend had been lucky; the cancer had been contained. But it was always there, hovering, waiting to strike. Tommy had learned to deal with his illness. Nick hadn't. If he could take the pain and suffering away from his friend, he would willingly give his right arm, but that wasn't how it worked. As Tommy had said, this was a war he had to wage alone, and all Nick could do was be there for him when he needed him.

Nick was suddenly anxious to see his friend again. He might even be able to talk him into taking off his priest collar for one night and getting roaring drunk with him the way they used to when they roomed together at Penn State.

And he would finally get to meet Tommy's only family, his baby sister, Laurant. She was eight years younger than her brother and had grown up with the nuns in a boarding school for wealthy young girls in the mountains near

31

Geneva. Tommy had tried several times to bring her to America, but the conditions of the trust and the lawyers guarding the money convinced the judges to keep her sequestered until she was of age to make decisions for herself. Tommy had told Nick that it wasn't as grim as it sounded and that by following the letter of the trust, the lawyers were, in fact, protecting the estate.

Laurant had been of age for some time now and had moved to Holy Oaks a year ago to be close to her brother. Nick had never met her, but he remembered the photos of her that Tommy had stuck up on the mirror. She'd looked like a street urchin, a scruffy-looking kid wearing a pleated black skirt and a uniform white blouse that was partially hanging out of her waistband. One of her knee-high socks had fallen down around her ankle. She had scabby knees and curly long brown hair that drooped down over one of her eyes. Both he and Tommy had laughed when they saw the photo. Laurant couldn't have been more than seven or eight years old when the picture was taken, but what stuck in Nick's mind was the joy in her smile and the sparkle in her eyes, suggesting the nuns' chronic complaints about her were true. She did look like she had a bit of the devil in her and a zest for life that was going to get her into sure trouble one day.

Yeah, a vacation was just what he needed, he decided. The key to all of his plans was getting back to his home base, Boston, and that meant he was going to have to get on the damned plane first. No one hated flying as much as Nick did. It scared the hell out of him, as a matter of fact. As soon as he entered the Cincinnati airport, he broke out in a cold sweat, and he knew his complexion was going to be green by the time he boarded the plane. The 777 was bound for London with a brief stop in Boston, where Nick would be getting off, thank God, and going home to his Beacon Hill town house. He'd purchased the building from his uncle three years ago, but he still hadn't unpacked most of the cardboard boxes the movers had dropped into the center of his living room, or hooked up the high-tech audio system his youngest brother, Zachary, had insisted on picking out for him.

He could feel his stomach tightening as he headed for check-in. He knew the drill. He presented himself, his credentials, and his clearance to the security officer. The prissy, middle-aged man named Johnson nervously chewed on his pencil-thin upper lip until his computer gave him Nick's name and code verification. He then escorted Nick around the metal detector the other passengers would have to pass through, handed him his boarding pass, and waved him down the ramp.

Captain James T. Sorensky was waiting for him in the galley. Nick had flown with the captain at least six times in the past three years and knew the man was an excellent pilot and meticulous in his job—Nick had run a background check on the captain just to make certain there wasn't anything suspicious in his past to suggest the possibility of a nervous break-down while he was flying. He even knew the kind of toothpaste the man preferred, but none of those facts made his nervousness subside. Sorensky had graduated from the Air Force Academy at the top of his class and had worked for Delta for eighteen years. His record was unblemished, but that didn't matter either. Nick's stomach was still doing somersaults. He hated everything about flying. It all boiled down to a question of trust, he knew, and even though Sorensky wasn't a complete stranger—they were on a first-name basis these days—Nick still didn't like being forced to trust him to keep almost 159 tons of steel in the air.

Sorensky could have been a model for an airline poster with his silver-tipped, immaculately trimmed hair, his perfectly pressed navy blue uniform with razor-edge creases in the trousers, and his tall, lean physique. Nick wasn't overweight by any means, but he still felt like a bull moose next to him. The captain radiated confidence. He was also rigid about his own rules, which Nick appreciated. Though Nick had the government clearance and FAA approval to carry his loaded Sig Sauer on the plane, he knew it made Sorensky nervous—and that was the last thing Nick wanted or needed. In preparation, Nick had already unloaded his gun. As the captain greeted him, he dropped the gun's magazine into his hand.

"Good to see you again, Nick."

"How are you feeling today, Jim?"

Sorensky smiled. "Still worried I'll have a heart attack while we're in the air?"

Nick shrugged to cover his embarrassment. "The thought has crossed my mind," he said. "It could happen."

"Yes, it could, but I'm not the only man on board who can fly this plane."

"I know."

"But it doesn't make you feel any better, does it?"

"No."

"As much as you have to fly, you'd think you'd get used to it."

"You'd think I would, but it hasn't happened yet."

"Does your boss know you get sick every time you get on a plane?"

"Sure he does," Nick answered. "He's sadistic."

Sorensky laughed. "I'm going to give you a real smooth ride today," he promised. "You aren't going on with us to London, are you?"

"Fly over an ocean? That's never going to happen." The thought made his stomach lurch. "I'm going home."

"Have you ever been to Europe?"

"No, not yet. When I can drive there, I'll go."

The captain glanced at the magazine he held in the palm of his hand. "Thanks for letting me hold on to this. I know I don't have the legal right to ask you to give it up."

"But it makes you nervous to have a loaded weapon on board, and I don't want a nervous pilot flying this plane."

Nick tried to get past Sorensky so he could get settled in his seat, but the captain was in the mood to chat.

"By the way, about a month ago I read a real nice article in the newspaper about you saving that poor boy's life. It was interesting to read about your background and how you're best friends with that priest...how the two of you ended up taking different paths. Now you wear a badge and he wears a cross. And saving that child...it made me proud to know you."

"I was just doing my job."

"The article also mentioned that unit you work with. What was it he called the twelve of you?" Before Nick could answer, the captain remembered. "Oh, yes, the Apostles."

"I still haven't figured out how he managed to get that information. I didn't think anyone outside the department knew about the nickname."

"Still, it's fitting. You saved that little boy's life."

"We were lucky this time."

"The reporter said you refused to be interviewed."

"This isn't a glory job, Jim. I did what I had to, that's all."

The agent's humility impressed the captain. With a nod, he said, "You did a fine thing. That little boy's back with his parents now, and that's all that counts."

"Like I said, we were lucky this time."

Sorensky, sensing Nick's unease with his compliments, quickly changed the subject. "There's a U.S. Marshal Downing on board. He had to give me his weapon," he added with a grin. "Do you happen to know him?"

"The name's not familiar. He isn't transporting, is he?"

"Yes, he is."

"What's he doing on a commercial flight? They've got their own carriers."

"This is an unusual situation according to Downing. He's taking a prisoner back to Boston to stand trial and he's in a hurry," he explained. "Downing told me they got the boy cold for selling drugs and that it's an open-and-shut case. The prisoner isn't supposed to be violent. Downing thinks his lawyers will plea him out before the judge ever picks up his gavel. Like you, they preboarded. The marshal's from Texas. You can hear it in his voice, and he seems like a real nice fella. You ought to go introduce yourself to him."

Nick nodded. "Where are they seated?" he asked with a quick glance into the main cabin of the mammoth plane.

"You can't see them from here. They're on the left side, back row. Downing has the boy shackled and handcuffed. I'm telling you, Nick, his prisoner can't be much older than my son, Andy, and he's just fourteen. It's a crying shame, someone that young is going to spend the rest of his life in prison."

"Criminals are getting younger and dumber," Nick remarked. "Thanks for telling me. I will go say hello. Is the plane packed today?"

"No," Sorensky answered as he tucked the magazine into his pants pocket. "We're only half full until we land at Logan. Then we'll be packed."

After insisting that if Nick needed anything he was to let him know, Sorensky went back to the cockpit, where a man wearing the navy blue uniform and identification of the airline's ground crew was waiting with a clipboard full of curled papers. He followed the captain into the cockpit and closed the door behind him. Nick put his suit carrier in the overhead compartment, dropped his old, scarred, leather briefcase in his assigned seat, and then crossed over to the left side of the plane and started down the aisle toward the U.S. marshal. He was halfway there when he changed his mind. The other passengers were quickly filing on board now, and so he decided to wait until they were in the air and he'd gotten his legs back before introducing himself to Downing. He did get a good look at him though, and the prisoner too, before he turned around. Downing had one leg stretched out into the aisle, and Nick could see the fancy scrollwork on his cowboy boot. Tall and wiry, the marshal was all cowboy with his weathered complexion, his thick brown mustache, and his black leather vest. Nick couldn't see his belt, but he would have bet a month's salary that Downing was sporting a big silver buckle.

Captain Sorensky had been on the mark in his evaluation of the prisoner. At first glance he did look like a kid. But there was a hardness Nick had seen countless times in the past. This one had been around the block more than once and had most likely killed his conscience a long time ago. Yeah, they were getting younger and dumber these days, Nick thought. The prisoner had been cursed with bad judgment and god-awful genes. His face was scarred with acne, and his marble cold eyes were so close together he looked cross-eyed. Someone had done a real hatchet job on his hair, no doubt on purpose. There were spikes sticking up all over his head, kind of like the Statue of Liberty, but then maybe he wanted to look that way. What did it matter what kind of punk haircut he had? Where he was going he would still have plenty of friends waiting in line for a chance to get to him.

Nick went back to the front of the plane and got settled in his seat. He was in first class today, and though the seat was wider, it still felt cramped. His legs were too long to properly stretch out. After shoving his briefcase under the seat in front of him, he leaned back, clipped his seat belt together, and partially closed his eyes. It would have been nice if he could have at least tried to get comfortable, but that was out of the question because he knew that if he took his suit jacket off, he'd freak out the other passengers when they saw his holstered gun. They wouldn't know it wasn't loaded, and Nick wasn't in the mood to calm anyone else down. Hell, he was hovering on the edge of a panic attack now, and he knew he'd stay that way until the plane had taken off. He'd be all right, sort of, anyway, until they began their descent into Logan Airport. Then the anxiety would start all over again. In his present, claustrophobic, neurotic state, he thought it was damned ironic that O'Leary wanted him to join the crisis management team.

Mind over matter, he told himself, and in a panic or not, he was determined to catch up on his paperwork while he was in the air. He'd already checked and knew that no one was going to be sitting in the window seat. Nick always took the aisle, even if it meant moving another passenger, so that he could see the face of every single person who came on board the plane. After takeoff he would be able to spread his folders out while he deciphered his notes and fed the information into his laptop.

Damn, he wished he weren't such a control freak. Morganstern had told him he'd taught him relaxation techniques while he was on retreat with the other team members during their isolated training period, but Nick didn't have any memory of anything that had happened during those two weeks, and he knew the others didn't remember anything either. They had all agreed to Pete's terms. He had sat them down, explained what he wanted to do, but not how, and then asked them to trust him. Nick had the most difficult time making up his mind because it meant he would have to give up his control. In the end, he finally agreed. Pete had warned them they wouldn't remember, and he'd been right about that. None of them did.

Sometimes a scent or a sound would trigger a thought about the retreat and he'd tense in reaction, but just as suddenly as it came into his mind, it vanished. He knew he'd been in a forest somewhere in the United States— he had the scars to prove it. There was one the shape of a crescent moon on his left shoulder and a smaller scar directly above his right eye. He'd left the retreat with cuts and abrasions on his hands and legs, and God only knows how many mosquito bites to prove he'd been stomping through the wilderness. Did the other Apostles have scars? He didn't know, and he could never seem to hold on to the question in his mind long enough to ask.

Once during a private meeting Pete had brought up the topic of the retreat and Nick had asked him if he'd been brainwashed. His boss had flinched at the word. "Good Lord, no," he said. "I simply tried to teach you how to maximize what God gave you."

In other words, Pete's mind games trained them to hone their naturally acute instincts, to focus or, like the army slogan said, to be all they could be.

The plane was moving. They taxied to the end of the runway and then stopped. Nick assumed they were waiting for their turn to get in line with the other planes for takeoff— Cincinnati was a national hub and was always glutted with traffic—but fifteen minutes passed, and they still weren't inching forward. When he leaned over the empty seat and looked out the window, he saw two planes taxiing at a hell of a fast clip in the opposite direction.

A young blond woman smiled at him from across the aisle and tried to engage him in conversation by asking him if he was a nervous flyer. His white-knuckle grip on the armrests had to have been a dead giveaway. He nodded in answer, then turned to look out the window again to discourage further chitchat. She wasn't bad-looking, and the spandex skirt and top she wore proved, without a doubt, that she had a fine body, but he didn't want to work at small talk, and he certainly wasn't in the mood to flirt. He must be more tired than he'd thought. He was becoming more and more like Theo. These days his brother wasn't in the mood for anything but work.

Nick spotted the fire truck and two police cars racing toward the plane at the same time that Captain Sorensky's voice came over the intercom. It was strained with good cheer.

"Ladies and gentlemen, there will be a slight delay while we wait our turn for takeoff. We should be in the air soon, so sit back, relax, and enjoy the ride."

No sooner were the words out of his mouth than the door to the cockpit opened and Sorensky, oozing confidence with his smile, stepped out into the galley. He hesitated for the barest of seconds, his gaze fully directed on Nick, and then started down the aisle. Following on his heels was the young, pasty-

42

faced airline crewman. The man was tailing the captain so closely he looked like he was holding on to the back of his jacket.

Nick slowly unfastened his seat belt.

"Captain, shouldn't you be flying this plane?" the leggy blond asked, smiling.

Sorensky didn't look at the woman when he answered. "I just want to check something in back."

The captain's hands were fisted at his sides, but as he passed Nick's seat, his right hand unfolded and he dropped the gun's magazine into Nick's lap.

In one fluid motion, Nick sprang out of his seat, grabbed the young crewman's arm, and pinned it to the back of the headrest behind him. The element of surprise was on his side. The man didn't even have time to blink before his gun was snatched out of his hand and he was facedown on the floor with Nick's foot pressed against his neck. The magazine was back in the Sig Sauer and the gleaming barrel was pointed at the man before the captain had fully turned around.

It all happened so fast, the other passengers were too stunned to scream. Sorensky raised his hands and called out, "Everything's okay, folks." Turning to Nick, he said, "Man, do you move fast."

"I've had some practice," Nick replied as he reholstered his gun and then knelt down and began to go through the man's pockets.

"He told me he's the prisoner's cousin, and he was going to get him off this plane."

43

"Didn't put a whole lot of thought into the plan, did he?" He flipped open the man's wallet and read the name on his Kentucky driver's license. "William Robert Hendricks." Nudging the man he asked, "Your friends call you Billy Bob?"

In response Billy Bob started squirming like a fish in a canoe and screaming at the top of his lungs for a lawyer. Nick ignored him and asked the captain to see if Marshal Downing happened to have an extra pair of cuffs he could borrow.

As the initial moment of shock wore off, the passengers began to react. A murmur went through the crowd, and like a snowball, gathered momentum as it rolled down the aisle. Captain Sorensky, sensing the panic that was spreading, took control. In a voice as smooth as good whiskey, he called out, "Settle down, settle down. It's all over now. Everyone sit back down and relax. As soon as this law officer takes care of this little matter, we'll be on our way again. No one's been hurt." The captain then asked one of the attendants to please fetch Marshal Downing from the back row.

The marshal, with prisoner in tow, strode down the aisle and handed Nick a pair of handcuffs. After Nick had snapped the cuffs in place behind the prisoner's back, he hauled him to his feet. He noticed that Marshal Downing was shaking his head and frowning.

"What's the matter?" he asked.

"You know what this means, don't you?" Downing muttered in a slow Texas drawl.

"What does it mean?" Captain Sorensky asked.

"More damned paperwork."

After stopping by his Boston office to drop off a couple of folders, tie up some loose ends, and take a little ribbing about the possibility that he had only squelched the hijacking to delay having to fly—everyone in the department seemed to think his fear of flying was hilarious—Nick finally headed home. Traffic was a bitch, but then it always was. He was tempted to head his '84 Porsche toward the highway and open her up just to see how the reconditioned motor would manage but decided against it. He was too tired. Instead, he maneuvered her through the familiar side streets. She handled like a dream. What did he care if his sisters, Jordan and Sidney, had nicknamed her "Compensation," implying that a man who drove such a sexy sports car was merely compensating for what was lacking in his love life.

He pulled into the basement garage of his brick town house, hit the remote control to close the door, and felt his entire body begin to relax. He was finally home. He climbed the steps to the main floor, dumped his Hartmann bag in the back hallway outside the laundry room door—his housekeeper, Rosie, had trained him well—and had his suit jacket and tie off before he reached the newly remodeled kitchen. He dropped his briefcase and his sunglasses on the shiny brown granite island, grabbed a beer from the Sub-Zero refrigerator that always made a weird sucking sound whenever he closed the door, and headed for his sanctuary, dodging the pyramid of unpacked boxes Rosie had stacked in the center of his living room with hostile notes Scotch taped to them.

The library was his favorite room in the house and the only one he'd bothered to furnish since he'd lived there. It was located in the back on the first floor. When he opened the door, the scent of lemon furniture polish, leather, and musty old books wafted about him, the scent not unpleasant. The room was large and spacious, yet still felt warm and cozy on harsh winter nights when a blizzard was raging outside his windows and there was a fire blazing in the hearth. The walls were a dark walnut that stretched twelve feet up to the ornately carved eighteenth-century moldings bracketing the ceiling. Two of the four walls bore shelves slightly bowed from the weight of the heavy texts. A ladder rolled back and forth along a brass pole across the bookcase so the volumes on the top shelves could be easily reached. His mahogany desk, a gift from his uncle, faced the fireplace, the mantel a clutter of photos his mother and his sisters had placed there after he'd moved in. Double French doors with a Palladian arch above them were straight ahead. When he pulled the draperies back and opened the doors to the walled garden with the old cherub fountain and paver-brick patio, that had been laid down God only knows how long ago, sunlight and scent filled the library. In the spring it was lilac first, then honeysuckle, but now the heavy smell of heliotrope was prominent.

He stood there surveying his peaceful haven for several minutes until the heat began to press in on him and he heard the central air conditioner kick on. He closed the doors, yawned loudly, and took a long swallow of his beer. Then he removed his gun, took the magazine out, and put it all inside his wall safe. He sat down at his desk in his soft leather swivel chair, rolled up his sleeves, and flipped on his computer. The tension in his shoulders was easing, but he let out a loud groan when he saw the number of E-mails waiting for him. There were also twenty-eight logged calls on his answering machine as well. With a sigh, he kicked off his shoes, leaned back in his chair, and began scrolling through his E-mail while he listened to his phone messages.

Five of the calls were from his brother Zachary, the youngest in the family, who desperately wanted to borrow the Porsche for the Fourth of July weekend and vehemently promised to take good care of the car. The seventh message was from his mother, who was just as vehement when she told him that Zachary was not to be given the Porsche under any circumstances. His brainy sister Jordan also called to tell him that their stock had just hit $150 per share, which meant that Nick could retire now and live the high life had he been so inclined. Thinking about it made him smile. His father, with his work ethic, would have heart failure if any of his children weren't productive. According to the judge, their purpose in life was to make the world a little better. Some days Nick was sure he was going to die trying.

The twenty-fourth message stopped him cold.

"Nick, it's me, Tommy. I'm in real trouble, Cutter. It's five-thirty my time, Saturday. Call me as soon as you get this message. I'm in Kansas City at Our Lady of Mercy rectory. You know where it is. I'm going to call Morganstern too. Maybe he can get hold of you. The police are here now, but they don't know what to do, and no one can find Laurant. Look, I know I'm rambling. Just call, no matter what time."

CHAPTER

3

Someone killed Daddy, and Bessie Jean Vanderman meant to find out who the culprit was. Everyone said it was old age and not poison that had done him in, but Bessie Jean knew better. Daddy was as fine as could be until he just up and keeled over. It was poison all right, and she was going to prove it.

One way or another, she would get justice. She owed it to Daddy to ferret out the criminal and have him arrested. There had to be proof somewhere, maybe even in her own front yard, where she kept Daddy chained on sunny days so he could take in some fresh air. If there was any evidence around, by God, she'd find it. The investigation was on her shoulders and hers alone. Sister had cut short her vacation in Des Moines and had made her cousin drive her home when she heard the news. She was trying to help, but she wasn't much use, not with her bad eyesight and her vanity making it impossible for her to put on the tortoiseshell bifocals Bessie Jean now regretted she'd ever told her made her look plumb bug-eyed. Certainly no one else was going to help look for evidence of foul play because no one else cared a hoot, not even that no-good Sheriff Lloyd MacGovern. He hadn't liked Daddy much, not since he'd gotten away from her and taken a bite out of Sheriff Lloyd's ample ass. But, even so, you'd think he would have had the decency to stop by her house and offer his condolences on Daddy's passing when there she and Sister were, sitting just one short block away from the town square where his office was located. Shame on him, Bessie Jean told Sister. It didn't matter if he liked Daddy or not, he should still do his duty and find out who murdered him.

Not everyone in Holy Oaks was being cal-

49

lous, Sister reminded her. Others living in the valley were being very thoughtful and sensitive. They knew how much Daddy meant to Bessie Jean. That uppity next door neighbor of theirs with her fancy French name, Laurant, had turned out to be the most thoughtful and sensitive of all. Why, what would they have done if she hadn't heard Bessie Jean wailing and come running lickety-split to help? Bessie Jean had been down on her knees, leaning over poor dead Daddy, and Laurant had helped her to her feet and put her and Sister in her car, then had run back, unchained Daddy and scooped him up in her arms, real gentle like, and put him in the trunk. Daddy was already stiff and as cold as a stone, but Laurant still had sped all the way to Doctor Basham's offices and had run Daddy inside as quick as she could on the hope that maybe the doctor could perform a miracle.

Since there weren't any miracles being dispensed that dark day, the doctor had put Daddy in the freezer to await the autopsy Bessie Jean insisted on. Then Laurant had driven her and Sister over to Doctor Sweeney's office to get their blood pressure checked because Bessie Jean was still terribly distraught, and Sister was feeling light-headed.

Laurant turned out not to be so uppity after all. In all her eighty-two years, Bessie Jean wasn't one to ever change her mind after she'd made it up, but in this instance she did just that. After she'd gotten past her initial shock and hysterics over losing Daddy, she realized what a kind-hearted soul Laurant was. She was still a foreigner, of course. She came to Holy Oaks from that city of sin and debauchery, Chicago, but that was all right. The city hadn't rubbed off on her. She was still a good girl. The nuns who had raised her at that fancy boarding school in Switzerland had instilled strong values. Bessie Jean, as rigid and set in her ways as she liked to think she was, decided that she could stand to have one or two foreigners for friends. She surely could.

Sister suggested they stop mourning Daddy's passing long enough to bake a tart apple pie for Laurant—it was the neighborly thing to do—but Bessie Jean chided her for having such a poor memory and forgetting that the Winston twins were looking after Laurant's corner drugstore while she drove all the way down to Kansas City. She'd said she wanted to surprise her brother, that good-looking priest with such nice thick hair that the young girls at Holy Oaks College were always drooling over. They would have to wait until Monday to bake because that was the day Laurant was expected home.

Once both sisters had decided that Laurant was no longer an outsider, they naturally felt it was their business to interfere in her life whenever possible and to worry about her, just like they would if they had married and had had daughters of their own. Bessie Jean hoped Laurant remembered to lock her car doors. She was young, and in their estimation, that meant she was also naive, whereas they were older and wiser and knew all about the sorry ways of the world. Granted, neither one of them had been any farther away from Holy Oaks than Des Moines to visit their cousins, Ida and James Perkins, but that didn't mean they didn't know all about the terrible things happening today. They weren't ignorant. They read the papers and knew there were serial killers out there waiting at all the rest stops to prey on beautiful young women who were foolish enough to stop, or who had unfortunate car troubles that put them in harm's way. As lovely as Laurant was, she would certainly catch any man's eye. Why, just look at all the high school boys hanging around that store that wasn't even open yet in hopes she'd come outside to have a word with them. Still, Bessie Jean reminded Sister, Laurant was every bit as smart as she was pretty.

Having made the decision not to fret about Laurant any longer, Bessie Jean sat down at the dining room table and opened the wooden stationery box her mama had given her when she was a young girl. She took out a sheet of pink, rose-scented paper embossed with her very own initials, and reached for her pen. Since Sheriff Lloyd wasn't going to do anything about Daddy's murder, Bessie Jean was taking matters into her own hands. She'd already written one letter to the FBI requesting that they send a man to Holy Oaks to investigate, but her first letter must have gotten lost in the mail because a full eight days had passed and she still hadn't heard a word from anyone. She was going to make certain this letter didn't get lost. This time she was going to address her request to the director himself, and as expensive as it was, she was going to spend the extra money to send it by certified mail.

Sister got busy cleaning house. After all, company was coming. Any day now, the FBI would be knocking on their door.

The wait was making her nuts. When it came to her brother's health, Laurant found it impossible to be patient, and sitting by the phone waiting for him to call her with the results of the blood tests required more stamina than she possessed. Tommy always called her on Friday evening between seven and nine, but he didn't call this time, and the longer she waited, the more worried she became.

By Saturday afternoon she had convinced herself the news wasn't good, and when Tommy still hadn't called her by six that night, she got into her car and headed out. She knew her brother was going to be upset with her because she was following him to Kansas

City, but while she was headed toward Des Moines, she came up with a good lie to tell him. Her background was art history, she would remind him, and the lure of the Degas exhibit on temporary loan to the Nelson Atkins Museum in Kansas City was simply too appealing to resist. There had been a mention of the exhibit in the *Holy Oaks Gazette*, and she knew Tommy had read it. Granted, she had already seen the exhibit in Chicago, several times as a matter of fact, when she had worked at the art gallery there, but maybe Tommy wouldn't remember that. Besides, there wasn't a rule that you could see Degas's wonderful ballerinas only once, was there? No, of course not.

She couldn't tell Tommy the truth, even though they both knew what that was, that she became consumed with panic every three months when he checked into the medical center for tests. She was terrified that the results weren't going to be satisfactory this time and that the cancer, like a hibernating bear, was waking up again. Damn it, Tommy always had the results of his preliminary blood tests by Friday evening. Why hadn't he called her? Not knowing was making her an emotional wreck. She was so scared inside she was sick. Before she had left Holy Oaks, she had called the rectory and had spoken to Monsignor McKindry, uncaring that she was acting like a neurotic mother hen. The monsignor had a kind, gentle voice, but his news wasn't good. Tommy, he'd explained, was back at the hospital. And no, he'd told her, the doctors hadn't been happy with the preliminary tests. Laurant was sure she knew what that meant. Her brother was undergoing another brutal round of chemotherapy.

Damned if she'd let him go through that ordeal without family by his side this time. Family...he was the only family she had. After their parents' deaths, she and her brother, children at the time, had been forced to grow up on opposite sides of the ocean. So much had been lost over the years. But things were different now. They were adults. They could make their own choices, and that meant they could be there for each other when times got rough.

The alternator light went on just outside the town of Haverton. The filling station was closed, and she ended up spending the night at a no-frills motel there. Before leaving the next morning, she stopped by the motel office and picked up a map of Kansas City. The clerk gave her directions to the Fairmont which, he informed her, was close to the art museum.

She still got lost. She missed her exit off of I-435 and ended up too far south on the highway that circled the sprawling city. Clutching the soggy map she'd accidentally spilled Diet Coke all over, she stopped at a gas station for more directions.

Once she got her bearings, getting to the hotel wasn't difficult at all. She followed the street marked State Line and headed back north.

Tommy had told her that Kansas City was pretty and clean, but his descriptions didn't do the city justice. It was really quite lovely. The streets were lined with well-manicured lawns and old, two-story houses with flowers in bloom everywhere. Following the gas station attendant's instructions, she cut over to Ward Parkway, the street that he had promised would take her directly to the Fairmont's front door. The parkway was divided by wide grassy medians, and twice she passed groups of teenagers playing football and soccer there. The kids didn't seem to mind the oppressive heat or the stifling humidity.

The street curved down a gentle slope, and just as she began to worry she'd gone too far, she saw a cluster of pretty Spanish-style shops up ahead. She guessed that this was the area the motel clerk had called the Country Club Plaza and she felt a sense of relief. A couple of blocks farther and there on the right was the Fairmont.

It wasn't quite noon yet, but the hotel clerk was gracious about her wilted condition and let her check into a room early. An hour later she was feeling human again. She'd been driving since early that morning, but a long, cold shower revitalized her. Even though she knew Tommy wouldn't mind if she showed up at the rectory wearing jeans or shorts, she'd brought along "church" clothes. It was Sunday, and noon mass would probably just be getting out when she arrived. She didn't want to offend Monsignor McKindry, who, Tommy had told her, was extremely conservative. He'd joked that if the monsignor could get away with it, he'd still be saying mass in Latin.

She put on a pale pink, ankle-length, linen, sleeveless dress with a high mandarin collar. The skirt had a slit up the left side, which she hoped Monsignor wouldn't think was too racy. Her long hair was still damp at the nape, but she didn't want to mess with it any longer, and after she fastened the dainty straps on her sandals, she grabbed her purse and sunglasses and went back downstairs.

The heat felt like a slap in the face as she stepped outside, and she couldn't quite catch her breath for several seconds. The poor doorman, an elderly man with salt-and-pepper hair, looked in jeopardy of melting, dressed as he was in his heavy gray uniform. As soon as the valet brought her car around the circle, the doorman stepped forward with a wide smile to open the door for her. But the smile vanished when she rechecked her directions to Our Lady of Mercy church.

"Miss, there are churches much closer to the hotel," he informed her. "Why, there's one just a couple of blocks away on Main Street called Visitation. If it weren't so hot, you could even walk there. It's a beautiful old church and it's in a safe neighborhood."

"I need to go to Our Lady of Mercy," she explained.

She could tell he wanted to argue with her, but he held his tongue. As she was getting into her car, he leaned forward and suggested that she lock her doors and not stop for any reason until she had reached the church's parking lot.

The area she drove into half an hour later was run-down and depressing. Abandoned buildings with broken windowpanes and boarded-up doorways lined the streets. Black graffiti on the walls screamed angry words at passersby. Laurant drove past a fenced-in, empty lot that some of the locals were using as a trash bin, and even with her windows up and the air-conditioning blasting away, she could still smell the stench of rotting meat. At the corner of the block were four little girls, about six or seven years old, dressed in their Sunday best. They were playing jump rope as they chanted a silly rhyme, giggling and carrying on like little girls do, oblivious to the destruction around them. In such decay, their innocence and beauty were jarring. The girls brought to mind a painting she had once seen during her studies in Paris. It was of a dirty brown field, fenced with black barbed wire, ugly and menacing with its sharp points. An angry gray sky swirled above. The mood was dark and bitter, yet in the left corner of the painting, entwined in the gnarled metal, a straggly yellow vine wound halfway to the top of the wire. And there, reaching toward heaven, was one perfect red rose just about to bloom. The painting was called *Hope,* and as Laurant watched the children at play, she was reminded of the artist's message—that life will go on, and even in such blight, hope can and will flourish. Laurant committed to memory the scene of the little girls playing, hoping one day, when she had her paints, to capture them on canvas.

One of the little girls stuck her tongue out at Laurant and then waved to her. Laurant retaliated in kind and smiled as the child dissolved into a fit of giggles.

Four blocks ahead, in the midst of the rubble, sat Our Lady of Mercy Church. Twin pillars, painted white, stood as sentinels guarding the neighborhood. Mercy looked worn out from her duty. She was in desperate need of repair. Cracked paint peeled at the top of the pillars and the side of the church, and warped, rotting boards curled along the foundation. Laurant wondered how old the church was and pictured her all spruced up again. From the ornate carvings along the roofline and the stonework in front, Laurant knew she had once been magnificent. She could be again, with a little care and money. But would Mercy ever be renovated to her former glory, or, as was the horrid fashion these days, would she be ignored until it was too late and then torn down?

A black wrought iron fence at least eight feet high surrounded the property on all sides. Inside the barrier was a large recently tarred parking lot and a whitewashed, stone house adjacent to the church. Laurant assumed this was the rectory and drove through the open gates, parking her car next to a black sedan.

She had just gotten out and was locking the door when she noticed the police car. It was parked in the rectory's driveway but was practically obstructed from view by the leafy branches of an old sycamore. Why were the police there? Probably more vandalism, she guessed, as Tommy had told her that the problems in the neighborhood had escalated in the last month. He thought it was due to the fact that the kids were out of school and there weren't any jobs or organized activities to keep them occupied, but Monsignor McKindry believed that the increased violence and desecration were gang related.

Laurant headed for the church. The doors were open, and she could hear organ music and voices raised in song. She was halfway across the parking lot when the music stopped. Seconds later people came pouring out. Some of the women were using the church bulletin to fan themselves, and several men were mopping the sweat from their brows with their handkerchiefs. Then Monsignor McKindry, looking as cool as a cucumber despite being dressed in long flowing robes, joined the crowd. Laurant had never met the monsignor, but she recognized him all the same from Tommy's description. The priest had shocking white hair and deep creases in his face. He was tall, and so thin as to appear sick. But, according to her brother, Monsignor ate like a lineman and was in the best of health, considering his advanced age.

His congregation obviously loved him. He had a smile and a kind word for every man and woman who stopped to speak to him, and he called each of them by his or her first name—impressive considering the number. The children adored him too. They surrounded him, tugging on his robes to get his undivided attention.

Laurant moved to the side of the steps in the shade of the building, waiting for Monsignor to finish his duties. Hopefully, after he had changed out of his vestments, he would walk over to the rectory with her while she questioned him in private about Tommy. Her brother tried to shield her from unpleasant news, so much so that she had learned not to trust him when he told her anything about his medical condition. From what Tommy had told her about Monsignor, she knew that, although the older priest was kind and compassionate, he was also honest to a fault. It was her hope that he wouldn't sugarcoat the truth if Tommy were no longer in remission.

Her brother worried about her worrying about him. It was ridiculous, the games they played. Because he was older and because there were just the two of them in the family now, Tommy tried to shoulder too much on his own. Admittedly, she had needed his guidance when she was a little girl, but she wasn't a little girl anymore, and Tommy needed to stop shielding her.

She happened to glance over at the rectory just as the front door opened and a policeman with a rather noticeable potbelly came out on the porch. He was followed by a taller, younger man. She watched as the two shook hands and the policeman headed for his car.

The stranger on the porch captured her full attention, and she blatantly stared at him. Impeccably dressed in a tailored white shirt, navy blue blazer, and khaki pants, he looked like he had just stepped off the cover of *GQ*. Yet he wasn't what she would call drop-dead gorgeous, or even handsome, at least not in the usual sense, and perhaps that was what appealed to her. She'd done a little bit of modeling for an Italian designer during her summer break from boarding school, before Tommy had found out and put a stop to it, but in those two and a half months she had worked with a fair number of pretty males. The man on the porch could never be called pretty. He was too rugged and earthy for such a label. And very, very sexy.

There was an aura of authority about him, as if he were used to getting his way. She stared at the sharp angle of his jaw, the hard line of his mouth. He could be dangerous, she thought, yet she couldn't define what it was about him that made her feel that way.

The stranger had an interesting face and a complexion that was unfashionably tanned. Interesting indeed.

One of Mother Superior's constant warnings rang like an alarm bell inside her head. *Beware of wolves wearing sheep's clothing. They'll steal your virtue every time.*

This man didn't look like he ever had to steal anything. She imagined women flocked to him and that he took only what was freely offered. He was something else all right. She let out a little sigh then, feeling guilty about having such thoughts just a few feet away from the holy church. Mother Mary Madelyne was probably right about her. She was going to go to hell in a handbag if she didn't learn to control her sinful imagination.

The stranger must have sensed her staring at him because he suddenly turned and looked directly at her. Embarrassed at being caught in the act of gawking at him, she was about to turn away when the front door opened, and Tommy came outside. Laurant was overjoyed to see him there, and not in a hospital bed as she had feared.

Dressed in his long black cassock and white Roman collar, he looked pale to her—and worried. She started weaving her way through the crowd.

Tommy and the stranger he was talking to presented a striking picture. Both were tall and dark-haired, but Tommy bore the Irish complexion with his ruddy cheeks and generous sprinkling of freckles across the bridge of his nose. Unlike her, when he accidentally stayed out in the sun too long, he didn't tan; he burned. He had an adorable dimple—at least she thought it was adorable—in his right cheek, and his boyish good looks had earned him the amusing nickname "Father What-a-Waste" from all the college and high school girls.

There certainly wasn't anything boyish

about the man standing next to her brother. He kept watching her make her way toward the porch as he listened to Tommy and occasionally nodded agreement.

He finally interrupted her brother when he tilted his head toward her. Tommy turned, spotted her, and shouted her name. Taking the stairs two at a time, his black robe flapping about his ankles, he raced to intercept her with a look of acute relief on his face.

Laurant noticed that his friend stayed on the porch, but he wasn't paying any attention to them now. He was thoroughly occupied watching the crowd disperse around them.

She was astonished by her brother's reaction to seeing her. She'd thought he'd be mad, or irritated at the very least, but he wasn't upset at all. In fact, he acted as though they'd been separated for years, even though she had seen him only a few days ago when he'd taken her on a tour of the abbey's attic.

Tommy engulfed her in a bear hug. "Thank God you're all right. I've been worried sick about you, Laurant. Why didn't you tell me you were coming? I'm so happy to see you."

His voice shook with emotion. Thoroughly confused by his behavior, she pulled away and said, "You're happy to see me? I thought you'd be furious that I followed you. Tommy, why didn't you call me Friday evening? You promised you would."

He finally let go of her. "And you've been worried, haven't you?"

She looked into his big brown eyes and

decided to tell him the truth after all. "Yes, I've been worried. You were supposed to call when you had the results of the blood work, but you didn't call and I thought...maybe the results weren't very good."

"The lab screwed up. That's why I didn't call. They had to redo the tests. I should have called, but damn it, Laurant, you should have let me know you were coming. I've got Sheriff Lloyd looking all over Holy Oaks for you. Come on inside. I've got to call him and tell him you're here, safe and sound."

"You called Sheriff Lloyd looking for me? Why?"

He grabbed hold of her arm and pulled her along. "I'll explain everything as soon as I get you inside. It's safer."

"Safer? Tommy, what's going on? I've never seen you so rattled. And who is that man standing on the porch?"

The question surprised her brother. "You've never met him, have you?"

"Who?" she asked, her frustration mounting.

"Nick. That's Nick Buchanan."

She stopped dead in her tracks and turned to her brother. "You're sick again, aren't you? That's why he's here...like the last time when you got so bad and you didn't tell me until—"

"No," he interrupted. "I'm not sick again." She didn't look like she believed him, and so he tried once again to convince her. "I promised you I would tell you when and if I had to have chemo again. Remember?"

"Yes," she whispered, her fear ebbing.

"I'm sorry I didn't call you Friday," he said. "It was inconsiderate. I should have let you know the tests got screwed up."

"If you don't have to have chemo again, why is Nick here?" she asked with a glance toward the porch.

"I sent for him, but the reason had nothing to do with my health." He rushed on before she could interrupt him. "Come on, Laurant. It's about time you met him."

With a smile she said, "The infamous Nick Buchanan. You didn't tell me he was so..." She stopped herself in time. She had always felt she could tell her brother just about anything, but it didn't seem appropriate now for her to admit that she thought his best friend was incredibly sexy. It was double jeopardy, she supposed, having an older brother who also happened to be a priest. There was no way he would understand or appreciate his sister having such ideas.

Nick and Tommy were more like brothers than friends. They met during a fistfight on the playground of St. Matthew's Elementary School when they were in second grade. They bloodied each other's noses and from that day on became each other's shadow. By an odd set of circumstances, Tommy ended up living with the Buchanan family of eight children most of his grade school and high school years, and then he and Nick went to Penn State University together.

"He's so what?" Tommy asked as he pulled her along.

"I'm sorry?"

"Nick's so what?"

"Tall," she said, finally remembering what they were talking about.

"I never sent you any photos?"

"No, you didn't," she said, casting her brother a frown for the oversight. Suddenly nervous, she took a deep breath, smoothed her skirt, and went up the stairs to meet him.

Lordy, lordy, he had blue eyes. Brilliant blue eyes that didn't miss a trick, she thought as Tommy made the hasty introductions. She put her hand out to shake his, but he wouldn't let her be formal. He pushed her hand away, pulled her into his arms, and hugged her. It was a brotherly embrace, and when she stepped back, he continued to hold on to her while he looked her over.

"I'm so happy to finally meet you. I've heard so much about you over the years," she said.

"I can't believe we haven't met before now," he replied. "I saw all the pictures of you when you were a kid. Tommy had them up on the wall of our dorm room, but that was years ago, and damn, Laurant, you sure have changed."

She laughed. "I hope I have. The sisters at the boarding school were thoughtful enough to send photos to my brother, but he, on the other hand, never sent me any."

"I didn't own a camera," Tommy said.

"You could have borrowed one. You were too lazy."

"Men don't think about things like that," he argued. "At least I didn't. Nick, we should get her inside, shouldn't we?"

"Yes, of course," he agreed.

Tommy held the screen door open and rudely shoved Laurant inside.

"What, in heaven's name, is the matter with you?" she demanded.

"I'll explain in a minute," he promised.

The foyer was dark and musty. Her brother rushed ahead and led the way into the kitchen at the back of the two-story house. There was a breakfast nook with a bay window overlooking Monsignor's vegetable garden, which took up most of the fenced-in backyard. An old rectangular oak table, one leg propped up with a coaster so it wouldn't wobble, and four spindle chairs sat in front of the three windows. The room had been recently painted a bright, cheerful yellow, but the blinds were torn and brown along the edges. They needed to be replaced, but she knew money was a precious commodity at Mercy.

Laurant stood in the center of the kitchen, watching her brother. He was acting like a nervous twit, pulling all the blinds down to the windowsills. Sunlight filtered into the kitchen through the cracks and tears, filling the room with soft light.

"What's the matter with him?" she whispered to Nick.

"He'll explain in a minute," he promised, repeating Tommy's exact words to her.

In other words, be patient, she thought.

Nick pulled a chair out for her and took the seat adjacent to her. Tommy couldn't seem to get settled. He sat down, then immediately jumped back up to get a notebook and pen from the linoleum counter. He was as jittery as a june bug.

Then Nick drew her attention when he stood up. His demeanor was just as serious as her brother's. She watched him loosen his tie and unbutton the top button of his shirt. The man oozed sensuality, she thought to herself. Was there a woman back in Boston waiting for him to come home? She knew he wasn't married, but he could be involved with someone. Surely he was.

Then Nick removed his jacket, and Laurant's fantasies came to a screeching halt.

As Nick draped the coat over the back of the empty chair next to him he watched the abrupt change in Laurant. Her back was now pressed against the chair as though she were trying to put as much distance between them as possible. He also noticed she was staring at his gun. Just a few seconds ago, she had been open and friendly, bordering on flirtatious. Now she looked guarded and uncomfortable.

"The gun bother you?"

She didn't give him a direct answer. "I thought you were an investigator."

"I am."

"Then why do you wear a gun?"

"It goes with the job," Tommy answered for his friend. He was shuffling through his papers, his head downcast while he tried to get organized.

Laurant's patience had run out. "I've waited long enough, Tommy. I want to know why you're acting so strange. I've never seen you this nervous."

"I have something to tell you," he began. "It's kind of difficult to know where to start." Looking past her, he said the last to Nick, who nodded.

"I think I know what it is," she said. "You did get your lab results, didn't you? And you're afraid to tell me about them. Did you think I'd make a scene, and that's why you waited? They weren't good, were they?"

He let out a weary sigh. "I got the results last night as a matter of fact. I was going to tell you later...after I explained what happened yesterday."

"Tell me now," she said quietly.

"Doctor Cowan felt real bad that the lab had screwed up the first time and so he made them rush the second blood work. He called from a wedding reception to let me know he finally got the results and everything's fine. Now will you relax?"

"So there's definitely no chemo this time?" Her voice sounded like that of a child, and she had so wanted to be adult about this. If anything happened to her brother, she didn't know what she would do. It seemed to her that she had only just found him and now this horrible illness was trying to take him away from her. "If everything's going so well, then why

70

are you so nervous? And you are nervous, Tommy. Don't tell me you aren't."

"Maybe you ought to just let her listen to the tape," Nick suggested.

"I don't want her to hear it yet. It'll be too much of a shock."

"Then let her read the transcript the police made."

Tommy shook his head. "I think it would be better if I just told her what happened first." He took a deep breath, then plunged in. "Laurant, this man came into the confessional just as I was about to close up." He paused for a few seconds while he collected his thoughts and then began again. "After I talked to the police, I made some notes, and while I was writing down what he said—"

Her eyes widened in disbelief, and she couldn't stop herself from interrupting him. "You wrote down a man's confession? You can't do that. It's against the rules, isn't it?"

He held up his hand to stop her. "I know what the rules are. I'm a priest, remember?"

"You don't need to snap at me."

"Sorry," he muttered. "Look, I'm just edgy and I've got a hell of a headache, that's all. This guy...all the while he was talking to me, he was making a tape."

She was astonished. "He recorded the conversation? Why would anyone want to tape his own confession?"

"He probably wanted a keepsake," Nick suggested.

Tommy nodded. "So anyway, he must have

gone right out and made a copy of the tape. We know it isn't the original because of the whirling sound in the background," he explained. "He dropped the copy off at the police station. Can you believe it, Laurant? He just sauntered inside and left it on a desk."

"But why would anyone go to so much trouble?"

"He wanted to make sure I could talk about it," he explained. "It's all part of a sick game he's playing."

"What's on the tape?" She waited for him to answer, and when he hesitated, she demanded, "Tommy, just spit it out for heaven's sake. It can't be as bad as you're making it sound. What did the man say that was so upsetting?"

Her brother pulled his chair closer to hers before he sat down again. Taking both of her hands in his, he said, "This man told me he's planning...he wants..."

"Yes?"

"He's going to kill you."

aurant didn't believe him, not at first anyway. Tommy recounted what the man had said to him in the confessional. She didn't interrupt, but with each new detail she could feel her body stiffen. For a second or two, she was actually relieved that she was the target and not her brother. Tommy had enough to deal with now.

"You're taking this awfully well."

Her brother had made the remark in an almost accusatory tone of voice. Both he and Nick were waiting for her to absorb the information, watching her intently as though she were a butterfly trapped under a glass.

"I'm not sure what to think," she responded. "I don't want to believe it's true...what he said."

"We have to take the threat seriously," Nick cautioned.

"This other woman he talked about...Millie. He told you he killed her a year ago?" she asked.

"He bragged about it."

A shiver ran through her. "But was her body ever found?"

"He said he buried her deep, where no one will find her," Tommy answered.

"We're running the name through VICAP,"

Nick interjected. "Their computer system stores information on unsolved homicides that have been reported. It looks for possible matches. Maybe we'll get a lucky break."

"I believe what he told me. I think he did kill that poor woman. He wasn't making it up, Laurant."

"Did you see him?" she asked.

"No," he replied. "I ended it when he told me you were his next victim. I jumped up and ran out." He paused to shake his head. "I don't know what I thought I was going to do. I was pretty shook up."

"But you didn't see him? He had already gone? How could anyone move that fast?"

"He hadn't left."

"He cold-cocked him," Nick told her.

"He what?" she asked, unfamiliar with the term.

"He knocked me out," Tommy explained. "He was waiting for me and he got me from behind. I don't know what he used, but I'm lucky he didn't crush my skull. I went down hard," he added. "And the next thing I knew, Monsignor was leaning over me. He thought I'd passed out from the heat."

"My God, you could have been killed."

"I've taken worse hits playing football."

Laurant made Tommy show her where he'd been struck. When she touched the lump at the base of his skull, he winced. "It still stings," he said.

"Maybe you should let a doctor look at that."

"I'll be all right, but damn, I wish I had seen his face."

"I want to listen to the tape. Did you recognize the voice?"

"No."

"Maybe I will."

"He mostly whispered."

Tommy was frightened. She could see it in his eyes and hear it in his voice when he next spoke.

"Nothing's going to happen to you, Laurant. We're going to make sure you stay safe," he fervently promised with a nod toward Nick.

She didn't say anything for a long while but simply stared at the dripping faucet in the sink across the room. Her head was reeling.

"You can't be blasé about this," Tommy warned.

"I'm not."

"Why are you so calm?"

She put her elbows on the table, bowed her head, and pressed her fingertips against her temples. Calm? She knew she was an expert at hiding her emotions—she'd done it for years—but she was surprised her brother couldn't see how shaken she was. She felt like a grenade had just gone off in her head. Her quiet, peaceful world had just been blown apart. She was anything but calm.

"Tommy, what do you want me to do?"

"I'll tell you what you can't do. You can't take any chances, Laurant, not until this is over and they've caught him. You can't stay in Holy Oaks."

"How can I leave? My best friend is getting married, and I'm her maid of honor. I'm not going to miss that. And you know my store is set to open in two weeks, and it still isn't ready. Then, there's the public hearing coming up about the town square. People are depending on me. I can't just pack up and leave."

"It would only be temporary, until they catch him."

She shoved the chair back and stood. She couldn't sit there another second.

"Where are you going?" Tommy asked.

"I'm going to make a cup of hot tea."

"Tea? It's ninety-eight degrees in the shade, and you want hot tea?" She scowled at him and he backed down. "Okay, okay. I'll show you where everything is."

They watched her fill the teakettle with water and put it on the burner. After she'd gotten a tea bag out of the canister and put it in the cup, she leaned her hip against the counter and turned back to her brother. "I have to think about this."

"There's nothing to think about. You've got to leave. You don't have a choice in this, Laurant. I won't have you—"

Nick quietly interrupted, "Tommy, you ought to call Sheriff Lloyd."

"Yeah, you're right." He'd forgotten about the sheriff until Nick reminded him. "And maybe while I'm gone, you can talk some sense into her," he added with a frown at Laurant. "She can't be difficult about this. She has to understand this is serious."

"I'm not being difficult," she argued. "Just give me a minute, all right?"

Reluctantly, he got up and went to make the call. Nick used his mobile phone to alert the police that Laurant was there. Then he called his superior. While he was talking to Morganstern, she made her tea and carried it to the table. Then she sat down again.

"You need to get one of these," he said as he put the phone back in his breast pocket. "We would have known where you were and could have gotten hold of you while you were on the road."

"In Holy Oaks everyone knows where everyone else is. It's like living in a fishbowl."

"The sheriff didn't know where you were."

"He probably didn't bother to ask anyone. He's very lazy," she said. "My neighbors knew where I was going and so did the two men who were looking after the store while the workmen were there."

She picked up the transcript of the conversation the police had made, began to read it, and then put it back down.

"I'd like to listen to the tape now."

Unlike her brother, Nick was anxious for her to do just that. He left the kitchen to get the cassette player, and when he returned he put it in the center of the table.

"Ready?" he asked.

She stopped stirring her tea. She put the spoon in the saucer, took a breath, then nodded.

He hit the play button and leaned back.

Laurant stared at the whirling cassette as she listened to the conversation that had taken place in the confessional. Hearing the stranger's voice made the horror more real to her, and by the time the tape ended, she was nauseated.

"My God."

"Did you recognize his voice?"

She shook her head. "It was such a low whisper, I didn't get all of what he said. I don't think I've heard him before. I'll listen to it again," she promised, "but not yet, all right? I don't think I can..."

"Some of what he said was deliberate...calculated. At least that's what I think. He wanted to spook Tommy."

"And he succeeded. I don't want my brother to worry, but I don't know how to stop him. It isn't good for him...the stress."

"You've got to be realistic, Laurant. A man tells him he's going to kill his sister after he gets his kicks, and you don't think he should worry?"

She threaded her fingers through her hair in agitation. "Yes, of course...it's just..."

"What?"

"It isn't healthy for him."

Nick had noticed her slight French accent when she first spoke to him, but now the accent was more pronounced. She might have looked calm and collected, but that facade, like a thin layer of ice, was cracking.

"Why me?" she asked, sounding genuinely bewildered. "I live such a boring...ordinary life. It doesn't make any sense."

78

"A lot of weirdos don't make any sense. There was this case a couple of years back. This pervert did six women before they finally caught him. You know what he told them when they asked him how and where he chose his victims?"

She shook her head.

"At the grocery stores. He'd stand out front and he'd smile at the women as they rushed past him. The first one who smiled back...that's the one he wanted. Ordinary women, Laurant, leading ordinary lives. You can't look for reasons with these guys, or waste your time trying to figure out how their minds work. Leave that to the experts."

"Do you think the man in the confessional is a serial killer?"

"Maybe," he allowed. "And maybe not. He could just be getting started. The profilers will know more after they've heard the tape. They'll have some insight."

"But what do you think?"

"There's a hell of a lot of inconsistencies here."

"Such as?"

He shrugged. "For one thing, he told Tommy he did the other woman a year ago, but I think he was lying about that."

"Why?"

"Because he also said he's gotten a real taste for it," he reminded her. "The one statement conflicts with the other."

"I don't understand."

"If he got off on it—torturing and killing the

woman—then he did her recently and not a year ago. He wouldn't have been able to wait that long."

"Nick, what about the letter he said he sent to the police?"

"*If* he wrote it, and *if* he mailed it, then they'll get it tomorrow or the day after. They're ready," he added. "And they'll run it for prints, but I doubt he left any."

"I don't suppose they found any prints on the cassette, did they?"

"Actually, there was one, but it wasn't our man's. The kid who checked him out at Super Sid's Warehouse had a record, so his prints were on file. It was easy to track him to the warehouse," he explained. "His probation officer helped him get the job."

"Did he remember who bought the tape?"

"Unfortunately, he didn't," he answered. "Have you ever been to one of those stores? The traffic going through there is unbelievable, and it was a cash-only counter, so there wasn't any credit card receipt or check to trace."

"What about the confessional? Did they find any prints there?"

"Yeah, hundreds."

"But you don't think any of them are his?"

"No, I don't," he replied.

"He's very smart, isn't he?"

"They're never as smart as they think they are. Besides..."

"What?"

"We're going to be smarter."

Nick radiated confidence, and it suddenly dawned on Laurant that he probably had been trained to present a calm demeanor so that witnesses and victims wouldn't panic.

"Does anything ever rile you?" she asked.

"Oh, yes."

"You're sure the man on the tape is serious, aren't you?"

"Laurant, no matter how many times you ask me the question, the answer's going to be the same. Yes, I think he's serious," he patiently repeated. "He's gone to a lot of trouble researching you and Tommy and me. Like I said before, his intent was to scare your brother, and he sure as hell succeeded. Tommy's convinced this guy's crazy, but I've got this feeling that most of what he said was carefully rehearsed. Now we have to figure out his real agenda."

She could feel her control slipping and clinched her hands. "I can't believe this is happening," she whispered, her voice cracking. "Did you hear what he did to that woman? How he tortured her? Did you..."

He took hold of her hand and squeezed. "Laurant, take a deep breath. All right?"

She did as he suggested, but it didn't help. The impact of what she had heard was finally hitting her full force. Chilled to the bone, she pulled her hand away and began to rub her arms.

She was covered with goose bumps and was visibly shivering. Nick grabbed his jacket and draped it around her shoulders. "Better?"

"Yes, thank you."

He had the sudden urge to put his arm around her and comfort her just like he would one of his own sisters if she were scared, but he didn't know how Laurant would react, and so he stayed where he was and waited for her to give him some sort of signal.

She pulled the jacket tight around her with a death grip on the lapels.

"How long have you been here?"

"About an hour."

Both of them fell silent, and for several minutes the only sounds were the ticking of the clock above the kitchen sink and Tommy's muffled voice from the living room. Nick noticed she hadn't touched her tea. Then Laurant looked up at him, and he saw the tears in her eyes.

"Are you feeling overwhelmed?" he asked.

She brushed a tear away and answered, "I was thinking about that woman...Millie...and what he did to her..."

The tea was cold, and she decided to make another cup. Then she decided to fix a cup for Nick too. The chore kept her busy and gave her a moment to try to get a grip on her emotions.

Nick watched her work and thanked her when she put the unwanted tea in front of him. Waiting until she sat down again, he said, "I was wondering how you're going to hold up."

"You're hoping I'm tougher than I look?"

"Something like that."

"Exactly what is it you do for the FBI?"

"I work for the lost-and-found department."

"What is it you find?"

"When I'm lucky?"

"Yes, when you're lucky."

He leaned over to hit the rewind button and then glanced back at her. "Kids. I find kids."

His eyes were the most intense shade of blue, and when he looked at her directly, she felt as though he were trying to see inside her mind. She wondered if he were analyzing her every move as though she were a chess piece. Was he trying to find her vulnerability?

"It's specialized work," he commented, hoping that would put an end to the discussion about his job.

"I'm sorry we had to meet this way...under these circumstances."

"Yeah, well..."

"Look how I'm shaking," she said as she put her hand out for him to see. "I'm so angry I want to scream."

"Then do it."

The suggestion brought her up short. "What?"

"Scream," he said.

She actually smiled, so silly was the notion. "Monsignor would have heart failure, and so would my brother."

"Look, just take a few minutes and try to chill out."

"How do you propose I do that?"

"Let's talk about something else, just for a little while...until Tommy comes back."

"I *can't* think about anything else right now."

"Sure you can," he advised. "Try, Laurant. It might help calm you down."

She reluctantly agreed. "What should we talk about?"

"You," he decided.

She shook her head, but he ignored it and continued on, "It's odd, don't you think, that we've never met before today?"

"Yes, it is odd," she agreed. "You've been my brother's closest friend since you were little boys, and he lived with your family all those years, yet I don't know much about you at all. Tommy came home for summer vacation, and you were always invited to come too, but you never did. Something always came up."

"My parents went over once," he said.

"Yes, they did. Your mother brought family photos with her, and there is one of you...actually it's the entire family...and Tommy... standing in front of a fireplace at Christmas. Would you like to see it?"

"You've got it with you?"

She didn't have any idea how telling it was that she carried the photo with her. He watched her dig her billfold out of her purse. She'd put the picture in one of the plastic covers that came with all the billfolds, and when she handed it to him, he noticed her hand wasn't trembling anymore.

He looked at the photo of the eight Buchanan kids clustered around their proud parents. Tommy was there too, squeezed in between Nick's brothers Alec and Mike. His brother Dylan was sporting a black eye. Nick figured he'd probably given it to him during one of their family football games.

"Your mother helped me learn all the names," she said. "You're a little blurry though, and Theo's elbow is blocking half your face. No wonder I didn't recognize you today."

He handed the billfold back to her, and as she was putting it away, he said, "I know a lot about you. Tommy had pictures up on the wall, the ones the nuns sent of you when you were little."

"I was very homely."

"Yeah, you were," he teased. "All legs. Tommy would read me some of your letters too. It used to tear him up that he couldn't bring you over to live with him. He felt so guilty. He had a family, and you didn't."

"I did all right. I spent my summer vacations with Grandfather, and the boarding school was really very nice."

"You didn't know any other way of life."

"I was happy," she insisted.

"But weren't you lonely?"

85

She shrugged. "A little," she admitted. "After Grandfather died."

"Are you comfortable with me?"

The question jarred her. "Yes, why?"

"We're going to be spending a lot of time together, and it's important that you feel you can relax around me."

"How much time will we be spending together?"

"Every minute of every day and night until this is over. It's the only way, Laurant." Without pausing to give her time to absorb that bit of news, Nick commented, "Your brother went crazy when he found out you were modeling."

She smiled again. "Yes, he did get a little crazy. That episode merited a long-distance call to the Mother Superior. I couldn't believe my own brother would tell on me."

"The Mother Superior...her name was Mother Madelyne, wasn't it?"

His memory was impressive. "Yes," she answered. "After Tommy told on me, Mother called the people I was supposed to be visiting during the summer break. They were very wealthy, and I had met an Italian designer through them."

"He took one look at you and wanted you, right?"

"He wanted me to model his spring fashions," she corrected. "And I was in several shows."

"Until Mother Madelyne dragged you back to the convent."

"It was mortifying," she admitted. "I was

put on probation, which meant pots and pans for six months. Overnight, I went from glitz to dishwater hands. Do we spend every minute together, Nick?"

He didn't miss a beat. "When you brush your teeth, I'll squeeze the toothpaste."

Once again he switched back to the topic of her past. "Eleven months later you were on the cover of one of those fashion magazines, and when Tommy showed it to me, I couldn't believe it was the same scrawny little kid with skinned knees."

He was giving her a compliment, but she didn't know how to respond, and so she said nothing at all.

"You and I are going to be inseparable," he said.

"Do you mean that first thing in the morning you'll be standing on my doorstep before I've even gotten dressed for the day?"

"No, that isn't what I mean. I'll be getting dressed with you. What side of the bed do you sleep on?"

"I beg your pardon?"

He repeated the question.

"The right side."

"Then I'm on the left."

"Are you joking?"

"About the bed? Yeah, I am. But I'm going to do whatever is necessary to keep you safe. I'm going to blatantly invade your privacy, and you're going to let me."

"For how long?"

"As long as it takes."

"What happens when I take a shower?"

"I'll hand you the soap."

"Now I know you're joking."

"Laurant, I'm going to be close enough to scrub your back. That's just the way it has to be. You need to understand that I'm going to be the first thing you see in the morning and the last thing you look at before you close your eyes at night. You and I are in this together."

"But if you're spending all your time with me, how are you going to catch him?"

"I work for a powerful organization, Laurant, remember? They're already investigating. Leave it to us to catch him. It's what we're trained to do."

She rested her chin in the palm of her hand. She didn't say a word for a long minute, and then she straightened up again and looked him right in the eyes.

"I won't let him scare me. I want to help. I promise I won't do anything stupid," she hastened to add. "No, I'm not scared now. Just angry. Furious, in fact, but not scared."

"You should be scared. Fear will keep you coiled, focused, on your toes."

"But it can also paralyze, and I won't let it paralyze me," she assured him. "This man...this monster," she corrected, "tells my brother how much fun he had torturing and killing a poor, innocent woman, and then he tells him the craving's come back and that he's chosen me for his next amusement. He's so clever, he knows Tommy wants to see his face, so he waits for him to come outside the confessional and then he hits him on the back of the head. He could have killed him."

"He didn't want to kill him or he would have," Nick said quietly. "He's using Tommy as his messenger now." He saw the look that crossed her face and immediately sought to reassure her. "Don't worry about your brother. We're going to keep him safe too."

"Night and day," she demanded.

"Of course," he agreed.

She nodded. "Doesn't it seem to you that this man is calling all the shots now? He tells Tommy to notify you and make you take me away and then *maybe* he won't follow. And my brother wants to do just that. Hide me."

"Of course he wants to hide you. He loves you and he doesn't want anything to happen to you."

She rubbed her temples with her fingertips. "I know," she said. "And I would probably react the very same way."

"But?"

"I know my brother, and right now he's in agony worrying about something else that man said to him in the confessional that neither you nor Tommy has mentioned in front of me."

"What's that?"

"He told Tommy he would try to find someone else to amuse himself with." Her voice shook as she continued. "For whatever reason, he decided to warn me so I could get away, but this other woman won't have any warning, will she?"

"No, she probably won't," he agreed. "But you've got to—"

She interrupted him. "Running away isn't an option. I'm not going to give anyone that kind of power over me. I won't be scared."

"I think we should discuss this later, after Pete's had time to go over the tape with the profiler."

Nick tried to get up from the table, but Laurant grabbed hold of his hand. She didn't want to wait. "I know that you must have some theories. I want to hear them. I need information, Nick. I don't want to feel powerless, and right this minute that's exactly how I feel."

His eyes bored into hers for several seconds before he made up his mind. Then he nodded. "All right, I'll tell you what we know. To begin with, my superior, Dr. Peter Morganstern, already has listened to a copy of the tape. He's a psychiatrist who heads my department and he's the best there is. If anyone can get into this creep's mind, he can. Just remember, Pete hasn't had time to sit down and analyze every word."

"I understand."

"Good. First, let's talk facts. The most important fact is that this wasn't random. You were specifically chosen."

"Do you know why?"

"We know he chose you because he's...dedicated...to you," he said, searching for the right word.

"What does that mean?" she asked impatiently.

"It means you've got a fan. It's what we call them...fans."

"That doesn't make any sense. I'm not a movie star or a celebrity. I'm just an average person."

"Look in the mirror, Laurant. There isn't anything average about you. You're beautiful. He thinks you're beautiful." He hurried on before she could interrupt. "And most victims these guys select aren't high profile."

She took a breath and then said, "Go on. I need to know exactly what I'm up against. You aren't scaring me," she added so he wouldn't continue to choose his words so carefully. "I want to know everything so I can fight back, and by God, I am going to fight back."

"Okay, here's what he's telling us. He's been stalking you for a long time now. He knows everything about you. Everything. He knows what kind of perfume you wear, what your favorite foods are, what kind of detergent you use in your laundry, what books you read, what your sex life is like, what you do every minute of every day. He wants us to know that he's been inside your house at least a couple of times, but probably more. He sat in your chairs, he ate your food, and he went through your drawers. It's his way of getting to know you," he explained. "He's probably taken something from your underwear drawer to keep, something you wouldn't miss right away. Think about it, and you'll remember some old nightgown or T-shirt that you haven't been able to find lately. The garment has to be something you wear close to your skin."

"Why?" she asked, shaken by Nick's description of the man he called a fan. She didn't want to believe that anyone had gone through her house uninvited and searched through her things, and the thought that she was being watched made her skin crawl.

"It has to have your scent on it," he explained. "It makes him feel closer to you. Whatever it is, he's sleeping with it," he added, remembering the man's words about wrapping himself in her fragrance.

"Anything else?" she asked, surprised at how normal she sounded.

"Yeah," he said. "He's watched you sleep."

"No, I would have known," she cried out.

He tapped the cassette player. "It's all there."

"What if I had opened my eyes...what if I woke up and saw him?"

"That's what he wants you to do," he said. "But not yet. He'd be upset if you forced him to hurt you now."

"Why?"

"You'd be speeding up his agenda."

"Go on. I'm not scared," she reiterated.

"What I just told you...that's what he wants us to know. Here's what we're theorizing at this point. He lives in Holy Oaks, and he's someone you come into contact with all the time, maybe even on a daily basis. You're friendly with him, but like I said before, he's reading all sorts of other messages. Pete says he's in the adoration stage. That means he thinks you're pretty damned perfect, and he wants to protect you. The guy's obsessing now, and he's clearly at war with himself. He wants us to believe he is anyway. He might genuinely like you, Laurant, and in that case he doesn't want to hurt you, but he knows he's going to because no matter what you do, you're going to disappoint him. In his mind, there's no way you can live up to his expectations—he'll make sure of that—and there's no way you can win."

"You said he's in the adoration stage but that's going to change. When do you think it will happen?"

"Are you asking me how soon? I don't know," he admitted. "But I don't think we'll have to wait long. You could already be...tarnishing...in his mind. Look, he's got to find something wrong with you so he can feel betrayed. Maybe it will be the way you smile. All of a sudden, he's going to think you're mocking him, or maybe he'll believe you're coming on to some other man. That would definitely enrage him. He'd like us to think he's tormented. Remember, he promised Tommy that if you ran away from him, he might not follow you. But he also boasted that he is brilliant and that he wants more of a challenge."

"Maybe he'll get tired of this...obsession."

"He isn't going to go away." Nick's voice had a sharp edge now. "The fantasy's controlling him. He can't stop. It's a cat-and-mouse game to him, and you're the mouse. He likes the hunt. The more challenging it is, the more fun. The game won't be over until you have begged for mercy."

He leaned forward and studied her closely. "Well, Laurant? Are you scared yet?"

What a delightful time he'd had toying with the priest. Delightful indeed. He really hadn't expected that he would have so much fun, because he'd learned from past experiences that sometimes the buildup—the planning stage in his schedule, as he liked to call it—turned out to be far more rewarding than the actual event—like when he was a boy and he was building his fort in the back-yard. The joy was in the anticipation for what he was going to do inside his isolated cocoon where no one could spy on him. Oh, he'd spend hours and hours getting ready, a busy little beaver sharpening the kitchen knives and scissors he'd stolen from his mother's drawer, and meticulously preparing the burial sites for the animals he'd trapped and caged. The killings always turned out to be anticlimactic though. The animals never squealed enough to satisfy him. But in this instance, good old Tommy boy hadn't let him down. No, no, he hadn't been disappointed in the priest at all.

As he was driving down the highway, he replayed the conversation in his head over and over again until he was laughing out loud and tears were streaming down his face. There wasn't anyone around, and so he could be as loud and raucous as he wanted to be, but then, come to think of it, he could pretty much do whatever he wanted to do these days, anytime, anywhere, as long as he was careful. Just ask pretty little Millicent. Oh, nope, you couldn't do that. No, sirree.

Father Tom's tortured cry when he realized the next victim was none other than his precious sister kept echoing in his mind. "My Laurant?" the priest had shouted.

"My Laurant?" he mockingly imitated. Priceless. Really priceless.

It was a pity he had had to leave so abruptly. He would have enjoyed tormenting Tommy a bit longer, but there simply hadn't been time, what with all those wasted minutes spent on that nonsense about not being able to tell anyone what had been said inside the confessional, even after he'd given him permission. By God, he'd ordered him to tell. It hadn't made any difference to the priest though. No, sirree. It hadn't. Oh, he'd known about the church's precious regulations guarding their sacraments—he *always* did his homework—but he'd misjudged Tommy because he hadn't counted on him being such a stickler for the rules. Who would have thought the priest would be so stubborn, when spilling the beans would save his own sister's hide? Who would have thought? A priest who wasn't morally bankrupt. My, oh my, what a dilemma that turned out to be. Had he been an ordinary man, his plans would have been ruined, and he would have had to start over again. But he wasn't ordinary. No, no, of course not. He was brilliant, and he had, therefore, anticipated every possibility. He'd almost blurted out, right there in the confessional, that he was taping the conversation, but he'd decided to let Tommy be surprised. He had hoped he wouldn't have to share the tape though, not yet anyway. It would be added to his impressive and certainly eclectic collection. Millie's tape was getting plumb worn out. Some insomniacs listened to the soothing sounds of the ocean or gentle rainfall when they went to bed; he listened to Millie's sweet voice.

The priest had forced his hand with that stupid confession rule, and the only way to get around it had been to break the rule himself by letting the police have a copy of the tape. Always thinking ahead, that was the ticket. One quick trip to Super Sid's Warehouse to pick up a three-pack of blank cassettes, a couple of manila envelopes, and he had taken care of the problem.

He would not allow anyone or anything to

interfere with his schedule, which was why he always had an alternative plan of action in mind. Anticipate and respond. That was the key.

He let out a loud yawn. There was so much to do in preparation, and because he was meticulous to a fault in everything he did, he needed every single minute of the next couple of weeks to get ready for his own special Fourth of July celebration.

It promised to be...explosive.

Now he was on his way to St. Louis, thanks to his helpful friend, the Internet. What a wondrous invention that was. The perfect accomplice. It never whined, complained, cried, or demanded. And he didn't have to waste precious time training it. It was like a well-paid whore, giving him what he wanted, when he wanted it. No questions asked.

Who would have imagined it would be so easy to learn how to make your own bombs in simple one-two-three steps a child of average intelligence could follow, with colorful illustrations to help the slow-witted along? If you had the money—which he did—you could order more sophisticated triggering devices—which he had—and lovely "enhancing" kits that turned little ear-tingling pops into ear-bleeding booms guaranteed to take out a city block, or your money back. He didn't have any desire to find nuclear ingredients, but he had a feeling that if he searched the subterranean rooms long enough and got real friendly with those stupidly dedicated anarchists, he would find everything but the plutonium. Weapons weren't a problem either, as long as you knew where to click on. And he did, of course. Yes, he did.

Although he had ordered lots of interesting little gadgets through the Internet, he hadn't ordered the explosives because he knew the mules could be monitoring the sight. Still, he'd gotten the connection he'd needed from one of his buddies who had hooked him up with an illegal dealer operating out of the Midwest, which was why he was now breezing down I-70 with his shopping list in his pocket.

He spotted a roadside rest area ahead and thought about stopping so he could get his copy of the tape out of the back of the van. He wanted to listen to the priest's voice again, but then he saw the police car parked there and he immediately changed his mind.

The mules were probably replaying the tape now while they made copious notes. It wasn't going to do them any good though. They weren't smart like he was. They wouldn't get anything from his voice except maybe the region he came from, and who cared about that? They would never figure out his game until it was over and he had won.

He knew what the mules were calling him. The unsub. He liked the sound of it and decided that Unknown Subject was about the best nickname he'd ever acquired. The simplicity of it appealed to him, he supposed. By using the word *unknown*, the mules—his nickname for the FBI agents—were admitting how inept and incompetent they were, and there was something honest and pure about their stupidity and their ignorance. The mules actually knew they were mules. How delightful.

"Are we having fun yet?" he shouted as he sped down the highway. And then he laughed again. "Oh, yes, we are," he added with another chuckle. "Yes, sirree."

CHAPTER

8

Two detectives from the Kansas City Police Department, Maria Rodrigues and Frances McCann, arrived at the rectory a little past two. As the interview got under way, Nick, silent and watchful, remained by Laurant's side. He let the detectives run the show and didn't interfere in the questioning or volunteer any opinions or suggestions. When he got up to leave the room, Laurant had to force herself not to grab hold of him to keep him there. She wanted him close by, even if only to offer moral support, but he'd gotten a phone call from a man named George Walker, a profiler assigned to the case.

Tommy joined them, and the first couple of minutes with him were very predictable. Like most women who met her brother for the first time, the detectives seemed captivated and had trouble taking their eyes off him.

"Are you a full-fledged priest?" Detective McCann asked. "I mean, have you been ordained and everything?"

Tommy gave her one of his grins, completely unaware of the heart flutters they caused in most women, and responded, "I'm full-fledged."

"Maybe we should stick to the investigation," Rodrigues suggested to her partner.

McCann flipped open her notepad and looked at Laurant. "Did your brother tell you how we got hold of the tape?" She didn't wait for an answer but continued. "The son of a bitch just strolled inside the police station sometime last night, dropped his little package, and then strolled right back out. I mean, it was the perfect time 'cause it was a zoo in there. Two big drug busts had just gone down, and they were dragging their drugged-out asses in for over an hour. The watch said he didn't notice the package until things had calmed down. Anyway, we figure he must have been dressed in blues, like a street cop, or maybe he was pretending to be a lawyer, come to bail his client out. No one remembers seeing anyone with a manila envelope," she added. "That's what the tape was in, and to be honest, it was such a hectic time, I doubt anyone would have noticed the envelope if the son of a bitch hadn't called."

"He called 911 from a pay phone in City

Center Square," Rodrigues interjected. "That isn't too far from here."

"The guy's got steel balls, I'll give him that," McCann remarked. She colored then and blurted, "Sorry about the language, Father. I've been hanging around Rodrigues too long."

"So what can you tell us?" Rodrigues asked Laurant.

Laurant raised her hands in a gesture of futility. She didn't have the faintest idea how to help them—she couldn't even come up with a viable theory as to why she had been targeted.

The detectives didn't have any leads yet, though it wasn't for lack of trying. They had already canvassed the neighborhood, searching for witnesses who might have noticed a stranger or a car in the vicinity late Saturday afternoon. No one had seen or heard anything out of the ordinary, which hadn't surprised the detectives.

"People around here are suspicious of the police," Rodrigues explained. "We're hoping that if anyone saw anything peculiar, he'll confide in Monsignor or maybe even Father Tom here. The parishioners trust their priests."

Neither Rodrigues nor McCann were optimistic about catching the unsub quickly. They would have to wait and see what developed. Maybe the letter the man had told Tommy he'd mailed would shed some insight. Then again, maybe not.

"Aside from assaulting Father Tom here, no

other crime has been committed," McCann said. "At least not yet anyway."

"Do you mean to tell me that if I'm murdered, then you'll look into it?" Laurant asked a little more sharply than she intended.

McCann, the more blunt of the two, responded. "Do you want me to sugarcoat it or be honest?"

"Be honest."

"Okay," she replied. "We're pretty territorial, kinda like big cats, and it would depend on where he dumped the body. If it's our city, we take the case."

"A crime has already been committed," Tommy reminded them.

"Yes," Rodrigues agreed. "You were assaulted, but—"

Tommy interrupted. "I didn't mean that. He confessed to killing another woman."

"Yeah, well, he says he killed her," Rodrigues countered. "He could have been lying about that."

McCann volunteered her opinion that the incident in the confessional was just a sick prank by an irate man who maybe had a grudge against Father Tom and wanted to get back at him. That was why, she explained, they had spent so much time on their first call questioning him about possible enemies.

"Look, we aren't going to sit on our hands," Rodrigues assured Laurant. "But we don't have a lot to go on yet."

"And it isn't our jurisdiction."

"How do you figure that, Detective McCann?"

Nick asked the question. He was leaning against the door frame, watching the detectives.

Her tone was antagonistic when she answered. "The unsub reported the crime here in Kansas City, but he made it clear on the tape, clear to us anyway, that he lives in or around Holy Oaks, Iowa. We'll share what we've got with the police there, and we'll keep the file open of course...in case he comes back."

"The way we see it, the FBI's involved. Right? You guys are bound to come up with something," Rodrigues offered.

McCann nodded. "We don't like to interfere in an FBI investigation."

"Since when?" Nick asked.

She smiled. "Hey, we're trying to get along here. I don't see why we can't work on this together. You give us what you've got, and if we come up with anything, we'll be happy to share it with you."

They weren't getting anywhere. After the detectives gave Laurant their cards, they left the rectory. Laurant was thoroughly frustrated by the lack of action, even though she realized her expectations had been unrealistic. She wanted answers and results—maybe even a miracle—to make this nightmare go away, but by the time the detectives left, she felt...hopeless. Because her brother seemed so relieved that something was being done— the cavalry had arrived after all—she didn't tell him how she felt. In fact, she didn't get a chance to talk to him for the rest of the afternoon. His attention was diverted elsewhere.

Tommy was so rattled by what was happening, he forgot it was Sunday afternoon. But then he happened to look out the window and saw the kids waiting for him. There was a tradition at Mercy parish on warm Sunday afternoons when Tommy was in town, and he wasn't about to let anything get in the way of the ritual that meant so much to the children in the neighborhood. At precisely quarter of three, all other duties and concerns came to a standstill, when a large number of neighborhood kids gathered in the church parking lot and began to clamor for Father Tom to come outside. Tommy put on a pair of shorts and a T-shirt, kicked his shoes and socks off, and grabbed a towel. He made Laurant stay inside—it was safer he told her—but she could watch the fun from one of the windows.

As was the custom and barring any unforeseen complications, a fire truck arrived at three o'clock, and two good-hearted off-duty firemen closed the gates to the lot and opened the fire hydrant. The children, including toddlers through high schoolers, eagerly waited while the firemen adjusted the heavy nozzle between the iron gates and clamped it to the rails so that the hose wouldn't go skittering every which way. Then the water was turned on. The kids wore cutoff jeans or shorts. None of them owned swimming suits—such apparel wasn't in their parents' budgets—

but that didn't diminish their excitement. After stacking their towels and shoes on the steps of the rectory, they played in the water until their clothes were soaked, splashing and shouting with as much enthusiasm as any children at a country club. There weren't any fancy kidney-shaped pools with diving boards and water slides at Mercy. They made do with what they had, and for an hour, while the firemen and any other adults who had tagged along with their little ones sat with Monsignor on the porch and sipped cold lemonade, chaos reigned.

When Tommy wasn't busy holding on to the smaller children so they wouldn't be swept into the bushes by the force of the spray, he manned the medical kit and dispensed Neosporin, glow-in-the-dark Band-Aids, and sympathy for skinned knees and elbows. After the firemen turned the water off and prepared to leave, Monsignor dispensed Popsicles. No matter how tight money was or how poor the collections were that week, there was always enough set aside for these treats.

After the pandemonium had died down and the waterlogged, worn-out children had all gone home, Monsignor McKindry insisted that Nick and Laurant join Tommy and him for a peaceful dinner. Tommy and Nick prepared the meal. Nick grilled chicken while Tommy fixed a salad and green beans fresh from the monsignor's garden. The table conversation revolved around the monsignor's reunion, and he entertained his guests with one story after another about the trouble he and his friends had caused during their seminary days. By unspoken agreement, no one discussed what the older priest called the "disturbing event" during dinner, but later as Monsignor McKindry and Laurant worked side by side washing and drying the dishes, he brought up the topic again when he asked her how she was handling the worry. She told him she was frightened, of course, but also so angry she wanted to start throwing things. Monsignor took her at her word and immediately snatched the plate she was drying out of her hands.

"When your brother found out he had cancer, I know he felt powerless and frustrated and angry, but then he decided to take charge of his medical care. He read as much as he possibly could about his specific type of cancer, and that was quite a challenge because his is such a rare type. He studied all the medical journals and he interviewed a good number of specialists in the field until he found the man who had set the protocol for treatment."

"Dr. Cowan."

"Yes," Monsignor replied. "Tom felt that Dr. Cowan could help him. He didn't expect any miracles, of course, but Tom had faith in Dr. Cowan, and the physician seems to know what he's doing. Your brother's holding his own in this battle," he added. "And that's why, when the oncologist transferred to Kansas Medical Center, Tom followed him. What I'm trying to advise you to do, Laurant, is take charge. Figure out a way you can do that and then you won't feel so helpless or afraid."

After they finished cleaning the kitchen, Monsignor brewed her one of his special toddies, guaranteed to soothe her frazzled nerves. Then he said his good nights and went upstairs to bed. The drink was bitter, but she dutifully drank it down because Monsignor had gone to so much trouble for her.

It had been a hell of a day. It was late now, almost ten o'clock, and the stress had worn her out. She sat on the sofa next to her brother in the rectory living room, trying to pay attention as they formulated their plans. But concentration was difficult, and she couldn't keep her thoughts from wandering. She couldn't even seem to block out the background noise. An old air conditioner propped in the window adjacent to the fireplace droned on and on like a swarm of angry bees, yet barely cooled the room. Occasionally the unit would shudder violently before returning to the monotonous droning again. She kept expecting the thing to leap out of the window. Icy condensation dripped down into a spaghetti pot Tommy had placed under the window to protect the hardwood floor he was determined to refinish one of these days, and the constant pinging noise was driving her to distraction

Nick was full of energy. He was pacing around the living room, his head down as he listened to what Tommy was saying. Her brother, she noticed, was quieter—he'd taken his tennis shoes off and propped his feet up on the ottoman. There was a huge hole in one of his white socks, but he didn't seem to notice, or care, that his big toe was sticking out. He was yawning every other minute.

Laurant felt as limp and lifeless as a rag doll. She put the china cup on the table, sank back into the soft cushions of the sofa, took a couple of deep breaths, and closed her eyes. Maybe tomorrow, after a good night's sleep, she'd be more clearheaded.

So lost was she in her own thoughts, she flinched when Tommy nudged her knee to get her attention.

"Are you falling asleep on us?"

"Just about."

"I think you and Nick should stay here tonight. We've got two extra bedrooms. They're Spartan but adequate."

"You've only got one extra bedroom," Nick said. "Noah's going to be here anytime now."

"Who's Noah?" Laurant asked.

"A friend," Nick answered. "He's coming in from D.C."

"Nick thinks I need a baby-sitter."

"Bodyguard," he corrected. "Noah's good at what he does. He's going to stick to you like gum on a shoe. No arguments. I can't be in two places at once, and since you want me to stay with Laurant, I'm putting Noah on you."

"Do you think Tommy's in danger?" Laurant asked.

"I'm not taking any chances."

"Is Noah with the FBI?"

"Not exactly."

He didn't go into detail, but she was too curious to drop the subject. "Then how do you know him?"

"We used to work together. Noah's...specialized...and Pete uses him every now and then. I had to call in a favor to get him. He's swamped with business these days."

"As a bodyguard?"

"You could say that."

"You aren't going to tell me what his specialty is, are you?"

Nick grinned. "No, I'm not."

Tommy yawned loudly. "It's settled then?"

"What's settled?" she asked.

"Haven't you been paying attention? We've been discussing the matter for the past fifteen minutes."

"No, I haven't," she admitted, and because he was her brother she didn't feel the need to apologize. "What did you settle?"

"You're going away with Nick." He glanced up at his friend and added, "That's what I decided anyway. Nick's ambivalent."

"Oh? Where would we be going?"

"Nathan's Bay," he answered. "You could stay with the family. They'd love to see you, and I know they've been begging you to come. It's a great place, Laurant, and it's isolated too. There's only one way in and out," he added. "Over a bridge. I'm telling you, you'll love it there. The front yard is the size of a football field, and just beyond is the water. Maybe Theo will take you sailing. You've met Nick's brother, remember?"

"Yes, of course I remember him. He stayed with Grandfather and me for a week after he finished law school."

"And aren't you still corresponding with Jordan?" he asked, referring to Nick's sister.

"Yes, and I'd love to see her again, and Judge and Mrs. Buchanan too, but—"

Tommy cut off any protest she was going to make. "And you'd finally get to meet all the others," he pressed. "I'm sure they'll come home to see you."

"That would be nice, but Tommy, now isn't the time."

"It's the perfect time. You'll be safe, and that's all you should be thinking about now."

"What makes you think this lunatic won't follow me? Have you considered Nick's family? I could be putting them in danger."

"We'd make it secure," Nick said. He sat down in the easy chair on the other side of the ottoman and leaned forward, bracing his arms on his knees. "But I think we're going to be staying here for another day, maybe two."

"To wait for the letter the man told Tommy he mailed to the police?"

"We don't have to wait on that."

"I want my sister out of here now," Tommy insisted.

"Yeah, I know you do."

"Then why do you want to hang around? It's dangerous," he argued.

"I doubt our man is still in Kansas City. He's done what he came here to do. He's probably gone back home. We're staying because Pete's coming here. He's personally overseeing the investigation, and he wants to talk to you."

"About what?" Laurant asked. "What can Tommy tell him he doesn't already know?"

Nick smiled. "Lots of things," he said.

"When is he coming?"

"Tomorrow."

"I was pretty shaken up when I talked to him," Tommy said. "I was real desperate to find you because I figured you'd know what to do."

"Do you still figure that?" Nick asked.

"Of course."

"Then let me do my job. Laurant and I will wait to talk to Pete before I take her away. I'm going to protect her, Tommy, and you're just going to have to trust me."

He slowly nodded. "I'll try not to get in the way. Is that good enough?"

The doorbell rang and the conversation came to an abrupt end. Nick told Tommy to stay where he was and went to open the door. Laurant noticed he unsnapped the flap over his gun on his way out of the room.

"I'm sure that's Nick's friend, Noah."

"Do you think he sleeps with it?" she asked her brother in a whisper.

"Sleeps with what?"

"His gun."

He laughed. "Of course not. You don't like it, do you?"

"I don't like guns."

"Do you like Nick?"

She shrugged. "I liked him before I met

111

him because he's been such a good friend to you, and he seems very nice."

"You think so?" he asked, and then he laughed again. "Nick would get a kick out of hearing that. When the chips are down, when things get bad, he isn't nice at all. That's what makes him good."

Before she could nag him into giving her specifics, Nick returned to the living room. His friend Noah followed him.

Tommy's bodyguard certainly made a strong first impression. Laurant suspected that if he were ever involved in a brawl, he'd come out the winner and relish the good time he'd had slamming heads together.

He was dressed in faded jeans and a light gray T-shirt, and his sandy blond hair was in desperate need of a trim. There didn't seem to be an extra ounce of fat anywhere, and the muscles in his upper arms strained the bands on his shirtsleeves. A scar below his eyebrow and a devilish grin gave him a rakish appearance, and she knew before he'd spoken a word that he was a flirt and a ladies' man. He'd already given her the once-over as he crossed the room to shake Tommy's hand, and his gaze, she'd noticed, had lingered on her legs a bit longer than was necessary.

"I really appreciate you taking the time from your busy schedule to come here," Tommy said.

"Yeah, well, to be honest, I wasn't given a choice. Nick asked."

"He owes me," Nick explained.

"True," Noah agreed, his gaze still on Laurant. "And he never lets me forget it."

When Tommy introduced him to his sister, he took hold of her hand and didn't let go. "You're a hell of a lot prettier than your brother," he drawled. Glancing at Nick, he added, "Say, I've got a great idea."

"Forget it," Nick replied.

Acting as though he hadn't heard him, he suggested, "Why don't I take her and you can have her brother."

"She's off limits, Noah."

"How come?" he asked, his eyes locked on Laurant's. "You married?"

"No," she answered, smiling over his outrageous behavior.

"Then I don't see the problem. I want her, Nick."

"Too bad," Nick snapped.

Noah's smile widened. He had obviously gotten just the reaction he wanted because he winked at Laurant, as though she were a partner in his game to irritate Nick. He finally let go of her hand and turned to Tommy again. "So what do I call you? 'Tom' or 'Tommy' or just plain 'priest'?"

"You call him 'Father,'" Nick interjected.

"But I'm not Catholic."

"Tom or Tommy will be fine," Tommy said.

"Pete told me you have a copy of the tape," Noah said then. His smile was gone now. "I think I'd better listen to it."

"It's in the kitchen," Tommy told him.

113

"Good," he replied. "I'm starving. Have you got anything to eat?"

"Would you like me to fix you something?" Laurant offered.

When Noah looked at her again, the smile was firmly back in place. "Yeah, I'd like that a lot."

Nick didn't like it at all. Shaking his head, he said, "You can fix yourself something to eat. Now that you're here, Laurant and I are going to take off. She's wiped out."

"What's the schedule tomorrow?" Noah asked.

"I've got to go back to the hospital for a couple of tests," Tommy said. "Just routine stuff," he added for Laurant's benefit.

"Hell, I hate hospitals."

"They ought to be sending you thank-you notes," Tommy remarked dryly. "From what Nick's told me about you, you send them a lot of customers."

"Nah, I cut out the middleman. I send them right to the morgue. Saves time and money." Noah glanced at his friend. "What'd you tell your priest about me?"

"That you shoot to kill."

Noah shrugged. "That's about right, but then, so do you. My aim's better, that's all."

"No, it isn't," Nick countered.

Laurant was fascinated by the conversation, but she couldn't tell if Noah was joking or telling the truth. "Have you killed a lot of people?"

"Now Laurant, you know better than to

114

ask me that. I can't kill and tell. Besides, it's a sin to brag, isn't it, Tom?"

Nick laughed. "Bragging is the least of your sins, Noah."

"Hey, I'm a good man. I like to think of myself as an environmentalist."

"How's that?" Nick asked.

"I'm doing my part to make the world a better place." Turning back to Tommy he asked, "Are we going to be at the hospital all day?"

"No, I've got an early appointment in radiology. We should be back here by eight or nine."

"Is it time for another MRI?" Nick asked with a mischievous twinkle in his eyes. "If so, I really want to be there for you."

"What's so funny about an MRI?" Noah asked.

Nick shook his head and Tommy actually blushed as he answered. "As a matter of fact, I am having another MRI, but Nick can't go with me. He's been banned from radiology."

Noah wanted details, and it didn't take Laurant long to realize she was the reason Nick and Tommy weren't giving him any. They squirmed around their explanation like naughty schoolboys hauled in front of the principal.

"If you'll excuse me, I'll just go and get my purse."

She hadn't even reached the kitchen before she heard the laughter. Tommy was telling the story, but because he was speaking in such a low voice, she could only catch a word or two. Whatever had happened with Nick in the radiology department was hilarious to the three men. She found her purse on the floor next to the chair, looped the strap over her shoulder, and then leaned back against the table and waited for the laughter to die down.

Nick came looking for her. "You ready?"

With a nod she followed him to the front door. Tommy stooped down so she could kiss him on the cheek, and Noah immediately imitated the action.

Laughing, she pushed him back. "You're a terrible flirt."

"Yeah, I am," he agreed. "And you're one hell of a beautiful woman."

Ignoring the compliment, she said, "Watch over my brother."

"Don't you worry. I've been bred to do just that. I come from a long line of law enforcement officers, so I'm a natural protector. It's in the genes," he added. "Sleep well, Laurant."

She nodded. Nick opened the door, but she paused on the threshold. "Noah? What's your last name?"

"Clayborne," he answered. "Noah Clayborne."

aurant's car was a piece of junk. The carburetor was clogged; the spark plugs needed to be replaced, and the transmission was slipping. Nick was surprised they made it across town to the hotel.

He had made reservations from the rectory. They were registered under the names of Mr. and Mrs. John Hudson. They stopped by the reception desk to pick up their keys and then went upstairs. In the elevator he told her he'd had her clothes transferred.

"Very efficient of you."

"I'm an efficient kind of guy."

He stepped out of the elevator first, made sure the hallway was empty, then walked by her side down the long, red carpeted corridor. It was as quiet as a tomb. Their suite was at the very end of the hall. Nick inserted the plastic card in the lock and pushed the door wide.

"Did I mention we've got the bridal suite? It's all they had available. Now Laurant, don't go all awkward on me," he hastily added when he saw her expression. "You look like you want to run."

She forced a smile. It *was* awkward, but

she was determined to get past it. "I'm too tired to run anywhere."

"Want me to carry you over the threshold?"

She didn't answer. He finally gave her a little nudge to get her moving. She hesitantly stepped into the one-bedroom suite. She heard the door click behind her, and she felt a sudden pang of nervousness. This wasn't the time to be embarrassed or shy, she reminded herself. Nick was standing right behind her. She could feel the heat from his body. She quickly walked away from him and looked around the living room. It was beautifully decorated in soft, soothing taupe colors. There were two chocolate chenille sofas facing each other with a black marble coffee table in between. In the center of the table was a large crystal vase filled with fresh spring flowers, and on the sideboard in front of the triple windows overlooking the plaza lights, was a silver tray laden with fruit, cheese and crackers, and a bottle of champagne submerged in a black onyx bucket of ice.

Nick was doing something funny with the door. He had a thin wire in his hand and was threading a loop around the door latch. On the end of the wire was a tiny square box about the size of a nine-volt battery, and after he twisted the wire around the doorknob, he turned the box, and a red light suddenly began to blink.

"What is that?"

"My own personal security system," he told her. "Jordan designed it for me. If anyone

118

tries to get in while I'm in the shower or asleep, I'll know about it."

He stood up, rolled his shoulders, and then suggested she get ready for bed. "I'll use this bathroom, and you can have the one off the bedroom."

Nodding, she walked to the door separating the living room from the bedroom and then paused. There was a king-size bed, and the white comforter and sheets had already been turned down for the night. A long-stemmed red rose was in the center of the bed, and Godiva chocolate squares, wrapped in gleaming gold paper, were on two of the pillows.

"What's the matter?" he asked when she continued to stand at the entrance.

"There's a rose on the bed."

He crossed the room to see for himself. "Nice touch," he remarked.

He was just a foot away, leaning against the door frame. She couldn't quite look at him when she said, "It *is* the bridal suite."

"Yep, it is," he agreed. "You feeling awkward again?"

"No, not at all," she lied.

"You can have the bed, and I'll take the sofa out here."

She heard a loud crunch. Nick had just taken a huge bite out of an apple. Juice dripped down his chin, and he casually wiped it away with the back of his hand and offered the apple to her. She leaned over and took a much smaller bite.

The tension left, and he was suddenly her

big brother's best friend again. She headed for the bathroom, and while she was sorting through her overnight bag, looking for her nightshirt, out of the corner of her eye she saw Nick dive on the bed and grab the TV remote.

She stayed in the shower a long time, letting the hot water beat down on her shoulders until all the tension of the day eased away. She was drained by the time she finished blowing her long hair dry. She put on an extra-large Penn State nightshirt, slapped on some moisturizer, and then grabbed her tube of Chanel body lotion and went back into the bedroom.

Nick had made himself at home. He was leaning back against the pillows he'd propped against the headboard, his long muscular legs sprawled out in front of him with one ankle crossed over the other. He had changed into a pair of old frayed shorts and a white shirt. His hair was still wet from his shower, and he was barefoot. A small notebook and a ballpoint pen were on his lap and the television remote control was in his hand. He looked completely at ease.

There were complimentary robes hanging in the closet, but she'd forgotten to take one of them into the bathroom with her, and since he'd just given her little more than a cursory glance and turned back to the television, she stopped worrying about being prim and proper. She wasn't scantily clad in a negligee after all. The nightshirt covered her from her neck to the top of her knees.

Nick didn't take his gaze off the television. Outwardly, he was immobile, concentrating on the TV screen, but inside his thoughts were turning somersaults. When Laurant had stepped out of the bathroom, he'd taken it all in, those incredible long legs, the soft swell of her breasts under the thin fabric, her beautiful neck, her flushed cheeks, and that perfect mouth of hers. He didn't think he could have been more aroused if she'd been wearing one of those lacy little teddies from the Victoria's Secret catalog.

Oh, yeah, he'd noticed it all and in just under three seconds max. It had taken every ounce of discipline he possessed to look away, and honest to God, if she'd asked him what he was watching on television right now, he wouldn't have been able to tell her.

He was a little shocked—and a lot disgusted—by his reaction to her.

"You're just like my brother," she remarked as she stretched her legs out, tugged the nightshirt down, and then propped two fat pillows behind her back. Imitating him, she crossed one ankle over the other and began to twist the lid open on her lotion.

There was a lot of room between them on the king-size bed, but it was still a bed. *Get over it,* he told himself. *She's Tommy's kid sister.*

"What did you say?" he asked.

She was rubbing the pink lotion on her arms when she answered him. "I said that you're just like my brother. Tommy always has the remote clutched in his hand."

Nick grinned. "That's because he knows the secret."

"What secret?"

"He who controls the remote, controls the world."

She laughed, and that only encouraged him. "Haven't you ever noticed how the President is always patting his vest pocket? He's making sure the remote's still there."

She rolled her eyes. "And all this time I thought it was just a nervous habit."

"Now you know the truth."

She put the lotion on the table next to the bed and slipped under the covers. She blankly stared at the television for a minute, but her thoughts were racing.

"Noah's good at what he does, isn't he? I know you told me that he is, but after I met him, I felt like I didn't have to worry about Tommy any longer. Noah made me feel confident that he'll watch out for my brother. Oh, I know he was teasing about all that kill-and-not-tell stuff...he was teasing, wasn't he?" she asked.

Nick laughed. "Yes, he was."

"You told me that Pete uses him every once in a while, but that Noah doesn't work for the FBI?"

"He does and he doesn't. It's kind of like being a little bit pregnant."

"There's no such thing."

"Exactly," he replied. "Noah likes to think of himself as a free agent."

"But he isn't?"

"No. Pete runs him."

She wasn't sure what he meant by that remark. "And because Pete works for the FBI and Noah works for him…"

"He works for the FBI too. We just don't tell him so."

Smiling, she said, "I can't tell when you're serious. I feel numb everywhere. Hopefully, in the morning I'll be clearheaded again."

Tomorrow, when her thoughts weren't playing Twister inside her head, she'd decide how to handle things. But for now, she was just too exhausted to think.

She fell asleep watching him watch the hockey game.

CHAPTER

10

When Laurant woke up, she could hear Nick moving around in the living room. Grabbing her bag, she hurried into the bathroom to get dressed. Her choice of clothing was limited. She'd left Holy Oaks in such a hurry, there simply hadn't been time to give her wardrobe consideration. When she'd packed, she'd thought she'd only be in Kansas City overnight, but she had thrown in a short black linen skirt and a white top just in case Tommy had been admitted to the hospital. The linen skirt was going to look like she'd slept in the thing once she sat down, but it was going to have to do.

She had just put on one shoe and was reaching for the other when Nick knocked on the bathroom door.

"Breakfast is here," he called. "As soon as you're ready, we've got work to do."

She came out holding a shoe in her hand. "What kind of work?"

He motioned to a notebook on the table. "I thought we'd make a list. It'll give me a head start, but I'll warn you now, we'll be going over all this several times."

"I won't mind. What exactly are we going to go over?"

He pulled the chair out at the table and waited for her to sit down. "A couple of things. First, we're going to make a list of people who might have a grudge against you. You know...enemies. Folks who would be happy if you just disappeared."

"I'm sure there are people who dislike me, but I honestly don't think any of them would wish me harm. Do I sound naive?" She bent down to put her shoe on. When she straightened up again, Nick was putting a croissant on her plate.

"Yeah, you do," he answered. "Do you want some coffee?" he asked as he reached for the carafe.

"I don't drink it, but thanks anyway."

"I don't drink it either. Odd, huh? We must be the only two people in the world who don't support Starbucks."

He straddled the chair across from her and pulled the cap off his pen.

"You said first we're going to make a list of enemies. What else?" she asked.

"I want to know about any friends who are maybe a little too attentive. But, first things first. How long have you lived in Holy Oaks?"

"Almost a year."

"You moved there to be close to your brother, and you're opening a store soon, right?"

"Yes. I purchased an old, run-down building in the town square and it's being renovated now."

"What kind of a store is it?"

"Everyone's calling it the corner drugstore, because that's what it used to be years ago, but I won't be selling any drugs, not even aspirin. It's going to be a place where the college kids can hang out, but also, hopefully, where town families can bring their children for ice cream. There's going to be a soda fountain with a lovely marble top and a jukebox."

"Fifties or sixties stuff, huh?"

"Sort of," she agreed. "I've done a lot of work for the sororities and fraternities designing logos and artwork for their T-shirts and banners, and I hope to get more. There's a loft above the soda fountain with wonderful windows and lots of light. That's where I plan to work. The store isn't big, but there's a veranda out front and I'm thinking about putting tables and chairs there during the warm months."

"You aren't going to make much money selling ice cream and T-shirts, but then, I guess with your trust you don't have to worry about that."

She didn't agree or disagree with his assumption. She merely added, "I also do a lot of design work for the local businesses, and I'm going to teach a course this fall."

"I know you studied art in Paris," he said. "You paint, don't you?"

"Yes," she said. "It's a hobby."

"Tommy told me you won't even let him see any of your work."

"When I get better, I will," she said. "*If* I get better."

"Is there anyone who doesn't want you to open your store?"

"Steve Brenner would love to see me fail, but I don't think he would hurt me or my brother just to get me to leave town. He even asked me out on a date once. He's a bother really. He doesn't like to hear the word no."

"I take it you didn't go out with him?"

"No, I didn't. I don't like him at all. Money means everything to him. He heads the Holy Oaks Advancement Society. Honest, that's what they call themselves, even though there are only two of them." She thought to add, "Steve Brenner is a realtor."

"And the other member of this society?" Nick asked as he added Brenner's name to the list.

"Sheriff Lloyd MacGovern."

"So what do the two of them want to do to advance Holy Oaks?"

"They want to buy all the buildings around the square for some developers," she said. "Steve's the brains in the scheme, the one trying to put it all together. Even if an owner sold directly to the developers, Steve and the sheriff would get a commission. It's the way Steve set it up, or so I'm told."

"And what do the developers want the property for?"

"They want to mow down all those beautiful old buildings and put up housing for the college expansion. Huge, ugly apartments for married students."

"Couldn't the developers build them somewhere else?"

"Yes, they could, but they also plan to put in a superstore right outside of town," she explained. "If they get rid of all the shops around the square..."

"They've cornered the market."

"Exactly."

"Who are the developers?"

"Griffen, Inc.," she answered. "I haven't met any of them. They're based in Atlanta. Steve's their spokesman. They're offering the owners a lot of money...top dollar."

"Is anyone else besides you holding out?"

"There are a lot of people in town who want to see the buildings restored and not torn down."

"Yeah, but how many of them own businesses around the square?"

She sighed. "As of last Friday there were four still on my side."

"The others caved?"

"Yes."

"I want you to draw a diagram for me and write in all the names of the owners. You can do it later," he added.

"All right," she agreed. "I've been calling it the town square, but it's actually a three-sided square. A little park leads in on the fourth side. There's a lovely old fountain. It's at least sixty, maybe seventy years old, but it still works...and there's a bandstand. During the summer months, the local musicians get together every Saturday night and play there. It really is charming, Nick."

She closed her eyes and began to recall the names of those who had signed on with Griffen, starting with the struggling hardware store owner.

"Margaret Stamp owns a little bakery in the center block," she explained. "And Conrad Kellogg owns the town pharmacy. He's on the block directly across from me. It's critical that they hold firm, because if one of them sells, Griffen can tear down their block, and once one apartment building goes up, the square's lost."

"What happens when Tommy gets transferred and leaves Holy Oaks? Will you sell your store then and follow him?"

"No, I'll stay where I am. I like Holy Oaks. I'm comfortable there. It has a rich history, and people care about one another."

"I can't imagine living in a little town. I'd go nuts."

"I love it," she said. "I felt...safe...until this happened. I believed that in a small town you knew who your enemies were. I guess I was wrong about that."

"I know you moved there after Tommy got so sick."

"He almost died."

"But he recovered. You could have taken a leave of absence from the gallery in Chicago and gone back there after Tommy got better, but you quit instead. How come?"

She looked down at the plate and nervously straightened the silverware on the table. "I wasn't running to my brother. I was running away from a very uncomfortable situation. It was a...personal matter."

"Laurant, I warned you that I was going to invade your privacy, remember? I'm sorry if it embarrasses you to talk about personal things, but you're still going to have to," he added. "Don't worry. I won't tell your brother."

"I'm not worried about that. It was just so...stupid," she said, glancing up at Nick again.

"What was stupid?"

"I met this man in Chicago. In fact, I worked for him. We dated for a little while, and I thought I was falling in love with him. That's what was stupid. He turned out to be..."

She was having trouble coming up with the perfect word to describe the man who had

129

betrayed her. Nick came to her aid. "Slime? Scum? Bastard?"

"Slime," she decided. "Yes, he was definitely slime."

He turned a page in his notepad and asked her for the man's name.

"Joel Patterson," she answered. "He was head of the department."

"And...? What happened?"

"I found him in bed with another woman, a friend, as a matter of fact."

"Ouch."

"It's not funny. At least it wasn't funny at the time."

"No, I don't suppose it was," he agreed. "Sorry, I wasn't being very sensitive, was I? Who was she?"

"Just a woman who worked for the gallery. Their affair didn't last long. She's involved with someone else now."

"Give me her name."

"Are you going to check her out too?"

"I sure am."

"Christine Winters."

He wrote her name on his pad, then looked at Laurant. "Let's go back to Patterson for a minute."

"I don't want to talk about him."

"Still wounded?"

"No," she answered. "Just still feeling stupid. Do you know that he had the gall to blame me?"

Nick lifted his gaze from the writing pad and gave her a sideways glance. "You're kidding?"

His astonished expression made her smile. "It's true. He told me it was all my fault that he went to bed with Christine. 'Men have needs,'" she quoted.

"And you weren't putting out, huh?"

"What a quaint way of stating it. No, I wasn't."

"Why not?"

"Excuse me?"

"You thought you loved him. Why didn't you go to bed with him?"

"Are you justifying—"

"No, of course not. The guy's a jerk. I was just curious, that's all. You said you loved him..."

"No, I said I thought I was falling in love with him," she corrected as she pulled the croissant apart and reached for the jam. "I was being very practical," she explained. "Joel and I shared the same interests, and I thought we had similar values. I was wrong about that."

"You still haven't answered my question. Why didn't you go to bed with him?"

She couldn't skirt the issue any longer. "I was waiting for...I wanted..."

"What?"

"A little magic. A spark anyway. There should be...shouldn't there?"

"Hell yes, there should."

"I tried, but I couldn't make myself feel..."

"Laurant, it's either there or it isn't. You can't manufacture it."

She laid the jam knife on her plate, then dropped her hands in her lap and slumped against the back of the chair. "I'm not very good with relationships," she said.

"Did Patterson tell you that?" He didn't wait for an answer. "He really messed with your head, didn't he? What else did good old Joel tell you when he was busy blaming you for driving him to another woman?"

She could tell he was getting angry, and the fact that it was on her behalf made her feel good. "He said my heart was made of ice."

"You don't believe that nonsense, do you?"

"No, of course not," she said. "But..."

"But what?"

"I've always been very reserved. Maybe I am a little cold."

"You're not."

His denial was given with conviction, as though he knew something she didn't. She would have asked him to explain, but their conversation was interrupted when the phone rang and Nick got up to answer it.

"That was Noah," he said when he returned. "Pete's plane just landed. Let's go."

Fifteen minutes after Noah's phone call, Nick was driving her back to the rectory.

"Your transmission's slipping," he commented as they started the climb up Southwest Trafficway. "I noticed it last night, but I was hoping I was wrong."

"I guess I'll have to have it looked at again."

It was another hot, humid day. The air-conditioning wasn't cooling the car well at all, and so she rolled down her window.

"I think your compressor's had it too," he told her. "She's got over ninety thousand miles on her, Laurant. It's time to trade her in."

"Trade *her* in?" she repeated, smiling. "It's a car, Nick, not a woman."

"Men like to bond with their machines," he explained. "Good men coddle them."

"Is that another one of the secrets you boys share?"

"Not boys," he corrected. "Men. Manly men."

She laughed. "Does Dr. Morganstern realize he has a nut working for him?"

"What makes you think *he* isn't nuts?"

"Is he?" She turned serious when she added,

"I imagine he's heard and seen some terrible things, hasn't he?"

"Yes, he has."

"And so have you."

"Yeah, well it goes with the job."

"Tommy worries about you."

They had just started up another steep incline and Nick was listening to the grinding sound as the transmission tried to shift gears. Wincing over the god-awful noise, he made up his mind to have a mechanic look her over before Laurant drove the car again. She was damned lucky she hadn't gotten stranded on the highway.

He glanced at her over the top of his sunglasses. "Tommy wants me to get married and settle down," he said. "He thinks a family will make my life more normal. It isn't going to happen though. With the work I do, marriage isn't in the equation, and having children of my own...that's definitely out of the question."

"Don't you like children?"

"Sure I do," he replied. "But I know I'd ruin them. If I had any of my own, I wouldn't let them out of my sight. Yeah, I'd ruin them all right."

"Because you'd be afraid that something might happen to them...because you've seen—"

He cut her off. "Something like that. What about you? Do you want to get married and have a child?"

"Yes, I do...someday. I don't want just one child though. I want a houseful of them and I don't care if it's fashionable or not."

"How many constitute a houseful?"

"Four or five or maybe even six. Does Dr. Morganstern have any children?"

"No, he and Katie weren't able to have any, but they do have lots of nieces and nephews, and they always have someone camping out at their house."

She watched Nick for a moment. "Why do you keep looking in the rearview mirror?"

"I'm a cautious driver."

"You're checking to make sure no one's following us, aren't you?"

"That too," he allowed.

"Where's your gun?"

With his left hand he lifted the holster he'd wedged between the seat and the door. "Never leave home without it," he said. "I'll have to put it on when we reach the rectory. Rules," he explained.

Propping her arm on the window, she stared out at the old buildings along the avenue. She was thinking about Dr. Morganstern, wondering what he was going to be like, if he would be reasonable when she told him what she wanted to do. She had already decided to go around Tommy and Nick—both were too emotionally involved to be practical about the situation—but she hoped that the doctor would understand and help her, with or without her brother's cooperation.

"Laurant, we'll finish making that list later," Nick said. "We probably should have started it last night, but you were pretty wiped out."

"About last night...I was wondering..."

"Yes?" he asked when she hesitated.

"I fell asleep while you were watching a game."

"Not a game, *the* game. The Stanley Cup play-offs," he explained.

"Did you watch all of it?"

"To the bitter end."

"And then what did you do?"

He knew what she was trying to find out, but the devil in him decided to make her ask. "I slept," he answered.

A long minute passed. "Where?"

He smiled. "With you."

The tone of his voice was self-assured. His aim, no doubt, was to make her blush, and she decided it was high time she turned the tables on him. She was always prim and proper, but not this time. "So was it good for you?"

He laughed. "Sure was. I slept like a baby. Now I'm worried though. What's your brother gonna say when I tell him I slept with his sister?"

"I won't tell if you won't."

"Deal."

They reached Mercy, and Nick parked the car in front of the church so that he wouldn't interrupt the basketball game in progress. They spotted Noah and Tommy right away. They were standing nose to nose in the center of a group of teenagers. Tommy was wearing a pair of khaki shorts and a white polo shirt. Noah had on torn jeans, a black T-shirt, and his brown leather shoulder holster and gun. The expression on his face was downright menacing. It didn't take Laurant long to figure out why. Tommy was holding a whistle to his lips, and Noah was in his face, arguing over a call he'd made. Her stubborn brother had never been one to back down, and he was now giving as good as he was getting. His face was beet red, and he was being every bit as belligerent as Noah. The boys were clustered around her brother like a small legion of warriors ready to strike on command.

Laurant got out of the car before Nick had time to open the door for her. She saw him slip on his gun and tried not to let it bother her.

"I thought Tommy had to go to the hospital for more tests today," she remarked.

"It's after ten now," he said. "They've probably already been there."

"Shouldn't you do something about that?" she asked with a nod toward Noah, who had just poked Tommy in the chest. Her brother retaliated by blowing his whistle in Noah's face.

Nick burst out laughing. "Look at the boys' faces."

"They don't like Noah shouting at their priest."

"He's just having some fun."

"But I don't think the boys understand that. Noah's outnumbered."

"You think so?"

She looked up at him. "You don't think so?"

"He can hold his own," Nick said.

"I'm going inside," she said, waving to her

brother as she crossed the parking lot. She saw Monsignor waiting for her in the open doorway and hurried toward him.

Noah spotted her out of the corner of his eye. He stopped shouting in midinsult and turned his back on Tommy so he could get a better view.

"What are you staring at?" Tommy demanded, still panting from the shouting match.

"Laurant," Noah answered. "She's got a great body."

"You're talking about his sister," Nick reminded him, giving his shoulder a shove from behind.

"Yeah, I know. It's hard to believe they're related. She's so damned pretty and sweet, and he's such a jerk. By the way, your friend's as blind as a bat," he added. "He can't even tell a ball's out of bounds when the line's two feet away from him."

The shouting match started all over again.

Ten minutes later the three of them came lumbering inside. Tommy was mopping his brow with the edge of his shirt, but Nick and Noah hadn't even broken a sweat. They were all laughing as they headed for the kitchen to get something to drink.

Laurant stepped back into the living room to get out of their way, shifting the heavy laundry basket she was holding to her other hip.

"I can't believe you offered those kids beers," Tommy chided.

"It's hot out," Noah defended. "I figured they'd want one."

"They're underage," Tommy pointed out in exasperation. "And it's not even noon yet."

Nick winked at her as he passed her again, carrying a six-pack of Coke. Noah told Tommy to stay inside while he and Nick talked to the boys on the porch.

"What was that all about?" she asked her brother.

"One of the boys told Monsignor he might have seen the car the guy was driving Saturday, so Nick is talking to him."

"Did the boy tell the police?"

"No, none of the kids talk to the police," he explained. "But they all heard what happened, and as Frankie—he's the leader of the pack—so eloquently put it, 'Nobody's gonna come in our 'f''ing parish and mess with one of our 'f''ing priests.'"

Laurant's eyes widened. Tommy nodded. "Frankie's a good kid," he said. "But he has to keep up appearances. Being tough is important to all of them. Anyway, they started talking to their friends. They all hang out on the street, day and night, and one did remember seeing a strange van parked on Thirteenth Street, next to that empty lot. Nick's hoping he can get a description of the guy driving. Keep your fingers crossed," he added. Then, switching the subject, he asked, "What are you doing with the laundry basket?"

"I can't stand waiting. I have to keep busy,

so I asked Monsignor if I could help with anything."

Tommy opened the door to the basement, turned on the light, and watched her go down the wooden steps.

Dr. Morganstern arrived five minutes later. She could hear him talking when she came up the stairs. The men were standing together in the front hall. His agents were a full head taller, and so was Tommy, but they were all deferentially "siring" him to death.

Laurant was nervous and apprehensive about meeting the doctor, and she hoped it didn't show when Nick pulled her forward to introduce her.

He shook her hand, insisted she call him Pete, and then said, "Why don't we go sit down and figure out what we're going to do."

Instinctively she looked at Nick. He gave her a quick nod, and she followed Tommy into the living room. Morganstern stayed behind to speak to his agents. He spoke to Nick first, but in such a low voice, Laurant couldn't hear what he was saying. Then he turned to Noah, and whatever he said to him so startled the agent he suddenly burst into laughter.

"God will strike me dead, sir."

"And lose one of his trusted soldiers? I think not," Pete responded as he led the two men into the living room. "Besides, I'm fully convinced God has a sense of humor."

Pete placed his briefcase on the table and flipped open the latches. Nick dropped down on the sofa next to Laurant, and Noah stood behind his superior, acting like a sentry, with his arms folded across his chest.

"I was wondering, sir, if you'd found out anything significant from that profiler you assigned to the case," Noah said. "What was his name, Nick?"

The doctor answered the question. "His name is George Walker, and yes, he does have a few ideas that can help us. Nothing concrete unfortunately."

"Don't profilers figure things out from crime scenes?" Tommy asked. "I read somewhere that that's how they get their information."

"Yes, that's true," Pete agreed. "However, there are other ways too."

"Like the tape?"

"Yes."

"Tommy, will you please stop pacing around and sit down," Laurant said.

Her brother motioned for her to move closer to Nick and then sat down on her other side. He didn't know quite how to phrase the question he wanted to ask, and so he decided to be blunt.

"Exactly why are you here, Pete?"

"We're very happy that you're here," Laurant interjected so that the doctor wouldn't think her brother was as rude as he sounded. "Isn't that right, Tommy?" she added as she nudged him in the side.

"Yes, of course," he agreed. "Pete knows I appreciate his help. We go way back, don't we?" he asked the psychiatrist.

Pete nodded. Tommy turned to Laurant to explain. "I called Pete a couple of years ago about a troubled kid I was trying to help. It was out of my league, and Pete helped get him into a treatment center. That was the first time I used my connection through Nick, but since then, Pete's come through for me with three other difficult cases. You never say no to me, do you?"

"I try not to," Pete answered. "I came here today to sit down with you, Tom. I wanted to review what happened in the confessional."

"You've heard the tape," Tommy reminded him.

"Yes, I have, and it's been very helpful with the investigation. However, it doesn't tell me what you were thinking while our unsub was talking. I'd like to take you through it again."

"I've told Nick everything I remember. I've gone over it at least ten times."

"Yeah, but Pete will be asking different questions," Nick said.

"Okay. If you think it will help, I'll go through it again."

Pete smiled. "Noah, why don't you and Laurant wait in the other room. Nick, I'd like you to stay."

Laurant followed Noah to the door then turned back just as Pete was opening his briefcase. "Pete? When you're finished, may I have a word in private with you?"

"Certainly."

Noah pulled the French doors closed behind

them. Monsignor was coming down the steps from the second floor with a basket of dirty linens. Without a word Laurant took the basket from him and headed down to the basement again. She could hear her brother's laughter and assumed the questioning hadn't begun yet.

Pete acted as though he had all the time in the world. He started by asking Tommy if he missed playing football. Tommy was sitting on the edge of his seat, obviously tense and worried. Pete eased him into the discussion about the confession, and by the time their talk had ended, they had two more little bits of information that might prove helpful. The unsub had been wearing Calvin Klein's Obsession. Tommy had forgotten about that. And, until now, he'd also forgotten about a click he had heard. He had assumed the man was snapping his fingers to get his attention. Pete suggested that the click was actually the recorder being turned on.

Pete ended the conference when he stood. "When you return to Holy Oaks, I would rather you didn't hear confession for a while."

"How long is a while?"

"Until we've devised a trap to snare him."

Tommy glanced at Nick and then back to Pete again. "You don't think he's going to come back to confession, do you?"

"I certainly think he'll try," Pete said.

Tommy shook his head. "I don't see that happening. It's too risky for him."

Nick, who had been unusually silent until

now, spoke up. "He'll see it as a challenge. He thinks he's vastly superior to all the rest of us, remember? He's going to want to prove it."

"Tom, like it or not, he's established a relationship with you, and I believe he's going to want to keep you apprised of what he's been up to," Pete said. "One thing I know for certain now," he continued. "This unsub is going to go to any lengths necessary to talk to you again. He wants your admiration, but he also wants your loathing and fear."

"In many ways, you're the perfect partner in his plan," Nick told him.

"How do you figure that?"

"He wants someone to appreciate how smart he is."

Tommy said, "I know you think I'm being stubborn about this, but I gotta tell you I still think you're wrong about this guy. It just doesn't make any sense to me that he would try to contact me again. I've listened to your arguments and I know you're experts..."

"But?" Nick prodded.

"But you've forgotten why he came to me in the first place. He wanted absolution and he didn't get it. Remember?"

Pete gave him a sympathetic look. "No, he came to you because you're Laurant's brother," he said. "And he never wanted forgiveness," he added softly. "He was mocking the church, the sacrament, and he was mocking you, Tom, especially you."

Tommy looked miserable. "You do realize he almost got Monsignor McKindry in that con-

144

fessional. I volunteered for the duty at the last minute."

"Oh, he wouldn't have gone to McKindry," Pete said. "He knew you were inside the confessional before he even walked into the church."

"He probably watched you cross the parking lot and go inside," Nick said. "And if Monsignor had taken the duty, then he would have patiently waited for another opportunity."

"Nick's right," Pete said. "This man is organized and very patient. He's put a lot of time and effort into stalking you and your sister."

Something Pete had said earlier began to nag Tommy and he asked, "What did you mean when you said he was giving us mixed messages?"

"I meant that he's deliberately trying to make us run in five different directions," he explained. "In the tape he's telling us he's a stalker, maybe a serial killer. He's telling us he's just getting started, but then he implies that he's been at it a long time. He says he's killed one woman, but he's hinted at the possibility that there have been others. He laughed, if you'll recall, when he told you that he'd only hurt the women before Millicent. Now it's our job to figure out what's real and what isn't."

"In other words, it could all be lies or it could all be true."

"Tommy, try to understand that with these creeps, it's always about fantasies. Always," Nick repeated emphatically. "The fantasy is what is driving this unsub. It could all still be in his head, but we have to assume that Millicent did exist and that he tortured and killed her."

"And now he wants to act out his fantasy with Laurant?"

Pete nodded. "The situation is urgent. He needs a reason to talk to you again."

"What are you trying to tell me?"

Pete's eyes, he noticed, were edged with sadness now. "If what he told us is true, then I'm certain he's out there looking for another woman right now."

"He said he'd try to find a substitute to replace Laurant...temporarily," Nick said.

Tommy bowed his head. "Dear God," he whispered. "And then he'll want to confess his sins, right?"

"No. He'll want to brag."

CHAPTER
12

Tiffany Tara Tyler was a slut and proud of it. She'd learned a long time ago that she was going to have to relax her moral code of behavior if she was ever going to get anyplace in this cold, hard world. Besides, not being a prude had carried her a long way from the trailer park in Sugar Creek—she was wearing the proof. And nothing, not even a blown-out tire on her rusted 1982 Chevy Caprice, was going to get her down. She was riding high and feeling good, and all because she was as sure as shit that her life was about to undergo a radical change. Oh, she knew she was always going to be a Jezebel in her mother's estimation—she'd decided her daughter was damned to the eternal fires of hell after she'd caught her in the bathroom with Kenny Martin—but Tiffany had made up her mind not to care a hoot what her crazy, old, worn-out mother thought of her anymore. She knew where her real talent lay, and she believed with all her heart that if she worked hard enough, she would succeed. Who knew? Maybe by the time she was thirty, twelve long years from now, she might even be a millionaire like that Heidi Fleiss madam she so admired because she got to meet all those famous movie stars. Tiffany bet they treated Heidi just like a star too, and maybe, after she finished having sex with them, they even took her out to dinner at one of those fancy, expensive restaurants.

Tiffany remembered the exact moment her life experienced an epiphany—she'd looked that word up in the dictionary after reading the article in *Mademoiselle* magazine. She'd been at Suzie's Hair Salon, getting a perm that fried her already fried, unnaturally blond, frizzy, long hair. To take her mind off her painful burning scalp, she'd picked up the magazine and begun to read the article that was all but screaming at her, "Know Your Assets." The message couldn't have been any more clear to her. Do what you're good at. Change what you don't like about yourself. And use your assets to get what you want. But, most of all, go for it.

She took every word to heart, and to this day she carried the stolen magazine with her wherever she went. It was always tucked inside her Vuitton rip-off bag next to the brand-new mobile phone she'd spent two whole hundred dollars on so she could get three months' free phone service, as long as it was in the U.S. of A.

Tiffany liked to think she was gifted with ESP, and after reading that article, she could plainly see she was destined for great things. It was all going to begin happening for her in just two days' time when she checked herself into the Holidome. The motel's rates were a little steep, but it was worth it. The Holidome sat across the highway from the doctor's office, and she wouldn't have so far to walk after the surgery was done.

Because she'd bought herself the phone— she'd seen a picture of Heidi Fleiss with a mobile phone in her hand and figured it was an important asset every girl ought to have if she was going to go places—she was still shy two hundred dollars of the twenty-four hundred she needed to get her boob job. She was carrying all of the twenty-two hundred with her. She didn't dare take the chance of hiding any of her money in the trailer, where her stepfather could sniff it out like a trained hound dog with his beet-red, twice-broken, alkie nose. He'd just go on another one of his drunken sprees, which always ended up in jail. If he didn't find it, her mother certainly would. She was always snooping through Tiffany's things looking for more damning evidence to prove her daughter was still a whore. Then she'd feel it was her duty to donate all the cash to that screaming redemption preacher she watched on television all the time. No, Tiffany didn't take any chances with the hard-earned money that guaranteed to change her future. She had it all with her and all in cash. She'd divided the money in half and stuffed eleven hundred dollars into each one of her size 32AA Wonderbra cups, which weren't doing anything remotely wonderful for her figure, as flat-chested as she was. New boobs were going to change all that, of course. She was sure of it.

Going for it and changing what you could change—that's what success was all about. Like most eighteen-year-old girls, she had big dreams. She had always been very goal oriented, and big boobs were an integral part of her future plans. She'd never told anyone, not even her best friend, Louann, that her biggest dream of all was to be the centerfold in *Playboy* magazine. *Penthouse* was a step down, and so was *Hustler*, but she'd settle for either one of those centerfolds too. All the men in Sugar

Creek read those magazines—well, they didn't really read them. They took them into the bathroom with them so they could get off while they gawked at naked women, and she just knew their eyes were going to bug right out of their heads when they saw her in all her naked beauty smiling coyly out at them with her new size 36D boobs.

She didn't have any idea what kind of money could be made in centerfold work, but it had to be a lot more than she was making now lap dancing. She was never the customer's first choice, and she <u>knew</u> it had to be because she was so flat-chested. Vera, one of the other girls, always made three times what she did in tips, but then Vera was full-figured, and the men liked to burrow their faces in between her enormous boobs. Tiffany had had to supplement her income by giving blow jobs out back, behind the Dumpster. She was real talented with her mouth—just ask any of the boys back in Sugar Creek, or for that matter the doctor who was going to give her new boobs. He'd been so impressed with her skill, he'd reduced the price of the implants. Tiffany guessed she'd have to impress the doctor again to get a further discount of the two hundred dollars she was lacking, and if he balked about it, she'd just have to threaten to have a chat with his prim little wife, who had been sitting a couple of feet away at the front desk answering the doctor's phone while Tiffany was inside the cubicle lathering up the good doctor's privates. One way or another, she was going to get her new size 36D boobs in just two days' time.

The flat tire was a temporary setback, and as she stood on the side of the highway furiously working the wad of gum in her mouth, she spotted a van coming toward her. She wasn't going to have to use her new phone to call a tow service after all. Tugging her hot pink, spandex skirt down, she propped her hand on the tilt of her hip, balanced herself regally on the hot pink stiletto heels that killed her feet but made her legs look good, and pretended to be a helpless woman in need of assistance.

She hoped a man was driving the van because she could always get any man to do anything she wanted once he understood how talented she was. Squinting into the sun, she let out a loud sigh of relief when the van pulled to a stop behind her car and she saw the handsome man smiling at her.

Tiffany Tara Tyler straightened up, put on her best come-hither expression, and sashayed over to the van.

Just as she had predicted, her life was about to radically change.

Forever.

This was about as close as Laurant was ever going to get to a therapy session with a psychiatrist. There weren't any of those in Holy Oaks. There were, however, several people she knew who could have benefited from a couple of long talks with a "head" doctor. Emma May Brie—as in the cheese—immediately came to mind. She was a perfect candidate for analysis. The sweet, but strange, woman wore a blue shower cap decorated with white daisies as a hat everywhere she went, rain or shine. She took if off for only one hour on Tuesday mornings when she got her hair done at Madge's Magic, the local beauty shop that guaranteed to give every customer "volume." Emma May wasn't the exception to their promise. When she stepped outside the shop, her thinning gray hair was indeed twice the size, that is, until she put her daisy cap on and squished it all down.

There were other residents who could also use a good psychiatrist, but the fact was, if the renowned Dr. Morganstern decided to go into private practice and hang his shingle out on Main Street, no one would ever go see him. It just wasn't done. Problems were never discussed with outsiders, and anyone who was thought to be peculiar was simply given a wide path when he was having one of his "spells."

What was taking Pete so long? He'd asked her to wait for him in the dining room, but that had been at least ten minutes ago, and she was now so fidgety she couldn't sit still. Just as she made up her mind to go back downstairs and finish sorting the laundry, the swinging door from the kitchen opened.

"I'm sorry I made you wait," Pete said as he entered, "but Monsignor and I got to talking and I didn't want to interrupt a story he was telling me about one of his parishioners."

He closed the double doors leading to the hallway to insure privacy.

Although she had requested the meeting, she was suddenly dreading it because she knew what she wanted to ask him, and part of her was worried sick that he would agree.

"There now," he remarked as he sat down.

She couldn't seem to sit still and was tapping her foot against the hardwood floor so vigorously her knee was making the table wobble. When she realized what a telltale sign that was about her mental state, she forced herself to stop. It was impossible to relax, so she sat ramrod straight, as stiff as a corpse, in the uncomfortable chair that made a squeaky sound of protest every time she moved.

Shards of sunlight filtered into the room through the old-fashioned, Victorian lace curtains, and the air smelled faintly of overly ripe apples. There was a large oriental bowl filled with fruit in the center of the table.

Pete didn't show any signs of rushing. He opened the conversation by asking her how she was holding up.

"I'm doing all right." Could he tell she was lying?

Silence followed her response. He continued to patiently wait for her to gather her thoughts and tell him what was on her mind. She felt like a fool because she was having so much trouble getting the words out. What had seemed like a perfectly sound plan a half hour ago now seemed deranged.

"Have you ever skied?"

If Pete was surprised by the question, he didn't let it show. "No, as a matter of fact, I haven't. I've always wanted to try it though. What about you?"

"Yes, I used to ski all the time. The school I attended was surrounded by mountains."

"You attended boarding school in Switzerland, didn't you?"

"Yes," she answered. "And I'd go up into the mountains every chance I could. I love skiing, and I actually got pretty good at it. Since I've been in America, I've gone to the slopes in Colorado a few times. I'll always remember how it felt that very first time I took the lift up to the top of a black...they rate the slopes by degree of difficulty, you see. Green is for beginners, blue is for the intermediate skier, and the blacks are reserved for the experienced who want more of a challenge. There are other ratings too, like diamonds and double diamonds," she rambled on. "Anyway, the first time I stood on the edge of what appeared to be a sheer drop-off, I took the longest time gathering my courage to push off. I felt like I was standing on the cliffs of Dover. It looked that steep to me. I was terrified...but determined."

"And talking to me is like standing on that precipice again?" Pete asked.

She nodded. "Yes, it is...because I know that, like that mountaintop, once I push off, there's no going back."

There was an uncomfortable pause before Laurant started again. "I guess I should start by being completely honest, shouldn't I? I'd be wasting your time otherwise. I told you I was doing all right, but that wasn't true. I'm a mess inside, and I feel like I'm tied in a thousand knots."

"That's understandable."

"I suppose so," she agreed. "All I can think about is...him. My concentration's shot," she added. "When I was doing the laundry for Monsignor, I was thinking about what I wanted to ask you, and I accidentally poured an entire bottle of bleach in with the sheets before I realized what I was doing. A very large bottle of bleach," she emphasized.

Pete smiled. "Think of the positive. They'll be nice and white."

"They were green and blue stripe when I put them in the washer."

He laughed. "Oh dear."

"I'll have to buy him a new pair," she said.

"But as you can see, I'm having a little trouble..."

"Staying focused?"

"Yes. My mind's racing, and I feel so...guilty."

Monsignor knocked on the door and poked his head inside.

"Laurant, I'm heading over to the hospital to make my rounds. I shouldn't be gone long, and Mrs. Krowski will be here soon. Would you mind catching the phone calls until she arrives? Father Tom can handle any emergencies."

"Yes, of course, Monsignor."

Pete stood. "Just a minute, Monsignor."

Excusing himself, he went into the hall and called for Noah. Laurant heard footsteps on the stairs and then Pete spoke again. "Ask Agent Seaton to drive Monsignor and stay with him."

The old priest balked at the idea of having an escort, arguing that he could drive his own car, but Pete gently cut him off and firmly insisted that the agent accompany him. Monsignor realized it was pointless to argue and reluctantly agreed.

Apologizing, Pete returned to Laurant. Nick followed him into the dining room, closed the door behind him, and then leaned against it. Folding his arms across his chest, he winked at her, and his body language told her in no uncertain terms that he wasn't planning on leaving anytime soon.

"Did you wish to speak to Pete?" she asked.

"Nick asked to join us," Pete said. "I told him it was up to you."

She hesitated a moment. "Okay. But, Nick," she demanded, looking him right in the eye, "I would appreciate it if you didn't interrupt or argue when you hear what I have to say. Promise me."

"No."

"Excuse me?"

"I said no."

Pete seized control of the conversation then. "You said you were feeling guilty. Why?"

Deciding to ignore Nick, she stared at the delicate rose pattern on the oriental bowl when she answered. "I want to run away and hide until you catch him, and I'm ashamed because I feel that way."

"You have nothing to feel ashamed about, and your desire to run away is quite natural," Pete said. "I'm certain I'd feel the same way."

She wasn't buying that. "No, you wouldn't. My reaction is cowardly and selfish."

Suddenly feeling restless, she got up and walked over to the front window. Lifting the lace curtain, she looked outside just as Monsignor was getting into the passenger seat of a black sedan.

"You're being too hard on yourself," Pete said. "Fear isn't a flaw, Laurant. It's a safety mechanism."

"He's out there now...looking for another woman, isn't he?"

Neither Pete nor Nick answered.

"Get away from the window," Nick ordered.

She immediately stepped back and let go of her tight grip on the curtain.

"Are you worried he's watching the rectory now?" She took a step toward Nick. "You told me you thought he'd accomplished what he came here to do and that he was on his way home."

"No," Nick corrected. "I told you he was probably gone. We aren't taking any chances."

"Is that why Monsignor has an escort today? Yes, of course it is."

"As long as you and Tom are here, Monsignor will have an agent watching out for him," Pete added.

"We're putting him at risk?"

"It's just a precaution," he insisted.

"This man...he's going to kill another woman soon, isn't he?"

Pete chose his words carefully. "Until we can prove otherwise, we must assume he was telling Tom the truth. Therefore, the answer is yes, he's going to take another woman soon."

"He'll torture her and kill her." The room seemed to be closing in on her, and she took a deep breath in an attempt to collect herself. "And he won't stop with just one more, will he? He's going to keep on killing and killing."

"Come and sit down, Laurant," Pete said.

She did as he requested, sitting sideways in the chair to face him. Her hands were clasped on her knees. "I have a plan."

He nodded. "You're ready to push off that mountaintop, aren't you?"

"Something like that," she agreed. "I still want to run away," she added. "But I'm not going to do that." Out of the corner of her eye she saw Nick straighten. "I want to catch him."

"We will get him," Pete assured her.

"But I can help you," she said. "And I have to help. For a lot of reasons," she added. "First and foremost are those women out there who don't have an inkling that this monster is looking for his next victim. They're the overriding reason I'm not going to hide."

Pete was frowning in anticipation. When he began to shake his head, she knew he had guessed what she wanted to do, and so she hurried to explain before he put an end to the discussion.

"I can be very stubborn and determined, and once I make a decision, I stick to it. All my life other people have tried to control what I do. After my mother died, the lawyers handling the trust made all the decisions for me. That made sense when I was young, but as I got older, I began to resent their totalitarian tactics. They certainly weren't interested in how I felt, and I wanted to at least have some input in the decision making, but that wasn't allowed. They decided what schools I would attend, where I would live, and how much or how little I could spend."

She paused to take a quick breath and then continued. "It took me a long time to get out from under their control, but I finally managed it, and I've found a place where I feel that

I belong...really belong. Now this monster is trying to take that away from me. I can't let him do that. I won't."

"What is it you want me to do?"

"Use me," she blurted out. "Set a trap and use me to get to him."

"Are you out of your mind?" Nick exploded.

She heard the anger in Nick's voice but tried to ignore him. She kept her gaze fixed on Pete. "Help me convince my brother that I should go back to Holy Oaks. That's the first step," she said. "You have no idea how scared I am, but the way I see it...I don't really have a choice."

"The hell you don't," Nick argued.

She glanced up at him. "The only way I can get my life back is to take control."

"It's out of the question," Nick insisted.

"No, it isn't out of the question," she said, surprised at how calm she sounded. "Pete, if I go back home after he's told my brother to hide me away, won't he see it as a challenge?"

"Yes, I'm sure he will," he agreed. "This is a game to him. Otherwise, why would he have mentioned Nick? He knows Nick is with the FBI, and he wants to prove that he is much more intelligent than any of us."

"Then if I go back to Holy Oaks, he'll think I'm playing into his hand, right?"

"Yes."

"There's no way in hell you're going back until this bastard is either dead or behind bars," Nick said.

"Will you please let me finish and then you can argue?"

She kept a wary eye on him. He looked like he wanted to pluck her out of her chair, drag her into the hall, and shake some sense into her. It was just the resistance she had expected.

"You can get into his mind, Pete. You can figure out what buttons to push and make him come after me, and if I make him angry enough...then he'll leave those other women alone. At least that's my hope. You and Nick could set a trap. You do this sort of thing all the time, don't you? And Holy Oaks is a small town. There's only one major highway leading in and out. I don't think it would be too difficult to close the town, if you needed to."

"Laurant, do you realize—" Pete began.

"Yes, I know what could happen, and I assure you I won't take any chances. I'll do whatever you tell me to do. I promise. Just let me help you catch him before he kills again."

"Using you as bait," Pete said.

"Yes," she answered quietly. "Yes," she repeated resolutely.

"You're out of your ever loving mind. You do know that, don't you?" Nick snapped.

"The plan makes sense," she argued.

"What plan?" he demanded. "You don't have a plan."

"Nicholas, calm down."

"Pete, we're talking about putting my best friend's little sister into a situation—"

"Maybe you should stop thinking of me as Tommy's sister," she suggested. "And start thinking like an agent. This is a golden opportunity."

"Using you as bait." He was repeating Pete's statement, but unlike his superior, his voice wasn't calm. Nick's bordered on a roar.

"Will you please lower your voice? I don't want Tommy to hear about this until we've made a decision."

Nick glared at her and began to pace around the room. Laurant was depending on Pete now to become her ally because, as bad as Nick was taking her plan, she knew her brother's reaction was going to be ten times worse.

She knew she had to convince Pete. "I'm not going to spend the rest of my life hiding. We both know you wouldn't even be here if it weren't for Nick and Tommy. With all the work you have to do, you couldn't possibly drop everything and go running every time you heard about a threat. Isn't that right?"

"Unfortunately, there aren't enough of us to handle the load these days," he admitted.

"Your time's valuable, and so I thought that maybe we could speed up this man's agenda."

She could have sworn she saw a speculative gleam appear in the doctor's eyes.

"What are you proposing?"

"Let's make him crazy."

Nick had paused in his pacing and was staring at her with an incredulous look on his face. "He's already crazy," he told her. "And so are you if you think Tommy and I are going to let you put yourself in the middle of his playground. Hell no, Laurant. It isn't going to happen."

She turned back to Pete. "What would do it? What would push him over the edge? How could we make him so angry he'll get careless?"

"Having listened to the tape, I can tell you that this unsub has quite an ego, and it's important to him that the world believe he's intelligent. It would infuriate him if he heard any criticism at all. If you were to discuss him openly in town, if you were to tell everyone about this fool of a man, then I believe he would speed things up. He'd want to get to you quickly just to shut you up. Mock him, and you'll incite him."

"What else could I do?"

"Make him jealous," he said. "If he thought you were romantically and intimately involved with another man, then he would view that as a betrayal."

She nodded. "I could make him jealous. I know I could. Remember what he said on the tape? How Millicent betrayed him by flirting with other men, and he had to punish her? I could flirt with every man in town."

Pete shook his head. "I believe it would be more effective if there was just one man, and the unsub believed you loved him."

She waited for him to continue. Pete began to drum his fingers on the table while he considered the possibilities.

"He mentioned Nick by name. He dared Tommy to get the FBI involved, so it's apparent he wants to play his game with us." Pete rubbed his jaw. "Let's play into his hand until we see where it leads."

"What does that mean?"

"Let him think he's calling the shots," Pete explained. "I wonder how he would feel if he thought his confession brought you and Nick together romantically. His carefully thought-out game would backfire, and he'd certainly feel like a fool. It's an interesting idea." He nodded and added, "You and Nick should behave like a couple in love. That should push the unsub right over the edge." Pete qualified his suggestion when he said, "If he is what he says he is."

"Nick...," she began.

"There's no way he's going to buy it," Nick said. "He brings us together and we fall in love overnight? I'm telling you, Pete, it won't work."

"We don't care if he believes it or not," Pete patiently explained. "The goal is to taunt him and his little game. If you and Laurant act like lovers, he'll believe you're mocking him. He won't like it one little bit. I guarantee it."

Nick shook his head. "No. It's too risky."

"You're not being reasonable," Laurant protested.

"*I'm* not being reasonable? You don't have a clue what these creeps are capable of...not a clue."

"But you know what they can do," she pointed out. "And you could make it safe for me."

Bracing his hands on the tabletop, he leaned forward and shook his head. "You aren't making an informed decision because you don't know what you're up against. There's no such thing as a fail-safe plan. Isn't that right, Pete? Remember the Haynes case? Why don't you tell her about that fail-safe plan."

Pete paused to consider how much he was going to tell Laurant before beginning.

"Before I started working for the FBI, men like Haynes were called psychopaths, and he certainly was that all right. Nowadays Haynes would be called an organized killer—as opposed to disorganized. He was meticulous in his preparation and planning, and he was highly intelligent. He always targeted a stranger, stalked her for months until he was very familiar with her habits. He would never have contacted her though or warn her the way this unsub has warned you," he thought to add. "And when he was finally ready, he lured the woman he'd chosen to a secluded area where no one would hear her scream. Like a lot of organized killers, Haynes enjoyed prolonging her agony as long as possible—it heightened his own pleasure, you see, and after he killed her, he always hid the body. That's an important difference between an organized and disorganized killer," he explained. "Most disorganized killers leave the body in plain sight, and often they'll leave the weapon they used as well.

"Haynes did keep souvenirs, however...most of them do, so that he could relive the fantasy,

165

but also so that he would have a reminder that he had fooled everyone, especially the authorities. If it weren't for his wife contacting us, I believe Clay Haynes could have gone on killing for years and years before he disintegrated. He was that clever.

"They set a trap to snare him. His wife had found the souvenirs in an old trunk, and she wanted to help us. She was terrified of her husband and for good reason, but she was determined to put him behind bars. Clay traveled during the week. He was a pharmaceutical rep, but he always returned home on Friday afternoon. They thought they had time, so they let Mrs. Haynes pack before they moved her to a safe house. An agent was with her and a couple of others were staked out front.

"Clay surprised everyone by coming home early. During interrogation he told us he went in through the basement, and he knew at first glance that someone else had touched his trophies. He came up behind the agent in the living room and killed him and then turned his wrath on his wife. When the agent in the house didn't answer the phone, the others rushed inside, but it was too late by then. Clay had done quite a job on her."

"He butchered her," Nick said. "And she sure as hell didn't die quick."

Laurant closed her eyes. She didn't want to hear any more details.

"Were you on that case?"

Pete answered. "Nick was a brand-new recruit. He had completed his training to work in my section, but at that time he was also working with the serial crime unit under a very capable man named Wolcott. Wolcott took Nick along to the crime scene."

Laurant saw the bleakness in Nick's eyes and felt a crushing tightness in her chest.

"I saw what that psychopath did to his wife and the agent," Nick said. "And all the while he was killing the man inside and carving on her, there were agents outside waiting for him. Don't you wonder what must have been going through her mind knowing that help was that close? I still think about it," he admitted. "It proved too much for Wolcott to handle. He resigned the next day."

"Haynes got away, but he was apprehended the following week," Pete interjected.

"A week and a day too late for anyone to help his wife," Nick said. "Things can go wrong and best-laid plans—"

"I understand the risks," she said. "This man who's stalking me, he's organized, isn't he?"

"Yes."

"If he's so clever and so organized, couldn't he go on killing for years?"

"Some do."

"Then how can either one of you believe we have any other choice? The woman he's hunting now...she's someone's daughter, or mother, or sister. We have to do this."

"Hell," Nick muttered. "Have you thought about Tommy's reaction? What's he going to say when you tell him about this half-cocked plan of yours?"

"Actually, I thought you might want to tell him about it. You could explain it much better than I could."

"No, I won't do it."

Pete was watching Nick closely. "Interesting," he remarked quietly.

Nick misinterpreted the comment. "You can't possibly think her idea has merit. It's crazy."

"No, I think your reaction is interesting. I've already told you how I feel about your involvement in this, Nick. You're too close to it."

"Yeah, well, I'm on vacation. I can do what I want."

Pete rolled his eyes and then tried to force his agent to be logical. "Laurant's right about one thing. You need to start thinking like an agent. This is a golden opportunity."

She knew then she had her ally. "Will you talk to my brother?"

"You're going to have to get Nick's cooperation first."

"That isn't going to happen," Nick assured her.

The phone rang, jarring her. Relieved by the interruption, she hurried to answer it.

"Three rings, Laurant. Let it ring three times before you pick up," Pete cautioned.

She didn't understand why Pete wanted her to wait, but she nodded agreement as she continued on into the hallway. There was a small alcove, an indentation really, on the opposite side of the steps. A Queen Anne table just fit inside the recess. A black desk phone was resting on top of a pair of phone books, and there were a pad and a pen beside it.

Nick stepped out into the hall as Laurant picked up the receiver.

"Our Lady of Mercy," she said as she reached for the pen. "May I help you?"

She heard the giggling, and then a little boy's voice asked, "Is your refrigerator running?"

She knew the joke and decided to go along. "Why, yes it is."

Another spurt of laughter followed, and then another voice shouted, "Then you better go catch it."

Laughter rang through the phone as Laurant hung up. Nick was watching from the doorway.

"Kids playing phone games," she explained.

The phone rang again. As she waited for the third ring to end, she said to Nick, "I guess I shouldn't have encouraged him. I'll be firmer this time."

"Our Lady of Mercy. May I help you?"

"Laurant." Her name was said on a low sigh.

"Yes?"

The voice on the other end of the line began to sing a bastardized version of "Buffalo Gal."

"Green-eyed girl won't you come out and play, come out and play, come out and play. Green-eyed girl won't you come out and play... Like my singing, Laurant?"

"Who is this?" As she asked the question, she whirled around and looked at Nick.

169

"A heartbreaker," the voice taunted. "I'm afraid I'm going to have to break your pretty little heart. Are you scared?"

"No, I'm not," she lied.

She cringed when she heard his laughter. It stopped as suddenly as it had begun and then he whispered, "Do you want to hear another song?"

She didn't answer. Nick was rushing toward her; she could hear sounds coming from upstairs, and out of the corner of her eye she saw Pete watching her from the dining room, yet she was frozen by the voice on the phone. She was gripping the receiver so tightly in her hand that Nick had to use considerable force to pull it away and listen with her.

It dawned on her then that someone was taping or tracing the call, and that was why Pete had told her to let it ring three times. She should keep him talking as long as possible she thought, but oh God, the sound of his voice made her want to throw up.

"Is the song as stupid as the one you just sang?" she asked.

"Oh, no, no, this one's sure to please. It's so pure and…original. Listen close now."

She heard a click, and then a woman's bloodcurdling screams. It was the most horrific sound she had ever heard. If Nick hadn't been holding her up, she would have dropped to the floor as the tortured screams pierced her ear. They were almost inhuman and seemed to go on forever. Then, Laurant heard another click, and the screaming stopped.

"Aren't you going to tell me to leave her alone? I have, you know. I've left her in a grave, even put a little stone on top so I'd remember where she is if I ever want to dig her up again. I do that sometimes, you know. I like to see what they've become. This one was a poor substitute for you, Laurant. Are you ready to play yet?"

Bile was rising to her throat. She could taste it.

"Play what?" she asked, trying her best to sound bored with him and with the conversation.

"Hide-and-seek. You hide and I seek. That's how the game is played."

"I'm not playing any games with you."

"Yes, yes, you are."

"No," she countered, her voice hard. "I'm going home."

He shrieked, but she couldn't tell if she'd just angered him or made him happy. Jerking the phone away from Nick's hand, she straightened up and shouted, "Come and get me."

Some things in life were simply too good to pass up. Like an icy cold glass of lemonade on a blistering hot and humid day. Or a lady in distress standing on the side of the highway, just begging for a little attention. Only this one hadn't been a lady, and he'd ended up feeling a bit sorry he'd wasted so much of his valuable time on her.

Still, he had put the tape to good use hadn't he? Perhaps his valuable time hadn't been completely wasted after all. By God, they'd gotten his message loud and clear. Heart-breaker was a man of his word.

He wondered how long it would take them to find her. Hell, he'd done everything but post directions. Poor, poor Tiffany. He burst out laughing then; he couldn't contain it. The bitch had never gotten to use the new phone she'd shoved in front of his face while she bragged about it. He'd used the phone though, to call his sweetheart, and he'd stayed on the line long enough for the mules to figure out whose name the phone was listed under.

He'd given her what he considered a fitting burial. He left her in a shallow grave near the highway. The scrub surrounding the gully obstructed the view. Eventually the mules would find her, and they'd know with one look what kind of woman she had been.

He broke her heart, and then he stole it. The spontaneous action worried him for a couple of minutes, but then he realized how careful he'd been not to get any of the blood in his van. Those amazing Ziploc bags really did do a good job, just like the commercials boasted. He'd have to remember to send the company a note praising their clever little product.

Filth. That's what she'd been. Pure filth. And that was why he hadn't kept the memento. He didn't want to remember her, so he'd thrown it away.

Usually, whenever he encountered a worthy prospect, he entertained the notion of keeping her and training her, but at first glance he could plainly see that this one had been used, and he immediately ruled her out. The replacement had to be pure and innocent, clean, and adoring. Oh, yes, she'd be adoring all right, or a lasting relationship would never, ever work. No sirree.

He had done it before and he could do it again.

A burst of raw anger caught him unaware, shocking him. He realized then that he was gripping the steering wheel and forced himself to relax. All his time and effort had been wasted. Wasted! He had created the perfect mate, and when she died, he grieved.

He didn't relish the chore of finding and training a replacement, but he couldn't put it off much longer. No, he'd have to get started soon, which meant hour upon hour of careful, meticulous planning. He would have to see to every detail, every tiny wrinkle. And research. There would be so much research involved. He would have to know everything about her. Everything! Who her friends and relatives were, who would miss her, and who wouldn't give a damn. Then he'd have to isolate her, alienate her, and once he finally took her, the real work would begin. He'd keep her locked away. The slow, agonizing training process would begin, day in and day out, endless training. He would be cruel and relentless until she became exactly what he wanted. There would be pain, lots of pain, but she would come to understand and forgive him once he had broken her and then molded her into the perfect mate. Why? Because she would adore him.

The anger wouldn't let him alone. Rage was steadily building, gnawing at his gut like hungry maggots. He couldn't let it get out of control, not now. He took a deep breath and ordered himself to think about something pleasant.

Little Tiffy had been as easy as she'd advertised. No challenge at all. He didn't even have to sweet-talk her into getting into his van. No, she'd just strutted over to the door and scrambled right on up inside, with her tight little skirt hiked up above her crotch. She'd wanted him to see she wasn't wearing panties. No modesty, that one. God only knew what diseases she'd been carrying. He'd had to wash three times just to get rid of the stench of her.

He made a mental note to remember to tell his buddies on the Internet that killing whores wasn't what it was cracked up to be.

She couldn't dirty talk her way out of what was happening to her. No, sir. Killing her had been a kick, but it hadn't given him the rush he craved these days. He knew why of course. She hadn't been clean.

"Green-eyed girl, won't you come out to play..."

Oh, how he hated to start all over again. Such time! Such work!

"Calm down, calm down," he whispered. "You've done it before, you can do it again."

It wasn't a project he was ready to undertake just yet. If he'd learned anything over the years, it was that you finished one job before you took on another.

The exit off I-35 leading to Holy Oaks loomed up ahead. An exemplary driver, he turned on the blinker and slowed the van.

"Green-eyed girl, I'm coming for you, coming for you, coming for you..."

He had a secret name for Holy Oaks. He called it "unfinished business."

chapter 15

The game was on.

A team of FBI agents swarmed into Holy Oaks to prepare the trap. Jules Wesson, their section leader, set up his command post in a spacious, well-appointed cabin owned by the abbey and located just eight blocks south of the town on the tip of Shadow Lake. Wesson, a Princeton graduate with a masters in abnormal psychology, was rumored to become Morganstern's replacement if and when Wesson completed his doctorate, and if and when Morganstern retired—rumors most of the other agents believed had been started by Wesson himself. He was a by-the-book, hard-nosed, pain-in-the-ass boss, surprisingly arrogant given the fact that the agents under his direction had far more experience in the field than he did.

Joe Farley and Matt Feinberg, one a field agent from Omaha, Nebraska, the other an electronic surveillance specialist from Quantico, were sent into town ahead of the others to scout Laurant's neighborhood and secure the premises. Both had been ordered to treat the property as a crime scene.

They knew they were going to have trouble

blending in. In a town the size of Holy Oaks, everyone knew everyone else, and everyone else's business, and the two agents didn't want to stand out like a pair of red shoes in a funeral procession. They had been told that there were other strangers in town working at the abbey on the restoration, and so both of the agents dressed in work clothes. Farley wore a baseball cap and carried a black duffel bag. Feinberg carried a toolbox.

No one paid them the slightest attention. No one, that was, but Bessie Jean Vanderman.

While Agent Feinberg slowly circled the perimeter of Laurant's two-story clapboard house, checking for possible hiding places, Agent Farley carried his bag up the front steps. He crossed the porch and paused at the door to put on a pair of gloves. An expert at getting in and out without leaving a trace, he used a very simple tool, his American Express card—he never left home without it—to open the door. It took him less than five seconds.

Sheriff Lloyd McGovern showed up five minutes later and burst in on Farley. Bessie Jean, Laurant's neighbor and unofficial watchdog now that Daddy had passed on, had called the sheriff when she spotted a squat-necked, square-framed man going inside Laurant's house.

Farley was more concerned about the sheriff messing up his crime scene than the gun the man was waving about.

Lloyd, scratching his balding head and still brandishing his gun—which, the agent could plainly see, had the safety on—shouted, "You put your hands up, boy. I'm the law here in Holy Oaks and you'd best do what I say."

Feinberg came inside the front door without making a sound. He walked up behind the sheriff and poked him in the back to get his attention. The sheriff mistakenly thought he had a gun. He dropped his weapon and put his hands up.

"I'm not resisting," he stammered, the bluster and hostility gone from his voice now. "You boys take whatever you want, but leave me the hell alone."

Rolling his eyes in exasperation, Feinberg moved to the side and waved his palms in front of the sheriff. Lloyd realized he was unarmed and scrambled to get his gun off the floor.

"All right now," he began, pleased he was once again in charge. "What are you boys doing here? You're just plain stupid if you think you're going to steal anything of value. Look around you, and you can see Lauren don't have much at all worth taking. I know for a fact that she doesn't have a VCR, and her television set is at least ten years old. It can't be worth more than forty dollars, and that sure ain't worth going to jail for. As far as I can tell, she's as poor as a church mouse. She ain't got much in the bank, and she had to take out a loan to pay for her store."

"How do you know how old her television set is?" Farley asked, curious.

"Harry told me. That's Harry Evans," he

explained. "He's my cousin twice removed. He tried to sell Lauren a brand-spanking-new television a while back. You know the kind with the picture inside the picture? She didn't want it, and she asked him to fix up an old television she bought at a garage sale instead. She was throwing good money away if you ask me. And that's how come I know how old her television is."

"And you've got a relative working at the bank too?" Feinberg asked. "Is that how you know about the loan?"

"Something like that," Lloyd answered. "I might remind you boys I'm the one with the gun here, and you're gonna start answering my questions. Are you robbing Lauren?"

"No," Feinberg answered.

"Then what are you doing in her house? Are you foreigner relatives of hers from France?"

Farley had been born and raised in the Bronx and hadn't been able to rid himself of his thick street accent. He sounded like a thug in a bad gangster movie.

"That's right," he managed to say with a straight face. "We're from France."

The sheriff liked to be right. His chest puffed up like a peacock. Nodding as he put his gun away, he said, "I thought as much. You talk funny, so I figured you boys had to be foreigners."

"Actually, Sheriff, we're both from the East, and that's why we have accents. My friend here was just joking when he said we're French. We're friends of Laurant's brother," he explained. "We're doing some work up at the abbey, and Father Tom asked us to stop by and fix her sink."

"It's clogged," Farley added to the lie.

The sheriff noticed the black bag near the front door. "Are you boys planning on spending the night here?"

"Maybe," Farley answered. "Depends on how much work the plumbing needs."

"She doesn't own the house. She's just renting. Where is Lauren?"

"She'll be here soon."

"And you think you boys are going to sleep here in the same house with her, and you're not related?"

Feinberg's patience was wearing thin. "Quit calling me boy. I'm thirty-two years old."

"Thirty-two, huh? Then answer me this. What's a grown man doing wearing braces? I never heard of such a thing."

The braces were the last step in the reconstruction of a shattered jaw Feinberg had suffered four years ago during a raid that had gone sour, but the agent wasn't about to impart that information to a man he had already surmised to be a complete moron. Besides, no one was supposed to know the truth, that they were FBI agents.

"We do things different in the east."

"I reckon you do," he agreed. "But you still shouldn't be staying here."

"Why? Are you worried about Laurant's reputation?" Feinberg asked.

"No, everyone knows Lauren's a good girl,"

the sheriff replied as he settled his broad rear end on the arm of the sofa.

"Then what's the problem?" Farley asked. "Why does it bother you if we sleep here?"

"Oh, it won't bother me none at all, but it's going to bother someone else you boys don't want to be messing with. I'm warning you. You'd best find some other accommodations because he isn't going to like hearing that Lauren's got two men living with her, even if it's just for a couple of days. No, he won't like hearing it at all."

"Who are you talking about?"

"Yeah, who won't like it?" Farley asked as he shut the door. The sheriff wasn't going to leave until they had an answer to that question.

"Never you mind who. I'm going to have to tell him though. Why don't you boys go on up to the abbey? They've got rooms you can use for free if you tell them you're here for retreat. You know what that is, don't you? You spend your time praying and contemplating."

"I want to know who's going to be upset about us staying with Laurant," Farley persisted. "And I also want to know why you think you have to tell him."

" 'Cause if he found out that I knew and I didn't tell him..."

"What?" Farley demanded.

"He can get real mean," the sheriff said. "And I don't want to make him angry."

"Make who angry, Sheriff?"

Lloyd pulled a stained handkerchief from

his back pocket and mopped his brow. "It's close in here, isn't it? Lauren's got herself a window air conditioner, and I don't think she'd mind if you boys turned it on. The living room will be nice and cool by the time she gets home. She is coming here today, isn't she?"

"We're not sure," Feinberg said.

Farley wouldn't give up. "We're still curious to hear that name, Sheriff."

"I'm not giving it to you, and I can be right stubborn when I want to, and I'm feeling stubborn now. I wouldn't get myself worked up about it if I was you, because you're going to be meeting my friend real soon. He'll come over here lickety-split as soon as he hears you're here. I guarantee it. He's a powerful man around these parts, so if you know what's good for you, you'll be real respectful to him. I wouldn't make him mad, that's for sure. The law can only do so much."

"Meaning we're on our own?" Farley asked.

The sheriff lowered his gaze. "Something like that." Shrugging, he added, "It's just the way things are around here. Progress comes with a price."

"And that means...?" Farley asked.

"Never you mind."

"You can tell your friend he has nothing to fear from us," Feinberg said. "Neither one of us is romantically interested in Laurant."

Farley guessed where Feinberg was heading and immediately nodded. "That's right," he agreed.

"Well, now, that's good to hear because my friend is planning to marry Lauren real soon, and he always gets what he wants. Make no mistake about that."

"He's talking marriage, huh?" Feinberg remarked.

"It ain't just talk. It's only a matter of time before she comes around to understanding that's the way it's going to be."

"Sounds like your friend thinks he owns Laurant," Farley said.

"He does own her."

Feinberg laughed.

"What in tarnation's so amusing?"

"Your friend," Feinberg explained. "He's in for a real disappointment."

"How's that?"

"When he finds out..." Farley deliberately let the sentence trail off.

"Finds out what?"

"Laurant met someone while she was in Kansas City."

"It was love at first sight," Feinberg interjected.

"That's not completely true." Farley spoke to Feinberg now as the agents continued to play the sheriff and feed him information. "She's known Nick all her life."

"No, she's known about him, but she never met him until last week."

"Who are you talking about?"

"Nick."

"Nick who?" the sheriff demanded, his frustration apparent.

"Nicholas Buchanan."

"The man Laurant's in love with," Farley explained.

"The funny thing is...," Feinberg began.

"What?"

"This guy...Nick..."

"What about him?"

"He's Father Tom's best friend. Guess it was meant to be."

"And this Nick lives in Kansas City? Long-distance relationships don't work out."

"Oh, he doesn't live in Kansas City. He lives on the East Coast."

"Then I don't think Brenner has anything to worry about. Like I just said, long-distance relationships rarely work."

The sheriff had unknowingly just given them his friend's name, but neither Feinberg nor Farley let him know it.

"Nick must have figured that too," Feinberg said.

"Which is why he's moving here to Holy Oaks to be with Laurant," Farley added.

The sheriff's eyebrows shot up. "He's coming here...with her?"

"That's right," Farley said. "Guess he doesn't want to take the chance of losing her."

"And it was love at first sight," Feinberg reminded him.

"Where's this fella going to stay?"

"Here with Laurant, until they get married. Then I'm not sure where they'll live," Farley told him.

"Get married, you say? Who'd you hear this from?"

"Laurant told us," Feinberg answered.

"People will talk."

"I imagine they will."

"I got to get going now." The sheriff hastily shoved his handkerchief back into his pocket and headed for the door.

For all his considerable bulk, the lawman could move fast when he wanted to. Farley and Feinberg stood at the window and watched the sheriff run to the car.

"What a piece of...," Farley muttered. "He didn't even ask us our names or ask to see our identification."

"He's got places to go, people to see...," Feinberg began.

"And a friend named Brenner to tell," Farley concluded as he pulled out his cell phone and dialed.

The phone was answered on the first ring. "You got him?" Farley asked. He listened for another minute, then said, "Yes, sir," and hung up.

Feinberg squatted down by the black case. "Let's get started," he said as he handed the other agent a pair of gloves. "This could take us all night."

Farley was the eternal optimist. "Maybe we'll get lucky."

An hour later, they did get lucky. They found the video camera tucked high in a corner of the linen closet outside of Laurant's bedroom. The camera lens was pressed

185

against a hole in the wall and was pointed toward Laurant's bed. He'd been watching her sleep.

Nick wasn't talking to her. Laurant assumed he was still furious because she had insisted upon returning to Holy Oaks. After she'd taunted the madman to come and get her, Nick had gone a little crazy. And that was putting it mildly. Tommy heard all the commotion and came running, with Noah hot on his tail. As soon as Nick told her brother what she'd done, Tommy joined in the shouting match, but she held her own and stood up to them. Pete and Noah came to her assistance, flanking her sides like protective guardians. They defended her plan, and after what seemed like an hour of battling, Tommy finally caved. The phone call convinced him that the man wasn't going to forget Laurant, and if the FBI didn't set a trap and catch the animal, then she would be on the run or in hiding for the rest of her life.

And while the unsub was playing his hide-and-seek game with her, he would, no doubt, be preying on other women.

They had no other choice.

Unfortunately, Nick hadn't seen it that way, and thus far she'd been unsuccessful in penetrating his anger. Pete had once again suggested that Nick step aside, repeating his earlier argument that he was simply too close to the situation and couldn't be objective. Nick refused to listen, but when Morganstern threatened to take the choice away from him and have him removed from the case, Nick saw Tommy's stricken expression, and then he too caved.

Pete made a call to Frank O'Leary to get the ball rolling.

Now, she was finally on her way home, sitting side by side with Nick on a US Air Express plane that was taking them from Kansas City to Des Moines. They would drive the rest of the way. Pete told her a car would be waiting at the airport. Her automobile was going into the shop for repairs in Kansas City, and as soon as the work was finished, Tommy and Noah would drive it back to Holy Oaks.

She didn't want to think about what was going to happen once she got there. She nervously flipped through the pages of *Time* magazine, even tried to read an article about inflation, but she couldn't concentrate, and after rereading the same paragraph three times, she gave up.

How long was Nick going to give her the silent

treatment? He had stopped talking the minute they'd entered the airport.

"You're being childish."

He didn't respond. She turned to look at him and noticed how gray his complexion was.

"Are you sick?"

A curt shake of his head was her only answer. Then she noticed his grip on the armrest. "Nick, what's wrong?"

"Nothing's wrong."

"Then why won't you talk to me?"

"We'll talk later, after the plane lands...unless..."

"Unless what?"

"We crash and die in a fiery ball."

"You're joking."

"No, I'm not."

She couldn't believe it. Macho Man was afraid of flying. He looked like he was going to throw up. His fear was real, and no matter how funny she thought it was, she forced herself to be sympathetic.

"You don't like flying much, do you?"

"No," he answered curtly before turning to stare out the window again.

"Want to hold my hand?"

"It isn't funny, Laurant."

She plied his hand away from the armrest and slipped her fingers through his. "I wasn't teasing. Lots of people don't like to fly."

"Is that right?"

His grip was firm and she could feel the calluses on his hand. Working man's hands, but today he was dressed like an executive on

Wall Street. Another contradiction, she thought, another layer of his personality she found puzzling and fascinating. Tommy and Nick seemed so different from each other. They certainly had chosen different paths. Her brother was dedicated to the church. He always looked for the good in others, and his primary goal was to save souls.

Nick seemed to have dedicated his life to fighting demons. His job was depressing and unending, and she wasn't sure if the rewards were worth the price he paid. He seemed so cynical to her. He expected people to be bad, and thus far, he hadn't been disappointed.

The urge to comfort him took her by surprise. She leaned close and whispered, "We're almost there."

"We aren't there until or unless we land."

He was proving to be difficult to comfort. "Landings aren't dangerous—"

He snorted. "As long as the pilot knows what the hell he's doing."

"I'm sure he knows what he's doing. Pilots are trained to land planes."

"Maybe."

"We've only got a few more minutes to go. We're making our final descent."

His grip on her hand tightened. "How do you know that?"

"The captain just told the attendants to sit down."

"Did you hear the landing gear go down? I sure as hell didn't hear it."

"I did."

189

"You're sure?"

"Yes, I'm sure."

He took a breath and told himself to calm down. "You do know that this is when most accidents happen, don't you? Pilots misjudge the runway."

"Did you read that somewhere?"

"No, I just figured it out. Simple physics. Things go wrong...human error. Think about it. One man's trying to ease down over a hundred fifty tons of metal on a couple of little rubber rollers. It's a damned miracle every time a plane lands."

She maintained a somber expression. "I see. Then you believe that if man were meant to fly, he would be born with wings."

"Something like that."

"Nick?"

"What?" Now he sounded surly.

"In your line of work...don't you have to dodge bullets...and don't you go into life-and-death situations sometimes? You're an FBI agent for heaven's sake. The cream of the crop. Yet you're afraid of a little plane ride."

"Ironic, isn't it?"

She ignored the sarcasm in his voice. "I think you should talk to someone about this. Pete could help. He's a psychiatrist, and he could surely help you get over this...worry."

He didn't feel like telling her that Pete's amusement at his phobia matched hers. "Maybe," he shrugged.

Because he was looking at her, he didn't notice the ground coming up to meet the plane. The landing was smooth and uneventful, and by the time they had taxied to the gate, Nick's complexion was looking healthy again.

"Don't you want to get down on your knees and kiss the ground?" she asked.

"It's plain cruel to make fun of a man's phobias, Laurant."

"I wasn't making fun."

"Sure you were," he replied. He moved into the aisle, flipped open the overhead compartment, and pulled the bags down. "You've got a real mean streak inside you."

He stepped back so she could stand in front of him. "I do?"

"Yeah. I like that."

She laughed. "Pretty cocky now that you've got your feet on the ground, aren't you?"

"I'm always cocky," he boasted as he nudged her toward the exit.

The airport was surprisingly crowded. As they threaded their way toward the baggage claim area, Nick noticed the number of men admiring Laurant. One man didn't even try to be subtle. He did a double take, then turned completely around and followed them. Nick responded by throwing his arm around Laurant's shoulders and pulling her into his side.

"What are you doing?"

"Making sure you stay close," he answered. He shot the gawker a hostile look, then grinned when the man turned and hurried the other way.

"You wear your skirts too short."

"I do not."

"Okay, then you wear your legs too long."

"What's the matter with you?"

"Nothing. Keep moving."

He continued to scan faces as they walked through the crowd. He had to let go of her when they reached the escalator. She was frowning at him, but it was too late to take back the comment about her skirt.

An agent was waiting for them outside the baggage area. The car, a 1999 Explorer, was parked in a No Loading zone. The agent handed Nick a folder stuffed with papers and the keys to the car, and then loaded their luggage into the back. Two airport security guards were huddled together on the sidewalk, shaking their heads and muttering over the fact that they couldn't do anything about the illegally parked vehicle.

The agent drew her attention then when he opened a large black case that was tucked into the rear corner of the cargo area. When she saw the display of weapons, she took an involuntary step back.

Nick noticed. "It's not too late to change your mind."

She straightened her shoulders. "Yes, it is."

The agent opened the passenger door for her, wished her good hunting, and then disappeared inside the terminal.

Nick tossed his jacket into the backseat and unbuttoned the collar of his shirt as he got in behind the wheel, pushing the seat back as far as it would go to accommodate his long legs. There was a leather console between them. Inside was a map of Iowa.

Laurant knew the way home, of course, but Nick still checked the route that someone had outlined with yellow Hi-Liter.

"Did you hear what your friend said to me?" she asked.

"What's that?" he wondered, glancing up from the paper he held in his hand.

"Good hunting."

Nick nodded. "Yeah, we always say that," he explained. "Superstition."

"Like 'break a leg' before you go onstage?"

"Yes."

She let him finish reading, and after he'd placed the file folder in the back, she asked, "Was there anything important?"

"Just some update stuff."

"We better get going."

"Are you in a hurry?"

"No, but those security policemen look like they want to cry because they can't give you a ticket."

Nick waved to the guards as he pulled out into traffic. "Are you hungry?"

"No," she answered. "What about you?"

"I can wait."

"Was there anything in the folder about the letter that man told Tommy he'd mailed to the Kansas City police?"

"No, they still haven't gotten anything."

"Why would he tell Tommy he'd mailed it when he obviously hadn't?"

"I don't know. Maybe he was toying with him. I'll let Pete figure that one out."

She was silent as Nick maneuvered through the heavy traffic. Once they were on the highway, he rolled up his sleeves and settled back in his seat. He had the next two hours to prepare her. He went through the list of all the things she wasn't going to do and ended with the same reminder he'd given her at least ten times now.

"You don't believe anything anyone tells you, and you don't go anywhere without me. You got that?"

"Yes, I've got it."

"Not even the ladies' room in a restaurant."

"I know. Not even the ladies' room."

He nodded, appeased for the moment. She wasn't fooled. She knew he'd go through the list again in another hour or so. "Let's go over your daily routine again."

"You should have it memorized by now."

"Okay, let's see if I do. We get up around seven o'clock every morning, do our stretching exercises—"

"To limber up," she supplied.

"Yeah, right, and then we go running... God help me...three and a half miles, start to finish. We take the path around the lake, beginning at the western tip, and we always go in the same direction."

"Yes."

"I hate running. It's bad for the knees, you know."

194

"I find it invigorating. Maybe you will too," she said. "You look like you're in good shape. You can run three and a half miles, can't you?"

"Sure I can, but I'm going to be bitching the entire time."

She laughed. "I'll look forward to that."

"Okay, so then we go back home and..."

When he paused, she assumed she was supposed to continue. "And we shower and change into work clothes, and then we walk two blocks to the town square. I'll spend most of the day getting my loft organized and unpacking boxes while the workmen finish up downstairs. With any luck at all, they should be done soon. I want to be open by the Fourth of July."

"That doesn't give you much time."

"You'll probably be back in Boston by the Fourth."

"You're being optimistic. I could be in Holy Oaks for a month, maybe longer."

"How can you afford to take so much time?"

"I promised your brother. I'm not leaving until we catch him...or..."

"Or what?"

"If he goes to ground, and I have to leave for whatever reason, I'm taking you with me. Don't even think about arguing about that," he warned.

"I won't, but you know what I think?"

"No, what?"

"I think it's going to happen fast. I don't think we're going to have to wait long."

Nick nodded. "I feel the same. The way he sounded on the phone...yeah, he's gonna be coming after you fast. Pete thinks so too."

"Good. I want this to be over as soon as possible."

"Yeah, well, God willing, it will be. You know, you're going to be sick of me by the time I leave."

"On the contrary, I'm sure you'll be sick of me."

"I doubt it. I'll warn you now. I'm going to be taking a lot of liberties. Fact is, I'm going to be all over you." He glanced at her before continuing. "The goal is to make the unsub crazed with jealousy. Right? And so angry, he'll make that one little mistake..."

"And then you can get him."

"That's the plan. But I probably won't be the one nailing him. Neither will Noah for that matter."

"Why do you think that?"

"Noah's going to be busy baby-sitting Tommy, and I'll be busy...mauling you. I'm kind of looking forward to that. So tell me something. What kind of kisser are you?"

She attempted a southern accent when she answered in a slow drawl, "I'm very...very... good."

He laughed. "How do you know you're good?"

"Andre Percelli," she said. "He kissed me, and he told me I was good. That's how I know."

"You never mentioned this Andre guy before. Who the hell is he?"

"We met in fourth grade. But alas, our love affair ended as quickly as it had begun. We were in the cafeteria line when he kissed me, and I ended it then and there."

Nick smiled. "How come?"

"He wasn't a good kisser."

"But you were."

"That's what Andre told me before I punched him."

He laughed. "You were a tough little kid, weren't you?"

"I could hold my own. I still can," she boasted.

"So, whatever happened to Andre?"

"Nothing happened to him. Last I heard, he was married with two babies."

Nick changed the subject back to her routine. "We never talked about the evenings. What do you do at night?"

Laurant was digging through her purse, looking for her hair clip. "Yes we did talk about the evenings," she reminded him. "And I told you that there's something scheduled every night for the next two weeks."

"Because of the wedding you're going to be in?"

"Partly," she answered. "But also because I promised the abbot I'd help clean out the attic. He's spring cleaning before the anniversary celebration."

"Which is also happening on the Fourth of July. Bad timing," he added.

"The wedding's the Saturday before," she told him. She found the clip at the bottom of her purse.

"This anniversary thing...it's going to be a mess. I hope to God we get this tied up before then. Tommy told me the town's going to be loaded with strangers coming in from all over the United States."

She pulled her hair back and clipped it in place. "Actually, they'll be coming in from Europe too," she said. "Assumption Abbey opened its doors one hundred years ago. There might even be a cardinal attending."

"Great," he muttered. "It's going to be a security nightmare. I'm telling you, Laurant, if we don't catch this creep quick, I'm getting you out of there until the celebration is over."

"Agreed," she replied. "Pete said to take it a day at a time, remember?"

"Until the first of July. Then we leave."

She put her hand up. "I'm not arguing with you, but it doesn't give us much time."

"Unless he makes his move fast. Listen, it's real important you don't...relax. You understand? Relaxing your guard can be dangerous."

"I know and I won't relax. Could I ask you something?"

"What?"

"If I weren't me...what I mean to say is...if I weren't your best friend's sister and we were complete strangers to each other before this happened, then would you have been as resistant to setting a trap?"

"You mean using you as bait?"

"Yes."

"The problem is, you *are* my friend's sister. I can't separate that."

"But what if...?"

Nick's immediate reaction was to tell her yes, he would have been just as resistant because he knew firsthand how plans could blow up in your face, but after mulling the theoretical question over in his mind for another minute, he admitted it was a golden opportunity and he probably wouldn't pass it up.

"It's fifty-fifty."

"Meaning?"

"I'd weigh the dangers against the possibility of catching this creep before he kills again. And then..."

"Then what?"

He sighed. "I'd go for the trap."

"Have you ever been scared?"

"Hell, yes. I've seen what can happen. We don't always get the bad guys, Laurant, no matter what you've seen on television. Sometimes, they stay on the loose for years. The son of a bitch on the top of the 'most wanted' list, Emmett Haskell, broke out of a high-security mental ward in Michigan over a year ago, and we still haven't caught up with him."

"What did he do?"

"He killed a lot of people. That's what he did. Seven dead so far, but those are only the ones we know about. There could be more. Haskell told the shrinks that killing brought him good luck. He liked to bet the horses and always went to the track the first Saturday of every month, so the first Friday of every month, he had to kill someone. Didn't matter who," he added. "Anyone would do.

Man, woman, child. He was real partial to women though. The prettier, the better...for luck, you see."

"Tommy told me..."

"What?"

"You hadn't told him in confidence or he never would have said anything, but I asked him why he was so worried about you and he mentioned..."

He knew where she was leading—the Stark case. He had told Tommy about that one, hoping that talking about it would help him forget. It hadn't helped him though, not one little bit.

"He mentioned I killed a woman, right?"

"Yes."

"I did what I had to do."

"You don't have to defend your actions to me, Nick."

"There really wasn't any other choice. Maybe if I'd been a little smarter about it, I could have gotten her cuffed...but I left the house, and that gave her time to get the kid and prepare."

A shiver ran down her arms. "Prepare for what?"

"Me. She knew I was coming back, and she wanted me to watch her kill the little boy."

Laurant saw the troubled look that crossed Nick's eyes. "How do you get rid of it?" she asked. "Do you block out the memories?"

"No, I don't block anything out. I deal with it."

"But how?"

He shrugged. "I keep busy."

"Keeping busy isn't dealing with it."

"Don't you tell Noah I said this, but sometimes I wish I were more like him. He can shrug it all off when he has to."

She disagreed. "He's paying a price, just like you. He's just got tougher shields."

"Yeah, maybe. But as long as animals like Haskell and Stark are out there, I can't relax. I want to get them."

"There's always going to be another one, isn't there? Nick, you need a normal life outside of your work."

"Now you sound like Pete, and this is damned heavy chitchat."

He picked up the phone, punched in a number, and then spoke into the mouthpiece, "We're taking the next exit and finding something to eat. By the way, you're following too close."

After he'd put the phone back, she turned around to look out the back window. "The blue car, right?"

"No, the gray Honda behind the blue."

"How long have they been following us?"

"Since we left the airport. This car has a tracking device with a fifty-mile radius, and once we're in Holy Oaks, Jules Wesson, the senior agent in charge of this operation, will always have us under surveillance."

"That won't do us much good. It's a little town, and we'll walk as much as we drive."

"You're going to be wearing a cute little

tracking device too. I'm not sure what it will be in, but probably a pin or a bracelet."

It was actually comforting to know that the FBI would be tracking her as she moved about town.

"I'm sure Jules Wesson is efficient, but I still wish that Pete were in Holy Oaks."

"He wouldn't be much good there. He's never been a field agent. Jules Wesson and Noah and I will feed him information as we get it, and hopefully Pete will be able to figure out the where and when and how. Think there's a decent place to eat in Sweetwater? That's the next exit."

"There's a diner in the center of town. The food's actually pretty good."

"What are you in the mood for?"

"A big, juicy hamburger with pickles. And fries. Lots of French fries."

"Sounds good to me."

She didn't need to give him directions. Sweetwater boasted one main street, aptly named Main Street, and the diner was located right smack in the middle of it.

Laurant slid into a booth by the front window. Nick sat down beside her. There wasn't much room.

"Don't you want to sit across from me?" she asked.

"No," he replied as he reached for the sticky, plasticized menu standing on end behind the salt and pepper shakers. "We're gonna start practicing this lovey-dovey stuff."

Nick ordered two double hamburgers, a

202

double order of fries, and two glasses of milk. She told him he ate like a farmhand, and that reminded him of a story about her brother involving the cafeteria line at college. By the time Nick finished recounting the incident, she was laughing so hard, there were tears in her eyes. She had no idea Tommy had been such a prankster.

"He started the food fight?"

"Tommy wasn't always a priest," Nick reminded her.

He told her another story, and then another. A couple of times the other patrons of the diner turned at the sound of their laughter. They saw a young couple completely at ease with each other.

Laurant was thoroughly relaxed by the time they got back into the car and headed out again.

"Maybe you should slow down. I don't see the gray car," she said.

"That's the way it's supposed to work. You aren't supposed to see them."

"Are they going to follow us all the way to Holy Oaks."

"Yes, they are."

"How many agents are there waiting for us?"

"Enough."

"Isn't this costing a lot of money?"

"We want to get him, Laurant. Cost isn't important."

"Yes, but what happens if it takes longer than everyone expects?"

"Then it takes longer."

Laurant removed the clip and let her hair fall around her shoulders, then she tilted the seat back. She had just closed her eyes when Nick said, "I don't get it."

"What don't you get?"

"You...living in such a little town."

"I like it."

"I don't believe it. You're a big-city girl at heart."

"Actually, I'm not at all. I grew up in a little village."

"Your grandfather happened to own the village," he pointed out. "You lived on an estate. You can call it a small town if you want."

"And I went to school in a tiny little town. It was almost cloistered. I really like Holy Oaks, Nick. The people there are good and decent. And it's beautiful. And peaceful...at least it used to be peaceful."

"Yeah, well if you like it so much, how come you rent the house you live in? Why didn't you buy it?"

"I wanted to concentrate on the business first," she explained. "And Mrs. Talbot didn't want to sell the house just yet. She raised her family there, and even though she's living in a nursing home now, she isn't ready to let it go. I'm thinking about buying a cabin on the lake. It needs a lot of work though."

"How come you haven't already purchased it?"

"Steve Brenner."

"The Holy Oaks Advancement Society guy?"

"He owns the cabin."

"I think the guy wants to own *you*."

"What?"

"It seems that when Agents Farley and Feinberg went into your house, the neighbor lady called the sheriff and he came running."

"L.A. doesn't run anywhere."

"The sheriff's name is L.A.?"

She smiled. "Lard Ass," she explained. "Everyone calls him that. He isn't highly thought of in Holy Oaks."

"I guess not."

"I didn't mean to interrupt. What happened when the sheriff showed up? Did he know they were FBI? They must have told him."

"No, they didn't and wouldn't tell him anything, but the odd thing is, he never asked. He was busy telling them all about Steve Brenner's designs on you. Seems Brenner's telling everyone he's going to marry you."

"He's such a jerk."

"Sounds like it. One of the agents told the sheriff all about our hot and heavy relationship, and he couldn't wait to leave."

"No doubt to tell Steve."

"No doubt."

"He's the kind of man who has trouble understanding he can't get everything he wants."

"I'll help him understand."

She wasn't sure how he planned to do that, but the tone of his voice indicated he was looking forward to it.

It seemed that the time spent driving to

Holy Oaks sped by faster than the actual miles. They were comfortable together. They discussed music—they both liked classical and country. They argued politics—she was a die-hard liberal, and he was a full-blown conservative. And he kept her fascinated with funny stories about growing up in a large family. Before she realized it, Nick was slowing down to take the exit to Holy Oaks.

"We'll be home before dark," she remarked.

Nick turned serious. "Laurant, there are a couple of things I need to tell you."

"Yes?"

"Farley and Feinberg...the agents I mentioned a while ago."

"Yes?"

"When they searched your house, they found a video camera."

"Where did they find it?"

"In the linen closet upstairs. There was a perfectly drilled little hole about half the size of an aspirin. The camera's eye was facing your bed. You never would have noticed it. It's right in the center of a flower in your wallpaper."

She felt as though all the air had been knocked out of her lungs. She spun around in her seat and unconsciously clutched his forearm. "And you're just now telling me?"

"I thought you could use a little respite from this nightmare. If I'd told you when we first got in the car, you would have been worrying about it all the way home. Am I wrong?"

"How long has it been there?"

"Awhile," he answered. "There was dust on

it, so it's been there for some time, at least a week or two, but I can't tell you exactly how many days and nights. The serial number was filed off."

"Don't ever hold back information again. All right? When you hear something new, you tell me right away."

"We're going to be living together. I'll tell you everything."

"Until death do us part?" she asked sarcastically, but her sarcasm was tinged with fear.

"No, until we catch him."

She released her grip on his arm. "I'm sorry I snapped at you. You did warn me. You told me he'd been in my house and that he'd watched me sleep. He's seen me..."

She didn't go on. She turned to look out the window so he wouldn't see how shaken she was. She pictured herself getting dressed and undressed. Some nights when the air conditioner wasn't cooling sufficiently, she'd slept in the nude. And all of it was on tape.

She looked down at her lap and saw that she'd broken the hair clip. "I feel like I've done something I should be ashamed of. There were nights when I didn't feel like wearing a nightgown. It was hot," she defended.

"What you do in the privacy of your own bedroom..."

"But that's just it," she cried out. "I haven't done anything. I slept. That's all. I certainly haven't been entertaining any men, but what if I had? God, this is so sick."

"Laurant—"

"Don't you dare say it."

"Say what?"

"That it isn't too late for me to change my mind."

He pulled over to the side of the road, put the car in park, and then nodded toward the sign to the right. It was the Holy Oaks city limit.

"Are you giving me one last chance to change my mind?" she asked.

"No."

"Then why did you stop?"

"To tell you that you've got to stop freaking out every time you hear something...unpleasant. There are going to be some surprises, and I'm going to try my damnedest to anticipate, but you've got to...handle it. You understand? I can't be worried about how you're reacting and try to put you back together every time you—"

She put her hand on his arm, gently this time. "I promise. I won't freak out. At least I'll try not to."

He could hear the determination in her voice, see it in her eyes. "You've got guts," he said as he changed gears and pulled out onto the highway.

She was suddenly cold. She turned the air conditioner down and rubbed her arms. "Did they find the tape? Was it in the camera? Those tapes don't last very long, do they? Just a couple of hours. How did he change it? Has he been going back and forth into my house...my bedroom? If he has, he's been taking quite a risk of being seen."

"The camera's operated with a transmitter,

which means he's watching your bedroom on a monitor somewhere. I'll show it to you when we get there. It's a fairly simple motion sensitive device." He added, frowning, "High school stuff really—and that's what bothers me about it. Whoever set up the equipment wasn't a pro, but he got the job done."

"Why does that bother you?"

"It just doesn't seem very clever for our boy," he explained. "Like I said, it isn't high-tech, and our unsub seems like the kind who would go to great lengths to make it slick...perfect. His goal is to impress us."

"And you weren't impressed."

"Exactly."

Nodding, she turned to look out the window again. "We're almost home."

Nick turned left onto Assumption Road, a two-lane highway. Someone had partially blackened the road sign with paint so that only the first three letters, *A-s-s,* were visible. Nick grinned when he saw it.

"The high school kids do that at least once a year," she explained. "They think it's funny."

"It is funny."

"Then you probably watch the *Simpsons* on television, don't you?"

"I never miss it."

"I don't either," she admitted. "Messing with the sign makes the abbot furious. Disrespectful and all that. Are we going home first, or do you want to go to the lake to see Jules Wesson? Tommy told me he arranged for the agents to use the abbot's cabin."

"Let's go check in with Wesson first. I turn on Oak Street, don't I?"

"Yes. You'd make a left on Oak if you were going to my house and a right to get to the lake."

The twin steeples of Assumption Abbey rose up in the distance. The gothic structure had been built on top of a hill overlooking the pristine little town. It was magnificent. The drab grayness of the massive stone edifice was intermittently broken by brilliant stained glass windows, and a long, winding path led up to the doors.

Nick slowed the car as he drove past the wrought iron fence that surrounded the property. There were giant oaks everywhere. They clustered protectively against the north and south sides of the structure, like flying buttresses strengthening the outside walls.

"It looks like a cathedral," he remarked softly, as though they were inside the church now.

"The renovation has been going on for a long time. It's become a town project to raise funds to restore it," she said. "It's almost finished," she added, "...the main church anyway. The chapel still needs work. We'll have to come up here and walk around. The gardens are beautiful this time of year."

"Which came first? The chicken or the egg?"

She understood what he was asking. "Assumption Abbey was founded by an order of priests from Belgium, and it was here long before the town developed. Our population is quite diverse. There was an influx of immigrants after World War II."

"Why would they come all the way to Holy Oaks, Iowa?"

"Didn't Tommy tell you anything about the history of this town?"

"No, he didn't."

"The immigrants followed Father Henri VanKirk. He died last year. I wish I could have known him. He was an incredible man. During the war, he helped countless numbers of families escape the Germans, but he was eventually captured and tortured by the Nazis. When he was finally released, he came to America, and his superiors sent him here to heal. Quite a few of the families he had helped had lost everything, and they followed him. They rebuilt their lives and made Holy Oaks their home.

"After Father VanKirk died, the abbot found his journals. He thought they would offer inspiration to people, and so he decided to have them all translated into English. Everyone's been so busy getting ready for the anniversary celebration, there hasn't been time, but as soon as it's over, I'm supposed to begin the translation and save it all on the computer."

"Is Father VanKirk buried here?"

"Yes, he is. There's a cemetery on the other side of the abbey. Magnificent oak trees, bigger than the ones you see beside the church, circle the grounds..."

"And that's why this place is called Holy Oaks, right?"

She smiled. "Right. They protect the ground where the angels sleep."

Nick nodded. "Where the angels sleep. I like that."

"What do you think of the town? It's pretty, isn't it?"

White clapboard houses lined the paved brick streets. The streetlights looked like old-fashioned gas lights. Nick knew they were electric. Still, they were a nice touch and made the town all the more quaint.

"Holy Oaks reminds me of a New England town. It's got that kind of charm. Does your house have a white picket fence?"

"No, but my neighbor's does."

They reached the stop sign on Oak. Nick turned right and headed down another tree-lined street. The branches formed a canopy from one side to the other. "I feel like I'm in a time warp. I keep expecting to see Richie Cunningham driving down the street in a '57 Chevy convertible."

"He lives two blocks over," she teased.

As they neared the lake, the houses became more modest. Built in the last half of the century, they sported more modern features, like brick facades and split levels, but, like their older counterparts, they were meticulously kept up. It was apparent that the families living here took pride in their homes and their town.

They passed a deserted baseball field, continued west, past a Phillips 66 filling station, through a pair of rough timber posts and into the park.

"This place is crammed with kids from the college in the spring and in the fall. The local high school kids take it over in the summer."

Nick rolled down his window. The earthy smell of the humus from the pine needles and the oak and birch leaves matted against the ground filled the air. They reached a fork in the road, and straight ahead was a clear lake. Shadows from the towering trees rippled on top of the glistening water with every faint breeze.

The cabin was tucked in between the trees. Nick pulled into the gravel driveway and turned off the motor.

"It doesn't look like anyone's home."

Laurant had just made the comment when the front door opened. Through the screen she could see a man with thick, black-rimmed glasses peering out at them.

Nick made her stay in the car until he came around and opened her door. His eyes were never still. He was constantly searching the area around them, barely paying her any attention at all as he offered her his hand.

"Is that man Jules Wesson?" Laurant asked.

"No, that's Matt Feinberg. He's our electronic nerd. He's a nice guy too. You'll like him."

The agent under discussion waited until they'd reached the porch, then opened the door and stepped back. He was average in appearance, medium height, brown hair and eyes, and he wore braces. He had a wonderful, sincere smile. He was holding a wad of wires in both hands, but he dropped them on the entry table so he could shake her hand.

After the preliminaries were exchanged, he asked, "Did Nick tell you that Farley and I went through your house?"

"Yes," she answered. "You're the one who found the camera."

"That's right. While we were inside, your neighbor called the sheriff, and he came running. He's something else," he said, and then he filled her in on what they had told the sheriff about doing some repair work on her house. Then he turned to Nick. "As soon as Seaton puts in another phone line, we'll be good to go. He's working on it now."

"How many agents are here?"

Feinberg glanced up at the balcony before he answered. "Wesson isn't sharing that information. I honestly don't know how many are here, and if and when more are coming."

"Where is Wesson?"

"In the bedroom getting some papers. This is a nice place, isn't it? If the circumstances were different, I'd want to camp out here. The lake reminds me of Walden Pond."

Nick nodded. "This is the cabin you ought to buy, Laurant," he said.

She agreed. The light was wonderful. Two-story picture windows brought the view of the lake inside. The living room and dining area had been combined into one large rectangle. The atmosphere was rustic, yet airy. It was cluttered now though. Computer boxes and other equipment were scattered about. The dining room table had been pushed against the far wall, and on top were two computers. It didn't look like either one had been plugged in yet.

She heard a door open and looked up to the balcony just as Jules Wesson stepped out. He was talking on his mobile phone and was carrying a stack of papers.

Wesson was tall, wiry, and partially bald. He had piercing eyes, but after giving her and Nick only a brief glance, he ignored them and continued with his phone conversation. She watched him go to the table and put the papers down. Then Feinberg drew her attention again.

He handed her a gold watch. It looked like an old-fashioned Timex with a stretch band. "We'd like you to wear this, and we don't ever want you to take it off, not even in the shower. It's water repellent, of course. You could even go swimming with it. There's a tracking device inside, and I'll be monitoring your every move on that screen behind me. We want to know where you are at all times."

Laurant removed her own watch and slipped on the new one. She'd left her purse in the car and didn't have any pockets, so she handed it to Nick, and he tucked it in the pocket of his shirt.

Wesson hung up the phone. He nodded to Laurant as Nick introduced her, but he didn't waste any time on pleasantries. "I'm ready for him," he announced briskly. "But I don't like surprises. You don't leave Holy Oaks without getting my permission first. Understand?"

"Yes," she replied.

Wesson finally got around to acknowledging Nick. The commander was establishing a pecking order, letting Nick and Laurant know he was the man in charge. Even in a crisis, games were still played. What bullshit, Nick thought. He knew Wesson considered him competition, and no amount of talking would ever convince him that Nick wasn't interested in fast tracking his way to the top.

Personally, Nick didn't like Wesson one little bit, but he was stuck working with him, and he would make the best of the situation. Wesson had an ego the size of Iowa, but as long as he didn't let it get in the way of the operation, Nick thought they'd get along just fine.

"Morganstern wants you to call him," Wesson said.

"They get anything on the phone call?"

Feinberg answered. "They were able to lock in on the call the unsub made to the rectory. The phone was owned by a woman named Tiffany Tyler, and the call was made just outside of St. Louis."

Feinberg stepped forward. "The highway patrol found her car parked on the shoulder of I-70. The left back tire was flat, and there wasn't a spare in the trunk. We think that she willingly got into the unsub's vehicle, but that's just an assumption. We also think he never touched her car, but even so, our techs went over it from top to bottom, inside and out. It's an old Chevy Caprice, and it was loaded with prints. They're running them now."

"We don't believe any of the prints belong to our unsub." Wesson directed his explanation at Laurant. "He's careful, real careful."

Feinberg nodded. "And methodical," he added as he removed his glasses and began to clean them with his handkerchief. "There wasn't a single smudge or half print on that tape or that envelope he left with the police."

"We want you to start irritating him," Wesson said. "Hopefully, he'll lose control and mess up, and we'll get a lucky break."

"Tiffany's the woman I heard screaming over the phone, isn't she?"

"Yes, she is," Wesson answered. "He used her phone to call you."

"Have you found her yet?"

"No." The answer was clipped, his lips pinched. He acted as though she had just criticized him personally.

"Maybe she's still alive. Do you think—"

"Of course not," Wesson impatiently cut her off. "She's dead, no doubt about it."

His cold attitude rattled her. "But why would he pick her up in the first place? If he's so careful and if he does study his clients before he takes them on like he bragged, then why would he do such a spontaneous thing?"

Feinberg answered her. "We're pretty certain he killed her to get our attention. He wants us to know he's the real thing."

Nick took hold of her hand. "And Tiffany

was…convenient. She was helpless and his for the taking."

Feinberg put his glasses back on, adjusted the rims around his ears, and said, "I forgot to mention that Farley and I went through your mail. It's piled up on the table by your front door."

Laurant took the invasion of privacy in stride. Although it hadn't occurred to her that the FBI would be opening her mail, the fact that they had didn't bother her. They were simply being thorough, and that was something she appreciated.

Wesson took a step closer to Nick and said, "Just so you understand. You're here solely as Laurant's bodyguard. Your job is to protect her every minute."

Wesson's tone had been antagonistic. Nick's was mild in comparison. "I know what my job is."

"And the plan is to enrage the unsub, so both of you have got to put on a show everyone in town will believe."

Nick nodded. Wesson wasn't quite finished putting Nick in his place. "My team will do the real work and catch this creep."

"The real work?" Nick repeated sarcastically. "We're working this together, like it or not."

"You wouldn't be here if it weren't for Morganstern," Wesson pointed out.

"Yeah, well, I am here, and you're going to have to deal with it."

The mood had turned hostile. They were like bulls getting ready to butt heads. Laurant

218

squeezed Nick's hand. "We should get going, don't you think?"

Nick didn't say another word. The phone rang just as he was opening the door to leave with Laurant. He turned back when he heard Wesson exclaim, "Hot damn."

Nick waited until he'd finished the conversation, then asked, "Hot damn what?"

Wesson smiled smugly. "We've got a crime scene."

CHAPTER

17

Wesson was a prick. He was also crass, obnoxious, rude, and arrogant, and his people skills sucked. Worse, he lacked compassion. The agent's response to hearing that a farmer had stumbled upon the mutilated body of eighteen-year-old Tiffany Tara Tyler had been grossly inappropriate. Wesson had been downright jubilant. Shouting with glee, the man had all but broken out in song, and what made his unbridled enthusiasm all the more obscene was that Laurant, a civilian, was there watching him.

Nick wanted to get her out of the cabin

before she saw or heard anything more, and deal with Wesson later, but when he took hold of Laurant's arm to lead her outside, she pulled away. What she did next not only surprised him, but raised his admiration a notch.

She made Wesson squirm. She got right in his face so he couldn't ignore her, and then she gave him hell. She reminded him that a young girl had been murdered, and if he couldn't feel any remorse or pity for poor Tiffany, then perhaps he should consider another line of work.

When Wesson began to argue, Nick took over, but his language was much cruder than hers.

"That's going in my report," Wesson threatened.

"See that it does," Nick countered.

Wesson decided to end the conversation. He resented that an outsider would offer an opinion about his behavior, and he wasn't about to waste any of his valuable time trying to placate her. That fell under Nick's job description.

"Just do what I tell you to do, and we'll catch him," he said.

She didn't back down. "And keep my opinions to myself?"

He didn't see any need to answer. Turning back to the computer, he ignored her.

Laurant swung around. "Nick, may I use your phone?" He handed it to her. "What's Dr. Morganstern's private number?"

Wesson did a one-eighty in the swivel office

chair and sprang to his feet. "If you have any problems, you bring them to me."

"I don't think so."

"Excuse me?"

"I said, I don't think so."

Wesson looked at Nick for help in dealing with the difficult woman. Nick simply stared back at him as he rattled off Morganstern's phone number. "Just hit thirty-two. It will speed dial the number for you."

"Look, ma'am, I know I sounded..."

She paused in dialing. "Callous, Mr. Wesson. You sounded coldhearted, cruel, and callous."

Wesson tightened his jaw and narrowed his eyes at her. "It doesn't do any of us any good to get personally involved. We're trying to catch this pervert so that there won't be any more dead bodies."

"Her name was Tiffany," Nick reminded.

"I'd like you to say her name," Laurant told him.

Shaking his head resignedly, as though he'd say or do anything just to get her off his back, he said, "Tiffany. Her name was Tiffany Tara Tyler."

She handed the phone back to Nick and marched out of the cabin. She was inside the car before Nick could open the door for her.

"What an obnoxious man," she said.

"Yes, he is," he agreed. "You made him sweat, and I didn't think that was possible."

"I don't understand why Pete would put someone like him in charge."

"He didn't. Pete is consulting on this case. O'Leary's the one in charge, and Wesson works under him."

Nick headed the car back toward town. The sun was just beginning to disappear behind the trees, creating a luminous glow on the lake's surface.

Laurant's thoughts were on Tiffany. "Wesson actually cheered when he heard about that poor girl."

Nick felt compelled to set the record straight. "No, he didn't cheer because a woman was murdered. He was excited because we now have a crime scene, and hopefully, that's going to change things. I'm not excusing Wesson's behavior," he added. "I'm just trying to explain it. He's supposed to be a good agent. I've only worked with him once in the past, but that was a long time ago, and we were both new and inexperienced. Pete says he's good. But Wesson's going to have to prove it to me."

"You said that now that you have a crime scene, things will change. How?"

"Every killer leaves what the profilers call his personal signature at his crime scene. It's an expression of his sick and violent fantasies, and it will tell us a lot about him."

"He's careful, you said so yourself. What if there aren't any clues at the crime scene?"

"There will be," he assured her. "Whenever one person comes into contact with another, he leaves something behind, no matter how careful he is. A hair follicle, a scale of skin, a bit of a fingernail, tread marks from the bottom of his shoes, or maybe a thread from his pants or shirt…there's always something left behind. The trick won't be finding the evidence. It's the analyzing what they find that's more difficult. It will take time and care. And while the criminologists are doing their job, the photos of the scene will be sent to the profiler and he'll tell us what fantasies the unsub's acting out."

He glanced over at her before continuing. "A killer's signature," he explained, "is his psychological calling card. He can change the methods he uses and the where and the when and the how, but he never changes his signature."

"You mean there's always a pattern."

"Yes," he agreed. "Like the marks on the body or the way the body is positioned. The profiler looks at that and figures out what the killer is really after. I can already tell you that, with this man, it's all about control."

Nick stopped the car at the corner of Oak and Main. A young woman pushing a baby stroller crossed the street in front of them. She paused to give Nick the once-over and to wave at Laurant before continuing on.

"My house is on the next block, second from the corner. But I don't want to go there. I wish we could just check into a motel."

"You've got to go home and act like nothing's wrong, remember?"

"I know, but I still don't want to," she said. "I don't ever want to go back into that house again."

"I can understand that."

They drove down the street, which was lined with trees older than any of the residents. The light of dusk, filtered by low branches, dappled the yards, but heavy storm clouds were just beginning to loom up on the horizon. Laurant saw her house and remembered how charming she'd thought it was the first time she'd driven up to it. It was old and worn, and she loved it. After she had moved in, the first thing she did was purchase a porch swing at the garden shop. Every morning she'd take her cup of tea and sit on the swing while she read the paper. In the evenings, she'd chat with the neighbors tending their yards.

The tranquility she'd felt, the sense of belonging, was gone now, and she didn't know if she would ever get it back.

"Is the camera still there, or did they take it away?" she asked.

"It's still there."

"Is it on?"

"Yes. We don't want him to know we found it."

"Then he didn't see the agents when they went into my bedroom?"

"No, they found it in the hall closet," he reminded her. "They kept out of the camera's eye."

He pulled into the driveway and turned the motor off. She was staring at the house when she asked, "Where would he get something like that? Do they sell transmitters in the stores?"

Before he could answer her, she blurted,

"Every time I go into the bedroom, he could be watching."

He put his hand on her knee. "We want him to be watching. This is a great opportunity to push him. You and I are going to be getting hot and heavy in front of the camera."

"Yes, I know what the plan is."

She wasn't getting cold feet, but she could feel her resolve slipping away. Her life had turned into one of those surreal movies where nothing was as it appeared, where everything that looked benign and innocent was only a mask hiding something sinister. Her charming little house looked inviting, but *he* had been inside, and there was a camera focused on her bed.

"Are you ready to go in?"

Her nod was brisk.

Nick could see her anxiety and decided to try to take her mind off the moment. As he opened his door, he said, "Holy Oaks is a pretty town, but I'd still go crazy living here. Where's the traffic? Where's the noise?"

She knew what he was doing. He was helping her cope. He could tell when she was getting overloaded, she realized, and that was when he lightened the conversation.

She opened her door and got out. "You like traffic and noise?"

"It's what I'm used to," he replied. They were looking at each other over the top of the car. "You don't get a lot of road rage here, do you?"

"Sure we do. When the sheriff's son, Lonnie, goes joyriding with his friends, a lot of people

225

would love to ram his car into a gully. He's a menace, and his father isn't going to do anything about it."

"The local thug, huh?"

"Yes."

She reached back into the car to get her purse while Nick surveyed the neighborhood. There was a big oak in the front yard, almost identical in size to the oak in the neighbor's yard on the corner. On the other side of the white, two-story house was an empty lot. At the end of the long drive was an unattached garage, which meant that when she put her car away, she had to walk to the back door. The two houses were close together, and there were trees and overgrown shrubs all along the sides—too many places for a man to hide. He also noticed there weren't any outside lights on the house or the garage.

"A burglar's paradise," he remarked. "Too many concealed areas."

"I've got a porch light."

"That's not enough."

"There are a lot of people here who don't ever lock their doors, even when they go to bed at night. It's a small town and everyone feels safe."

"Yeah, well, you're locking your doors."

"Yoo-hoo, Laurant. You're home."

Nick turned as a white-haired old lady wearing a bright purple dress with a wide lace collar opened her screen door and stepped out onto her porch. She was clutching a white lace handkerchief in her hand. She appeared to be around eighty years old and was as thin as a lightning rod.

"We had some excitement while you were away."

"You did?" Laurant called back. She went to her neighbor's picket fence and waited to hear what happened.

"Don't make me shout, dear," Bessie Jean gently chided. "Come over here and bring that young man with you."

"Yes, ma'am."

"She wants to know who you are," she whispered.

Nick grabbed Laurant's hand and whispered back, "Show time."

"Lovey-dovey stuff?"

"You got that right, babe." And with that, he leaned down and lightly kissed her.

Bessie Jean Vanderman stood on her porch, taking it all in. Her eyes were as wide as saucers as she watched the smiling couple.

The picket fence ran the perimeter of the front yard. Nick let go of Laurant's hand to open the gate. As he followed her down the cement walk and up the stairs to the porch, he noticed another elderly woman peeking out at him through the screen. It was dark inside the house and the woman's face was cast in shadows.

"What was the excitement?" Laurant asked.

"A hooligan broke into your house." Bessie Jean lowered her voice, as if sharing a confidence, and leaned toward Laurant. "I called the sheriff and demanded that he come right over and investigate. I don't believe there were any arrests made. The sheriff left the hooligan inside and went running to his car. That was certainly a sight to see. He didn't have the good manners to come and tell me what was happening. You'd best see if anything's missing." She straightened up and backed away to get a full view of Nick. "Now who is this handsome man standing so close to you? I don't believe I've ever seen him in Holy Oaks before."

Laurant quickly made the introductions, but Bessie Jean Vanderman took her time sizing him up. This one doesn't miss a thing, he thought, spotting the shrewdness in her clear green eyes.

"And what is it you do, Mr. Buchanan?"

"I'm with the FBI, ma'am."

Bessie Jean's hand flew to her throat. She appeared startled for about two seconds, then recovered. "Why didn't you say so in the first place? I'd like to see your badge, young man."

Nick produced his identification and handed it to her. She gave the badge only a cursory glance before handing it back.

"You took your sweet time."

"Excuse me?"

The criticism was there in her brisk tone when she responded, "Sister and I don't like to be kept waiting."

Nick didn't have the faintest idea what she was talking about, and he could tell from Laurant's puzzled expression that she didn't have a clue either.

Bessie Jean pulled the screen door open. "I don't see any reason to waste any more time. Come on inside and you can get started investigating."

"What exactly is it that you want me to investigate?" he asked as he followed Laurant.

Bessie Jean's sister was waiting for them. Laurant again made the introductions. Viola took off her glasses and tucked them in the pocket of her apron as she came forward to shake his hand. She was shorter, rounder, and a much softer version of her sister.

"We waited and waited," she said. She patted Nick's hand before she let go. "I'd almost given up on you, but Bessie Jean never lost faith. She was just certain her letter was misplaced, and that's why she wrote another one."

"It's not like the FBI to drag their feet," Bessie Jean said. "That's why I knew my letter must have been lost in the mail. I wrote a second letter then, and when I still didn't hear—"

"She wrote to the director himself," Viola explained.

Bessie Jean led the way into the living room. It was cool and dark and smelled of cinnamon and vanilla. One of them had been doing some baking, and his stomach rumbled in response. He was hungrier than he'd realized.

Dinner would have to wait. It took his eyes a second to adjust to the darkness, then Viola opened the front window curtains, and he was squinting again. The room was cluttered with antiques. Directly ahead of him was the fireplace. The mantel was lined with candles, and above was a huge oil painting of a gray-haired dog sitting on a burgundy cushion. The animal appeared to be cross-eyed.

Bessie Jean ushered Nick and Laurant to the Victorian sofa, then removed the needlepoint pillow from the wicker rocker and sat down, crossing one ankle over the other as she'd been trained to do by her mother. Her posture was so stiff, she could have balanced a couple of encyclopedias on her head.

"Get your pad out, dear," she ordered.

Nick barely heard her. His attention had been arrested by all the photos cluttering the tables and the walls. The subject was the same in every one of the silver frames—the dog—a schnauzer he guessed, or maybe a mixed breed.

Laurant touched his arm to get his attention and said, "Bessie Jean and Viola wrote to the FBI for help in solving a mystery."

"Not a mystery, dear," Viola corrected. "We know exactly what happened." She was sitting in a big floral print easy chair and was busy repinning the doily on one of the arms.

"Yes, we know what happened," Bessie Jean agreed with a nod.

"Why don't you give him the particulars, Sister."

"He doesn't have his pad and pen out yet."

Viola got up and went into the dining room while Nick patted his pockets, looking for a pad he knew he didn't have. It was in the car with his folders.

The sister came back with a pink notebook about the size of a pocket calculator and a pink pen with a purple feather sticking out from the end.

"You may use this," she said.

"Thank you. Now tell me what this is all about?"

"The director was remiss in not telling you what your assignment was," Bessie Jean said. "You're here to investigate a murder."

"Excuse me?"

Bessie Jean patiently repeated her announcement. Viola nodded. "Someone murdered Daddy."

"Daddy was a family pet," Laurant explained with a nod toward the oil painting looming over them.

"Daddy was named after our daddy, the colonel," Viola added.

To his credit, Nick didn't smile. "I see."

"We demand justice," Viola told him

Bessie Jean was frowning at Nick. "Young man, I don't mean to criticize..."

"Yes, ma'am?"

"I've just never heard of a law officer not having a pad and pen. That gun clipped to your belt is loaded, isn't it?"

"Yes, ma'am, it is."

Bessie Jean was satisfied. Having a gun was important in her opinion because, once he caught the culprit, he might very well have to shoot him.

"Have the local authorities looked into the matter?" Nick asked.

"Not a matter, dear. It was murder," Viola corrected.

"We called Sheriff L.A. right away, but he won't do anything to help us find the criminal," Bessie Jean explained.

Viola, wishing to be helpful, interjected, "That's Lard Ass, dear. Now write it down."

Nick couldn't decide which was more jarring—a pet named Daddy or a sweet old lady using the words *lard ass*.

"Why don't you tell me exactly what happened."

Bessie Jean gave her sister a relieved glance and then began. "We believe Daddy was poisoned, but we can't be absolutely certain. We kept him chained to the big oak in the front yard off and on during the day and sometimes into the evening on bingo night so he could take in the fresh air."

"We have a fence, but Daddy could jump it, so we had to use the chain," Viola explained. "Are you writing that down, dear?"

"Yes, ma'am."

"Daddy was in the best of health," Bessie Jean told him.

"He was only ten and in his prime," Viola supplied.

"His water bowl was completely turned over," Bessie Jean said as she rocked back and forth, fanning herself with her handkerchief.

"And Daddy could never have managed to turn that bowl over, because it was weighted down so he couldn't."

Bessie Jean nodded again. "That's right.

Daddy was clever, but he couldn't get his nose under that bowl."

"Someone had to have turned the bowl over," Viola said emphatically.

"We think poison was added to his water, and then after poor Daddy took a big drink, the culprit got rid of the evidence."

"We know how he got rid of it too," Viola announced. "He threw the poisoned water into my impatiens," Viola said. "He killed my beautiful flowers. They were in glorious bloom one day and shriveled up and brown the next. They looked like someone had poured acid on them."

A bell started ringing in the back of the house. Viola struggled to get out of the chair. "If you'll excuse me, I'll go get my buns out of the oven. Could I get you anything while I'm up?"

"No, thank you," Laurant said.

Nick was busy writing on his pad. He looked up and said, "I could use a glass of water."

"We often take a gin and tonic in an evening," Viola said. "It's quite refreshing on such hot humid days. Would you like one?"

"Water will do," he answered.

"He's on duty, Sister. He can't drink."

Nick didn't contradict her. He finished making a note to himself and then asked, "Did the dog bark at strangers?"

"Oh my, yes," Bessie Jean answered. "He was a wonderful watchdog. He was quite persnickety about letting strangers get near the house. He barked at everyone. Why, he took

233

exception to anyone who walked down the street."

The topic of the dog was obviously still distressing to Bessie Jean. As she talked about him, she gradually increased the pace of her rocking. Nick half expected her to fling herself out of the chair.

"There are some strangers in town now, working up at the abbey. Three men moved into the old Morrison house across the street and are renting it while they're here," she said. "And two more moved in with the Nicholsons at the other end of the block."

"Daddy wasn't partial to any of them," Viola interjected from the dining room. She carried a glass of ice water across the room to the coffee table and set it on a napkin she pulled from her pocket.

Nick was rapidly getting the idea that Daddy wasn't partial to anyone.

"Those Catholics are always in such a rush," Bessie Jean remarked. She had obviously forgotten that Laurant was Catholic and that her brother was a priest. "They're an impatient lot if you ask me. They want to get the renovations completed on the abbey so it will be ready for the open house during the July Fourth celebration."

"It's the abbey's anniversary celebration as well," Viola said.

Bessie Jean realized they were getting away from the investigation. "We had the doctor put Daddy in the freezer so you could oversee the autopsy. Are you getting all this down on your pad?"

"Yes, ma'am, I am," Nick assured her. "Please go on."

"Just yesterday I received a bill from the doctor for cremation services. I was thunderstruck, and I called him up right away. I was certain there had been a mistake."

"The dog was cremated?"

Bessie Jean dabbed at the corners of her eyes with her handkerchief and then began to fan herself again. "Yes, he was. The doctor told me that my nephew had called him and told him we'd changed our minds and to go ahead and cremate poor Daddy."

The rocking chair was really moving now, the floor creaking beneath it.

"And the vet followed those instructions without consulting you?"

"Yes, he did," Viola said. "It just never occurred to him to check with us first."

"Your nephew—"

"But that's just it," Bessie Jean cried out. "We don't have any nephews."

"If you ask me, the culprit wanted to get rid of the evidence," Viola said. "Isn't that right?"

"It would seem so," he agreed. "I'd like to look at those flowers."

"Oh, you can't do that, dear," Viola said. "Justin helped me dig out the roots and plant new flowers. He saw me out there, down on my knees, struggling so, and even after the hard day he'd put in doing carpentry work up at the abbey, he was kind enough to come over and help me. I simply can't keep up with the yard anymore."

"And who is Justin?"

"Justin Brady," Bessie Jean answered, impatiently. "I do believe I already mentioned him."

"No, you didn't," Viola said. "You told Nicholas that three workmen moved into the Morrison house and two others lived with the Nicholsons. You didn't say their names. I heard every word you said as clear as a bell."

"Well, I meant to," Bessie Jean replied. "I've only met the three across the street. There's Justin Brady. He's the only one we like."

"Because he helped me," Viola said. "And then there's Mark Hanover and Willie Lakeman. They were all sitting on the porch steps together drinking beer, and all of them saw me struggling, but Justin's the only one who crossed the street to help me. The other two kept on drinking."

"Well, young man, do you believe Daddy was murdered, or do you think we're just a couple of dotty old ladies making up stories?"

"Based on what you've told me, and assuming that it's accurate, I agree that your dog was killed," Nick said.

Laurant's eyes widened. "You do?"

"Yes," he answered.

Bessie Jean clasped her hands together. She was elated. "I knew the FBI wouldn't fail me. Now tell me, Nicholas, what are you prepared to do about it?"

"I'm going to look into this myself. Some samples of the soil where those flowers were planted would help. And the water bowl...you do still have it, don't you?"

"Yes, we do," Viola said. "It's packed away in the garage with all of Daddy's favorite toys."

"Will you keep us apprised of developments?" Bessie Jean asked.

"I most certainly will. You didn't happen to wash that water bowl, did you?"

"I don't believe we did," Viola said. "We were so upset, we just put it away so we wouldn't be...reminded."

"Viola wanted to take the painting down and pack up the pictures, but I wouldn't let her do it. It's a comfort having Daddy smiling down at us."

In unison, everyone paused to look up at the oil painting. While Nick was wondering how the women could tell that the dog was smiling, Laurant was pondering how the sisters could feel such affection for the nasty-tempered animal that snapped at everyone who came into the yard. He'd bitten so many people, the vet kept his shot record posted on the waiting room bulletin board.

"We do hope the culprit turns out to be someone from outside our peaceful valley. We don't like to think that one of our own could do such a terrible thing," Viola said.

"I wouldn't put such cruelty past the sheriff's boy. Lonnie's always been trouble. The boy's got a real mean streak inside him that runs deep. He gets it from his father, of course."

"He's a sneaky one all right. His mother passed on several years ago. I don't mean to speak ill of the dead, but she was a mousy woman. She didn't have any backbone at all, not even when she was a young girl. She was a whiner too, wasn't she, Bessie Jean?"

"My yes, she was."

"You said there were a lot of strangers in town," Nick said. "Have you noticed anyone hanging around your house or Laurant's?"

"I spend a good deal of my time sitting on my porch and I will occasionally look out the windows at night, just to make certain things are as right as they should be. Except for the man I saw going into Laurant's house yesterday, I haven't noticed anyone in the yard or lurking about. Like I said before, most of the strangers are workmen helping out at the abbey. Some of them come from as far away as Nebraska and Kansas."

She planted both feet on the floor and brought the rocker to an abrupt stop. Leaning toward Nick and Laurant expectantly, she asked, "You'll stay to supper?"

"It's macaroni night," Viola announced as she pushed against the cushions with both hands to raise herself out of the low chair and then headed for the kitchen. "Macaroni and brisket and homemade cinnamon rolls, and I'll make company salad."

"We don't want to put you to any trouble," Laurant protested.

"We'd love to join you," Nick said at the same time.

"Laurant, why don't you help Sister, and I'll keep Nicholas company," Bessie Jean suggested.

"Come and set the table, dear," Viola said. "We'll eat in the kitchen, but we'll use the Spode."

Bessie Jean didn't waste any time. As soon as Laurant disappeared, she leaned even farther out of the rocker and demanded to know how Nick and Laurant had become so friendly.

He'd been waiting for the opportunity. In the barest of details, he told her about his friendship with Tommy and how he had been called in to help when a man came into the confessional and threatened to harm Laurant.

"The unfortunate incident brought us together," he explained. "Our experts are all in agreement that the man was just a blowhard out to get some kicks. You know the kind. He wants to scare people, to stir up things and cause trouble. He wants attention, that's all. They figure he's not real bright. He probably has a low IQ," he added, "and is most likely impotent."

Bessie Jean blushed. "Impotent, you say?"

"Yes, ma'am. That's what they figure he is."

"Then you didn't come here to investigate Daddy's murder?"

He'd wondered how long it would take her to figure that out. "No, but I'm going to look into it all the same," he promised.

She sat back in the rocker. "Tell me a bit about your background, Nicholas."

She wouldn't let him skim over it. She drilled him with the expertise of a master interrogator. She wanted to know everything about his family too.

Laurant saved him by appearing in the doorway and calling them to dinner. Nick followed Bessie Jean into the kitchen. The delicate, flowered china rested on a white linen tablecloth that almost completely covered the chrome legs of the kitchen table. Nick charmed the ladies with his gentlemanly manners by rushing to pull out their chairs for them. They beamed with pleasure.

Company salad turned out to be a square of lime Jell-O nestled on a bed of iceberg lettuce with a dab of mayonnaise on top. He hated Jell-O, but he ate it anyway so he wouldn't hurt their feelings, and while he was gulping it down, Bessie Jean filled Viola in on the incident that occurred in Kansas City.

"The things people will do for attention these days. Terrible, just terrible. Father Tom must have been very upset."

"Oh, he was," Laurant said. "He wasn't sure what to do, so he called Nick for help."

"Something good came out of it," Nick said. He winked at Laurant across the table and added, "I finally met Tommy's sister."

"And you were taken with her, weren't you?" Bessie Jean nodded, as though stating a foregone conclusion.

"Of course he was," Viola said. "She's the prettiest girl in Holy Oaks."

"It was love at first sight," he told them, casting an adoring look at Laurant. "I didn't believe in that stuff until it happened to me."

"And you, Laurant?" Viola asked. "Was it love at first sight for you as well?"

"Yes, it was," she answered breathlessly.

"How romantic," Viola said. "Don't you think it's romantic, Bessie Jean?"

"Of course it's romantic," Bessie Jean said. "But sometimes fires that start fast burn out fast. I wouldn't want our Laurant to get her heart broken. Do you understand what I'm saying, Nicholas?"

"Yes, ma'am, I do, but it isn't like that."

"Then tell me, what are your intentions?"

"I'm going to marry her."

Viola and Bessie Jean looked at each other and then burst into laughter.

"Are you thinking what I'm thinking, Sister?" Bessie Jean chuckled.

"I'm just sure I am." Viola gave her sister a knowing smile.

"This is thrilling news," Bessie Jean announced. "I assume Father Tom has given his blessing?"

"Yes, he has," Laurant replied. "He's very happy for us."

Laurant and Nick looked at each other, puzzled by the ladies' laughter.

"Nicholas, we weren't laughing over your wonderful news. It's just...," Viola began.

"Steve Brenner," Bessie Jean supplied. "He's going to have a tantrum when he finds out about you two. Oh my, yes, and I do so hope Sister and I are there to see it happen. Mr. Brenner has grand plans for you, Laurant."

"I've never even gone out with the man, and

241

I don't believe I did anything to encourage his attention."

"He's infatuated, dear," Viola explained.

"No, he's obsessed," Bessie Jean corrected. "You're the prettiest girl in Holy Oaks, so he's got to have you. He thinks that having the best of everything will make him the best man in town. That's why he bought the big old house over on Sycamore. If you ask me, Mr. Brenner's nothing but a big old rooster, strutting around town." She turned to Nick. "He thinks he can take anything he wants, including your Laurant."

"Then he's in for a surprise, isn't he?" Nick asked.

Bessie Jean smiled. "My, yes, he is," she agreed. "You may have noticed that Sister and I don't have a high opinion of the man."

Nick laughed. "I noticed."

"Everyone else likes him just fine," Viola said. "We know why too. Mr. Brenner donates money to all the local charities, and that makes people appreciative. He isn't a bad-looking fellow either. He has a nice head of hair."

Bessie Jean scowled disdainfully. "I'm not so easily impressed. I don't care for showy people, and Mr. Brenner throws money around like it's grass seed. I'm going to lose my appetite if we keep talking about him. Now, Laurant, is your engagement official, or do you want us to keep quiet about it? We can keep a secret when we have to," she assured her.

"You may tell anyone you want to tell.

Nick and I are going to be looking for an engagement ring tomorrow or the day after." She was brimming with excitement as she put her hand out and wiggled her fingers. "I don't want anything too big."

"Don't forget to put the announcement in the paper. I could help you with that," Bessie Jean suggested.

From the eagerness in Bessie Jean's voice and the glint in her eyes, Laurant knew she was dying to give the news to her friend's daughter, Lorna Hamburg, who just happened to be the editor of the society page.

"I could ring Lorna up right after supper."

"That would be very helpful," Laurant agreed.

"Should I mention the problem in Kansas City?"

Laurant wasn't sure and looked at Nick who quickly answered. "Of course you should mention it. The editor will probably want to know all the details of how we met. Right, sweetheart?"

The endearment wasn't planned. It just slipped out, and he was more surprised than she appeared to be.

"Yes, darling. I think Bessie Jean should also tell Little Lorna that the FBI experts have concluded that they're dealing with a man who's obviously disturbed...and inferior."

"Oh, she'll be sure to tell Little Lorna everything," Viola said. She passed the platter of brisket to Nick, insisting that he take a second helping. Nick pushed his chair back, patted his full stomach, and told her that he couldn't eat another bite.

"There are so many disturbed people in the world today," Bessie Jean remarked with a shake of her head. "It will be a comfort to know an FBI agent is close by."

"Where exactly will you be staying?" Viola asked.

"With Laurant," he answered. "She's a strong woman, and she can take care of herself, but I want to be there to help make sure she's safe from men like Steve Brenner and anyone else who thinks he's going to bother her."

The sisters both raised their eyebrows and shared a look that Nick couldn't interpret. He'd said something they didn't like, but he didn't know what it was.

Bessie Jean put her fork down, pushed her plate back, then folded her hands on the table and collected her thoughts for a moment before turning to look directly at Laurant.

"Dear, I'm going to be blunt. I know a thing or two about raging hormones in young bodies. I may be old and set in my ways, but I keep up with the changing times by watching my stories on the television. Now, you don't have a mother or a father to guide you. Oh, I know you're an adult, but you still need someone who's older and wiser to counsel you every now and then. Every young woman does. Sister and I have grown quite fond of you, and with that fondness comes worry. Now, I'm going to ask you straight out. While Nicholas

244

is busy protecting you from other men, how do you propose to protect yourself from him?"

"She's talking about your virtue, dear," Viola said.

"We've made a commitment to one another," Nick began. "I won't do anything...dishonorable...and neither will Laurant."

"People will talk, but they'll do it behind your backs," Viola told him.

"They'll talk anyway," Bessie Jean said. "The best intentions sometimes get pushed to the side of the road in the heat of the moment. Do you understand what I'm saying?"

Laurant opened her mouth to speak, but nothing came out. She shot Nick a pleading look.

"Get to the point, Bessie Jean," Viola urged as she folded her napkin neatly on the table and stood.

"All right then, I will," she said, delicately dabbing at the corners of her mouth with her napkin. "Safe sex, Nicholas."

"Yes, dear," Viola agreed. She circled the table, collecting the plates. "We want you to practice safe sex...shall we have dessert?"

Steve Brenner was in a cold rage. The bitch had gone too far this time. No one, man or woman, was going to make a fool out of him. It was high time Laurant was taught a lesson, and he was just the man to inflict it. Who the hell did she think she was to humiliate him in front of his associates and his friends by bringing another man home?

How could anyone fall in love in the space of one weekend?

Infuriated over the news Sheriff Lloyd had just given him, he picked up a chair and hurled it across the room, knocking a desk lamp to the floor. He watched it shatter, and then, still enraged, he slammed his fist into the wall. Fresh paint splattered in every direction, spraying white mist on his freshly laundered, bloodred, Polo shirt. The drywall crumbled under his hand, and the skin on his callused knuckles ripped wide open when he struck the cement block behind the wall. Oblivious to the pain or the mess he'd just made, he jerked his hand back, then shook himself like a wet dog ridding itself of excess water.

He couldn't think when he was this angry, and he knew he needed to be clearheaded so that he could figure out his options. He was the master of the game, after all. The bitch didn't understand that yet, but she soon would. Yes, indeed.

Sheriff Lloyd was sprawled in a chair behind an empty desk. He appeared to be relaxed, but inside he was as nervous and tense as a cornered possum because he knew firsthand what Steve was capable of when he was riled. God help him, he never wanted to see that side of his new associate again.

Lloyd's brand new, silver, mustang belt buckle was digging painfully into his gut, but he was afraid to move. He didn't want to do anything that would draw attention to himself until Steve had gotten his temper under control.

Fat red drops of blood were steadily dripping down on Steve's pressed khaki pants and turning into black streaks all the way down to his knee. Lloyd thought about telling Steve—he knew how important his appearance was to him—but he decided to keep quiet instead and pretend he didn't notice.

Most of the women in town thought Steve was a handsome man, and the sheriff supposed he was, with his wavy brown hair and good bone structure. His face was a little long, but when he smiled, the women didn't see anything but charisma. He wasn't smiling now though, and if those same women could see the frost in his eyes, they wouldn't think he was handsome at all. They might even be as afraid of him as Lloyd was.

Steve clenched and unclenched his fists as he stood at the window, looking out at the square with his back to the sheriff. Three teenagers were riding their skateboards along the sidewalks, ignoring the posted signs prohibiting bicycles and skateboards as they sped along. The pharmacist, Conrad Kellogg, came running outside waving his hands when one of the freaks with dyed-orange, long, straggly hair accidentally rammed into his window.

Directly across the square, the door opened to Laurant's store, and the Winston twins, dressed in bib overalls, came outside. They were working late tonight. The streetlights were already on, which meant it was after seven. All the stores but the pharmacy closed at six. The twins were working overtime to get the store ready. Steve watched as they adjusted the seals around the window they'd just installed in her storefront.

"A damn waste of money," he muttered.

"What'd you say, Steve?"

He didn't answer. Since the brooding man wasn't paying any attention to him now, Lloyd decided it was safe to get comfortable. He eased his belt down below his extended belly, unbuttoned his pants to give him a little more room, and then dug his pocketknife out of his pocket. Flipping the rusty blade open, he began to dig the dirt out from under his ragged nails.

"I take off for a couple of days to get in a little fishing, and what happens? She falls in love with another man. Son of a bitch. If she had only given me a chance...if she had let herself get to know me, she would have fallen in love with me. No question about that. I can be fucking charming when I want to," Steve snapped.

Lloyd didn't know if he should try to placate him now or commiserate with him on this latest development. Saying the wrong thing could be worse than saying nothing at all, and so he settled on a loud grunt, leaving it to Steve to interpret.

"But she wouldn't give me the time of day," Steve railed. "All I wanted was a chance. I figured I'd give her some time to get used to the idea, then maybe send her some more flowers and ask her out again. Did you see the way she ignored me at the fish fry last month? No matter what I did, she wouldn't let me get near her. She acted like I was a pesky fly. That's how much attention she gave me. People noticed too. I saw the way they were watching me."

"Now, Steve, it ain't like that at all. Everyone in Holy Oaks knows you're going to marry Lauren. She's got to know it too. Maybe she's just sowing some wild oats before she settles down."

"Men sow wild oats, not women."

"Then maybe she's just playing hard to get." He winced when he poked tender skin under his thumbnail with the pocketknife. "You're going to be the richest man in the valley and she knows it. Yeah, that's what she's doing. Playing hard to get."

"I thought she was...better than that."

"Than what?"

"If he's staying there with her, then she's letting him touch her."

Rage was back in his voice, and Lloyd tried to deflect it. "I think she's just testing you. Women like men to chase them. Everybody knows that."

"Who were those men at the house?" He whirled around and regarded the sheriff malevolently while he waited for an explanation. He got an excuse instead.

"I was in a hurry to tell you about Lauren bringing home another man. I didn't think to ask their names. They told me they were friends and they were there to fix her sink. They had tools and I figured they were probably on their way to the abbey."

"But you didn't bother to get their names or see some identification."

"I was in a hurry," Lloyd whined. "I wasn't thinking."

"For God's sake, you're the sheriff in this two-bit, shantytown. Don't you know how to do your job?"

Lloyd dropped the knife and put his hands up in a conciliatory gesture. "Don't take your anger out on me. I'm just the messenger. If you want, I'll go right on back there and get all the information you want."

"Forget it," Steve muttered before turning his back on the sheriff again. "Maybe that old, dried-up biddy next door was right. Maybe they were robbing Laurant's house."

"Now, Steve, you know she doesn't have nothing worth stealing. I'm telling you they're just friends."

Steve couldn't get his anger under control. Laurant sharing her bed with another man. It was unforgivable. Maybe she was just trying to assert her independence...playing a little game with him. Oh, yes, she needed to be taught a lesson all right. He'd let her rudeness go unpunished in the past, and so he could only blame himself for this latest insult. The first time she had given him the cold shoulder he should have put the fear of God into her then and there. Some women required a heavy hand until they learned where their place was. His first wife had been like that, but he'd believed Laurant was different. She'd seemed delicate and almost perfect, but he realized now he'd used the wrong approach. He'd been too damned polite and nice, but that was going to change.

"No one falls in love in a single weekend."

"According to her friends, she's real taken with this Nick Buchanan," Lloyd remarked. His head was down, his concentration on getting the dirty paste out from under his pinky nail. "These friends...they told me Nick and Lauren were gonna get married."

After blurting out the last bit of information, Lloyd glanced up to see how Steve was reacting.

"Bullshit," Steve muttered. "That isn't going to happen."

Lloyd nodded. "But you know...if they should get married, they'd probably move away…what with his job and all… I didn't think to ask what it was this Nick fellow does for a living…but then don't you see? She'd have to sell her store."

Steve's gaze turned glacial as he watched Lloyd. The fat man reminded him of a monkey in the zoo, grooming himself in public without a care in the world. He was disgusting, but he was useful, and for that reason, Steve put up with him.

Lloyd put his penknife away, noticed all the dirt on the white desk pad, and brushed it to the floor. Glancing out the window he remarked, "Looks like Lauren's store is going to open real soon."

"That isn't going to happen either," Steve said. His face was contorted with anger, and he took a threatening step toward the sheriff. "Do you have any notion in that pea brain of yours how much money we stand to lose if she gets her way and convinces the other shop owners not to sell? I'm not letting anyone screw this deal."

"What are you going to do about it?"

"Whatever it takes."

"Are you talking about breaking the law?"

"Screw the law," he roared. "You're already in this up to your ass," he added in a snarl. "So what if you have to go in a little deeper."

"I haven't broken the law."

"Yeah? Tell that to old lady Broadmore. You're the one who forged her name on that legal document."

Lloyd began to sweat. "That was all your idea,

and what was the harm? The old lady was already dead and her relatives will get the money, so they sure don't care. Hell, they would have sold her store, but you said they'd hold us up for a lot more money if they knew about our deal with the development company. I don't look at what we done as criminal."

Steve's laugh sounded like a nail going down a chalkboard. "It might have been my idea, but you're the man who signed her name, and I noticed you couldn't wait to spend your bonus money buying yourself a new car."

"I only did what I was told to do."

"That's right, and you're going to keep on doing what you're told. You want to retire a rich man, don't you?"

"Sure I do. I want to leave this town...get away from..."

"Lonnie?"

The sheriff averted his eyes. "I didn't say that."

"You're afraid of your own son, aren't you, Lloyd? As mean and bad-tempered as you are, you're still afraid of him."

"Hell, no, I'm not," he blustered.

Steve hooted with laughter, and the sound was even more grating than ten fingernails scratching at a chalkboard. Lloyd had to force himself not to cringe.

"You chicken shit. You're scared of your boy."

At the moment, what scared Lloyd more than his son was knowing that Steve could see through his "big man" veneer. "Lonnie's going on nineteen years now, and I'm telling you, he ain't never been right in his head, not even when he was little. He's got a real mean attitude and a nasty temper to boot. I'll admit I do want to get away from him, but not because I'm scared. I can still beat the crap out of him. It's just that I'm sick and tired of the messes he's always getting himself into. I've had to sneak him out of trouble more times than I can count. Lonnie's going to kill someone one of these days. He came damn close with the Edmond girl. She ended up in the hospital, and I had to do some pretty fancy talking to get that doctor to keep quiet. I convinced him that Mary Jo would kill herself if folks heard she'd gotten herself raped. She'd never be able to hold her head up in this town again."

Steve cocked his head. "You threatened him too, didn't you? I'll bet you told him you'd sic Lonnie on him or his wife if he said a word. I'm right, aren't I?"

"I did what I had to do to keep my boy out of jail."

"You know what everyone in town calls you? Sheriff Lard Ass. They're laughing at you behind your back. If you want things to change, keep your mouth shut and do what I tell you to do. Then you can leave Holy Oaks and Lonnie, and never look back."

Lloyd was slowly tearing strips from the paper on the blotter. He kept his gaze averted when he asked, "You aren't gonna tell Lonnie what I'm planning to do, are you? The boy thinks he's gonna get a big cut of the money, and I want to be long gone before he figures out he ain't getting a dime."

"I won't tell him anything as long as you continue to cooperate. Do we understand each other? Now about this Buchanan—"

Lloyd's neck snapped back. "Who?"

Brenner's hand clenched into a fist again with the intent of smashing it into Lloyd's fat face, but he felt the sting in his knuckles this time, and glancing down, saw the bloodstains on his pant leg. Shit. He was going to have to change clothes again. Appearances had to be maintained, and he couldn't stand to look the least bit imperfect.

"Never mind," he muttered as he strode to the bathroom in the back of the office to wash his hand.

Lloyd finally remembered who Buchanan was. "I still wish you'd let me go on back to Lauren's house and have a talk with those friends. They could still be there."

Lloyd's nasally whine was getting on Steve's nerves. He didn't have any patience for slow-witted people, and if the sheriff weren't a necessary ingredient in his grand scheme, he would have taken great delight in beating the hell out of him. Better yet, he'd order Lonnie to do it for him while he watched. The boy would do whatever Steve told him to do because, like his father, he was motivated by greed and hate, and failure.

He finished washing, patted his hands dry with a paper towel, then folded it neatly into a perfect square before tossing it into the trash can. Reaching into his back pocket, he pulled out his comb and stood in front of the mirror, smoothing his hair back. "Where's Lonnie now?" he called out.

"I don't know. He never tells me where he's going. If he's gotten his lazy ass out of bed, then he's probably down at the lake, fishing. Why do you want to know?"

It was time for the lesson. Laurant was going to learn he wouldn't put up with any competition.

"Never you mind. Go find him and send him to me."

"I've got to go pick up my new car first."

"You've got to do what I tell you first, then you can get your damned car. I said, go find Lonnie."

The sheriff shoved his chair back and stood. "But what should I tell him?"

Steve came back into the office. He was smiling when he answered. "Tell him I've got a job for him."

aurant deliberately prolonged her visit with the Vandermans. She needed the time to psych herself up for the ordeal ahead of her.

In the blink of an eye, everything had changed. She used to think of her home as her safe haven, a sanctuary really, where she could find peace and tranquility after putting in a hard day's work. He had taken that away from her, the man the FBI nicknamed the unsub. The unknown subject who was tearing her mind into shreds.

How long had he been watching her? Would he be sitting in a comfortable chair watching her tonight? Laurant blanched at the thought. Soon now she would go into her bedroom and get ready for bed while the camera tracked her every movement.

She had a sudden urge to put on her tennis shoes and go running. She couldn't, of course, it was dark out, and it wasn't part of the approved-by-Wesson schedule. Laurant still wanted to do it though. She had started her running regimen after she heard about her brother's cancer. It was an outlet, a way of dealing with her fear. She loved the physical exercise, pushing herself to the limit, faster and faster, until her mind cleared and all she could concentrate on was the pounding of her heartbeat, the crunch of the scrub under her feet, and the rhythm of her breathing as she raced along the broken path around the lake. She became oblivious to her surroundings as she pushed and pushed, harder and harder, until the blessed endorphins kicked in, energizing her. For a brief time, the panic was gone, and she felt gloriously alive and completely free.

She longed for that feeling now, and oh God, how she wanted control over her life again. She hated being afraid, and alternating between fury and terror was making her crazy.

"Dear, be careful with that cup. You don't want to chip it."

Viola's caution pulled Laurant back to the present. Viola continued to tell her the latest gossip she'd picked up at her ladies' bridge club. Laurant tried to pay attention as she finished hand drying the blue Spode. When the kitchen was cleaned, she followed the elderly woman out onto the porch and sat side by side with her in the glider while Bessie Jean, her hand tucked into the crook of Nick's arm, took him on a stroll around the property to show off her petunias and her vegetable garden. The streetlight barely lit the backyard.

Nick was more interested in the dark, vacant, tree-lined lot behind Laurant's house than the garden. Cluttered with thick shrubs and bushes, it was a paradise for the unsub to hide and watch, or creep up on Laurant's house without being seen.

"Do kids ever play in that lot?" he asked Bessie Jean after complimenting her on her garden.

"They used to, but they don't go back there anymore, not since Billy Cleary got a fierce case of poison ivy. He was wearing shorts and he sat in it, you see, and from what his mother told me, it was a very painful experience. The child couldn't sit down for two weeks. Once he was feeling better, Billy and his friends turned to playing by the lake."

They had made a full circle of the house. Bessie Jean called out to Viola, "I was just telling Nicholas about Billy Cleary and how he used to play in the lot behind Laurant's house until he got poison ivy." She climbed the steps and sat down in a wicker chair.

Viola leaned toward Laurant. "His privates were covered in it," she whispered.

"I told Nicholas no one goes near that lot anymore," Bessie Jean explained.

"That's not true," Viola said. "Don't you remember, Sister? Several weeks ago there were children playing back there. Daddy stood on his hind legs at the back screen, barking and barking. We had to shut the door to calm him down."

Bessie Jean nodded. "I don't believe those were children," she said. "It was going on dark. It was probably just a raccoon or possum back there. Actually, now that I reflect upon it, I believe that a wild animal was making a home back there because Daddy put up a fuss several times that week."

Viola nodded. "Yes, he did," she agreed.

Nick leaned against the railing. "How long ago did this happen? Do you remember?"

"I can't be sure," Bessie Jean said.

"I remember," Viola announced. "I'd just put in the Big Boys."

"Big Boys?"

"Tomatoes," she explained.

"And that was when?" Nick asked patiently.

"Almost a month ago."

Bessie Jean didn't agree. She thought Viola was mistaken and that it hadn't been quite that long. The sisters bickered about it for several minutes before Laurant stood, drawing their attention and putting an end to the budding argument.

"Nick and I should be heading home."

"Yes, dear, you'll want to get unpacked and settled, won't you?" Viola remarked.

"She looks tuckered out, doesn't she, Sister," Bessie Jean commented.

Nick was in full agreement. Laurant did look worn-out. There were dark circles under her eyes. She looked completely different from the first time he'd seen her at the rectory. When she had learned that Tommy was all right, she completely relaxed, and for a short while, she didn't appear to have a care in the world.

But that was before her brother had told her about the sick bastard who wanted to kill her. To her credit, she hadn't collapsed or gotten hysterical like some would. And Nick remembered the strength she'd shown later when she'd talked Pete into letting her set a trap. How much strength and endurance did she have stored inside her? He hoped to God she had enough to see this nightmare through.

"Thank you so much for dinner. It was lovely," Laurant said.

"I'll give you my recipe for my macaroni dish," Viola promised.

Bessie Jean scoffed. "What recipe? You followed the directions on the Kraft macaroni and cheese box. Just get her one at the store, Sister."

Nick added his thank-you, then casually draped his arm around Laurant's shoulders. Bessie Jean escorted the couple to the end of her walk and opened the gate for them.

"Your eyes never settle, do they, Nicholas?" So that the young man wouldn't take offense, she hastened to explain. "I notice little things, you see, and from the moment you stepped out on my porch, you've been surveying the neighborhood. It's not a criticism," she added. "It's just that I noticed. You're always on your guard, aren't you? I imagine you were trained to do that at the FBI school."

Nick shook his head. "Actually, I'm just nosy."

She smiled up at him, her green eyes sparkling. Nick guessed she must have given the men in Holy Oaks a merry chase when she was a young girl.

Leaning around Nick, she whispered loudly, "I like your young man. Don't chase this one off, dear."

Laurant laughed. "I'll try not to," she promised. "I like this one too."

"Sister and I know all about a woman's biological clock," she said. "A good number of women your age already have two or three children. It's time you got started on a family."

"Yes, ma'am," she answered for lack of anything better to say. She knew it was pointless to argue with Bessie Jean or mention that plenty of women waited until they were in their thirties to start a family and that Laurant had several years to go before that momentous birthday. Bessie Jean was outspoken, opinionated, and as subtle as a sledgehammer, but Laurant still liked her. As flawed as she was, she was also honest and kind...on occasion anyway.

"Why, look, there's Justin Brady and Willie Lakeman."

The neighbors across the street were carrying a long extension ladder around from the backyard. One of them propped it against the side of the house and began to climb up while the other held it in place.

Bessie Jean called out a greeting and smiled when the two men waved.

"It's late to be painting," Nick remarked.

He'd only just made the comment when the floodlights were turned on from inside the house.

"Justin's the young man on the ladder," Viola said. "I told you about him. When he saw me working in my flower bed, he came right over to lend a hand. I didn't much care for any of them starting out, but I've since changed my opinion."

"Why didn't you like them starting out?" Nick asked, eyeing the tall, muscular man who was leaning into the ladder and reaching for the putty knife in the back pocket of his jeans.

"I thought they were all useless, but they're just ornery, not shiftless. They're keeping their promise," she added with a nod. "The owner, Mr. Morrison, made an arrangement with the boys to paint his house in lieu of paying rent. He's off in Florida taking in the sun until after the celebration."

"This is the first time I've seen any of them working on the house," Bessie Jean said. "I'll tell you what I have seen though. Almost every single night for the past couple of weeks, they've been walking down to the bar and grill on Second Street and drinking until closing time. They don't care about their neighbors trying to sleep. They sing and laugh and carry on, making a terrible racket when they're coming home. I've watched them from my window, and just two weeks ago one of them passed out in the front yard. I believe it was Mark Hanover. He slept there all night. It's shameful the way they carry on, getting drunk as skunks."

The sisters obviously had different opinions on the renters.

"But now they're keeping their word," Viola reminded her. "And Justin told me that, as soon as they finish working at the abbey, they're going to fix the house up, even if it means working from sunup to sundown. I believe they'll do it too."

Nick kept trying to get a better look at Willie Lakeman, but his back was turned to the street and he was wearing a baseball cap. Even if he turned around, Nick doubted he'd see his face clearly. Willie appeared to be about the same height and weight as Justin.

He decided to walk over and say hello. Maybe he could get the third renter to come outside and he could size him up too. His plan changed when he heard Laurant yawn. She was falling asleep on her feet.

"Come on, sweetheart. Let's get you to bed."

She followed him to the car and helped carry in the bags. The house was dark except for a small desk lamp by the phone, and all the draperies were closed. The phone rang just as she started up the stairs with her overnight bag. She dropped it on the floor, switched on a light, and hurried into the living room. Nick had warned her that there would always be at least one FBI agent inside her house at all times, so she wasn't taken by surprise when the swinging door to the kitchen opened and a man dressed in black pants and a long-sleeved white shirt rolled up to his elbows came hurrying toward her. There was a gun clipped to his belt and a sandwich in his hand.

He beat her to the phone, which was on the desk between her living room and dining room, checked the caller ID, and picked up a headset attached to the base of the phone, then motioned for her to answer.

From the number displayed, she knew it was Michelle Brockman calling. She was Laurant's best friend and would soon be a bride.

"Hi. How'd you know I was back?"

"This is Holy Oaks, remember?" Michelle said. "So tell me, is it true? Did some man actually threaten you in Kansas City? I'm never letting you leave this town again if it's true."

"Don't worry," Laurant assured her friend. "It was just some guy thinking he was funny. The authorities looked into it and said he's not to be taken seriously."

"That's a relief," Michelle sighed. "Okay then, tell me, who is the hunk?"

"Excuse me?"

Michelle's laughter erupted over the phone. The sound always made Laurant smile. It came from deep in her belly, and it was filled with such joy and mischief. They had met at the monthly fish fry. Laurant had only been in town a week and hadn't even unpacked her things before Tommy volunteered her services in the kitchen at the fund-raising event. Michelle had also been commandeered.

An instant friendship developed. They were complete opposites. Laurant was reserved, and Michelle was exuberant. She was also considerate. Lorna Hamburg had cornered Laurant and was trying to get as much personal information as she could for an article she wanted to write about the newcomer, or as she called her, the foreigner from Chicago. Michelle dragged Laurant away from the busybody and wouldn't let Lorna harass her. They became best friends from that moment on.

"I asked, who is he?"

"I don't know what you're talking about," Laurant replied, deliberately tormenting her friend.

"Stop playing games. I'm dying of curiosity. I want to know. Who is the hunk you brought home with you?"

"His name is Nicholas Buchanan. Do you remember I told you that my brother lived with the Buchanans when he was growing up?"

"I remember."

"Nick's Tommy's best friend," she explained. "I never met him until last weekend."

"And?"

"And what?"

"Have you gone to bed with him yet?"

Laurant could feel herself blushing. "Hold on a minute, will you?"

She put her hand over the mouthpiece of the old-fashioned phone and whispered to the agent, "Do you need to listen in on this private conversation?"

The agent was trying hard not to smile. He put the headset down and walked away. She pulled the chair out and sat down at the desk, facing the wall.

"All right, I'm back," she announced as she picked up a ballpoint pen and began to click it open and shut.

"Did you?"

"Did I what?"

"Stop being evasive. Did you go to bed with him yet? I heard he's gorgeous."

Laurant laughed. "Michelle, you shouldn't be asking questions like that."

"I'm your dearest friend, aren't I?"

"Yes, but—"

"And I'm worried about you. You need sex, Laurant. It's good for your complexion."

Laurant began to scribble on the notepad. "What's wrong with my complexion?"

"Nothing sex wouldn't help. It will bring color to your cheeks."

"I'll use blush."

Michelle let out a loud, exaggerated sigh. "You aren't going to tell me, are you?"

"No, I'm not."

"Is he really just a friend of your brother's?"

Laurant bowed her head. She felt horrible about lying to her best friend, but she knew that when this was over and she could finally tell Michelle the truth, she would understand.

"No, he isn't just a friend." She turned in the chair to look at Nick. He was standing in the front hallway with the other agent and nodding at something the man was telling him. His expression was somber until he caught her staring at him. Then he smiled.

She turned back to the wall. "The oddest thing happened, Michelle," she whispered.

"What?"

"I fell in love."

Michelle was immediately skeptical. "No,

you didn't. You actually allowed yourself to fall in love? I don't believe you."

"It's true."

"Honest? It happened awfully fast, didn't it?"

"I know," she replied. She picked up the pen again and began to draw.

"He must be something else to get through all your defenses. I can't wait to meet him."

"You will, and I know you'll like him."

"I can't believe this. He must have knocked you over to get your attention. You fell hard, didn't you?"

"I guess I did."

"This is mind-blowing," Michelle exclaimed.

"It's not *that* shocking," she said defensively.

"Puh-lease."

Laurant laughed. Michelle always put her in a good mood. She was so dramatic and very open in her feelings and attitudes, whereas Laurant kept everything close to her heart. Michelle was the only friend since high school whom she had ever confided in.

"I know what goes on in that warped head of yours. You're always trying to figure out what's wrong with the guy, and you're always playing it safe. Just because you got burned once—"

"Twice," she corrected.

"I don't count the college guy," Michelle said. "Everyone gets her heart broken in college at least once. I'm only counting the creep from Chicago."

"He was a creep," Laurant agreed.

"And just because you misjudged him, you concluded all men were scum. Except my Christopher. You never thought he was scum."

"Of course I didn't. I love Christopher."

She sighed. "I do too. He's so sweet and wonderful."

"So is Nick."

"Don't mess this one up, Laurant. Go with your feelings this time."

"What do you mean, don't mess this one up?"

"With your history..."

"What history?"

"Don't go all irate on me. I'm simply telling it like it is. You don't have a very good record with men around here. Want me to go through the list of men you've rejected?"

"I didn't love any of those men."

"You never let yourself get to know any of them long enough to find out if there was a future or not."

"I wasn't interested."

"Obviously. Everyone in town was so certain that Steve Brenner would be able to get through that thick shell of yours. I heard he was telling people he wanted to marry you."

"That's what I heard. I don't even like the man, and I certainly never encouraged him. He gives me the creeps."

"I like him, and so does Christopher. Steve is charming and funny and witty. Everyone likes him but you."

"Bessie Jean Vanderman and her sister don't like him."

"Please. They don't like anyone."

Laurant laughed. "That's not true."

"Yes, it is. They dislike the Catholics because they're too pushy, and I just heard that Viola thinks Rabbi Spears is running a crooked bingo game."

"You're kidding."

"Would I make that up?"

"Tell me something. How did you find out so quickly that Nick was with me?"

"The hotline. While Bessie Jean was standing out front, her sister snuck back inside, called my mother, and she told me. We all know how Viola loves to embellish. She said you were getting engaged, but mother and I didn't believe her. Do you think you will marry Nicholas one day, or is it too soon to ask that question?"

"You just asked me if we slept together," she reminded her.

"No, I asked you if you had sex."

"Actually, Viola wasn't embellishing. I am going to marry him."

Michelle shrieked again. "Why didn't you tell me right away. You're serious? You're really... I can't believe this. It's happening too fast for my little brain to take in. Have you set a date yet?"

"No," she admitted. "But Nick wants to get married real soon."

"Oh, God, this is so romantic. Wait until I tell Christopher. You're my maid of honor," she said then. "So?"

The hint wasn't subtle. "Will you be my maid of honor?"

Michelle paused to shout the news to her parents. Both of them had to take a turn on the phone congratulating Laurant, and by the time Michelle was back, ten more minutes had passed.

"Yes, I'll be your maid of honor. I'm honored that you asked me. Oh, that reminds me. I called you to tell you your dress is ready. You can pick it up tomorrow. Try it on one more time, okay? I don't want any screwups on the day of my wedding."

"All right. Anything else?"

"The picnic," she said. "I expect to meet Nick then."

"What picnic?"

"What do you mean, what picnic? The abbot's throwing a big thank-you party at the lake for everyone who worked so hard on the renovations."

"When was this decided?"

"Oh, that's right. You were out of town. It was in the Sunday bulletin, but you were in Kansas City. Oh, my God, I forgot to ask. The news about Nick turned me into a blithering idiot I suppose. It was so...un-you...that it was all I could think about. I forgot to ask. Is your brother all right?"

"Yes, he's fine. He got a clean bill of health this time."

"Then no chemo?"

"No chemo."

Michelle sounded relieved. "Thank goodness. Is he back home yet?"

"No, he and a friend are going to drive my

271

car back as soon as the repairs are done. The transmission was slipping."

"You need to buy a new car."

"I will, one of these days."

"When you can afford it, right?"

"Right."

Laurant suddenly dropped the pen. She hadn't been paying attention as she scribbled on the pad, but now she saw what she had done. There were hearts all over the paper, broken hearts. She ripped the paper from the pad and began to tear it up.

"Father Tom still doesn't know all the money's gone, does he?"

She glanced over her shoulder to see if Nick and the other man were still in the hallway, but they were gone.

Even though she was alone in the room, she still lowered her voice when she answered, "No, Tommy doesn't know the money's gone. You and Christopher are the only ones I've told."

"Heaven help you if Tommy finds out. Put yourself in his place. He assigned his interest in the trust to you when he entered the seminary, thinking that your grandfather's estate would be secure and that you would be set for life. How is he going to feel when he finds out those slimy lawyers were stealing every cent in the trust by charging exorbitant fees," Michelle railed. The more she talked about the injustice, the angrier her voice became. "Millions of dollars in fees," she reminded Laurant. "They should rot in jail. What they did to you was criminal."

"Not to me," Laurant corrected. "To my grandfather. They betrayed him, and that's why I went after them."

It had taken her a year to find an attorney who was willing to take on one of the largest and most powerful law firms in Paris, and even he had resisted at first, until he looked over her papers and saw what they had done. His position radically changed then. He wanted to put them out of business. The suit was filed the following morning.

"Don't lose hope. You have to keep fighting to get what's rightfully yours." She sighed over the phone. "Lawyers are scum buckets."

"Shame on you. You're marrying a lawyer, remember?"

"He wasn't a lawyer when I met him."

"Michelle, pray this is settled soon. I've spent almost every dime I have on legal fees and renovating the store. I had to borrow money from the bank too. God only knows how I'm going to pay it back."

"The lawyers you're fighting are hoping you'll give up and go away. Remember what Christopher said? That's why they keep filing all those motions or whatever to delay the final court hearing, but if you win again this time, they have to pay up."

"And within ten days," Laurant said.

"Well, hang in there. You're close to the finish line now."

"Yes, I know."

"Mother's yelling at me. I have to hang up. The picnic's at five. Don't be late."

"I don't understand why the abbot scheduled the party so soon. The renovations aren't
finished yet, and I'll just bet the scaffolding
is still in the church."

"It's the only time that would work with his
busy schedule," Michelle explained. "And
the abbot promised me the scaffolding would
be gone before the wedding. Do you realize,
in less than a week I'll be an old married
woman. Oh, hold on, Laurant."

She heard Michelle shout to her mother
that she'd be right down, and then she spoke
into the phone again. "Mother's becoming a
nervous wreck with the preparations."

"I should let you go."

"You sound tired."

"I am," she admitted.

Laurant's mind was racing even as she
talked to Michelle. Agent Wesson was using
the abbot's cabin as his command center,
and no one was supposed to know that he
and his men were in Holy Oaks.

"Where exactly is the picnic? At the abbot's
cabin?"

"No," Michelle answered. "He has some relatives or friends staying there. It's across the
lake. Just follow the traffic."

"Okay," she said. "I'll talk to you tomorrow."

"I won't be here, remember? I'm going to
Des Moines to pick up my new brace, so I'll
see you at the picnic."

"Who's driving you?"

"Dad," she answered. "If this one doesn't
fit, he's going to raise holy hell. Because of their

screwups, I have less than a week to learn how to walk without a limp."

"If anyone can do it, you can. Want me to do anything for you while you're away?"

Michelle laughed. "Yes. Go get some color in your cheeks."

Laurant heard Nick coming down the stairs, and when she finished saying good-bye to Michelle and hung up the phone, she saw him leaning against the door frame watching her. His hair was tousled on his forehead, and she was once again struck by how sexy he was. Maybe Michelle was right. Maybe she should think about putting some color back in her cheeks.

What would he be like in bed? My God, she couldn't believe she was letting her mind conjure up such thoughts. She quickly pushed the budding fantasies aside. She wasn't a teenager in the throes of a hormonal rebellion. She was an adult, and there wasn't anything wrong with being celibate until the right man came along, was there? Nick didn't fit her requirements. No, he wasn't the right man.

"Sorry I was on the phone so long."

"That's okay. Joe says you've got a bunch of messages stored on your machine. Go ahead and listen to them."

Nick carried her bag upstairs while Laurant replayed the tape. There was only one disturbing message, from Margaret Stamp, the owner of the local bakery. She was calling to tell Laurant that Steve Brenner had upped his offer to buy Margaret's store by 20 percent, and that Steve had given her a week to consider. She ended the message with a question. Did Laurant know that Steve wasn't going to pay out any of the money to those who had sold until all the stores had signed?

A clap of thunder rumbled in the distance. Laurant slumped against the back of the chair, concentrating on the droning whir of the tape as it rewound. Her resolve had taken another beating, yet she knew she would have to summon the energy to deal with this latest crisis. Poor Margaret. Laurant knew she didn't want to sell, but business at the bakery was poor these days, and the money Steve was offering would be enough to ensure Margaret a comfortable retirement. How could Laurant, in good conscience, talk Margaret into holding firm when there was a good chance she would lose everything?

She jumped when Nick touched her shoulder.

"Laurant, I'd like you to meet Joe Farley. He's going to be staying with us."

276

The agent came forward to shake her hand. "It's nice to meet you, ma'am."

Laurant's mind switched gears. The fight to save the town square would have to be put on the back burner for now.

"Please call me Laurant."

"Sure," he replied. "And you can call me Joe."

Joe was a thickset man with a bushy mane of red hair and a round face that lit up when he smiled. One of his front teeth was slightly crooked, and that humanized him somehow. Even though he too was wearing a gun, he didn't seem as imposing or as rigid as Mr. Wesson.

"Do you usually work with Nick?"

"I have a few times," he answered. "I'm usually stuck in an office, so this is quite a change for me. I hope you don't mind, but Feinberg and I have made a couple of changes in your alarm system. It isn't fancy, but it will get the job done."

She glanced at Nick. "I don't have an alarm system."

"You do now."

Joe explained. "We've wired all the windows and the doors so that when anyone comes inside, we'll know it. A red light will flash, but the alarm won't make any noise," he assured her. "We don't want to spook the unsub. We want to draw him inside and nail him. Hopefully, he won't know he's triggered the setup. Of course, any stranger that comes near your house is going to get marked by the agents outside."

"The house is being watched?"

"Yes, it is."

"How long will you be staying here?" she asked.

"Until the first of July...if we haven't caught the unsub before then. I'll leave when you do."

Her head was spinning. It was becoming more and more difficult to push one crisis aside while she concentrated on another. She turned around and headed for the kitchen, the men trailing behind her. "I need a cup of tea," she said wearily.

"Laurant, you're not waffling about leaving, are you? We did talk about this," Nick reminded.

"Okay, I know," she answered weakly.

"I mean it, Laurant. You're out of here—"

She cut him off. "I said okay." Her irritation was loud and clear. "Mind telling me where I'm going?"

"With me."

"Will you stop doing that?" she demanded loudly.

The burst of temper surprised Nick. He raised an eyebrow as he leaned back against the kitchen table and folded his arms. "Stop doing what?"

"Giving me dumb answers," she muttered. She grabbed the white teakettle from the counter and went to the sink to fill it with water.

It didn't take a trained eye to see that the pressure was getting to her, but the timing couldn't have been worse because Nick was also feeling like a cranky, caged animal. Now that they were in Holy Oaks, the waiting game began, and God, how he hated that part of his job. He'd rather have a root canal than wait around for something to happen.

Working with Jules Wesson was already turning out to be a problem. Nick had spent ten minutes on his mobile phone trying to get Wesson to give him information, but every time he asked a question, Wesson hedged. Nick knew what he was doing, pushing him out of the loop.

Joe dragged a chair out from the table and sat down, but Nick followed Laurant to the sink. "What the hell does that mean? Dumb answers?"

She bumped into his chest when she turned. Water sloshed out of the mouth of the kettle, splashing his shirt.

"You never give me a direct answer," she told him.

"Yeah? Like when?"

"Just now was a good example. I asked you where I was going, and you answered—"

He cut her off. "With me."

"That isn't a direct answer, Nick."

Without a thought as to what she was doing, she grabbed a towel and began to blot the water off his shirt. He snatched it out of her hand and tossed it on the counter.

"I'm not sure where we'll be going," he told her. "When I know, I'll tell you. All right? And by the way," he added, leaning down until they were nose to nose, "that's the only damned time I haven't given you a straight answer."

"No, it isn't," she countered. "I asked you how many agents were here in Holy Oaks, and do you remember what your answer was? Enough. Now, what kind of a straight answer was that?"

The muscle in his jaw flexed, indicating the price he was paying for holding his temper. "If I knew the exact number, I wouldn't tell you. I don't want you to see them or look for them."

"Why not?" She pushed him out of her way and went to the stove, put the kettle on the front burner, and turned it on.

"Because then you'll be staring at them or looking for them every time we go out, and if the unsub's watching you—which, by the way, we're pretty damned sure he's going to be doing—then he'll notice you noticing the agents."

"You two fight like an old married couple."

Laurant and Nick turned as one to frown at Joe.

"We weren't fighting," Nick told him.

"We were simply having a difference of opinion," she insisted. "That's all."

Joe grinned. "Hey, I'm not your kid you're trying to convince. I don't care if you fight or not. The fact is both of you probably need to let off a little steam, and you might as well clear the air right now."

Laurant noticed the stack of dirty dishes piled up in the sink. Joe had obviously made himself at home but hadn't bothered to clean up. She scowled at him, then got the Palmolive soap from the cabinet and filled the sink with water.

Joe noticed what she was doing. "I'll wash those. I was going to put them in the dishwasher, but you don't have one."

"It's an old house."

Nick picked up the towel and started drying the plate she handed him, as Joe leaned back in his chair and got comfortable.

"Nick, about leaving on the first...," Joe began.

"Yeah?"

"Wesson wants her to stay."

"Tough. She's leaving on the first."

"He's gonna pull rank."

"He can try."

"How come you're so firm on that date?"

"Because Tommy estimates a couple of thousand people are going to be flooding in here on the second and third. There's a big university reunion going on while the town celebrates the anniversary. I'd like to get her out of here before, but she's got to be in this wedding, and she won't leave."

"I'm telling you, Wesson's determined to keep her here for as long as it takes."

"And I'm telling you she's leaving. There's no way in hell I'm letting Laurant stay with a crowd that size coming here. How can I protect her?" Shaking his head, he added, "It isn't gonna happen."

Joe raised his hands in a conciliatory gesture. "I'm easy with whatever you decide. I just thought I should warn you you're in for a

281

fight, that's all. As far as I'm concerned, you're calling the shots."

Laurant handed Nick another dish to dry and asked, "What about Tommy? Will he also be leaving on the first?"

"You know how stubborn your brother can be. He thinks it's important that he help the abbot."

"But you'll make him leave, won't you?" she pleaded. "He won't listen to me, but he *will* listen to you."

"Yeah? Since when?"

"You've got to make him leave when we do. If he doesn't go, then I don't go. Tell him that. Then maybe he'll stop arguing."

"Calm down," he said when he saw the stricken look in her eyes. "Noah promised me he'd get him out of here one way or another. He may have to coldcock him and drag him out," he added. "But hitting a priest isn't gonna faze him. Noah gave me his word, so you can relax. Trust him."

"Is anyone hungry?" Joe asked hopefully. As if on cue, his stomach growled.

"I guess you are," Nick remarked.

"I'm starving. Feinberg was supposed to figure out a way to bring in some groceries, sneaking in through the back lot behind your house, but man oh man, those two old ladies next door are always looking out their windows. He hasn't been able to get past them. They should be working for the FBI."

"They don't know you're still here, or they would have said something to me or Nick."

"I haven't left the house since I came in," Joe explained. "Those old ladies went out that afternoon, and I'm assuming they think I left while they were gone. I've been real careful about the lights at night," he added.

"Couldn't Feinberg bring the groceries from the other side of the house?" she asked.

"He couldn't get to a door that way, and it was too much of a risk to try to hand them through the window."

Laurant let the water out of the sink, dried her hands, and then began to look through the refrigerator for something for Joe to eat.

"You find anything in there? I sure couldn't. I just ate the last of your cold cuts, and all that's left is cereal," Joe said.

"So the cupboards are pretty bare, huh?" Nick asked.

Laurant closed the refrigerator. "I'll go to the grocery store tomorrow," she promised.

"I was hoping you'd offer. I've got a list made up…if you don't mind."

"If you're really starving, we could go out and get you something," Nick offered.

Laurant shook her head. "Everything's closed this time of night."

"It's not even ten o'clock. Nothing's open?" Nick asked.

"Sorry. All the stores close at six."

"I honest to God don't know how she handles living here," he told Joe. He straddled the chair across the table from the agent and added, "There's not even a bagel shop within fifty miles. I'm right, aren't I, Laurant?"

She'd just finished searching through her pantry and closed the door, empty-handed. "Yes, you're right, but I get along just fine without fresh bagels."

"I don't suppose there's a Krispy Kreme donut shop in town," Joe lamented.

"No, there isn't," she said.

Laurant opened the freezer on the bottom of the refrigerator and began to search through the frozen vegetables.

"Did you find something in there?" Joe asked eagerly.

"Some frozen broccoli."

"I'll pass."

The kettle started whistling, and Nick reached for a cup and saucer. "You want any of this, Joe?"

"I'd rather have iced tea."

"We aren't here to serve you, buddy. If you want it, fix it."

Nick made Laurant sit down and served her a cup of the tea.

"Neither one of you should criticize the town until you've been here at least a week. You have to get into the swing of things first. The pace is different," she said.

"No kidding," Nick drawled.

She ignored the sarcasm. "Once you learn how to slow down, you'll like it."

"I doubt that."

She was getting angry. "You should keep an open mind. Besides, if I want a bagel, I buy a package at the store and defrost them."

"But those aren't fresh," he complained.

"Everyone eats bagels, Laurant. They're a national staple. What do all those college kids do? Bagels are healthy, damn it. Kids know that."

"Oh, stop whining. You're acting like one of those Americans who would come all the way to Paris and insist on eating at McDonald's."

"I wasn't whining."

"Yes you were."

"Whatever happened to the sweet sister I met in Kansas City?"

"I left her there," Laurant answered.

Joe got up from the table, grabbed the box of Rice Krispies from the cabinet, got the skim milk out of the refrigerator, and then reached for a tablespoon and the biggest bowl he could find. "This Brenner guy increased his offer by twenty percent to buy the woman's bakery, huh?"

Laurant gave him a surprised look.

"I listened to your messages," he stated. "And it sounded to me like Margaret's close to folding. The deal could be too good to pass up, especially if she's as old as she sounded over the phone."

"She isn't that old, but you're right. The money would be her retirement."

"You're trying to save the town, aren't you?" Joe asked.

She shook her head. "No, I'm only trying to save the town square. I don't understand why people think progress means tearing down beautiful old buildings to put up slick new ones. It doesn't make any sense to me. The town will be fine with or without the square, but the charm...the history...that will be lost."

Nick watched her stir the tea. She'd been doing that for the last couple of minutes, but she hadn't taken a drink yet. She sat motionless, staring pensively at the swirling liquid in the cup. The sound of the spoon clinking against Joe's empty bowl eventually drew her attention.

Laurant noticed that he glanced at his wrist as he carried the dish to the sink.

"Joe, why do you keep looking at your watch?" she asked.

"'Cause I've got it wired," he answered. "If the red light goes off on the panel I've hooked up in the guest room, it will trigger the alarm on my watch."

Thunder cracked close by, and it began to rain. Joe was thrilled by the sound. "Mother Nature's going to help us out tonight. Let's just hope the storm's a bad one."

"You want a bad storm?"

"I sure do," he answered. "Because Nick wants to disable the camera after you two have put on your little performance for our unsub. I'm gonna make the lights flicker a couple of times, and then I'm gonna turn everything off. I'll hit the main switch," he explained. "When the lights come back on, the camera won't."

"I figured you wouldn't be able to sleep with the camera watching you," Nick said.

"No, I wouldn't. Thank you," she said, relieved.

"The camera's plugged into an outlet up in the attic," Joe told her. "We're hoping he'll come inside to turn it back on, thinking that the breaker just needs to be reset."

She nodded. "And you'll be waiting for him."

She propped her elbow on the table, rested her chin in the palm of her hand, and stared at the back window with its blinds closed. Was he out there now, watching and waiting for his opportunity? How would he come at her? While she was sleeping? Or would he wait until she was outside and try to grab her then?

Rain began to pelt the windows.

"You guys ready to go upstairs?" Joe asked. "The storm could slow down any time, and I want to take advantage of this opportunity while it lasts. I'll go down to the basement and mess with the circuits. You two wait here until after I've turned the lights off and flipped them back on. Then you go upstairs and do your thing. I'll give you five minutes and then I'll turn everything off again. Nick, you dismantle the camera and when you've done that, shout down to me, and I'll turn the lights back on."

"Got it," he agreed.

"There's a flashlight on the hallway chest," he said. "So you'll be able to see what you're doing." Joe pushed the chair back and stood. "Okay, just sit tight until the lights come back on. I'm going to keep flickering them every couple of seconds. I'll yell when you can go up."

He hurried around the corner into the back hall and down the basement steps. Nick stood in the doorway, waiting.

"You didn't drink any of your tea. I figured out why you made it."

She glanced up at him. "What's there to figure out?"

The lights flickered twice, then went completely out. It was suddenly pitch black in the kitchen.

"Don't get spooked." His voice was a soothing whisper in the darkness.

"I won't," she assured him.

A flash of lightning lit the room for the briefest of seconds, and Laurant half expected to see a face looming in the gray light. She *was* getting spooked, sitting in that tiny room where *he* had made himself at home. God, how she wished she could jump in the car and run away. Why oh why had she come back?

Nick's voice eased her budding panic. "Making tea is how you cope, isn't it?"

She turned in his direction and tried to see him in the darkness. "What did you say?"

"When you get stressed, you stop everything you're doing and make yourself a cup of hot tea. You did that a couple of times in Kansas City while we were at the rectory. You never drink it though, do you?"

Before she could answer, the lights came back on and Joe shouted, "Let's do it."

Nick took Laurant's hand and gently pulled her from the chair. He didn't let go of her as they went through the house and up the stairs. With each step she took toward the bedroom, her heartbeat escalated until it felt like it was slamming against her rib cage. The linen closet door was open, but she couldn't see the camera.

Nick paused with his hand on the doorknob. "This has to look real. You understand what I mean? We want to provoke him, remember? That means we've got to get hot and heavy in there, and you've got to act like you're enjoying it."

"You're going to have to act like you're enjoying it too," she pointed out. Lord, she was suddenly so nervous her voice cracked.

"Nah, I'm not going to have any trouble at all. I've been wanting to get my hands on you for a long time. Ready?"

"Just try to keep up with me."

He wanted a seductress, and by God, that's what he was going to get. She was determined to give the performance of a lifetime. They had the same goal in mind, to make the madman so jealous he would forget caution and come after her. They hoped his fury would drive him to do something careless. It was too late for second thoughts.

"Hey," Nick whispered. "Smile." He grinned as he added, "Maybe we ought to practice a little first. How long has it been since you've been tossed in the hay and mauled."

"A couple of days," she lied. "How about you?"

"Longer than that. Any surprises inside?"

"Like what?"

"Oh, I don't know. The usual stuff all young ladies keep at their disposal. Chains and whips on the walls. The standard equipment handed down from mother to daughter."

She kept a straight face. "What kind of girls have you been hanging out with?"

"Good girls," he assured her. "*Real* good girls."

Laurant knew that Nick was trying to get her to laugh so she wouldn't have stage fright.

As she pushed past him, she said, "Sorry, no surprises inside. Every girl has mirrors on her ceiling, doesn't she?"

He was laughing when she opened the door. She went in first, flipped on the lights, and headed for the bed.

It turned out to be easier than she'd expected. She simply pretended she was modeling again. In her mind, the bed was the end of the runway, and it was her job to get there using every part of her body. She moved with easy grace, her hips swaying to the music she could hear in her mind, a pouty look on her face.

Nick watched from the doorway, stunned by the swift change in Laurant. She tossed her long thick curls provocatively over her shoulder as she glanced back at him with a sultry come-and-get-me look. When she reached the foot of the double bed, she turned and beckoned him forward with the crook of her finger. He had to remind himself that it was all an act.

If eyes could smolder with passion, hers could burn down the house.

He walked toward his temptress, but she wasn't quite finished shocking the hell out of him. As he reached for her, she shook her head, took a step back away from him and then slowly began to unbutton her blouse. She never took her gaze off him, staring directly into his eyes, waiting, teasing, beckoning.

He let her unbutton the blouse, but when she started to take it off and he saw the hint of her lacy bra and the soft swell of her breasts, he roughly pulled her into his arms, acting impatient and eager now. His hand moved to the back of her neck. He wound her hair around his fist as his other hand pressed against her spine, bringing her up close against him. Tilting her head back, he leaned down and kissed her long and hard.

The touch was electric. Her mouth was so soft, pliable, willing—damn, could she kiss. Her lips parted without prodding, and it was then that Nick gave in to his curiosity and desire. His tongue thrust inside to taste the sweet interior of her mouth. She stiffened in response, but only for a second or two, and then her arms found their way around his neck, and she was pressing against him, clinging to him as she matched his fervor.

The kiss went on forever. His mind knew it was all a performance for the camera, but his body didn't care about that distinction. He reacted like any other man would in the arms of a beautiful woman.

He dragged his mouth away from hers and began to nibble on her earlobe. "Slow down," he whispered, panting.

"No," she whispered back. Then she tugged on his hair, pulling his head back so that she could kiss him on the mouth again. When her tongue touched his, he growled low in his throat.

She smiled with smug satisfaction against his lips and then kissed him passionately again, thoroughly getting into the role of aggressor now, but Nick wasn't going to let her outdo him. He unsnapped her jeans and his hands moved to her spine and slipped inside the fabric. Cupping her backside, he jerked her up against his hard arousal. Shocked, her eyes opened, and she tried to pull back. He wouldn't let her. His mouth took absolute possession, and within seconds her eyes were closed again, and she was pressing against his hard, warm chest. Pelvis to pelvis, the fit perfect, she rubbed against him. The way he stroked and caressed her with his hands and his tongue made her forget that she was supposed to be acting. She gripped his shoulders to keep from collapsing and kissed him back with honest longing.

From the darkened living room across town, the Peeping Tom watched. His roar of rage echoed through the house. Shaking, he picked up a lamp, ripped it from the socket, and hurled it at the stucco wall.

Retribution was at hand.

She had trouble looking Nick in the eye the following morning. As soon as the lights had gone out the night before, Nick had abruptly pulled away from her and had gone into the hallway to dismantle the camera. She was thankful for the darkness then because she knew she looked dazed and disoriented. She had trouble getting her legs to work. She'd wanted to hide in the bathroom until she regained her wits, but that had been out of the question. She fell back on the bed instead and stayed there until her heartbeat slowed down and she could draw a proper breath.

Nick and Joe came into her darkened room and told her to get some rest. They would take turns staying awake. She didn't know if Nick slept or if he got any rest at all. The only thing she remembered was the exhaustion that overtook her.

She woke up at daybreak and dressed in her jogging clothes, a snug-fitting, blue-and-white-striped spandex top that didn't quite cover her belly button, blue spandex shorts, socks, and her comfortable but worn-looking white Reeboks. After securing her hair into a ponytail, she went into the bedroom to begin her stretching exercises.

Nick came into the bedroom as she was coming out of the bathroom. He took one look at her outfit, and his heart skipped a beat. Every curve of her body was evident. "Jeez, Laurant, does your brother know you wear stuff like that?"

She began her waist bends and didn't look at him when she answered, "There's nothing wrong with my clothes. I'm not going to church. I'm going running."

"Maybe you ought to put a big T-shirt over..."

"Over what?"

"Your chest."

The shirt wasn't going to cover her amazing long legs. He was having trouble taking his eyes off them. "And long pants," he muttered. "This is a small town. You're going to shock folks."

"No I won't," she assured him. "They're used to seeing me run."

He didn't like it, not one little bit, but who was he to complain? If she wanted to dress like a...runner...ah, hell, what was the matter with him? He had no business telling her what to wear. Even if they were in a relationship—which they weren't, he quickly qualified—he still wouldn't have the right to tell her how to dress.

Nick had already put on his running clothes, a faded navy blue T-shirt, gym shorts, white socks, and his battered, used-to-be-white running shoes. While she stretched her legs, he slipped his gun into the holster at his hip and pulled the T-shirt down to cover it. Then he picked up a small earpiece and tucked it in his right ear. Moving in front of the mirror above her dresser, he pinned a circular disc to his neck band just above his clavicle.

She was retying one of her shoelaces when she asked, "What's the pin for?"

"It's a microphone," he answered. "So no dirty talking today. Wesson will hear whatever I say, and just for the record, Jules, I still think this is a badass idea."

The voice inside his ear spoke back. "Duly noted, Agent Buchanan, and it's sir to you, not Jules."

Nick mouthed the word "jackass" to himself and then turned to Laurant, "You ready?"

"Yes," she answered, and for the first time since he'd come into the bedroom, she looked into his eyes.

"I wondered how long that was going to take."

She didn't bother to pretend to misunderstand. "You noticed?"

"Now you're blushing."

"I am not." Shrugging to cover her embarrassment, her voice dropped to a whisper so that Wesson, hopefully, wouldn't hear her, "I don't think we need to talk about what happened..."

"No, we don't need to talk about it," he agreed. Then he grinned an adorable lopsided grin and added, "But I'll bet we're both gonna be thinking about it all day long."

He was staring at her mouth, and so she stared at the floor.

"Let's go," he said.

Nodding, she brushed past him. On the way down the stairs, he said, "I want you to stay directly in front of me, and don't worry, I'll slow down to keep pace with you."

She laughed. "You'll slow down? I don't think so."

"I've been running almost every morning since I joined the FBI. We agents have to keep in top shape," he told her.

"Uh-huh," she agreed. "Then how come you told me you weren't a runner?"

"No, I didn't say that. I told you I hated to run."

"You said it was bad on the knees and that you were going to complain the entire time."

"It is bad on the knees, and I do plan to complain."

"And how many miles do you run every morning?"

"About a hundred, give or take."

She laughed. "Is that right?"

Joe was standing in front of the living room window, looking outside through the crack in the drawn drapes.

"Nick, I think you better have a look at this. We've got a situation here. You might want to reconsider running today."

Laurant beat him to the window. She peeked out and then said, "It's all right. It's just the boys waiting for me. We run together every morning."

Nick looked over her head and saw seven young men cluttering the sidewalk in front of her house. There were two more jogging in place in the middle of the street.

"Who are they?"

"High school kids," she answered.

"And they run with you every day? Why the hell didn't you mention them to me?"

He sounded incredulous and angry. "Don't get upset. It's no big deal. I'm sorry I forgot to mention them. The boys are on the track team at Holy Oaks High School...well, some of them are," she explained. "And they don't really run with me, at least not around the lake. They all peter out by the time I hit the path. Then they wait for me to come back and..."

"And what?" he demanded. Before she had a chance to answer, he muttered, "Wesson, are you getting this?"

"I'm hearing you loud and clear," came the staticky reply.

"And what?" he asked Laurant again. "They wait for you to come back around the lake, and then what?"

"And they jog home with me. That's all. They want to stay in shape during the summer so that when school starts, they'll be in top form."

Nick glanced outside again and noticed another boy running down the street to join his friends.

"Oh, yeah, they're serious runners all right," he remarked sarcastically. "Especially the kid eating the donut. He's definitely headed for the Olympics."

Joe got a glimpse of himself in the hall mirror. His hair was sticking up every which way. He hadn't bothered to comb it since he'd gotten out of bed, or rather, since he'd gotten off the sofa, and he self-consciously tried to pat it down as he said, "Uh...I don't believe any of those boys dragged themselves out of bed and came over here to run, Laurant. No, I'm pretty sure running isn't on their minds."

"Then what did get them out of their beds this early in the morning?" she asked, exasperated.

Nick answered. "Hormones, Laurant. Raging hormones."

"Oh, for heaven's sake. At this time of day? Boys their age have a whole lot more on their minds besides sex."

"No, they don't," Nick argued.

She looked at Joe who sheepishly nodded. "They really don't," he agreed with Nick.

Nick jerked his thumb toward the window. "At that age, I didn't think about anything else but sex."

Joe nodded. "I'd have to agree with Nick again," he said. "It's all I ever thought about. Mostly I thought about how to get it, and when I finally did get it, then I thought about how to get it again."

She didn't know whether to laugh or be angry. The conversation was ludicrous. "You're saying that every second of every waking hour that's what you both were thinking about when you were teenagers?"

"Pretty much," Nick said. "So we know

where they're coming from and what they're after. Maybe I ought to go outside and have a little talk with them."

"Don't you dare."

Nick came up with a better idea. He'd intimidate them. He pulled his T-shirt up over his gun and tucked the material behind it so that the weapon was clearly visible.

Joe watched him. "That ought to discourage them."

As Nick was opening the front door for Laurant, he smiled and said, "Maybe I ought to shoot a couple of them."

Laurant rolled her eyes as she went past him, ignoring his scowl. Waving to her entourage, she jogged across the street and introduced Nick to the boys. She told them that he was her fiancé. The kids all noticed Nick's gun, of course, but they gave it only a cursory glance before returning their full attention to Laurant's considerable assets. They didn't even look at him when Laurant explained that Nick worked for the FBI.

It all came down to spandex versus a loaded weapon, and spandex won.

Nick stayed right behind her as she ran. The boys fell into step around the two of them, taking turns trying to engage Laurant in conversation.

Donut boy was the first to fade. Three others quickly followed. Laurant gradually picked up the pace, her long legs eating up the pavement as she gracefully glided forward. She'd been right about her fan club's endurance. By the time they reached the entrance to the park, the last two boys were doubled over and panting for breath. Nick heard one of them gag and got an inordinate amount of pleasure from the sound.

Laurant loved this time of day. It was so peaceful and quiet and lovely. For an hour she forced herself to forget about everything and concentrate only on the path. The rain last night had left the leaves damp, but she knew that by noon, they would all be dried out again. A drought had hit Iowa hard, and the weeds and scrub were brown. As she rounded the bend around the blue water lake, the entrance to the nature preserve was on her right. There were a good ten acres of tall brown prairie grass. Like wheat, it swayed in the gentle morning breeze.

She passed the abbot's cabin and had the feeling that Agent Wesson was watching her, but she couldn't see him because the blinds were drawn. The dock to the right of the cabin and behind was sitting up high out of the water, another sign of the lack of rain.

Sweat trickled down the back of her neck and between her breasts by the time she'd made a complete circle around the lake. She slowed down, then stopped, doubled over and took long deep breaths. She could hear Nick panting behind her.

Standing there, they were easy targets. He did a quick survey of the dense forest and overgrown brush around them, and moved closer to her. His T-shirt was covered with sweat. With the back of his arm he wiped his forehead. She could catch her breath when they were back home. "Let's get out of here. Do we walk or run home?"

"We jog."

The boys were waiting at the park entrance. Grinning like idiots, they once again fell into step around Nick and Laurant.

"Wimps," Nick muttered as Laurant waved good-bye to the boys and sprinted up the front walk.

Once the door was shut behind them, Nick relaxed. "Damn, it's humid out there."

"What did you think of our lake? Isn't it beautiful?"

"I saw it yesterday," he reminded her. "When we went to see Wesson."

"But isn't it lovely? It's a fisherman's paradise. You can actually see the fish in the clear, rock-bottomed water."

"Yeah? I didn't notice."

She had her hands on her hips and was still panting a bit. "How could you not notice? What were you looking at?"

"All the places the bastard could hide. He could have had you in his sights from the moment we entered the park until the moment we left, and I never would have spotted him. I can't let you do that run again. You hear me, Wesson? The unsub could have been hiding anywhere. There's too much territory to cover."

Her mouth went dry when she tried to speak. "You think he'll use a gun to..."

"He's an up close and personal kind of guy," Nick said. "He might try to wing you to slow you down though."

"There were other agents keeping both of you in their sights all the while you were in the park," Joe added as Laurant passed him on her way to get some bottled water. He followed her into the kitchen and continued. "You both were safe."

Laurant returned to the living room, tossed Nick a bottle of Evian, and opened her own. She took a big drink and headed for the stairs.

"I'm going to take a shower."

"Wait," Nick said as he went up the stairs ahead of her. He looked in the bathroom to make sure there weren't any surprises waiting.

He was being overly cautious, and she was thankful for it.

"Okay, go ahead."

"You could shower in the other bathroom down the hall," she suggested.

"I'll wait."

Nick was sitting on the bed talking on the phone when she came out of the bathroom fifteen minutes later. Her hair was dripping down her back, and she was wearing a short cotton robe that had seen better days. He took one look at her and promptly lost his train of thought. He knew she was naked under that thin material, and he had to force himself to turn away so he could concentrate on his conversation.

"Look, Theo, we'll talk about this when I get back to Boston. All right?" He hung up the phone and slowly turned his head to get a glimpse of Laurant out of the corner of his eye. He watched her open the dresser drawer and take out two little wisps of lace. Immediately, his mind went to visions of her wearing them.

Get a grip, he told himself. She was off-limits, and he had no business fantasizing about her. What the hell kind of a friend was he to lust after Tommy's sister?

Berating himself didn't do any good. He wanted her. Simple as that. There, he finally admitted the obvious. Now what was he going to do about it? Nothing, he decided. Not a damned thing. Even if she weren't his friend's sister, he wouldn't get involved with her. A relationship between the two of them was impossible. It would never work out, and she'd end up hating him. She wanted what she had never had, a family and kids, lots of kids, and he didn't want any of that. He'd seen too much to ever let himself become that vulnerable. Even though he came from a family of eight, he was still a loner, and that's the way he liked it.

He never should have kissed her. Bad idea, he decided. He hadn't been prepared, hadn't realized how good it was going to be. God, he was arrogant. He actually thought he could remain distant and professional, but when she wrapped her arms around him and he felt her soft lips, thoughts of being professional went flying out the window, and he'd turned into one of those perverted teenagers outside. All he could think about was getting her flat on her back.

Maybe Morganstern was right after all. Maybe Nick was too close and personal for this assignment. His boss had been referring to his friendship with Tommy though. What would Pete think if he knew that his agent was lusting after the friend's sister? Nick already knew the answer to that question. Pete would have his hide.

The phone rang again. Nick answered it, listened for a minute, and then said, "Yes, Monsignor. I'll be sure to tell him. Thanks for calling."

Laurant was standing in the closet doorway, shifting from bare foot to bare foot as she searched through the clothes crammed together on the single, bowed rod.

When Nick hung up, she asked, "Was that Monsignor McKindry?"

"What? Oh, yeah, it was. Tommy left his Daytimer in the kitchen, and Monsignor said he'd mail it to him."

"Did he mention when Tommy and Noah left?"

"Yes," he answered. "At the crack of dawn. Laurant, for the love of God, put some clothes on."

She kept sorting through her clothes as she answered him. "As soon as you give me a little privacy, I'll be happy to get dressed."

He could hear the embarrassment in her voice. "Okay, okay," he said, feeling like an idiot. Heading for her shower, he added,

"Don't leave the bedroom until I'm dressed, and keep the door locked."

"Joe's downstairs."

"Yeah, well, I still want you to wait for me." His voice didn't leave room for argument.

She ran after him. He was peeling his T-shirt off as she reached behind him to grab her hair dryer and brush from the counter behind the sink. Her hand accidentally rubbed against the base of his spine, and he reacted as though she'd just burned him with her curling iron. He flinched.

"Sorry," she stammered.

He sighed as he tossed the T-shirt into the sink. "I made you feel awkward again, didn't I?"

They were standing toe to toe, facing each other. She clutched the robe to her chest with one hand and gripped the hair dryer and brush with the other hand.

"Is Mr. Wesson listening?" she whispered.

He shook his head. "The pin's on the dresser with the earpiece."

"I don't want it to be awkward, but it's just that we kissed. I know we were supposed to, but I..."

"What?"

Shrugging, she said, "It just made things awkward again. That's all."

"We both got..."

"What?" she whispered.

"Hot."

She'd been staring at his toes until he'd said that word. Her eyes flew to his.

"Yes, we did. What do we do about it?"

"Get past it," he suggested. "I know one way."

The sparkle in his eyes should have been a warning. "How?" she asked.

"Take a shower with me. That should get you past your shyness."

She was so shocked by the suggestion she laughed, which was exactly what he wanted her to do. The tension vanished. His grin was comical. "You've got that leer down perfectly," she told him as she turned around and left the bathroom.

Because the mirror was still clouded with steam, and the bathroom was sweltering, Nick told her to leave the door open. She waited until she heard the shower running, then hurried to get dressed and dry her hair. Since they were going shopping for an engagement ring, she decided to dress up a little, and she put on her white pleated slacks and a peach silk blouse. Then she found her white canvas slip-ons in the back of the closet.

Nick made the bed while she brushed her hair. The coverlet was all lopsided when he was finished, but she didn't criticize his effort.

Nick wore jeans and a white polo shirt. He clipped the leather holster to his belt. Then he pinned the red disc back on, added the earpiece, and shoved his wallet in his back pocket.

"Okay, so what's the schedule?" he asked after he gave her a quick once-over.

"Some breakfast first because I'm starving, then the grocery store for Joe. After that, I want to check on my store to see if they've started on the floors yet. If they haven't, I'll work there all afternoon."

"Then the jewelry store," he suggested as he slipped on a pair of leather loafers.

"I've got to pick up the bridesmaid dress too," she remembered. "And I should spend an hour or two at the abbey. I've got to get started on the attic."

They spent the morning doing errands. It was all so ordinary, tasks that couples did together all the time, but there wasn't anything ordinary about their situation. She was constantly looking over her shoulder, even when they were in the grocery store getting supplies for Joe. Laurant was stopped by a friend or neighbor on almost every aisle, and each time, she introduced Nick as her fiancé.

He put on quite a show. He was attentive and affectionate, and it was all so natural, she had to remind herself that it was just an act.

She relaxed only when they were inside the car. She felt safe then. Nick drove through McDonald's to get breakfast and headed home again. He turned on the radio, and they listened to Garth Brooks croon about a love lost and found again.

She was eager for Nick to see her store. She helped him carry the groceries inside, and left them in the hall for Joe to put away. Then they got back in the car again. Since they were going up to the abbey after they purchased an engagement ring, he decided to drive to the square.

He stopped at the fountain so that he could see all the buildings ahead of him. None of them were historical treasures by any means, but the old structures were charming. Most of the facades needed work, but nothing major.

"Do you see what it could be?" she asked.

"Yeah, I do," he agreed. "Why would anybody want to tear this down?"

"Exactly," she said enthusiastically. "Years ago, this is where everyone did their shopping and their socializing. I want it to be like that again."

"Sprucing up the stores won't be enough," he said. "There's got to be something inside to draw the people in."

"The president of the college is considering moving the bookstore into the corner building on your right. It's more than big enough, and they're running out of room on campus. The kids would have to come into the square to get their books."

"That will help."

"Yes," she agreed. "And they can walk. The campus is only a couple of blocks away. Let's go," she urged. "I want you to see my store."

Her enthusiasm made him smile. He parked in the center block, near the jewelry store. He put his arm around her as they walked along the street.

She couldn't show off her store after all. The first coat of polyurethane had just been applied to the floor. Since the windows were coated, Nick couldn't even look through to see the lovely marble countertop. He would have to wait at least four days until the second and third coats had been applied and dried.

They backtracked to Russell's Jewelry Store. Nick impressed the socks off of Miriam Russell when he picked out a two-carat diamond ring—the biggest in the store. Laurant didn't want that one though. She liked the one-and-a-half-carat, marquise diamond. Since it didn't need to be sized—it fit her finger perfectly—Nick said it was meant to be.

She held out her hand, waving her fingers so the light would catch the sparkle in the diamond, ooh-ing and ah-ing like a woman in love. She worried she might be overdoing it a bit, but Miriam seemed to be buying the act. Her hands were clasped together, and she was beaming with satisfaction.

When Nick handed Miriam his American Express card to pay for the purchase, her expression sobered. She asked Laurant if she could have a word in private before she ran the charge. She led Laurant to the back of the store while Nick waited at the counter. He didn't know what they were discussing, but whatever the topic was, it embarrassed Laurant. Her face turned pink, and she kept shaking her head.

A few minutes later, after Nick signed the purchase slip, he picked up the ring, put it on Laurant's finger again, and then leaned down and kissed her. It was a gentle, undemanding kiss that left her thoroughly shaken. He had to nudge her away from the counter.

As they were leaving the store, Miriam

called out, "Remember what I said, Lauren. I'll keep my fingers crossed for you."

Clearly mortified, Laurant hurried away. Nick caught up with her. "What was that all about?"

"Nothing important."

"She's gonna keep her fingers crossed for you?"

"It's nothing, really."

"Come on, Laurant. Tell me."

She stopped trying to outrun him. "Fine, I'll tell you. That little conference we had in the store was all about Russell's return policy. She thinks I'm going to botch this one up. Those were her words, not mine. You do realize, don't you, that when this is over and you've gone away, they're all going to think I screwed up again. This isn't funny, Nick, so you can stop grinning."

He wasn't at all sympathetic. Laughing, he said, "You've got a real strange reputation here, don't you? Exactly what is it you do to the men who try to get close to you?"

"Nothing," she cried out. "I don't do anything. I'm just...discriminating. There's a small group of women in town who have nothing better to do than gossip, and if one of them happens to see me talking to an available man, she assumes all sorts of things that aren't true. Before I know what's happened, that nosy editor, Lorna Hamburg, is printing it in the local paper. It's ridiculous," she added. "When I'm not seen socializing with the same man, everyone assumes I've gone and botched it again."

"She actually prints stuff like that in the paper?"

"She runs the society page," she explained. "It's all gossip and rubbish. There isn't a whole lot going on here, and so she..."

"Embellishes?"

"Oh, God, speaking of the devil," she whispered. "Let's get out of here. Move it, Nick. She's spotted us."

Lorna Hamburg caught sight of them a block away and came running. Long, curly, platinum hair dwarfed her already small features, and huge pendulum earrings dangled from her lobes and flapped madly to and fro with each step. She carried a leopard print canvas bag the size of a suitcase looped over her left shoulder, and as she ran, she tilted to that side, like a drunk who couldn't walk a straight line.

She was sprinting now to intercept them, her fuchsia-colored, four-inch heels clipping along the sidewalk. The sound was like teeth chattering.

"Man, can she move," he remarked.

As she bore down on them, Nick couldn't help but notice her eyebrows, or rather the lack thereof. Lorna had plucked hers out and used a pencil to draw a straight line above her deep-set eyes.

Thanks to Nick's lack of cooperation in running for cover, Laurant was stuck.

"I thought FBI agents were supposed to be fast," she muttered as she patiently waited to introduce him to the woman she secretly called *Gazette* Gorilla.

"Keep the goal in mind. This is a golden opportunity. Now stop frowning and look like you love me."

Nick was disgustingly charming, and that only encouraged Lorna to be pushier than ever. She demanded an on-the-spot interview. Whipping her eight-by-ten notebook out of her bag, she wanted to know all the details of how the two of them had met.

Within fifteen seconds, Nick knew two things about the woman. One, she detested Laurant, and two, she wanted him. It wasn't an arrogant assumption. Nor was it a shrewd observation. Hell, the way she was looking at him while she repeatedly moistened her lips with her tongue darting in and out made it real apparent. Disgustingly so.

The knot in Laurant's stomach twisted tighter and tighter as Lorna's questions became more and more personal, but she didn't reach her unraveling point until Lorna asked if she and Nick were already living as man and wife.

"That's none of your damned business, Lorna."

Nick squeezed her shoulder and then said, "Honey, show Lorna your engagement ring."

Laurant was still fuming as she lifted her hand and waved it in front of Lorna's face.

"That must have cost a fortune. Everyone in town knows you work for the FBI," she said then. "Why, I must have gotten six phone calls about you already. It's true," she added when he looked skeptical. "It's the gun, you

312

see. People wondered about it. They're much too polite to ask you, of course."

"So they whisper behind his back," Laurant interjected.

Lorna ignored her. "FBI agents don't make much money, do they?"

"Are you asking me if I can afford the ring?" Nick wondered.

"I wasn't going to be that forward."

Nick squeezed Laurant's hand. "I live a comfortable life. Family trust," he added.

"Then you're rich?"

"For heaven's sake, Lorna. It's none of your—"

Nick placed his other hand on Laurant's shoulder and said sweetly, "Now, darling, don't get all bent out of shape. Lorna's just curious."

"Yes," she agreed. "Curious. Where are you from, Nick? You don't mind if I call you Nick, do you?"

"No, of course not. I live in Boston. I was raised on Nathan's Bay."

"Will you be taking Laurant to Boston after you're married?"

"No. We're going to be living here. I'll be doing a lot of traveling, but I can be based anywhere, and Laurant loves this town. It's growing on me too."

"But Laurant won't have to work after you're married, will she?"

"I'm not selling the store, Lorna, so give it up," Laurant snapped.

"You're holding up progress, Laura."

"Tough." It wasn't a great comeback, but it was the best she could do on the spur of the moment. "And I happen to want to work."

"Of course you do." Her tone was condescending.

"If Laurant wants to work, she will," Nick said. "She's a modern, independent woman, and I'll support whatever she does."

Lorna closed her notebook and stuffed it in her bag. Then she turned her full, patronizing attention on Laurant.

"I want to believe this one's the real thing, but honestly, I have my doubts. I certainly don't want to be forced to print yet another retraction. I just hate doing that. People believe that what I print in my column is true, so you can understand my concern."

Nick draped his arm around Laurant's shoulders and pulled her into his side.

"You've had to print a retraction about Laurant?"

"Twice I've had to do it," Lorna said.

"It's not important," Laurant blurted. "We really need to get going. I've got a lot to get done this afternoon."

"I'm sure you've noticed what a small town Holy Oaks is," Lorna began. "But I'm actually quite important here. I'm the society editor at the *Gazette*. People depend on me to keep them abreast of the latest happenings about town. They also expect me to be accurate, but your fiancée has made that task extremely difficult. I've gotten to the point where I just hate writing anything about her. I really do."

"Then don't," Laurant suggested.

Turning back to Nick, Lorna continued, "As I was telling you before I was so rudely interrupted, Laura keeps changing her mind. I mentioned in one of my articles that Steve Brenner and Laura were a serious item and that marriage appeared to be on the horizon, but I was forced to print a retraction."

She paused to smirk at Laurant before continuing. "She made me do it. Can you imagine? My credibility was on the line, but she didn't care about that. She still insisted I print a retraction."

"Because it wasn't true," Laurant pointed out in exasperation. "I've never dated Steve Brenner and you know it, but you didn't care about being accurate, Lorna. Did you?"

Laurant's French accent was getting thicker, a dead giveaway that she was upset.

"Must you be insulting? I am accurate. I print what I'm told."

"If memory serves, you wrote about my wedding plans."

Laurant was backing her into a corner, and Lorna didn't like that one bit. "I can't remember the details now, but I'm sure I must have gotten it straight from the horse's mouth or I wouldn't have printed it," she muttered, her lips puckered with distaste now.

"The horse being Steve Brenner?" Nick asked.

"I'll admit I might have...exaggerated a bit, to make the article newsworthy," she explained. "But I certainly didn't make it all up, no matter what Laura's told you. I have my reputation to protect."

"What did Steve have to say about the article?"

Lorna shrugged. "He didn't say anything about it. Have you met him yet?"

"No, I haven't."

"You'll like him," Lorna predicted. "Everyone likes him, everyone but Laura," she said, waving her hand at Laurant. "Steve wants to improve the economy here, and he's done so much to help this town. I know he must have been as embarrassed as I was about the retraction, but he never said a word. He wouldn't, of course. He's such a gentleman. I wouldn't have printed that retraction at all if Lauren hadn't threatened to go over my head. She can be a very...difficult woman."

"We really need to get going," Laurant said again. She had had enough of Little Lorna.

Nick didn't budge. "Just for the record...since you want to be accurate and all..."

"Yes?" Lorna asked, her pen poised to strike.

"Her name's Laurant. That's Laurant, not Laura, not Lauren. We're in love," he added. "So you aren't going to have to worry about printing another retraction. Isn't that right, sweetheart?"

When she didn't answer right away, he squeezed her shoulders.

"Yes," she said. "Nick loves me and I love him."

Lorna had that ugly smirk on her face

again. It was apparent she didn't believe Laurant, and all of a sudden it became imperative to Laurant that the obnoxious woman be convinced.

"It happened just like that," she said, snapping her fingers in front of Lorna's nose. "I didn't believe in love at first sight, but then I met Nick. I thought it was just plain old lust, didn't I, darling? But then I realized it was real. I'm madly in love with him."

Lorna's small eyes were darting back and forth between Nick's complacent grin and Laurant's earnest expression.

"I'm going to quote you." She made it sound like a threat.

"That'll be just fine," Nick told her as he turned toward the car with Laurant still tucked against his side.

Fortunately the car wasn't parked far away. Nick opened the door for Laurant and then went around to the driver's side and got in. Lorna stood on the sidewalk, watching them with a malevolent glare.

"I get the feeling Little Lorna doesn't like you much," Nick said, glancing back at the society editor in the rearview mirror.

"I can see why the FBI wanted you. You're very observant."

"My article's going to be in the Sunday paper," Lorna shouted. "Please try to stay in love until then."

Infuriated because the woman wouldn't believe her, Laurant hit the button to roll the window down and then leaned out. "I'm telling you for the last time, Lorna. This is true love. It's the lasting kind."

Lorna stepped off the curb. "Really."

"Really," Laurant repeated.

"Have you set a wedding date?"

It was a challenge, and it didn't go unanswered. "As a matter of fact we have," she said. "We're getting married on the second Saturday in October at seven o'clock."

"Is there a reason the wedding's so soon?" she asked.

"We don't want a long engagement. Besides, everything's planned. Honestly, Lorna, everyone knows about this. You really should keep up, shouldn't you? I mean, you are the society editor after all."

Lorna's response was a loud snort. "Still...planning a wedding in so little time. You don't *have* to get married, do you? Is that the reason for the rush?"

"That's it," Laurant snapped as she reached for the door handle.

Nick grabbed her arm and hit the door lock. He was trying not to laugh, but he was dying to ask her what she would do if he let her get out of the car. Was she going to deck Little Lorna?

It suddenly occurred to Laurant that she was acting like a complete lunatic. She slumped down in her seat and rolled the window up.

"Will you please start the car. I want to get out of here."

Neither one of them said another word until they had driven away from the town square and were heading for the abbey. Then Laurant exploded in a tirade. "Lorna Hamburg is the most opinionated, gossipy, nasty-spirited woman in Holy Oaks. I can't abide her. She's mean and cruel, and she loves to stir up trouble. How dare she not believe me," she cried. "I've never, ever lied to her before. Never. But she didn't believe me, did she? You saw the look on her face. She thought I was lying."

A minute passed in silence and then Nick glanced at her. "Laurant?"

"What?" she asked, sounding downright surly.

He pointed out the obvious. "You were lying."

"But she didn't know that, did she?"

"Apparently she did."

"Drive, Nick. Just drive."

He laughed. He simply couldn't help it.

She ignored him and stared out the window while she struggled to get her temper under control.

"You aren't being very logical," he pointed out. "What's going to happen when this is over and I go back to Boston? Are you going to make Lorna print another retraction, or are you just going to admit that you lied to her?"

"I'm never going to admit I lied. Never. I won't give that vile woman the satisfaction of knowing she was right. I've got a horrible reputation with the men in this town because of her lies."

She folded her arms and stared down at her

lap. She knew she wasn't being reasonable, but she was too angry with the Gorilla to care.

"Lorna doesn't have any ethics. None at all. I swear I'll go to any lengths to avoid admitting I lied. I'd even marry you," she exaggerated. "And you're totally unsuitable."

Nick slowed the car. "What do you mean, I'm unsuitable? What's the matter with me?"

"You aren't safe. That's what's the matter with you. You wear a gun, for heaven's sake."

"I told you before, it goes with the job."

"Exactly."

"There aren't any guarantees in life, and there's no such thing as completely safe, at least not the way you mean it. Bus drivers can be killed while they're doing their job."

"Oh? How many bus drivers do you think get involved in shoot-outs?"

He gritted his teeth. "I don't know all that many FBI agents who get into shoot-outs, as you so quaintly put it," he muttered. "You're being completely illogical. You do know that, don't you?"

Her spine stiffened. "Maybe I don't want to be logical. What's wrong with that?"

"Let me get this straight. Even though you know it's illogical, you'd still marry me just to spite Lorna?"

Of course she wouldn't do such a thing. And of course she wasn't going to admit it to Mr. Always-logical-know-it-all. "What's your point?" she asked

"Nothing. If you don't see anything wrong with it, then I don't either."

She folded her arms and gave him a belligerent nod. "Good. October fourteenth...seven P.M.... Pencil it in."

One man's trash could become another man's treasure. That was Laurant's hope, anyway, as she sorted through a dozen mildew-infested boxes of old, moth-eaten linens and broken knickknacks someone had stored in the attic over fifty years ago. By the time she stopped for the day, she was covered in a layer of dust, her white slacks were gray, and she was sneezing every other second from the moldy cardboard. Unfortunately, she didn't find a priceless van Gogh or Degas painting tucked in with the trash. In fact, she didn't find anything she didn't consider old junk, but she refused to lose heart. She'd only just started the job, after all, and there were over sixty boxes still sealed for her to sort through.

Nick helped her haul the trash down four flights of steps on their way to the car.

"Do we have time to stop by the seamstress to pick up my bridesmaid dress?" she asked.

"Sure, if we hurry. We're supposed to pick up Tommy and Noah in an hour. That's enough time to shower and change."

The minute they arrived home, she ran up the stairs, passing Joe on his way down.

"Just made the rounds and everything's locked up tight," he assured her.

Nick carefully draped the dress over the dining room table and headed for the kitchen to grab a cool drink.

Laurant rushed to get ready. She wasn't going to make the same mistake twice and come out of the bathroom wearing an ugly, old, ragged robe, and so she gathered up everything she would need, including her sling-back shoes.

Twenty-five minutes later she decided she was as good as she was going to get. She was pulling out all the stops tonight, and so she wore *the dress*. It was short, it was black, and it had just enough spandex in the material to make it cling in all the right places. The flattering square neckline showed only a hint of cleavage. She'd worn the dress only once since moving to Holy Oaks, and that was when she had taken Michelle and Christopher out to dinner to celebrate their engagement. Michelle had nicknamed the outfit "the killer dress," said it was indecently decent, and insisted that it was the sexiest thing Laurant owned. Christopher had been emphatic in his agreement.

Laurant stood in front of the mirror primping.

She even curled her hair, but because she was so out of practice, she burned her ear in the process. She stared at her reflection and let out a loud groan. Why was she going to so much trouble to look pretty? She wasn't a teenager in the throes of her first love, but she certainly was acting like one.

My God, was she falling in love with him? The possibility sent chills down her spine. When his job was over, he would leave.

"This is nuts," she whispered as she slammed the brush down on the counter. She had a stupid crush on her big brother's friend. That was all there was to it.

Her ego took a real beating when Nick entered the room. He barely noticed her. After giving her one quick once-over—probably making sure her shoes were on the right feet—he told her Pete was on the phone, and when Joe finished talking to him, Pete wanted to speak to her. Nick's voice sounded strained, and she wondered why he seemed so preoccupied.

He was looking over her head. "Nothing important," he said. "He just wants to hear how you're doing."

Nick got a whiff of her perfume as he passed her on his way to the bathroom. He pretended not to notice, just as he'd pretended not to notice how incredibly sexy she looked in that tight black dress. Until he closed the door. Then he leaned against it, bowed his head, and whispered, "Damn, am I in trouble."

They were fifteen minutes late picking up Noah and Tommy. Nick drove the car up the back driveway behind the abbey and pulled up to the steps. He and Laurant were getting out when Tommy appeared in the doorway and came running down the steps. Noah was nowhere in sight.

He hugged Laurant. "You okay?"

"I'm fine," she assured him.

"Get back in the car." He let go of her, opened the door, and tried to shove her inside, his anxiety apparent. "Nick, this is a bad idea."

"Where's Noah?" Nick asked. He waited until Tommy had gotten into the backseat, then slid in behind the wheel again.

"He's coming," Tommy said. "Why don't we get carryout and go to Laurant's house and eat. I don't like the idea of her being out in public. It's dangerous."

She turned in the seat so she could see his face. "Tommy, I can't stay locked in the house."

"I don't see why not."

"The plan is to be seen, remember?"

"I know what the plan is," he snapped. "Incite the madman to come after you."

"He's going to come after her," Nick said quietly. "But we'd like it to happen sooner rather than later. We'll be ready for him."

"Like I said, this is a bad plan. Things can go wrong—"

Laurant interrupted him. "Did you know there are agents watching us right now?" She didn't know if that were true or not. She was trying to calm her brother.

"Where are they?" he asked, craning his neck to look out the back window.

"You aren't supposed to see them," she said, sounding like an authority.

Tommy seemed to relax a little then. "Yeah, okay. Ah, heck. I forgot my wallet."

"You're not supposed to say that until the check comes," Nick joked.

"I'll just be a minute."

Laurant watched her brother run up the steps and go back inside. "He's more nervous than he was in Kansas City."

"It's understandable."

Tommy came back outside a minute later and took the steps two at a time with his long stride. Noah was hot on his tail. It was then that Nick and Laurant saw what Noah was wearing. Nick started laughing first, but Laurant quickly joined in.

Noah was dressed like a priest in a black suit, black clerical shirt, and a white Roman collar.

"He's gonna go straight to hell," Nick said.

She had to look away so she could stop laughing. "Do you think he's wearing a gun?" she asked.

"He has to carry a gun," Nick said.

"All the time?"

"All the time," he answered.

Noah didn't bother with a greeting. He was determined to make Tommy agree with him on a subject the two of them had obviously been arguing about.

"I'm telling you, it isn't normal."

"Maybe not for you," Tommy answered.

Noah snorted. "Not for any man."

Nick guessed what they were quarreling about. "Celibacy, right?"

"Yeah," Noah answered. "A priest never getting to have sex...that's just not right."

Nick laughed. Tommy shook his head and then tried to change the subject. "Where are we eating?"

Noah wouldn't let the matter go. He couldn't seem to get past the celibacy rule. "It's just not healthy," he said. "You don't even notice all those women coming on to you. Do you?"

Tommy's patience was wearing thin. "Yes, I notice," he said. "And I ignore them."

"That's what I mean. It's just not—"

Tommy cut him off. "Yeah, I know. It's just not normal. Now let it go, Noah."

Noah decided to accommodate him. "Damn, you smell good, Laurant. Or is that you, Nick?" he joked.

Before either one of them could answer, Noah said, "Have you noticed the ungodly number of vans in this town? Hell, they're everywhere. I figure Wesson's running the plates. He is, isn't he?"

The question broke the carefree mood and the conversation became serious.

"I called him earlier to find out if he had any news. I figured he had run the plates on the cars of the workmen on Laurant's block, but Wesson wouldn't tell me anything."

"What did he say?"

" 'I'm doing my job.' That's a quote."

Noah sighed. "So, we're the hired guns, is that it? He's gonna keep us out in the cold."

"It looks that way."

"The hell with that. I'm not going to work blindfolded."

Tommy began to grill Nick with questions and suggestions, and by the time they parked in the back of the Rosebriar Restaurant, Laurant had lost her appetite.

Noah grabbed Tommy's arm when he tried to get out of the car. "Listen up, priest. You stay close. You go running off again, and I'll shoot you myself."

"Yes, all right. It won't happen again."

Noah smiled, his good mood restored. Tommy got out of the car and opened Laurant's door for her. She swung her legs out and stood, self-consciously tugging on her skirt.

Noah let out a low whistle of appreciation. "You've got a beautiful sister, Tom."

"It's inappropriate for priests to whistle at pretty women."

Noah glanced at Nick. "It's been nonstop criticism since I put on this collar. I'm trying to be patient and helpful, but he's making it tough."

Tommy walked ahead with Laurant, his head bent down toward hers as they talked, and Nick fell into step beside Noah.

"Helpful in what way?" he asked.

Noah shrugged. "I offered to hear confession for one of the other priests, but Tom got all bent out of shape and wouldn't let me."

Tommy heard the comment and glanced back. "Of course I wouldn't let you."

"Your friend takes this priest stuff seriously."

"All priests are supposed to take their job seriously," Nick said. "I should have warned Tommy about your warped sense of humor."

"He's easy to rattle."

"That's because you know what buttons to push."

"What about Laurant?"

"What about her?"

Noah winked. "Have you been pushing any of her buttons? I noticed the way you've been looking at her."

"She's off-limits. Wait up, Tommy," he called out. "Let one of us go inside first."

"Off-limits for you, or for me?"

"For both of us. She's not the kind of woman you mess around with unless you've made a commitment."

The cobblestone path curved around the building. Noah strode ahead of Tommy and Laurant while Nick trailed behind. Both agents were busy looking at the terrain.

Terra-cotta pots brimming with red and white geraniums lined the path to the door. The Rosebriar was an old sprawling Victorian-style house that had been converted into a restaurant. The dining room was richly appointed with crystal vases filled with spring flowers on all the white linen tablecloths. The china looked old and expensive.

The room they were shown into was in the back of the house, overlooking a duck pond and the woods. They were led to a round table in front of the window so they could enjoy the view, but Noah nodded toward a corner table and asked to be seated there instead.

The room was quite full. It was noisy with laughter. Quite a few families were dining with their children. As they threaded their way to the corner, heads turned to watch Laurant. Even the children were mesmerized by her. Laurant seemed oblivious to the admiring gazes of every man in the restaurant.

The waiter pulled the table out so that Laurant could sit in the corner. Nick sat beside her. Noah and Tommy faced them, but Noah hated having his back to the room, and so he angled his chair to see the other diners. He started to take his jacket off, realized his gun would show, and pulled it back up over his shoulders.

Tommy couldn't sit still. Every other second he turned to look around the room. His head snapped up each time he heard a burst of laughter.

"Sit still and try to relax," Noah ordered. "You're drawing attention squirming in your chair like that. And quit staring at the other people. Don't you know most of them?"

Tommy shook his head. "No, I don't. That's why I'm watching them."

"Let us watch them," Nick suggested. "Now get with the program. Okay?"

"I think you should try to smile, Tommy," Laurant whispered. "We're supposed to be celebrating tonight."

"I'm going to order a bottle of champagne," Nick said.

"What are we celebrating?" Noah asked.

Laurant held up her hand. "Nick and I are officially engaged."

Tommy did smile then. "So that's why you got all decked out tonight."

"I'm not all decked out."

"And you've got makeup on too, don't you? You never wear makeup."

She knew her brother wasn't deliberately trying to embarrass her, but she still wanted to kick him under the table to get him to stop.

"Your hair's different too."

"I curled it. All right? Honestly, it's no big deal. And by the way, if anyone asks, you're thrilled that I'm going to marry your best friend."

"Okay," he said.

"Actually, I may have to marry your sister after all," Nick said with a grin.

"How's that?"

"She ran into a friend—"

"Lorna isn't my friend."

Nick nodded. "And Laurant will do anything to keep Lorna from saying I told you so."

Tommy laughed. "Lorna's always rubbed Laurant the wrong way. I guess you will have to marry her."

He leaned back in his chair. His gaze

bounced from Laurant to Nick, and then back again, and then he said, "You know that wouldn't be bad at all. You're kind of suited for each other."

"She doesn't want to marry me. I'm not safe enough for her."

"The wedding's at seven o'clock on the second Saturday in October, and you're marrying us," Laurant said. "I just know Lorna's going to talk to you, so act happy and don't forget the date."

"Yeah, yeah, the second Saturday in October," he agreed. "I won't forget. But when this is over, you're going to have to tell Lorna the truth."

Laurant was vehemently shaking her head. "I'll move first."

"I thought you were going to marry me to save face."

She shrugged. "I guess I could."

"Marriage is a holy sacrament," Tommy reminded them.

"Lighten up, Tommy," Laurant suggested. "Go with the flow."

"In other words, lie through my teeth, right?"

She smiled. "Right."

"Okay, let me ask you this. If I'm marrying you and Nick, who's going to walk you down the aisle?"

"I hadn't thought about that," she admitted.

"I've got an idea," Noah said. "How about if I marry Nick and Laurant, and Tom, you can walk your sister down the aisle."

"Now that's a plan," Nick agreed.

Tommy looked exasperated. "Okay, Noah, let's go over the rules one more time. You're not really a priest. You're just pretending to be one, and that means you can't marry anyone, you can't hear confessions, and you can't date."

Noah laughed, drawing stares from the other diners. "Damn, it doesn't take much to get you riled up. We're pretending that Nick and Laurant are getting married, aren't we? So I'm pretending I'm going to marry them."

Tommy looked at Nick. "Help me out here, will you? The abbot went out on a limb for Noah. Pete talked to him and convinced him to go along with this plan. He agreed to tell everyone that Wesson's a cousin and that he's letting him stay in the cabin. The man's being real accommodating," he added. "But we don't like people impersonating priests, and Noah promised he wouldn't do anything to discredit the collar. Five minutes after we leave the abbot's office, Noah's winking at Suzie Johnson and calling her darling."

"I'm pretending to be a friendly priest," Noah explained. "And I still think priests ought to have one day off a week to go—"

Tommy stopped him. "Yeah, I know. A day off to have sex. That's not the way it works."

Nick's phone rang. He listened for half a minute, then said, "Yes, sir," and hung up.

"The sheriff just got out of a new, red Ford Explorer. He's headed this way."

"Is he alone?" Noah asked.

"Looks that way."

"The lodge holds its weekly meetings here," Laurant explained. "The others are probably upstairs in one of the smaller dining rooms."

"Is Brenner a member of the lodge?"

"I think so," she answered.

"Maybe after we eat, I'll go up and say hello," Nick said. "I'd sure like to meet good old Steve Brenner."

A minute later the sheriff strutted into the entry. Dressed in his gray uniform and cowboy boots, he didn't bother to remove his hat when he entered the restaurant. Nick watched the hostess pick up a menu and lead the sheriff up the stairs.

"Brenner's the local talent, isn't he?" Noah asked.

"It looks that way," Nick said.

"What do you mean, 'the local talent'?" Tommy asked.

"The guy who tries to run the town. The bully," Noah explained. "There's always at least one in every town this size."

"Then that's what Brenner is," Tommy said. "He is trying to run the town, and my sister is the only person here who's willing to stand up to him." He noticed Laurant was admiring her ring and smiled. "I wouldn't get too attached to that ring, Laurant."

"I'm putting on a show, Tommy," she whispered. "But the ring is lovely, isn't it? I had no idea Russell's carried so many beautiful things." She began to wonder what it would be like to be married to Nick. To know that when she woke up every morning, he would be there? To be loved by—

"What kind of return policy does the store have?" Tommy asked, practical to the bone.

She put her hand back in her lap. "It's usually ten days, but Mrs. Russell is making an exception for me. She's giving me thirty days. Do you know what she said to me? 'Because of your sorry history with men, dear, I'll allow you a whole month to change your mind.' "

Tommy laughed. "My sister's got quite a reputation in town for scaring men away."

"Thanks to all the lies Lorna prints in the paper about me."

"Be honest, Laurant. You do scare men, and just for the record, I think that's just fine. It keeps the creeps from hounding you."

Tommy glanced over his shoulder once again when he heard a commotion behind him. Then he smiled.

"That's Frank Hamilton. He's the high school football coach, and those other two are assistants. They've all been dying to meet you, Nick. Come on. Let's say hello before they head upstairs."

"How do they know Nick?" Laurant asked.

"The football tape the sports channel runs a couple of times a year."

"Ah, hell," Nick muttered. He tossed the napkin on the table and followed Tommy out of the room.

"Nick's never going to live that game down, and he hates all the fanfare."

"What exactly happened during the game?"

"You never saw the tape?"

She shook her head. "No, and Tommy's never mentioned it."

"Nick scored the winning touchdown."

"That's nice."

Noah laughed. "There's a little more to it than that. Nick caught the short pass, then zigzagged his way through the defense, which he was real good at doing. He could turn on a dime, and that's why he got the nickname Cutter," he explained. "Anyway, his head was turned and he was looking up at the top of this cement wall. When you see the tape, you hear the announcer asking, 'What's number eighty-two looking at?' That was Nick's number," he added. "So then, while the one camera was focused on Nick, there was another camera searching the stands to see what had grabbed his interest, and after the game was over, they spliced those two tapes together."

He paused to take a drink of water before continuing. "There was this guy leaning over the cement wall. Turns out he was real drunk, and he was shouting like all the other fans, holding a beer in one hand, and a little kid in the other. He had the toddler sitting on the ledge. Can you believe how stupid that was?" he asked. "But like I said, he was drunk."

"Did he drop the baby?"

"He sure did, but Nick had been watching. He told me later that, when he was running, he saw the man grab at the kid once, but he didn't pull him back. He just kind of hung on to him and let him dangle half off the wall. Nick was running like there was no tomorrow at this point, and he didn't have anyone on his tail. He scored the touchdown but kept on running as he was turning. He thought he'd stand under that wall until someone made the father remove the kid, but when he was about ten feet away, the guy lost his grip and the kid came flying down. The fall would have killed him. Nick caught him, and honest to God, it was a beautiful thing to see."

The story astounded her. She thought of a hundred questions to ask, but Noah turned her attention when he said, "After the game, Nick was suspended."

"What?"

"It's true," he insisted. "After the game was over, the father came into the locker room with the cameramen. He was still drunk, of course, and some of the guys told me he was loving the attention he was getting. Anyway, he wanted to thank Nick for saving his kid, but Nick came around the corner, saw him, and hauled off and decked him. He knocked him out."

"And that's why he was suspended."

"Yeah, but it didn't last. The public outcry swayed the coach, who probably really didn't want to suspend Nick anyway. I could understand where Nick was coming from. He didn't want to hear any excuses from the drunk."

The waiter appeared and placed a basket of rolls between them. Noah grabbed one as he said, "Okay, it's your turn. You tell me something."

"What would you like to know?"

"How come Tommy lived with Nick's family while he was growing up?"

"My father was opening an office in Boston and had come over to set up a house, and he'd brought Tommy along so that he could get registered at school and start a new term. I was just a baby then, and I stayed with Mother. She was going to finish packing and follow Father. But then everything changed. Father was killed in a car crash, and for a while, Tommy was left in the care of the housekeeper. Mother couldn't cope with the loss. Tommy was only supposed to stay in Boston until the school year ended, and Mother was supposed to fly over and stay with him until then, but she wasn't stable enough to go anywhere. Grandfather told me she was drinking heavily and taking pills. Some of the pills were to help her sleep, and some were to help her wake up. She died of an overdose."

"Suicide?"

"I think so, yes. Grandfather said it was a combination of alcohol and sleeping pills. He wanted to believe it was an accident."

"That's a deadly combination."

She nodded. "After she died, Grandfather was stuck with Tommy and me. He wanted to do the right thing, and he knew Tommy was happy in Boston. Judge Buchanan called him out of the blue and suggested that Tommy live with his family until things settled down. Nick and Tommy had become best friends, and Tommy spent most of his time with the family anyway. The judge can be very persuasive. Like Mother, Grandfather thought it would be for a little while, but then he died."

"And Tommy got to stay where he was."

"Yes."

"What about you?"

She lifted her shoulders. "I was placed in a boarding school. After I graduated from university, I went to Paris for a year to study art, then I came to the United States and took a job in Chicago. I lived there for nine months, and then I moved to Holy Oaks. Nothing razzle-dazzle about my background."

"You were left out in the cold, weren't you? Tommy had this nice big family to call his own, but you didn't have anyone."

"I was happy."

"You couldn't have been happy."

"Here they come," she said. "I don't want to talk about this anymore. All right?"

"Sure."

Nick was chuckling as he sat down. "What's so funny?" Noah asked.

He looked at Laurant before he answered. "The men in town have given Laurant a nickname."

"Yeah? So what do they call her?" Noah asked.

"Ice Woman, or just plain Ice," Tommy said.

All three of them laughed, but Laurant wasn't amused. "You're a blabbermouth, Tommy."

"Hey, he asked."

She gave her brother a look that told him she

was going to give him hell later. Then Nick drew her attention when he leaned close to her and whispered in her ear. "You sure don't kiss like ice."

The waiter appeared to take their orders, but as soon as he left, the men took turns teasing her. Finally, when she had had enough, she took the upper hand.

"I heard Penn State is going to have a real bad football season. They lost their star quarterback."

She hadn't heard any such thing, of course, but that didn't matter. As soon as she said the word *football,* their minds clicked into sports mode. It was as easy as getting a baby to eat candy. She leaned back in her chair and smiled complacently.

Nick and Tommy had played ball for Penn State, and Noah, as it turned out, had been a running back for Michigan State, so each one of them believed he was the authority. During dinner they argued about draft choices and pretty much ignored her. She couldn't have been happier.

On their way out of the restaurant, a family of six called Tommy over to their table. Noah stayed with him, and Nick and Laurant went on outside.

Lonnie was waiting for them. His Chevy Nova careened into the parking lot as Nick and Laurant were heading toward their car. The Chevy came to a screeching halt in the center of the lot, just a few feet from them. Nick pushed Laurant between two cars, then got in front of her, waiting to see what the driver was going to do.

Lonnie wasn't alone. There were three others in the car with him, all from the nearby town of Nugent, and all with juvenile records. Whenever Lonnie had an important job to do for Steve Brenner, he made sure his friends were included. He gave them only a pittance of the money Steve paid, but they were too stupid to think that he might be screwing them out of their fair share. Besides, they were in it for the fun, not the cash, and Lonnie had another reason for involving them. If things went bad, they'd take the rap. His good-for-nothing father would have to let him go. How would it look if the sheriff's son were tossed in jail? Being a big man around town meant everything to him, and Lonnie figured he could get away with murder as long as he was careful.

Steve had told Lonnie that Laurant and her boyfriend were driving an Explorer, and they were standing next to a new, red Ford Explorer. Steve hadn't told him anything about Nick, just that he was claiming to be Laurant's fiancé. Since Steve planned to marry Laurant, Lonnie needed to put the fear of God into Nick. "Run him out of town," Steve had ordered, and Lonnie, salivating over the wad of cash Steve dangled in front of him, promised to do just that.

"That's the sheriff's son, Lonnie," Laurant whispered. "What's he up to?"

"Looks like we're going to find out real

soon," he whispered back. Then he shouted, "Hey, kid, move your car."

Lonnie left the motor running as he opened the door and jumped out. He was tall and gangly, his complexion marred by acne scars. His thin lips disappeared inside his sneer, and his hair hung down in his face in long, oily strands. Nick judged him to be around eighteen or nineteen years old.

This one was already a lost cause. He could see it in his eyes.

"Let's start with the car," Lonnie told his friends. "Trash it." He pulled his switchblade knife out of his back pocket. Snickering, he boasted to his friends, "I'm going to scare the shit out of Mr. Big City. Watch and learn." He flipped the dirty blade open as he slowly advanced. "Laura, you're gonna be riding home with us, 'cause your boyfriend's car's going to be a piece of shit by the time I get finished with it."

Nick laughed. It wasn't the response Lonnie had anticipated. "What's so damned funny?"

"You," Nick answered. He spotted Noah shoving Tommy behind him as he rushed down the stairs toward them. He called out to him. "Hey, Noah, the local thug wants to trash the new car."

"But that's...," Tommy began.

"Sure it is," Nick interrupted.

"Lonnie, what do you think you're doing? Put that knife away," Tommy ordered.

"I got some business with Laura," Lonnie said. "You and the other priest go on inside."

"Is this guy stupid or what?" Noah asked incredulously.

"I'm thinking he must be," Nick drawled as he reached inside his jacket and flipped the snap holding his gun in place.

Furious that he was being mocked in front of his friends, Lonnie lunged forward and thrust the knife into the left front tire. Then he stabbed it again, smiling when he heard the hiss of air.

"Still think I'm stupid?"

"Thank the Lord we have a spare," Noah called out. He was busy keeping Tommy behind him and trying to watch the morons at the same time.

Lonnie reacted just the way Noah hoped. He sliced the other tire. His friends hooted with laughter, and that only encouraged him. He carved a jagged line in the grille, then did the same to the hood.

Then he stepped back to survey his handiwork. "Now how are you going to get home?" he taunted.

Nick shrugged. "I figured I'd drive my car."

"With two flat tires?"

Nick smiled. "This isn't my car."

Lonnie blinked. Nick took a step toward him as he called out, "Noah, maybe you ought to go inside and get the sheriff. He'll want to know his kid's been messing with his car."

"Shit!" Lonnie shouted.

"Drop the knife. Do it now," he ordered. "Don't make this any worse than it already is.

You've destroyed private property, and threatening a federal—"

He was about to tell Lonnie he was an FBI agent but wasn't given the chance.

"Nobody makes a fool out of me," Lonnie hissed.

"You did that all by yourself," Nick countered. "Now drop the knife. This is your last warning."

Lonnie lunged, shouting, "I'm going to cut you up into pieces, you asshole."

The boast was empty. "Yeah, right," Nick said as he kneed Lonnie, then snatched the knife and tossed it to the ground. He slammed him into the car, setting off the alarm.

It happened so fast, Laurant didn't have time to blink. Lonnie was doubling over, screaming in agony. She saw the knife and stepped back so she could kick it under the car.

The second the alarm went off, Lonnie's buddies scrambled to their car and piled in. Nick let go of Lonnie and watched him collapse.

"You asshole. I'm going to—"

"Oh, look. Here comes Daddy," Nick said cheerfully.

The sheriff was running down the stairs, his big stomach jiggling up and down. In the meantime, the three boys in the car were all frantically trying to find the keys. Noah strolled over to the driver's side and said, "Looking for these?"

"We didn't do nothing. It was all Lonnie's idea."

"Shut up, Ricky," the boy in the backseat shouted.

"Get out of the car," Noah ordered. "Nice and easy, and keep your hands where I can see them." He didn't want to blow his cover, but he had his hand in his jacket on the butt of his Glock just in case one of them pulled a gun on him.

The sheriff looked like he wanted to cry. "My new car? Look at my new car. Did you do this, boy? Did you?"

Lonnie struggled to his feet. "No," he sneered. "That asshole did it," he added, pointing to Nick. "And he kicked me in my knee too."

"I was going to tell you I bought myself a new car," the sheriff continued, as though he hadn't heard a word Lonnie had said. "I was going to tell you. I was going to let you drive it too." He trailed his hand along the deep scratches in the hood, his eyes misty. "It wasn't even perfect for one whole day. I just picked it up."

"I'm telling you, the asshole did it," Lonnie said again.

"The kid needs some work on his vocabulary," Noah said.

"Are you going to believe me or not?" Lonnie shouted at his father. "I'm telling you for the last time, he cut your tires and scratched the paint."

Laurant was incensed. She pushed past Nick to face the sheriff. "I know he's your son and that this is difficult for you, but you are the sheriff, and you have to do your job. Lonnie's lying. He did the damage. He thought your new car belonged to my fiancé. Like it or not, you're going to have to arrest him."

Lloyd put his hands up. "Slow down, Laura. No reason to be hasty. It's my car and I'll make sure my boy pays the consequences *if* he did the damage, but he's saying your boyfriend—"

Laurant cut him off. She was so angry, she was sputtering. "He's lying," she repeated. "There are four witnesses. My brother, Father Clayborne, Nick, and me. You have to arrest him."

"Well, now, the way I see it, that's four against four, 'cause I'm sure Lonnie's friends are going to back him up, and I don't have any reason at all not to believe them."

"Lonnie threatened us with a knife."

Looking past Laurant to Nick, the sheriff demanded, "You'd best get your woman under control. I'm not going to put up with her yapping at me. Now you just back away, Laura, and hold your tongue."

Laurant couldn't believe the sheriff was talking to her as though she were a naughty child. "Hold my tongue? I don't think so," she said. "Do something," she demanded.

The sheriff glared at her. "I am going to do something," he announced. "You there," he muttered, pointing to Nick. "I want to see some identification, and I want to see it now."

Laurant's temper exploded. She turned to Tommy and spoke in rapid French, telling him what an incompetent fool she thought the sheriff was. In fluent French, Nick told her to calm down.

The sheriff's hands were balled into fists, and he kept glancing at his son. He wanted to kick some sense into the boy, and it took a good deal of discipline to control his fury. Besides, if he did give in to his temper, there was a good chance that Lonnie would strike back and beat the crap out of him. Lonnie had done it before, and Lloyd knew he would do it again.

"I said I want to see some identification."

"No problem," Nick replied as he pulled out his badge and flipped it open. "Nicholas Buchanan, Sheriff. FBI."

"Ah shit," the sheriff moaned.

"You're going to have to lock him up. I'll come by tomorrow and fill out the paperwork."

"What paperwork, Mr. FBI agent? It was my car that got damaged. Lonnie, stop your snickering or I swear I'll backhand you."

Noah came up behind the sheriff. "I'm not real familiar with the law, being a priest and all," he said, "but it seems to me that a crime was committed here by your son. Lonnie threatened an FBI agent with a knife, and that's some kind of a crime, isn't it?"

"Well now, maybe it is and maybe it isn't," the sheriff hedged. "I don't see a knife, so what you're claiming might just be fabrication. Do you see my dilemma?"

"The knife's under the car," Noah told him.

Trying to buy some time while he figured

346

out what he was going to do, the sheriff muttered, "How'd it get under the car?"

"I kicked it there," Laurant said.

"What were you doing with a knife?"

"Oh, for the love of...," she began.

The sheriff took his hat off and scratched his head. "Now here's what I'm going to do. You all go on home now and let me deal with this. You can come on by the office tomorrow, but you call me first," he told Nick. "I'll have it all sorted out by then. Go on home now."

Laurant was so furious she was shaking. Without a word, she turned her back on the sheriff and walked to Nick's car, her high heels clicking hard on the pavement.

Nick could hear her muttering under her breath. As he opened the passenger door for her, he took hold of her hand. "Are you all right? You're trembling. You weren't scared, were you? I wouldn't have let anything happen to you. You do know that, don't you?"

"Yes," she said. "I'm just angry, that's all. The sheriff isn't going to do anything about Lonnie. He certainly won't arrest him. You just wait and see."

"You are angry."

"He had a knife," she cried out. "He could have hurt you."

Nick was taken aback. "You were worried about me?"

Tommy and Noah were getting into the backseat, and she didn't want them to hear her. "Of course I was worried about you. Now

347

will you stop grinning like an idiot and get in the car? I want to go home."

He wanted to kiss her, but he settled on squeezing her hand instead. It was a sorry substitute.

"Sheriff," Nick called out as he walked around to the driver's side. "I'm going to want to talk to your son tomorrow."

Tommy was craning his neck to look out the back window when Nick drove the car out of the parking lot. He could see the sheriff arguing with Lonnie.

"You don't think Lonnie could be the guy who's stalking Laurant, do you?"

"We're going to check him out," Nick answered. "But I don't think he's the man we're after. Lonnie doesn't strike me as real intelligent."

"The kid's a moron," Noah said.

"Yeah, well, you did your part to spur him on," Nick said.

"How'd I do that?" he asked innocently.

"Thank the Lord we've got a spare? Isn't that what you said to Lonnie after he cut the first tire?"

"Maybe," Noah allowed. "I wanted to keep him busy so he'd leave you and Laurant alone."

"Is that right? I figured you wanted to see how far he'd go."

Noah shrugged while he tugged on his stiff collar. It was chafing his neck. "This thing feels like a noose," he told Tommy.

"Nick, were there any agents at the restaurant? And if there were, why didn't one of them come forward to help?" Laurant asked.

"It was under control," Nick answered.

"Wesson ordered me to let Tommy hear confession," Noah told Nick.

"Pete doesn't want him to," Nick responded. "It's a bad idea."

"That's what I told him."

From Noah's tone of voice, Laurant knew he didn't like Wesson any more than Nick did. She turned in her seat to ask him why.

Nick pressed his thumb against the disc so Wesson couldn't listen in.

Noah noticed what he was doing. "You don't have to do that. I want Wesson to hear me. For the record, I think he's a glory seeker and power hungry. He doesn't give a damn who he steps on to get to the top, including Morganstern."

Noah was on a roll and wasn't going to stop until he'd spilled all of his pent-up frustration with the man running the operation. "He sure isn't a team player," he added. "But then neither am I. Still, I avoid publicity just as much as you do, but Wesson goes looking for it. Remember the Stark case?" he asked, and before Nick could answer, he added, "Of course you do. You have to kill someone...you don't forget that. Not ever."

"What about the Stark case?" Nick asked, looking in the rearview mirror at Noah.

"I'll bet you were surprised when you opened your newspaper a couple of days later and read that human interest story about you saving that kid. Didn't you think it was damn odd that the reporter wrote all that stuff about you, your family, and your best friend, Tom?"

"You're saying that Wesson leaked the story?" Nick asked. He was getting mad just thinking about the possibility.

"Hell, yes, I'm saying it," he replied. "You did notice Wesson's name was splattered all over that article, didn't you? If I could get that reporter alone in a room for a couple of minutes, I could prove it too."

"Why would Wesson do it?" Laurant asked. "What does he have to gain?"

"He's got a grudge. Plus, he wants to run the Apostles," Noah said. "That's always been his goal, and I think he figures the more publicity he can get for himself, the better his chances will be. I'm telling you, Nick, as soon as Morganstern retires or accepts a promotion, Wesson's going to move in. When that day comes, you'd be smart to get out."

Nick pulled the car into the parking lot behind the abbey and stopped.

"Let's just concentrate on our jobs for now. Get some rest, Tommy. You look worn-out."

"See you tomorrow at the picnic," Tommy said. He reached over the seat and squeezed Laurant's shoulder. "You still doing okay?"

"I'm fine. Good night, Tommy."

Noah climbed over the seat and got out on Tommy's side. Leaning back in, he said, "Nighty-night, Icy."

The picnic was in full swing by the time Nick and Laurant arrived. He could hear the band playing as he took Laurant's hand and walked across the dirt road toward the crowd gathered around the bandstand and the picnic tables. The hill beyond the flat area was littered with colorful blankets, and from the distance it looked like a patchwork quilt. Children were running wild, ducking in and out between couples dancing to the music of The Hilltops. The aroma of smoking barbecue hung heavily in the air.

Tommy and Noah were busy turning hamburgers on the grill, but Tommy spotted them and waved hello. Laurant carried a blanket over her arm. She found a vacant spot under a gnarled tree and spread the blanket out there.

Nick didn't like the size of the crowd. It appeared that most of the town had turned out for the affair. It was twilight now, and someone plugged in the Christmas lights that had been strung from tree to tree around the wooden bandstand.

"Isn't the band great?" she asked.

"Uh-huh," he said as he continued to look over the crowd.

"Herman and Harley Winston started the group," she explained. "Herman's the one playing the sax, and Harley's on the drums. They're the twins I told you about who are doing the remodeling on my store. They're so sweet. You should meet them."

Nick looked at the bandstand and smiled. There were six members in the band, and all of them appeared to be in their seventies. The twins were identical and dressed alike in red checkered shirts and white pants.

"They're old men," he remarked.

"They're young at heart," she corrected. "And master craftsmen. In Holy Oaks, we don't put the elderly out to pasture. The contribution they make to this town is very important. When you see my store and my loft, you'll understand how talented these men are."

"Hey, I wasn't criticizing," he said. "I just noticed, that's all."

The bandleader, a bald-headed gentleman with a toothy smile, sparkling eyes, and terribly stooped shoulders, thumped on the microphone to get everyone's attention.

"Ladies and gentlemen, as you all know, this here picnic is the abbot's way of saying thank you to all of you folks out there who have worked so darn hard to get the church finished in time for the anniversary. The abbot expects you to have a fine time tonight," he added. "Now as you know, me and the boys in the band only play the oldies, because those are the only songs we know how to play. We just love to take requests, so if you got a special gal you want to impress, come on up and write the name of the song on a piece of paper and stick it in that hat over there on that card table. We got plenty of pencils and paper. We'll be drawing the requests out of that hat till we have to shut down. Now the first song is going out to Cindy Mitchell and her husband, Dan. This is Cindy's first outing since she had that gallbladder taken out, and it's real good to see her up and about. Come on, Dan, bring her on out to the dance floor. This song is one of my favorites," he added as he stepped back and lifted his hands like a symphony conductor. Tapping his foot, he counted, "One, two, three. Hit it, boys."

Silence followed the command. The band-leader turned around to find out what was wrong, then chuckled. Speaking into the microphone, he sheepishly explained, "I guess I ought to tell the boys the name of the song we're playing. It's 'Misty.' Now let's try it again."

Nick didn't like the idea of Laurant being in such a large crowd. He knew the picnic was a good place for them to be seen together, and for him to observe the people around her, but he was still having trouble with it. The crowd could swallow her up, and he didn't want her out of his sight, not for one second.

Her friends made his job difficult. As soon as they spotted her, they wanted to pull her away from him. They were, of course, very curious about him. Several men came up to shake his hand and introduce themselves. They were open and friendly, and they tried to draw him into their group of friends around the beer kegs while Laurant was being tugged in the opposite direction. To keep her close, Nick anchored his arm around her waist and held tight. He wouldn't let her budge.

She didn't put up with his behavior for long. Leaning up on tiptoes, she whispered into his ear, "You're going to have to let me talk to my friends and neighbors."

"Don't disappear on me," he whispered back, and then, because he knew they were being watched, he kissed her softly on her lips. "Try to stay between Noah and me."

"I will," she promised, and then she kissed him. "Now please smile, Nick. This is a party, not a funeral."

Someone called her name, and Nick reluctantly let go of her. She hadn't taken five steps away from him before she was surrounded by women. They were all talking at the same time, and he was pretty sure he was the topic, because they kept glancing at him. He put his hands in his pockets and kept his gaze locked on Laurant. She had the most incredible smile.

One of the women screamed, and Nick took a quick step forward, but then he saw that Laurant was showing off the ring, and that was what had excited the young woman. He backed off and once again looked over the crowd. When he turned back to Laurant, she was slowly threading her way toward the bandstand. As

Nick watched her mingle with the young and the old, he realized how vital she was to their community. She was also loved. The towns-people could obviously see what a gentle and caring woman she was. They responded to her the same way he did, by wanting to get closer to her. He could tell that she was genuinely interested in what they were saying. She made people feel good, and what a hell of a gift that was.

Nick was smiling as he watched her, but the smile vanished when she was stopped yet again by two men about her age. From the way they were drooling, he knew neither one was put off by her reputation. He felt a surprising burst of jealousy. Then one of the men put his hand on her arm, and Nick wanted to punch him. He knew his response was totally inap-propriate. It wasn't like him to be so posses-sive.

He couldn't figure out what was the matter with him. A relationship with her was impos-sible. He knew that, and he accepted it.

Why was he having so much trouble main-taining his distance? Because he was damn hot for her, he admitted. This wasn't lust. He was old enough and had been around long enough to know the difference. Lust he could control with cold showers, but this feeling was totally different. It worried the hell out of him.

"Are you Nick Buchanan?"

Nick turned. "That's me all right."

"My name's Christopher Benson," the man

said as he stuck his hand out to shake Nick's. "Laurant's my fiancée's best friend. Mine too," he added with a grin. "I wanted to meet you and say hello."

Christopher was a likeable, easygoing man. He was built like a linebacker. He was as tall as Nick, but outweighed him by at least fifty pounds.

After they exchanged small talk, Christopher admitted sheepishly, "Michelle sent me over to get as much information out of you as I could. She thinks that because I just finished law school, I should be able to grill anyone I want."

Nick laughed. "What exactly does she want to know?"

"Oh, the usual stuff, like how much you make, where you're going to live after you marry Laurant, and most important, are you always going to be there for her. You might be getting the idea that Michelle's nosy, but she isn't. She's just looking out for Laurant."

They both turned to watch Laurant. There were men standing in line to take a turn dancing with her. She was circling the floor now with donut boy.

He answered as many questions as he could and hedged on others.

When Christopher was finally satisfied, he remarked, "Laurant's an important part of this town. People depend on her. She and Michelle are like sisters," he added. "They bring out the devil in each other, and, man, do they like to laugh."

Nick was wondering when he was going to get a chance to dance with Laurant. He sure as certain wasn't going to get in line. Being a fiancé had a couple of perks, didn't it? Even if he was all pretend.

Christopher seemed to read his mind. "Why don't you go get Laurant. The food's going to disappear fast."

"Good idea," Nick said.

He shouldered his way through the crowd, tapped donut boy on the shoulder, and pulled Laurant into his arms. "I'm cutting in, kid."

Laurant softened the teenager's disappointment. Leaning to the side, she asked him to save her a dance later, after dinner.

"You're only encouraging him," Nick told her.

"He's a sweet boy," she said.

He didn't want to talk about the kid. He pulled her closer and continued to dance.

"Look like you love me, honey," he instructed.

She laughed. "I do love you, sweetheart."

"I like that thing you're wearing."

"That thing is called a dress. A sundress to be exact, and thank you. I'm glad you like it."

"Tell me something. If all the men in this town are afraid of you, how come they're lining up to dance with you?"

"I don't know," she said. "Maybe because they know I won't say no. They don't ask me to go out on dates though. I think Tommy might be right. I might scare them."

"That's good," he said with smug satisfaction.

"Why?" she asked.

He didn't answer her question. "Let's eat,"
he said.

"Viola and Bessie Jean are waving at us. I
think they want us to sit with them."

"Son of a bitch," Nick hissed.

His reaction startled her. "I thought you liked
them."

"Not them," he answered impatiently. "I just
spotted Lonnie. What the hell is he doing
here?"

"Do I get to say I told you so?" she asked.
She found Lonnie in the crowd, sitting alone
on a picnic table, an insolent expression on
his face. No one else was sitting at the table,
and Laurant noticed several people, obviously nervous around the bully, who were
avoiding making eye contact with him.

Nick was searching the crowd for the sheriff.
"I don't see dear old dad," he said.

"Oh, I doubt he's here. He wouldn't answer
your phone calls all day, and the jail was
locked up when we stopped by. I think he's
hiding from you, Mr. FBI Agent," she said.

Nick shook his head. "I'm going to have to
do something about him."

"You'll have to find him first."

"I'm not talking about the sheriff," he
replied. "I'm going to have to do something
about Lonnie. He's a complication we don't
need now."

"What can you do?"

Nick draped his arm around Laurant's shoulders and headed for the buffet that was set up behind the bandstand.

"Noah."

"Noah's what you're going to do?"

"Uh-huh."

"Okay. What can Noah do?"

He grinned. "Lots."

"Go make Lonnie get off that table first," she suggested. "Then we'll eat. People need places to sit."

"Okay," he agreed, but as he turned to the tables, he saw Tommy heading for Lonnie from the opposite direction. He had a spatula in his hand and a look on his face that indicated he wasn't going to put up with any of Lonnie's terror tactics today. Noah was busy scooping up burnt hamburgers, but he kept his eye on Tommy while he worked, which explained why two of the hamburgers ended up on the ground. Lonnie's friends materialized out of nowhere and stood by the table as Tommy approached.

"Shouldn't you go help my brother?" she asked, the worry there in her tone of voice.

"He can handle himself."

Lonnie had a cigarette dangling out of his mouth. Tommy said something to him, and Lonnie shook his head, then flicked the cigarette at him. Tommy stepped on it. Then as quick as a blink, he grabbed Lonnie by the scruff of his neck and jerked him off the table.

Lonnie's hand slipped into his pants pocket, and that's when Noah came running. So did a good number of the men attending the picnic. They ran to Tommy to help. The show of solidarity infuriated Lonnie, and within seconds, his face had turned purple with rage. Noah shoved his way through the men just as Lonnie pulled the switchblade out. Noah whacked him hard on the wrist with his spatula and tripped him at the same time. Howling in pain, Lonnie dropped the knife. Tommy picked it up and tossed it to Noah, then hauled Lonnie to his feet and ordered him and his friends to leave.

Laurant let out a sigh of relief. As Tommy and Noah headed back to the grill, several men stopped them to shake their hands. One enthusiastic man pounded them on their shoulders.

"Now can we eat?" Nick grabbed two plates, handed one to her, and headed for the hamburgers.

After they had filled their plates with salads and chips at the buffet table, they joined the Vandermans. The sisters were sitting with the three men who were temporarily living in the house across the street. Bessie Jean scooted closer to Viola so Laurant and Nick could sit on the bench with them.

Viola made the introductions, adding information she'd gleaned from the weary-looking workmen. Two of the men, Mark Hanover and Willie Lakeman, owned farms in northern Iowa and were supplementing their incomes with carpenter jobs. Justin Brady had just purchased his uncle's land in Nebraska and was diligently trying to pay off the mortgage as soon as possible by picking up extra work. All three men were in their early thirties and all three were wearing wedding rings. The calluses on their hands proved they were hard workers, and the empty cups lined up in front of them proved they were also hard drinkers. Nick leaned his elbows on the table and listened to the three men describing the work at the abbey, all the while sizing them up.

Mark downed a sixteen-ounce plastic cup of beer in two long gulps. Nick understood why the man was drinking so much when Bessie Jean asked him if he had any children.

Mark lowered his gaze to his cup in his hands. "My wife died last year. We didn't have any kids. We were waiting until we got some of our bills paid off."

Viola reached across the table and patted Mark's hand. "We're all terribly sorry about your loss, but you've got to get on with your life and try to look to the future. I'm sure your wife would have wanted you to."

"I know, ma'am," he replied. "With the drought, we all have to pick up work whenever we can. I've got my parents to look after, and Willie and Justin have families depending on them too."

Willie pulled out his wallet to show off his family, a redheaded wife and three carrot-topped little girls. Justin wasn't going to be outdone. He carefully removed the photo of his wife and handed it to Bessie Jean.

"Her name's Kathy," he said, pride radiating

in his voice. "She's due to have our first baby August first or thereabouts."

"Are you expecting a boy or a girl?" Laurant asked.

Justin smiled. "Kathy and I decided we didn't want to know. We want to be surprised." Glancing over his shoulder at the bandstand, he said, "Kathy loves to dance. I sure wish she could be here."

"We're all putting in fourteen-hour days," Mark said.

"It's good money, so none of us mind," Justin interjected.

"Justin, we haven't properly thanked you for helping us with our garden," Viola said. "As busy as you are, you made time to lend us a hand. I believe I'll bake you a nice chocolate cake. It's my specialty."

"That's very kind of you, ma'am, but we're putting in long hours at the abbey, and I won't be getting home until after dark. I sure do love chocolate cake though."

Viola beamed. "Well then, I'm baking you one. I'll just leave it on your doorstep or put it in your kitchen."

Mark started talking about all the work they still had to get done before the anniversary. Willie ribbed Justin, teasing him about getting the easy work in the choir loft while they had to climb up and down the scaffolding with their paint cans.

"Hey, I'm doing my part," Justin said. "The fumes from the varnish collect in that loft and make me light-headed. That's why I take more breaks than you guys."

"At least you've got your feet planted on the floor while you're working. Willie and I are hanging by our necks half the time."

"What are you doing in the loft?" Laurant asked.

"Tearing out the old, rotting wood and replacing it. There was a lot of water damage around the organ," he added. "It's tedious work, but it's going to look real nice when I'm finished."

"How do you like living at the Morrison's house?" Bessie Jean asked.

"It's okay," Mark said, shrugging. "Justin thought we all should split the chores, so we each took a room to keep clean. It makes it easier."

Nick devoured two hamburgers while he listened to the conversation. Feinberg had told him that Wesson had already ruled out these three men. He'd run a background check on all of them. They were farmers working as carpenters and racing against the clock to get renovations finished, but as far as Nick was concerned, they were still suspects. So was every other man attending the picnic. He wasn't about to rule out anyone in Holy Oaks.

One of the high school boys tapped Laurant on her shoulder and asked her to dance. She graciously accepted before Nick could come up with a reason to object. He followed them to the edge of the dance floor and stood there with his arms folded across his chest, watching.

The band was playing an old Elvis Presley song. Laurant swayed to the music while her enthusiastic dance partner gyrated wildly in a circle around her. She had to duck his elbow a couple of times because the kid's arms and legs were going every which way. Nick thought he looked like an extra in a bad karate movie, and he knew Laurant was having trouble maintaining a straight face. Other couples were giving the kid a lot of room, probably so they wouldn't get kicked.

For the next hour she was dragged onto the dance floor again and again as the band-leader called out the dedications and played the requested songs. When Laurant wasn't dancing, she helped clean up, and she was constantly being stopped by men and women, children too, to say hello. She moved through the crowd with an ease and comfort he envied.

She had told him that in Holy Oaks, people cared about one another, but now he was seeing it firsthand. He used to think it would drive him crazy if everyone knew what he was doing. Now he wasn't so sure. It might be kind of nice. He didn't know any of his neighbors in Boston. When he came home at night, he drove into the garage, went in his house, and stayed there until it was time to leave again. He had never had the time nor the inclination to interact with any of his neighbors. He didn't even know if there were any children on the block.

Laurant was dancing with Justin now and was laughing at something he'd said. The song ended and Nick spotted a man about his age heading toward Laurant. He decided she'd done enough dancing for one night. He got to her first, pulled her into his arms, and kissed her.

"What was that for?"

"Because we're in love," he reminded her. "Have you been telling people how we met?"

"Oh, yes," she answered. "I've told the story at least twenty times now."

"And did you tell them what the experts are saying about your stalker?"

She nodded against his chin, then put her head down on his shoulder and closed her eyes so that anyone watching would see her snuggling up to her lover while she danced with him.

"I've said it so many ways, I've run out of adjectives. I've called him stupid and sloppy, and I've told them the FBI's convinced he has a very low IQ, that he's to be pitied because he's so dysfunctional. You name it, Nick. I've said it."

"That's my girl."

"What about you? Have you been telling people how we met?"

"Yeah, every chance I get," he answered. "I met Christopher," he added. "I liked him."

"I haven't seen Michelle yet. Uh-oh, here comes Steve Brenner."

"You aren't gonna be dancing with him."

"I don't want to dance with him."

The song ended. As Nick and Laurant were

leaving the dance floor, they were intercepted by Brenner.

Nick sized him up with just one quick look. The man was all about control. The way he moved and the way he dressed were give-aways. The man's appearance was extremely important to him. His Ralph Lauren shirt and pants were crisply pressed, and there wasn't a hair out of place. The only concession he made to casual picnic attire was not to wear socks with his new Gucci loafers. As Nick shook his hand, he noticed Brenner was sporting a Rolex watch.

Brenner touched Laurant's shoulder sympathetically. "Laurant, I want you to know how sorry I am about that article Lorna wrote. I was embarrassed when I read that nonsense about the two of us. I have no idea where she came up with that story, and I hope it didn't cause you any distress."

"No, it didn't," she said.

He smiled. "Lorna told me that you and Nick are engaged, or was that another fabrication?"

"She got that right. Nick and I are getting married."

"Well, I'll be damned. Congratulations to both of you. You're getting a good woman," he said to Nick. Looking at Laurant again, he asked, "Have you set the wedding date?"

"Second Saturday in October," she told him.

"Where are you going to live?"

"In Holy Oaks," she said. "And I'll still be fighting you on the town square."

The smile went out of his eyes. "I expect you

will, but I think I've come up with an offer you won't want to refuse. I'd like to drop it off tomorrow after work. Are you going to be home? We could sit down and discuss it."

"No, I'm sorry, I won't be home. Nick and I are going to the rehearsal at the abbey for the wedding. And then there's dinner after," she explained. "We won't be getting home until after midnight."

Brenner nodded. "Why don't I give you a call next Monday. That should give you time to recover from Michelle's wedding."

"That would be fine."

"Getting engaged and setting a wedding date...that happened pretty quick, didn't it?"

Nick answered, "I've known Laurant a very long time, since she was a little girl."

"And when we saw each other again in Kansas City, we just...knew...didn't we, darling?" Laurant added.

Nick smiled. "Yes."

"Congratulations again," he said. "I guess I better go get a hamburger before they're all gone."

Nick kept his eye on Brenner as he walked away.

"What do you think of him?" she asked.

"He's got a lot of anger pent up inside."

"How could you tell that?"

"When he was congratulating us, his hands were fisted."

"I'm making his life miserable right now. He was probably clenching his fists to keep from wringing my neck."

"You're single-handedly blocking his plans."

"Is he a suspect?"

"Everyone is," he replied. "Come on. Let's go sit on the blanket and make out like teenagers."

The suggestion made her laugh. Several men and women turned and smiled at the happy couple.

"Sounds like a plan," she said. "But I don't think the abbot would approve."

"There you are. I've been looking everywhere for you."

Michelle came hurrying across the grass. Her fiancé, Christopher, had hold of her hand and was grinning from ear to ear.

Michelle was a beautiful woman. Petite, with delicate features, she had long golden hair that framed her heart-shaped face. She had a killer smile that demanded a response.

Laurant's friend wore a metal brace on her right leg, and when she tried to sit down at the picnic table, she winced in pain. Christopher was telling Nick a joke he'd just heard as he swept Michelle up into his arms and then sat down with her in his lap.

"I'm still limping," Michelle said to Laurant.

"But barely," she insisted.

"You think so?"

"Oh, yes. I noticed the difference."

"I shattered my knee in a car accident," she explained to Nick. "I shouldn't be able to walk at all, but I beat the odds."

"Michelle knows all about percentages,"

Christopher explained. "She has degrees in mathematics and accounting, and she's going to get her CPA after we get married."

"I'm keeping Laurant's books for her store," Michelle added.

The bandleader caught everyone's attention when he thumped on his microphone and announced that the next song would be the last for the evening.

"We've got to dance, honey," Christopher insisted.

"And so do we," Nick said. As he was pulling Laurant toward the dance floor, he said, "I like your friends."

"They like you."

The bandleader opened the piece of paper and smiled. "Ah, now folks, this here song is a slow one, and it's one of my favorites," he announced. "And so is the little girl it's dedicated to. It's for our own sweet Laurant Madden, and it's from Heartbreaker."

Nick had just taken Laurant into his arms when the bandleader made the announcement. He heard her drawn-in breath and felt her stiffen. He pulled her close, an instinctive response to danger.

He saw Noah and Tommy moving toward the bandstand. Another man separated from the crowd and came forward from the opposite direction. Nick knew at once that he was an agent. Damn, none of them knew who they were looking for, and the crowd was watching them, surrounding them, smiling because the song was for Laurant.

"Son of a bitch," he muttered.

"Nick, what do we do?" she whispered in a shaky voice.

"We dance," he said.

Laurant felt as though the world was closing in on her. She couldn't catch her breath, couldn't think. She tucked her head under Nick's chin and closed her eyes. *He wants me to know he's here, watching me. Oh God, make him leave me alone. Please God...*

"Now folks, grab your partner 'cause like I said, this is our last request. The name of the song is 'I Only Have Eyes for You.'"

CHAPTER 24

He stood in the crowd and watched, the intoxication building to a feverish pitch inside him. Laurant, his sweet Laurant. She mesmerized him. So lovely, so untouchable. For now. *Soon, my love. Soon you will be mine.*

Out of the corner of his eye he saw the mule walking toward her. He smiled then. He had snapped his fingers, and they had come. He was the spider now, and they were caught in his web.

He couldn't take his eyes off the mule. He watched him cross the grass and pull Laurant into his arms. It was all a game. Oh yes, he knew what they were doing. Trying to upset him, as though he were a simpleton.

And still he couldn't turn away. They were dancing, and he didn't like the way the mule was holding her. It was too close...too intimate. Then Nick kissed her. He felt such a burst of rage explode inside him his knees buckled and he had to sit down. It was a game, a game. They were playing with him, tormenting him. Yes, he knew what they were doing...and yet, he was livid.

How dare they torment him!

The surprises weren't over. He was blatantly staring at them now, studying them, and he could see the way Laurant was looking at the mule. He jerked back against the bench. She loved him. It was as plain as day to someone as clever and astute as he was. She couldn't hide it, not from him. Green-eyed girl had fallen in love with a mule. Lordy, lordy, what was he going to do about that?

She was ruining his good time. When the last song was announced and it was for Laurant, he'd felt flushed and dizzy. The joy and the rage were almost more than he could bear. And while he stood there in plain sight and watched his prey on the dance floor, smiling and laughing and acting like they were having a mighty fine time, he knew there must be mules rushing through the crowd searching for him. Fools, all of them. They didn't know what he looked like, or who he was, so how were they expecting to find him? Did they think he was going to pull out a gun and point it to himself? He laughed just thinking about it. Priceless, he thought. Their stupidity was truly priceless.

Then he spotted good old Father Tom, running toward his sister with another priest by his side. There was a beautiful look of terror in Tom's eyes. He savored it and sighed with pleasure. Now what in tarnation did those silly priests think they were going to do? Pray him into giving himself up?

Vengeance is mine sayeth the Lord. Was Father Tom thinking about vengeance now? The possibility amused him. Perhaps the next time he went to confession he would ask him. A priest should understand. That was his job, wasn't it? To understand and forgive? Maybe understanding would come with death. He mulled over that philosophical possibility and then shrugged. What did he care if Tommy understood or not?

My, oh my, he hadn't had this much fun in a long, long time. And it was only going to get better, as long as he kept the anger reined in, controlled it, soothed the beast with promises of the havoc to come. How dare they think they could outwit him? Ignorant mules, all of them.

Still, caution was called for now. Bide his time, that was the ticket. He certainly wasn't afraid or even worried about the mules. He had invited the FBI boys to Holy Oaks, now hadn't he? But he so wanted to be a gracious host, a regular Martha Stewart, if you will, and so he needed to know the exact number he would be entertaining. There had to be enough refreshments to go around. Did he bring enough C-4 with him? He thought about it for a minute and then smiled. Why, yes, as a matter of fact, he did.

Heartbreaker was always prepared.

His goal was to eliminate as many of the mules as he could, as long as it didn't interfere with his primary objective. The target. Get the target and have a little old-fashioned fun at the same time, while he proved to the world that he was The Superior Being. None of the FBI boys were a match for him. And soon now, very soon, when it was too late and they couldn't run and hide, they would realize it.

He would take care of his unfinished business and at the same time let the world mock them all on national television. Prime time. KABOOM. Film at eleven. Yes, sirree.

Another day passed and the pressure was mounting.

The thought of another crowded gathering was making Laurant physically ill, but she wasn't about to disappoint Michelle on one of the biggest nights of her life, her wedding rehearsal and the dinner that followed.

After the first course, Michelle noticed that Laurant hadn't touched her food. Leaning across the table, she whispered, "You don't look so good, sweetie."

"I'm fine," Laurant answered, forcing a smile.

Michelle knew better, and she turned to Nick for help. "Why don't you take Laurant home and put her to bed," she suggested.

When Laurant opened her mouth to protest, Michelle stopped her. "I don't want you getting sick. I am *not* walking down that aisle tomorrow without you."

Laurant and Nick said their early good-bye's and headed home.

A dozen red roses were waiting on the front porch when they arrived. Nick picked up the vase on his way inside the house.

"They were delivered right after you left," Joe said.

Nick read the card out loud. "Please forgive me and come home. Love, Joel."

Laurant took the vase and put it on the dining room table. Nick and Joe followed. The two men stood side by side frowning at the roses.

"It seems such a waste to throw them out," she said. "But that's what I usually do. I don't want to be reminded of Joel Patterson every time I walk through this room."

"How often does this creep send you flowers?" Nick asked, trying not to let his irritation show.

"About once a week," she said. "He won't give up."

"Yeah? We'll see about that." He picked up the vase, went into the kitchen, and emptied the water in the sink, then dropped the vase and the roses into the trash can. "He's a tenacious bastard, isn't he?"

"Patterson's the man in Chicago who was doing his secretary while he was chasing you, right?" Joe asked.

His frank assessment didn't faze her. "Yes, he's the one."

"I'd say he's having trouble letting go," Joe remarked. "But don't worry. Nick will take care of him."

"No, he won't take care of him," she countered, a bit more sharply than she'd intended. "Joel Patterson is my problem, and I'll deal with him."

"Okay," Joe said, surprised by the burst of anger. "Whatever you decide is fine with me."

"I'm ignoring him."

"That doesn't seem to be working," he pointed out.

"Let him spend his money on flowers. I don't care. Now can we please drop the subject?"

"Yes, sure."

She put her hand to her brow. "Look, I'm sorry I snapped at you. It's just...after what happened at the picnic...he was there, Joe. And he wanted me to know he was watching me. 'I Only Have Eyes for You.' That was the song he requested. Cute, huh?"

"I heard all about it," Joe said as he followed her into the kitchen. He had already guessed what she was going to do. Make tea. Joe knew the strain was getting to her. In the harsh kitchen light, she looked pale, as though she hadn't had a good night's sleep in weeks.

Joe blurted out what he was thinking. "You've got to stay strong."

She whirled around to face him, one hand defiantly on her hip. "You don't have to worry about me."

Easier said than done, Joe thought. "Why don't you go into the living room and watch a little television?"

"I'm going to make a cup of hot tea. Would you like some?"

"Sure," he said. It felt like it was 110 in the kitchen, but if she wanted to make hot tea for him, he'd drink it.

He sat down and watched her work. Nick was in the back hallway, talking on his phone, his head bent, his voice too low to make out any of the conversation. Joe figured he was either talking to Morganstern or Wesson.

Laurant took the kettle to the sink and held it under the faucet. She stared at the fleur-de-lis painted on the white tile above the splash guard while she thought about the picnic.

Nick had finished his call and came back into the kitchen in time to hear her say, "Lonnie was there at the picnic. He left early, but he could have put that piece of paper in the hat before Tommy chased him away."

Nick got a Diet Pepsi out of the fridge and popped the lid. He took a long swallow and then said, "Yeah, Lonnie could have done that, but he couldn't be in two places at once, and we know he hasn't left Holy Oaks in the last month. He was in town when the unsub talked to Tommy in the confessional."

"When did you find that out?" Laurant asked.

"I got that bit of information from Feinberg this morning."

She turned back to the sink. "So who wasn't here?" she asked.

The kettle was filled, and water was now pouring down the sides. Nick took it out of her hands, poured out half the water, and then put the kettle on the stove top.

"The sheriff was out of town," Joe told her. "And so was Steve Brenner. He told friends he was going fishing."

Laurant got out the tea bags and cups from the cupboard and put them on the table. She didn't seem to notice that Nick was drinking a Pepsi. She was still going to make him a cup of tea. He smiled while he watched her work. The quirky habit of hers was odd but sweet.

She sat down to wait for the water to heat. Restless, she picked up the deck of cards Joe had left and began to shuffle them.

"What about the crime scene Wesson was so excited about? Shouldn't we have heard something by now?"

Joe answered. "The lab's working on the evidence they've collected. I do know the scene was contaminated."

"Contaminated by what?"

"Cows," Joe said.

She couldn't block the picture Joe had just evoked and whispered, "Oh, God."

"Deal the cards," he suggested, hoping to turn her attention. "We'll play gin."

"Okay," she whispered, but she continued to sit there, shuffling the cards. Joe finally took them out of her hands and dealt them for her.

"I know it seems like a lot of time has passed, but—" Nick began.

She didn't let him finish. "They won't find his fingerprints. They won't find any evidence that could lead them to him."

Nick sat down, straddling the chair with his arms braced against the back. "Don't make him superhuman. He bleeds like the rest of us. He's going to mess up, and then we'll nail him."

She picked up her cards and looked them over. "The sooner the better, right?"

"Right."

"Okay, then why don't we make it happen sooner. I think Wesson's right. Maybe I should go running alone tomorrow, and maybe I should spend the day doing errands on my own. Don't shake your head at me. He's looking for an opportunity, and I think we should accommodate him. You could make sure I was safe."

"No." He was emphatic.

"Don't you think we should discuss this before you—"

"No."

She held her temper. "I really think—"

He cut her off. "I promised your brother I wouldn't let you out of my sight, and that's the way it's going to be."

"Hey, Nick, chill out," Joe suggested.

The burst of anger was short-lived. "Yeah, right," he agreed.

The tension was getting to both of them. Laurant knew why she was feeling so frustrated. Her every movement was being controlled by a lunatic. Yes, that was exactly what was happening, and God, how she hated it. But why was Nick losing his temper? He should be used to working under this kind of strain, shouldn't he? Up until tonight, he'd been very laid-back and as steady as a rock. How in God's name was he able to do it, day in and day out? The special unit he worked for searched for abducted children. She couldn't think of anything more terrifying than a child in danger. The pressure had to be tremendous.

"You're the expert. I'll let you decide what's

to be done. If you don't want me to run alone, then I won't," she said.

She'd done a complete turnaround in a matter of seconds, and Nick couldn't figure out why she was suddenly being reasonable again. "How come?" he asked suspiciously.

"I don't want to make your job any more difficult than it already is," she said.

"Now that you two are calm, I kind of hate to bring this up," Joe said. He discarded a card and picked up a new one. " 'Cause I know Nick's going to get upset again, but—"

"I don't get upset. What do you need to tell me?"

"If the unsub doesn't poke his head out of the woodpile within the next couple of days, I'm going to be reassigned."

The muscle in Nick's jaw flexed.

"How do you know you'll be reassigned?" Laurant asked Joe.

Nick answered. "Wesson. I'm right, aren't I?"

Joe nodded. "He thinks maybe the unsub knows I'm here, and if I make a big deal about leaving, then maybe—"

"Give me a break," Nick snapped.

"And I suppose if the unsub still doesn't try to grab her, then Wesson will reassign the other agents so the unsub will feel more comfortable? I've got an idea. Why don't we all pack up now and leave? Laurant can leave the front door open so he won't have any trouble getting inside. That's pretty much Wesson's game plan, isn't it, Joe. He'll stay in Holy Oaks though, you can bet your ass on that."

Joe pointed at the disc to remind Nick that Wesson could be listening in. Nick couldn't have cared less. He wanted him to know what he thought of his methods.

Nick unpinned the disc and held it up so he could speak directly into the microphone. "You want to be the big man to catch the unsub, don't you, Jules? At any cost. That's the plan, isn't it? It'll look great on your record, and your political ambitions are far more important than Laurant's safety."

Feinberg's voice responded. "Sorry to disappoint you, Nick, but I'm monitoring the line, not Wesson, and as far as I'm concerned, you guys are talking about the weather."

The agent was doing his best to protect Nick, but the effort wasn't appreciated. Wesson couldn't hurt Nick professionally, and even if he could, Nick wouldn't have cared. How would he feel if he got fired? Maybe relieved, he thought. Bad attitude, he decided, but he couldn't make himself care about that either.

Morganstern was right. Nick needed a vacation, and he needed sex. Lots of sex, but not with just any woman. He wanted Laurant.

"Gin." Laurant smiled at Joe when she showed him her cards. He groaned.

The kettle began to hiss. Laurant got up to fix the tea. She poured water into all three cups, then put the kettle back on the stove and turned to walk out of the kitchen.

"Hey, what about your tea?" Joe asked.

"I'm going upstairs now. I think I'd like to take a hot bubble bath."

Nick gritted his teeth. Now, why in the hell did she think they needed to know that? Damn. His mind went wild, and all he could think about was her lush body covered in a mist of bubbles. He wanted to follow her and dive into the tub with her. He headed to the guest room instead and took a cold shower.

Joe was watching a movie downstairs, so Nick, dressed in his jeans and his favorite old T-shirt, went into Laurant's room to watch *Sports Roundup*.

Theo called to check in. It was late in Boston, but his brother never slept. He was in the mood to talk about the latest bizarre case he was prosecuting. Nick tried to pay attention, but his eyes were locked on that bathroom door, and x-rated images kept flashing through his mind.

"What'd you say?" he asked Theo.

"Is everything okay with you?"

Hell, no. "Sure," he answered. "You know how it goes. It's the waiting that makes me nuts."

"How come you haven't mentioned Laurant? I haven't seen her in years. I'll bet she's changed. What's she like?"

"She's Tommy's sister. That's what she's like." Big mistake, Nick realized as soon as the words were out of his mouth. He'd sounded defensive, and Theo's reputation for being a top-rate prosecutor wasn't just talk. He immediately went for the jugular.

"So that's how it is."

"I don't know what you're talking about."

"Uh-huh."

"Nothing's going on."

"Does Tommy know?"

"Know what?" he hedged.

"That you've got the hots for his sister."

Before Nick could answer, Theo laughed. "You're going to have to tell him."

Nick pictured his hand going through the phone and grabbing his brother by the throat. "Theo, if you know what's good for you, you'll stop fishing. There's nothing to tell. Laurant's fine. Just fine. Okay?"

"Okay," he agreed. "Tell me something."

"What?"

"Does she still have those long legs?"

"Theo?"

"Yeah?"

"Go to hell."

He came in through the back door.

He'd tried using the key he had duplicated, but the bitch had obviously changed the locks. Now why had she done that, he wondered. Had she found the camera? He stood on the back stoop nervously flipping the key over and over in his hand while he pondered the possibility and finally decided no, she couldn't have found it. It was too well hidden. Then he remembered how old and rusty the lock was, and he assumed that it had simply broken.

Fortunately, he had worn his black windbreaker, and he could use it to protect his hand and break the glass. He'd put on the jacket so that he could blend into the night and wouldn't be seen by the two, dried-up old hags living next door to Laurant. They were like cats sitting in their windows looking out. He'd parked the car three blocks away, another precaution against her nosy neighbors, and walked over to her house, making sure he stayed away from the streetlights and close to the bushes.

Twice he felt like someone was following him, and he got so spooked he considered turning around and going back home, but the rage inside of him kept propelling him forward. The need to strike out was eating at him like acid, forcing him to take the calculated risk. He craved hurting her the way an alcoholic craved a drink of whiskey. The need wouldn't leave him alone, and he knew he would take any risk to get even.

He slowly removed his jacket, carefully folded it to double thickness, wrapped his hand inside the material, and then, imagining the glass was Laurant's face, he slammed his fist through the window, exerting far more force than was necessary. The glass imploded, shattering fragments into the back hallway.

The rush of adrenaline felt like an orgasm, and he almost shouted God's name in vain just for the sheer thrill of it. He suddenly felt powerful and invincible. No one would touch him. No one.

He certainly wasn't concerned about being heard, for he was sure the house was empty. Nick and Laurant had been picked up by her brother and another priest and had gone to the rehearsal dinner. He'd watched them leave before he'd gone back home to wait and then get ready. It was just after eleven now, and they wouldn't be back until well after midnight. Plenty of time, he thought, to do what he wanted and get out.

He reached in, unlocked the dead bolt, opened the door, and came inside. He had to resist the urge to whistle.

The silent alarm began to flash the second

the door opened, but Nick already knew someone was inside the house. He and Laurant had returned home earlier than expected, and he had taken the watch while Joe caught up on his sleep. Nick was upstairs on the landing and had just started down the steps when he heard the sound of glass breaking. The noise was distant but unmistakable.

He didn't hesitate. Drawing his gun, he flipped the safety off and headed for the guest room to alert Joe. He was reaching for the doorknob when the door opened and Joe stepped out, his Glock already in his hand, the barrel pointed to the ceiling. He nodded to Nick to let him know he was ready, then faded back into the darkness of the room, leaving the door wide open. Nick pointed to the flashing alarm, and Joe quickly unplugged it.

Without making a sound, Nick turned and hurried into Laurant's room. He quietly closed the door behind him. She was sound asleep on her back, her hands at her sides, an open Frank McCourt memoir resting on her chest. He went to the side of the bed, squatted down next to her, and put his hand over her mouth so she wouldn't make any noise when she woke up.

"Laurant, wake up. We've got company." His hushed voice was calm.

She woke up trying to scream. Her eyes flew open, and she tried to focus as she instinctively shoved his hand away. Then she realized it was Nick touching her. His words registered at the same time that she saw the gun.

"I need you to be real quiet," he whispered.

She nodded. She understood. Nick pulled his hand back and she pushed the sheets aside as she bolted upright. The forgotten book went flying and would have struck the hardwood floor had Nick not grabbed it in midair. He put it down on the bed, reached up to switch off the reading lamp, then took her hand and gently pulled her to her feet.

Her heart was pounding frantically, and she had trouble catching her breath. The room was so dark they had to feel their way along the wall. Nick led her into the bathroom, and she was reaching for the light switch when his hand covered hers.

"No lights," he whispered.

He stepped back into the bedroom and quietly pulled the door closed behind him.

"Be careful," she whispered.

She wanted to beg him to stay with her, but she knew he wouldn't and couldn't do that.

It was pitch black inside, and she was afraid to move for fear she would accidentally knock something over and let the intruder know the household was awake. Head bowed, she folded her arms across her stomach and stood frozen while her mind raced. How could she help? What could she do that wouldn't be a hindrance?

She was terrified for Nick. The unexpected could trip up even the most experienced man. Everyone had a vulnerable point, and Nick was no exception. If anything happened to him, she didn't know what she would do. Please God, keep him safe.

It was deadly quiet. She pressed her ear against the door and strained to hear any little sound. She stood that way for over a minute—it seemed like an eternity to her—and still nothing but the sound of her heart pounding in her ears.

Then she heard it. A scratching noise, like a branch scraping across a window, but the sound wasn't coming from inside the house. It was above her. The roof. My God, was the intruder on the roof? No, no, he was already inside downstairs. She tried then to convince herself that the noise she had just heard had simply been a branch swaying in the wind.

She strained to listen. She heard the sound again. It was closer now to where she stood, and it didn't sound like a scraping noise at all this time. Now it sounded like an animal, a raccoon or a squirrel, she thought, scurrying across the roof ledge outside the bathroom window.

Was the window locked? Yes, of course it was. Nick would have seen to that. Calm down. Don't let your imagination run wild.

She stared at the window. It was above the bathtub, but it was too dark to see if the lock was latched. She needed to check it. If she moved slowly and carefully, she wouldn't make any noise. She was beginning to inch away from the door when she saw a red, pencil-point beam of light shine through the windowpane.

It danced across the vanity mirror, closing in on her. Searching...looking for a target.

She dropped to her knees, then to her stomach, and edged over to the bathtub. She pressed the length of her body against the cool porcelain, her eyes glued to the red beam. Too late, she realized she should have gotten out of the bathroom when she had had the chance. The beam would catch her if she moved now. It was bouncing along the door, back and forth, back and forth. My God, if Nick opened the door and tried to come inside, whoever was on the ledge would have him clearly in his sights.

Calm down. Think. How could he have gotten on the roof without being seen? Nick had told her that there were agents watching the house night and day, but there was a treed lot next to her bedroom and bath, and another empty lot behind her backyard. It would be easy to climb up one of the hundred-year-old trees and make his way from the treetops to her roof. Easy, she thought.

But without being seen? It would be daring, tricky, but it could be done. Don't panic. Wait. Maybe it was one of the FBI agents on the roof. Yes, that could be it. He could be covering the bathroom window to make certain the madman didn't try to escape. All the windows were probably being covered by the FBI now.

As desperate as she was to believe that was true, she wasn't about to stand up to test her theory.

The beam was moving again, back to the mirror. Laurant seized the opportunity, thanking God there wasn't a moon tonight. The darkness was a blessing. She scrambled to her knees to get the door open, then crawled into the bedroom, scraping her knee on the metal threshold.

She never took her eyes off the beam. She could see it closing in on her as she swung the door shut. Grimacing over the faint click the lock made, she leaned back against the wall and tried to catch her breath.

She would be able to hear the window opening. It was old and warped, and it would make a lot of noise if it were pried up. And so she sat there listening, waiting, every muscle in her body tense in anticipation, ready to spring.

Nick heard the faint rustle as she crawled out of the bathroom. What the hell was she doing? Why hadn't she stayed inside?

He stood, pressed against the wall adjacent to the bedroom door and quietly pulled it open a crack. He could see out into the hallway that was faintly lit by the night-light on the chest at the far end of the wide landing. He waited for the intruder to either pass Laurant's door or come inside.

He could hear him creeping up the steps. He knew when his foot struck the fifth stair. It creaked. If he'd been inside the house the number of times Nick thought he had, he would have remembered the noise the step made and avoided it. Was Nick giving him too much credit? No, he didn't think so. This man was careful. He was a planner, every bit of information they had on him indicated as much. And he was organized. Methodical too. Yet, he hadn't been quiet when he'd broken into the house, and his method had been crude, not sophisticated. A tiger doesn't change his stripes. There were instances where an organized killer became disorganized, like Bundy and Donner, but it took time for them to disintegrate, get sloppy. This unsub was exhibiting a radical change.

The back door opened and then slammed shut. Whoever was coming up the stairs went running back down. Nick heard quick footsteps on the first floor, then harsh whispers. There were two of them in the house now. What the hell? That didn't make any sense at all. Everything they knew about the unsub pointed to a loner.

Until now. No, this was all wrong. The two intruders were arguing, but their voices were muffled whispers, and Nick couldn't catch any of what they were saying. They were by the front door, but only one of them rushed up the stairs. Nick could hear the other one moving around below. Then a crash, maybe a vase, Nick thought, followed by a shredding noise, like material being ripped apart. The son of a bitch was either looking for something or trashing Laurant's house.

The adrenaline was pouring through his veins now, and he couldn't wait to get his hands on both of them.

The other intruder was on the landing now. He had a penlight. First the beam, then the shadow crossed the threshold of Laurant's bedroom. He continued on to the hall linen closet. He was going for the camera, Nick decided. He was either going to remove it or turn it back on.

Joe flipped on the hall light as Nick swiftly moved into the hall to block any retreat.

"Freeze," Joe ordered, his gun trained on the suspect.

Steve Brenner yanked his hand back from the closet ceiling and shielded his eyes from the blinding light. "What the...," he shouted as he turned and tried to charge past Nick.

Nick clipped him on the side of his head with the butt of his gun. Stunned by the blow, Brenner reeled back, then attacked, his fists flailing like a drowning man. Nick easily dodged the assault, then threw an uppercut to his nose and heard the crunch of bone. Blood spurted as Brenner, screaming in pain, staggered back and went down on his knees. Both his hands cupped his nose as he began to shout obscenities.

"You got him?" Nick shouted as he turned and raced toward the stairs.

"I'm on him," Joe yelled back. He shoved Brenner to the floor on his stomach, then held him there with his knees pressed into his spine. "You have the right to remain silent..."

Nick took the flight of stairs in two leaps. He swung over the banister, dropped to the floor in the front hallway, and raced on. The caustic smell of gasoline was heavy in the air, and by the time he was halfway across the living room, his eyes were tearing. He saw the gallon can of gasoline on the floor near the dining room table and Laurant's pink bridesmaid dress in a heap next to the overturned can. The gown had been shredded into a wad and was soaked. Nick muttered an expletive as he ran on.

He caught a fleeting glimpse of Lonnie's profile as he turned the corner into the kitchen. He didn't see the matches though.

Lonnie struck one match in the back hallway, then lit the rest and threw the flaming pack behind him into the kitchen. Frantic to get away before he was caught, he clawed at the doorknob, but his hands were sticky with gasoline. On the third try he got the door open. He ran outside, tripped on the back step, and went flying into the yard. Scrambling to his feet he ran into the back lot, hooting with laughter because he knew he'd trapped Nick inside, and he had gotten away scot-free.

The floor was slick with gasoline, and the fire was instantaneous as the match flames ignited the fuel with a loud, greedy swoosh. The breeze coming in through the open back door whipped the fiery wall into a frenzy, and within bare seconds, the kitchen was a raging inferno. Nick stumbled back into the dining room. He tried to shield his eyes with the back of his arm as he regained his balance, but the heat was so intense he couldn't go forward. The fire was loud, almost deafening. Popping, crackling, hissing. The kitchen floor had turned into liquid fire, moving like a ferocious wave toward the dining room, drowning everything in its path.

"Laurant!" Nick shouted her name as he raced back through the living room. He thought he heard the squeal of tires out front and he stopped at the front door long enough to unlock the dead bolt, but he didn't open the door because he knew the fresh air would only feed the fire.

Joe had handcuffed Brenner and was trying to get him to his feet, but his prisoner was fighting him every inch of the way.

"Get him out through the front door, but hurry. The fire's out of control."

"That son of a bitch," Brenner screamed. "That miserable little piece of shit. I'm going to kill him."

Joe pulled Brenner to his feet and shoved him ahead of him down the stairs.

Nick burst into Laurant's room. She had already put on jeans and loafers and was pulling a T-shirt down over her midriff.

She'd packed too. He couldn't believe it. The empty overnight bag she'd left on the floor by the closet door was now on her bed and stuffed full. The bathroom door was wide open, and he could see that the counter had been swept clean.

"Let's go." He had to shout to be heard over Brenner's screams. "Leave it," he ordered when he saw her reach for the bag. "We've got to get out of here. Now."

Ignoring his order, she grabbed the bag and slung the strap over her left shoulder. Then she noticed he was barefoot. She grabbed his loafers and shoved them in the bag on top of the photo album.

Nick flipped the safety on his gun and slipped it into his holster. That gave her two more seconds to grab his wallet, the car keys, and her purse from the top of the dresser. She was shoving them into the side pocket of the bag when Nick grabbed her. He pulled her tight into his side and half carried her along the hallway and down the stairs. She had a death grip on the strap, and she could hear the bag banging on the steps behind her.

Black smoke rolled up the stairs to meet them. Nick shoved her head down against his chest and continued on.

She heard an unearthly sound behind her, like a dragon wheezing, and then a crackling roar followed. The air conditioner in the dining room window crashed to the floor and exploded. The force was so great the walls shook, and the hardwood shivered beneath her feet. The living room window shattered then, and shards of glass the size of butcher knives shot out onto the porch. The fire hissed and then roared again as it fed on the gust of wind that rushed inside the open doorway.

They made it outside just in the nick of time. Another few seconds and they would have had to climb out one of the bedroom windows. The fire chased them outside, the flames licking at their heels. They stumbled down the steps and onto the front walk, coughing from the inhaled smoke.

She squeezed her eyes shut to try to get rid of the stinging. Nick recovered much quicker than she did. He spotted Wesson leaping out of his car and running toward Joe and Brenner. The agent and his prisoner were standing in the empty lot beside Laurant's house. Feinberg was still in the car, the motor running.

How had the agents gotten here so soon, Nick wondered. First things first, he thought. He squeezed Laurant. "Are you okay?" he asked, his voice hoarse from coughing.

She leaned into him, thankful for his strength. "Yes," she answered. "Are you all right?"

"Good to go," he said.

She looked around her in a daze. The entire neighborhood was waking up. Families up and down the street began to spill out of their houses onto their front porches and lawns to watch the fire. She could hear the sirens wailing in the distance. She saw Bessie Jean and Viola standing by the big old oak in their front yard where they had kept Daddy chained. Both ladies were dressed in heavy, fuzzy robes, one pink, the other white, that made them look like giant bunny rabbits. Bessie Jean, her hair in pin curls, was wearing an old-fashioned hairnet, the knot she'd tied in the netting hanging down on her forehead. Viola was dabbing at her eyes with her lacy hand-kerchief and shaking her head as she watched the fire.

Laurant turned back and saw the flames shooting through the roof over her living room. It had been a near miss, she realized then. But Nick was all right, and so was she, without a blister between them.

She watched the fire and thanked God no one had been hurt. Suddenly, the fog lifted and the truth settled. She began to shake.

"Laurant, what's the matter?"

"You got him. It's over Nick. The nightmare's over."

She dropped her bag and threw her arms around him. He held her close. Then he heard her whisper, "Thank you."

"We aren't going to celebrate just yet. Let's take this a step at a time."

She looked up at him. "I still can't believe it. When I heard him shouting at you in the hallway, I recognized his voice and I knew it was Steve, but I just couldn't put it together in my mind. I was so shocked." She took a deep breath and tried to be more coherent. "You told me he was a suspect, and you were right all along."

She couldn't stop trembling. Impatiently wiping the tears away with the back of her hands, she remembered the man on the roof. "There were two of them," she said. "Yes, two," she repeated.

"The other man was Lonnie. He started the fire."

"Lonnie?" She didn't know why she was stunned to know the sheriff's son had been involved. Brenner had obviously been the brains. He had been the one to plan the nightmare from start to finish.

Nick was looking around for Lonnie. Where the hell was he? He should have been cuffed by now with at least one agent on him.

Willie and Justin came running across the street to help. Justin immediately went to Bessie Jean's yard to turn on her garden hose to try to contain the fire. It was pitifully inadequate.

Nick pulled Laurant toward Wesson. The agent was talking on his phone.

"I got him, sir. I certainly did, and as soon as I get the warrant, I'm positive I'm going to find more evidence to nail him."

"*I* got him?" She repeated Wesson's boast to Nick.

"Yeah, I heard what he said."

Joe had obviously also heard. He was glaring at Wesson, letting him see his hostility. The agent in charge ignored him and continued to speak into his slick, palm-size phone. Wesson could barely contain his enthusiasm.

"By the book, sir. That's how I got him. And for the record, instinct didn't have anything to do with the apprehension. It was careful planning and following through. No, sir, that wasn't a criticism of your methods. I'm simply telling you that it was hard work and not anything else."

The fire truck barreled down the street, the siren blaring. Feinberg moved his car out of the way of the fire hydrant and parked it in front of Bessie Jean's house, then got out and ran over to Joe. Like everyone else, he watched the blaze.

Volunteer firemen wearing yellow slickers and hats jumped from the truck and raced to hook up the hoses. The driver turned off the siren and then shouted, "Is everyone out of the house?"

"Everyone's out," Joe shouted back.

Nick was seething inside. He swore that if Wesson didn't get off the damn phone in the next five seconds, he was going to rip it out of his hand and beat the hell out of him if that was what it would take to get some answers. Where was Lonnie? And where were the agents who were supposed to be watching the house?

"Laurant, I want you to get in the car and stay there. I'll move it onto the street," he said as he grabbed her hand and pulled her along.

She could hear the anger radiating in his voice. He was still acting as though he was supposed to protect her and she couldn't understand why. They had caught Brenner, and they knew who his accomplice was.

"Nick, it's over." Maybe it hadn't sunk in yet. Yes, that was it, she thought. "You did it. You and Joe got him."

"We'll talk about it later," he said curtly as he reached down and picked up the bag.

When they reached the car, he muttered, "Ah, hell, the keys."

"I've got them."

He held the bag while she dug until she found them. Her hands were shaking so much she couldn't get the key in the lock.

Nick took the keys from her, unlocked the car door, and tossed the bag into the backseat.

"Hey, Laurant, how come that guy's handcuffed?" Willie asked.

Justin jogged over from the Vandermans' yard. He too was curious to hear the details.

"Isn't that Steve Brenner?" Justin asked. "He's a big shot in town."

"But how come he's cuffed? What'd he do?"

"He broke into my house."

"Get inside the car, Laurant," Nick said. He took hold of her elbow to get her moving, but she turned back when Brenner started screaming.

"Take these handcuffs off me. You can't hold me. I haven't done anything illegal. I own that house, and if I want to put a camera inside, you can't stop me. I signed the papers two weeks ago. It's my house, and I've got the right to know what goes on in there."

Joe had used up all his patience. "What you've got is the right to remain silent. Now shut the hell up."

Justin's mouth dropped open. "He put a camera in your house?"

"Where'd he put it?" Willie asked.

She didn't answer. She sagged against Nick's side. Her eyes were fixed on Brenner. He turned, saw her watching him, and sneered. There was dried blood caked on his perfectly capped teeth and more smeared on his lips. He was a reptile.

Brenner couldn't control his fury. He blamed

everyone but himself for getting caught. If the bitch hadn't brought the FBI boyfriend home, he wouldn't be in this predicament. Most of all he blamed Laurant. Joe grabbed him when he lunged toward her. Brenner tried to shove himself free while he shouted profanities at her. All his plans were ruined. Damn her.

"You bitch," he shouted. "This is my house now. I paid that old lady a lot of money and you know what? There isn't a damned thing you can do about it. When I'm finished suing everybody, I'm going to own the FBI. I have rights," he added in a roar. And then, hoping to humiliate her, he added, "I've been watching you undress almost every night. I've seen everything you've got to offer."

She saw the evil radiating like hot coals in his eyes, and she didn't have any doubt at all that he had killed those women. Brenner was clearly demented.

"Joe, put a gag in his mouth," Nick shouted.

"Get her away from here," Wesson ordered.

The profanities Brenner hurled at her didn't shake her as Nick led her back to the car. Some of the women in the crowd weren't so indifferent, however. One mother cupped her hands over her son's ears. Her neighbors might be shocked by Brenner's conduct now, but when they learned the truth about the Dr. Jekyll and Mr. Hyde living in their midst, they were going to be sickened.

Nick got her inside the car, then backed into the street and parked it behind Feinberg's vehicle.

"Listen to me. I want you to stay in the car with the windows up and the doors locked." He flipped on the air conditioner so she wouldn't swelter.

"I want to get out of here. Could we please leave now?"

She sounded close to tears. "In just a minute," he promised. "Okay? I've got to talk to Wesson."

She woodenly nodded. "Yes, all right."

She watched him sprint across the yard, then she turned to look at the house. The fire seemed to have been contained, and she thought it was odd that she didn't feel much emotion at all while she surveyed the destruction. It had been her home, but now that Brenner owned it, she never wanted to go inside again.

The flashing lights, the noise of the crowd, Brenner's screams—it was all too much. She put her hand to her forehead and slumped down in her seat. And then she began to cry for the two women Brenner had murdered.

They could rest in peace now. The monster couldn't hurt anyone else.

The sheriff was the last to arrive at the scene. His Ford Explorer rounded the corner on two wheels. Swerving to avoid hitting Little Lorna, the car skidded to a stop.

Lloyd left his SUV in the middle of the street. Grunting as he eased his bulk out from under the steering wheel, he got out of the car and stood there with his hands on his hips, surveying the crowd. He tried to look important. Frowning so that anyone who might be watching him would know he considered this situation a serious matter, he hiked his pants up with his belt, straightened his shoulders, and strutted into Laurant's front yard.

"What's going on here?" he shouted.

"What do you think is going on?" Joe asked. "The house is on fire."

Lloyd scowled at Joe to let him know he didn't appreciate his sarcasm. Then he noticed Brenner's hands were behind his back and there was blood all over his face. Leaning to the side, he saw the handcuffs.

"Hey, now, what's Steve wearing those cuffs for?"

"Breaking the law," Joe replied.

"Bullshit," Brenner ranted. "Lloyd, I didn't do anything illegal. Make them take these damn cuffs off me. They're chafing my wrists."

"In due course," Lloyd assured him. Then his eagle-eyed gaze homed in on Joe, and he took a threatening step toward him. "Aren't you that fella who was fixing Lauren's sink? What are you doing here? Did you strike this citizen? His nose looks to be broken. Now I'm asking you straight out, boy, and I want a straight answer. Did you hit him?"

"I hit him," Nick said. "I should have shot him."

"Don't you be a smart mouth, boy. This here is a serious matter."

"Yes, it is," Nick agreed. "And if you call me boy one more time, I'm going to handcuff you. Got that, Lloyd?"

Lloyd nervously took a step back to put some distance between him and Nick, and acted like he was contemplating the situation. In reality, the sheriff was getting the feeling that he was in over his head, but he knew that Brenner would kill him if he didn't get him out of this mess. He warily looked up at Nick. The FBI agent reminded him of a mountain lion, relaxed one second, and sinking his teeth into his prey the next.

"Lloyd, do something," Brenner demanded. "He broke my nose. I want him arrested."

Lloyd nodded and forced himself to look Nick in the eyes. The frost there gave him a chill. He was proud of himself for resisting the urge to look away. "That's battery, hitting a

404

citizen," he said. "You don't think I can arrest an FBI agent?"

Nick's answer was immediate. "No, I don't think you can."

"Shit," Brenner muttered.

"We'll just see about that," Lloyd blustered. "Steve's got to get to the hospital and get that nose fixed, and I'm going to take him there. I'm in charge, 'cause this here is my jurisdiction."

Joe looked at Nick before answering. "This here is my prisoner, and you aren't touching him."

Nick moved to stand beside Joe, a show of unity against the sheriff, but also he wanted to be able to keep his eye on Laurant.

"Say now, what are you wearing a gun for?" Lloyd asked Joe, seeing for the first time the weapon and holster attached to his belt. "You got yourself a permit for that thing?"

Joe smiled. "I sure do. I've got a badge too. Want to see it? I'll bet it's bigger than yours."

"You being a smart-ass, boy?"

"He's FBI," Nick said.

Lloyd was losing ground fast and needed to find at least one area over which he could take control.

"Are you responsible for this here fire?" he asked Nick.

Nick didn't think the question merited an answer. He shoved his hands in his pockets to keep himself from grabbing the sheriff by the neck.

Lorna was standing about five feet away from the two men, taking furious notes on a Big Chief tablet. She took a tentative step toward Nick, saw the look in his eyes, and backed away.

Joe motioned for Wesson to join them.

"What do you think you're going to arrest Steve for?" the sheriff demanded. "Burning down his own house?"

"He's already been arrested," Joe informed him.

"On what charges?" Lloyd asked.

"Is there a problem here?" Wesson called out as he came running over.

"Who the hell are you?" Lloyd asked.

"Senior officer in charge," Wesson responded.

Joe grinned. "He's FBI too."

"How many of you fellas are there in Holy Oaks? And what are you doing here anyway? This is my town," he stressed. "And you all should have come directly to me if you knew about a problem here."

A heated exchange followed. Lloyd kept insisting that he was taking Brenner with him, but there was no way that Wesson was going to let that happen. He also wasn't going to tell the sheriff what the charges were, despite Lloyd's protests that Wesson's secrecy was plain unconstitutional.

"It's an ongoing investigation."

"Investigation of what?"

Nick was seething, but his anger was fully directed on Wesson. He wasn't going to wait much longer to get some answers, and if that meant having an argument in a public forum, then that's the way it was going to go down.

"Can you believe this?" Joe whispered. "The two of them are in a pissing contest."

"Yeah, well, they can figure out who's the bigger man later. Hey, Sheriff, where's your son?"

The question distracted Lloyd. "Why do you want to know?"

"I'm going to arrest him."

Lloyd's bushy eyebrows shot up. "The hell you are. My boy hasn't done anything wrong." Making a wide sweep with his arm he added, "You can see for yourself, he ain't even here."

"He was here."

"Bullshit." Lloyd dragged the word out. "I'm saying he wasn't here, and I'm not gonna let you pin this on my boy. He was home with me all evening. We watched wrestling together on the television."

"I saw him," Nick said.

"You couldn't have seen him 'cause, like I just told you, he was home all evening with me."

Nick addressed Wesson. "I want a word in private with you. Now."

He saw Lorna start toward them and turned around and walked toward the empty lot, away from prying ears. Wesson looked perturbed but followed Nick.

"What is it?"

Anger punctuated Nick's words. "Where the hell were the agents you told me you assigned to watch the house? If they were here, then how come Lonnie got past them? The kid went out the back door."

Wesson's lips formed a thin line of disapproval. He didn't like anyone questioning his decisions.

"They left yesterday."

"They what?"

"They were given new assignments."

The muscle in Nick's jaw clenched. "Who gave the order?"

"I did. Feinberg and Farley were sufficient backup. I felt that was all the manpower I needed."

"And you didn't think it was necessary to inform Noah or me?"

"No, I didn't," Wesson answered very matter-of-factly. "You volunteered to be Laurant's bodyguard, and you're the one who brought in Noah to guard her brother. Frankly, if you hadn't gotten Morganstern's approval, you wouldn't even be on this case. I certainly wouldn't have approved it. You're too personally involved, but because you're one of Morganstern's golden boys, he bent the rules and let you in. I don't bend the rules," he added. "And I don't want or need your input. Have I made myself clear?"

"You really are a son of a bitch. You know that, Wesson?"

"Your insubordination is definitely going to be reported, agent."

The threat didn't faze Nick. "Be sure to spell it right."

"You're off the case."

Nick exploded. "You put Laurant in jeopardy by trying to make this a one-man show. That's what's going in *my* report."

Wesson was determined not to let Nick know how furious he was. "I did no such thing," he said coolly. "When you have had time to calm down, you'll realize that I didn't need a dozen agents running around town, sticking out like sore thumbs. It's the bottom line that counts. I got the unsub and that's all the boss is going to care about."

"You don't have enough evidence to prove Brenner's the unsub."

"Yes, I do," he insisted. "Look at the facts. Not everything has to be as complicated as you think it should be. Brenner was out of town and cannot account for his whereabouts. He had plenty of time to get to Kansas City, threaten the priest, and get back to Holy Oaks. He was careful about filing off the serial number on the camera, but he admitted he placed it in her house, and the only reason he went there tonight was because he thought you and Laurant were at the party. He's been careful, but he made a mistake. They all do," he added sagely. "We also know from witnesses that he was obsessed with Laurant and that he had plans to marry her. We can make a strong case that he snapped when she spurned him."

"What witnesses?" Nick asked.

"Several people in town I've already gotten statements from. Brenner's always been the primary suspect. You knew that. One of my agents is on his way back from the judge now with a warrant, and when he gets here, I'm personally going to go through Brenner's house. I'm sure I'm going to find more evidence to convict him. By the book," he added smugly.

"It's too pat, Wesson."

"I disagree," he countered. "It was solid investigative work that nailed Brenner."

"You're letting your ego cloud your judgment," he said. "Don't you think it's odd that he decided to bring another man in?"

"You're referring to Lonnie, and the answer is no, I don't think it's odd or out of character. Brenner simply took advantage of an opportunity. He probably figured he could pin the crime on the kid."

"What are you going to do about Lonnie?"

"I'll let the local authorities take care of him."

Nick gritted his teeth. "The local authority happens to be his father."

Wesson didn't want to be bothered with that detail. Tying up all the loose ends was a job for the underlings. "If everything goes according to schedule, Feinberg and I will be pulling out of here by tomorrow night at the latest. Farley's leaving now," he added. "And I really don't see any reason for you or Noah to hang around. I meant it when I said you were off the case."

Without a word or a backward glance, Nick walked away from the complacent bastard. Wesson was in his glory, and Nick knew he wasn't going to listen to anything he had to say. Brenner was the unsub. Case closed.

When Nick got into the car, Laurant took

one look as his face and asked, "What happened?"

"I'm officially off the case. Not that I was ever really on it," he added derisively. "Wesson's convinced that Brenner's our guy. He's waiting for a warrant so he can go through his house."

"But that's good, isn't it?"

He didn't answer her. Wesson was waving at him, trying to get his attention, but Nick ignored him and started the car.

"Nick, talk to me."

"This is all wrong."

"You don't think it's Brenner."

"No, I don't. I don't have any concrete reasons, but my gut's telling me he isn't the unsub. It's too easy. Maybe Wesson's right. Maybe I'm trying to make this more complicated than it really is. He's kept Noah and me in the dark, so I don't know what evidence they've got that convinces them. Hell, let's get out of here. I've got to get some distance so I can think."

"The Vandermans offered us their extra bedroom, and Willie and Justin also offered us beds. I told them we were going to sleep at the abbey."

Nick pulled out into the street. "Do you want to go there?"

"No."

"Okay. Then let's get the hell out of Dodge."

They headed north into lake country. As soon as they left town, Nick called Noah to tell him what had happened. He suggested that he wait until the morning to tell Tommy.

"Be sure to stress that Laurant is okay," he said.

As soon as he disconnected the call, Laurant asked, "What about the house? I saw you talking to the fire chief. Is everything gone?"

"No," Nick answered. "The south side of the house is trashed, but the upstairs on the north side is still intact."

"Do you think the closets are okay?"

"You worried about your clothes?"

"I had some of my paintings stored in the guest closet. It's okay," she hurried to add. "They aren't very good."

"How do you know they aren't good? Have you ever let anyone see them?"

"I've told you, painting is just a hobby," she answered.

She sounded so defensive, he decided to drop the subject. Their clothes smelled like smoke, and so he rolled his window down and let the breeze clear the air.

He stayed on the main two-lane highway for over an hour. Finding lodging wasn't a problem. There were billboards crowded together near every crossroad advertising seasonal rates. He finally turned onto a tributary leading to the west and chose a strip motel located two miles from Lake Henry. The garish purple and orange neon sign was still flashing vacancy, but the office was dark. Nick woke the manager, paid for the room in cash, and to the old man's delight, purchased two extra-large, red T-shirts sporting a white wide-mouth bass on the front and the name of the motel in bold white block letters on the back.

There were twelve units and twelve vacancies. Nick chose the end unit and parked the car behind the motel so that it wouldn't be seen from the road.

The room was sparse but clean. The floor was gray and white linoleum squares; the walls were cement blocks painted gray, and there were two double beds against the far wall with a wobbly, three-legged nightstand in between. The shade on the chipped ceramic lamp was torn and had been patched with duct tape.

It was well after two in the morning, and both of them were exhausted. Laurant dumped the contents of the overnight bag on the bed and then gathered up their toiletries and put them on the shelf in the bathroom. She took her shower first, and when she was finished, she washed out her lacy underwear and hung the bra and panties on a plastic hanger to dry. She

413

didn't know what to do about her jeans and T-shirt. If she tried to use the bar of soap to wash them it would take forever, and she knew they wouldn't be dry by morning. She was going to have to wear them again, but maybe they could find a Wal-Mart or Target on their way back to Holy Oaks, and she could buy clean clothing and change. There certainly weren't any department stores this far north.

She put the concern aside and dried her hair with the blow dryer the owner had chained to the wall next to the mirror.

When she came out of the bathroom wearing the new T-shirt with the giant bass covering her chest, Nick smiled, the first bit of emotion he'd shown since they'd left town.

"You look good, babe."

She tugged the T-shirt down to her knees. "I look ridiculous."

He grinned again. "That too," he admitted as he headed for the bathroom. "I can't believe you got the charger for my phone. I'm damn glad you did though."

"It was on the nightstand next to my glasses. I just grabbed everything I could get my hands on. I'll tell you, it was scary going back into that bathroom, and I just threw things in the bag."

She pulled the covers back and got into one of the double beds. Nick left the bathroom door open while he showered. The clear plastic shower curtain didn't conceal much, but she tried not to stare. She only put on her glasses so she could write a shopping list. Of course, glancing into the bathroom every now and then was just natural curiosity on her part, that was all. Liar, liar. If she'd been wearing any pants, they'd be on fire now.

Nick was built like a Greek god. He was turned away from her, so she could only see his backside. The muscles in his upper arms and thighs were incredibly well defined. She thought his body was just about perfect.

When she realized her behavior bordered on that of a voyeur—and how disgusting was that—she took her glasses off so she couldn't see anything if the temptation became too irresistible again. The man deserved a little privacy, didn't he?

She picked up the remote, smiling when she saw that it too was chained to the wall, and then turned on the television and squinted at the screen.

They were acting as though they'd been married for years. At least Nick was. He seemed thoroughly relaxed with her and hadn't even given the double beds a second glance. He was taking their situation in stride.

She wasn't. She was a nervous wreck inside, grossly uptight, as Tommy would say, but she was determined not to let it show. If Nick guessed anything was wrong, she was fully prepared to lie and tell him that it was the trauma tonight that had put her on edge. She couldn't tell him the truth because it would be a terrible burden for him, but she couldn't help but wonder how he would react if he knew what was going on inside her head.

Did he have any idea how she felt about him? What would he say if she told him she wanted him, and damn the consequences? One wonderful night together, and the memory could and would last her a lifetime. Not an affair or a fling, she qualified. Nick couldn't handle that, and neither could she. But one night and no regrets. Not ever. Oh, how she longed to have his arms around her. To have him hold her and caress her.

It wasn't going to happen, though. Nick had been up front with her from the very beginning. He didn't want marriage or children, and because he knew she did, he would never touch her.

Even though she was certain a lasting relationship was out of the question, she still ached to touch him. She loved him, God help her. How had she allowed herself to be so vulnerable? She should have seen it coming and done something, anything, to protect herself. It was too late now. When he left her, he was going to break her heart, and there wasn't anything she could do about it.

Knowing the pain that lay ahead didn't change how she felt about him. One night, she told herself. That was all she would ever need, but she knew Nick wouldn't see it that way. He would see it as a betrayal of her brother, and yet she still considered all the arguments she could give him to try to sway him.

They were consenting adults. What happened between them wasn't anyone else's business.

Laurant knew what Nick's answer to that argument would be. She was Tommy's kid sister. End of story.

Laurant knew Nick cared about her. But did he love her? She was afraid to ask.

Nick came out of the bathroom wearing a pair of plaid boxer shorts. He was towel drying his hair but paused when he saw her frowning. "What's wrong?"

"Nothing. I was just thinking..."

He tossed the towel over a chair, then went to the side of the other bed and pulled back the covers as he asked, "About tonight?"

"Not exactly."

"Then what were you thinking about?"

"Trust me. You don't want to know."

"Sure I do. Tell me what you were thinking," he prodded as he stacked the pillows against the headboard and then reached over to turn the lamp off.

"All right, I will. I was trying to figure out how to seduce you."

His hand was halfway to the lamp when he froze. She couldn't believe she'd blurted out the truth that way. But she certainly had grabbed his full attention. He stayed perfectly still, like a deer caught in the headlights, then slowly straightened and turned to stare at her.

His expression was priceless. Had she not been mortified, she would have laughed. Nick looked dumbfounded. He was obviously waiting for some kind of a disclaimer or clarification, or maybe even a punch line, she

417

supposed, but she honestly didn't know what to tell him, and so she lifted her shoulders in a shrug, as if to say, there it is, believe it or not, take me or leave me.

"Are you joking?" His voice was hoarse.

She slowly shook her head. "Have I shocked you?"

He took a step back, shaking his head. He'd obviously decided not to believe her.

"You did ask me to tell you what I was thinking about."

"Yeah, well..."

"I'm not embarrassed."

Her face was the color of the red T-shirt.

"No reason to be," he stammered.

"Nick?"

"What?"

"What do you think about what I just said?"

He didn't answer her. She pushed the covers aside and got out of bed. He quickly backed away from her. Before she could blink, he was halfway across the room.

"I'm not going to attack you."

"Damn right you're not."

She took a step toward him. "Nick..."

He cut her off. "Stay right where you are, Laurant." He pointed his finger at her as he gave the order...or, rather, shouted it. And he kept backing away until he bumped into the television, which would have crashed to the floor had it not been bolted to the wall.

She was mortified. He was acting as though he was afraid of her. She certainly hadn't anticipated such a bizarre response. Disbelief maybe, even anger. But fear? Until this moment, she hadn't believed Nick was afraid of anything.

"What's the matter with you?" she whispered.

"It's out of the question. That's what's the matter with me. Now stop it, Laurant. Stop it right this minute."

"Stop what?"

"Talking crazy."

Too embarrassed to look him in the eyes, she bowed her head and stared at the floor tiles. It was too late to take the words back or pretend she hadn't said them, and so she decided to make everything a hundred times worse and tell him everything.

"There's more," she said, her voice whisper soft.

"I don't want to hear it."

She ignored his protest. "When you kiss me, I get this funny, tingling feeling in my stomach, and I don't want you to stop. I've never felt that way before. I just thought you should know." She heard him groan but couldn't make herself look at him yet. "And you know what's really odd?"

"I don't want to—"

She interrupted him, desperate to get the declaration out before she lost her courage. "I think I'm falling in love with you."

She dared a quick look up to see how he was taking the announcement and wished to God she hadn't bothered. To his credit, he didn't look like he was afraid of her any longer. No, now he looked like he wanted to kill her. It wasn't what she would consider a step in the right direction.

She seemed driven to make it worse. "No, I'm not falling in love with you. I do love you," she stubbornly insisted.

"When the hell did that happen?" he demanded. The anger in his voice stung like a whip. She flinched and blinked away the tears in her eyes.

"I don't know." She sounded bewildered. "It just did. I certainly didn't plan it. You're all wrong for me," she said. "I couldn't handle an affair. I want it all, marriage till death do us part, and I want babies. Lots of babies. You don't want any of that. I understand we don't have a future together, but I thought that if I could persuade you to make love to me just this one time, that it would be enough. It wouldn't change anything."

"The hell it wouldn't."

"Oh, for heaven's sake, stop shaking your head at me. Forget I mentioned it. And by the way, I find your reaction insulting. I thought that you felt...that you cared as much as I...oh, never mind. A simple 'no thank you' would have sufficed. You didn't need to let me know how appalled you are by the notion of sleeping with me."

"Damn it, Laurant, try to understand."

"I do understand. You've made your position perfectly clear. You don't want me."

"Are you crying?" The question sounded like a threat.

She'd die before she admitted it. "No, of

course not." She wiped the tears from her face, but it didn't stem the tide. "It just looks that way."

"Ah, Laurant, don't cry," he begged.

"It's my allergies." A sob escaped. "I need a tissue."

She tried to walk past him to the bathroom, but he reached for her and pulled her toward him. She collapsed against his chest and let the tears come. He wrapped her in his arms, kissed the top of her head, then her forehead.

"You listen to me, Laurant." He sounded like a drowning man desperate for help. "You don't know what you're saying. You don't love me. You've been through hell and you're frightened, and your emotions are all mixed up now."

He knew what was happening to her. She was mistaking gratitude for love. Easy to do, given the circumstances. Yes, that was it. She couldn't love him. She was too good for him, too sweet, too perfect. And he didn't deserve her. He had to stop this now, before it was too late.

"I know what's in my heart, Nick. I love you."

"Stop saying that."

He sounded angry, but he was kissing her fervently at the same time, and he was being so very gentle. She didn't know how to interpret the mixed signals. She couldn't stop holding him, touching him.

"Sweetheart, please stop crying. It's making me crazy."

"My allergies are acting up," she cried against his collarbone.

"You don't have allergies," he whispered as he brushed his lips against her neck. He loved her scent. She smelled like flowers and soap and woman.

He was lost and he knew it. He cupped the sides of her face with his hands and gently kissed the tears away. "You are so lovely," he whispered, and his mouth covered hers, demanding and urgent now, unrelenting, his tongue stroking hers. He began to tremble like a young man experiencing his first attempt at lovemaking. Only this wasn't awkward. It was perfect.

God, how he wanted this. And yet there was still a part of him that tried to pretend he was merely offering her comfort. Until his hands slid up under her T-shirt and he was caressing warm, silky skin. The hell with comfort. He wanted her with a burning intensity that shook him to the core and scared the hell out of him.

He couldn't stop stroking her. She felt so good against him, so soft, so right. He was pulling her T-shirt over her head and trying to kiss her at the same time, even as he told her that they couldn't do anything they would regret in the morning light.

She frantically agreed as she tugged on the snap of his shorts, and then pushed them down. Her hands slid back up his thighs and began to caress him intimately.

Her fingers were magical, the feather light

422

touch against his groin exquisite torture. He was hard and throbbing, and when he knew he wouldn't last another minute if she kept stroking him, he grabbed her hands and lifted them up around his neck. Then he roughly pressed against her, and the feel of her soft full breasts against him was damn near his undoing. Velvety skin rubbed against his as he tried to devour her with his mouth.

He pulled away from her. "Wait, I've got to protect you," he whispered and then went into the bathroom to get what he needed from his shaving kit. He returned and paused for a moment. "Laurant, I..." Any second thoughts he may have had vanished when she wrapped her arms around him and kissed him.

They fell into bed together, all legs and arms. He shifted positions so that he lay on top of her, nudging her thighs apart so he could rest between them. He lifted his head and looked at her swollen lips and was suddenly overwhelmed by her beauty.

His hand cupped one breast, his fingers slowly circling the hard nipple. She let out a little gasp and closed her eyes, letting him know she liked that, and so he did it again and again as he watched her aroused response.

He was determined to slow the tempo, to give her as much pleasure as he could before he surrendered.

"I have wanted you for the longest time," he whispered. "From the moment I saw you, I wanted those long legs of yours around me. It's all I could think about."

His face was dark with passion, and his blue eyes glittered dangerously. She gently trailed her fingertips down the line of his hard jaw, then his throat.

"You know what else I've wanted?"

And then he showed her with his hands and his mouth what he had been thinking about. He knew where to touch, how much pressure to exert, when to withdraw. She moved restlessly against him, her caresses soon becoming more and more demanding, until her nails were biting into his shoulders and she was begging him to end his teasing.

His mouth was driving her crazy while his hands slid down the sides of her body. His fingers stroked her inner thighs, so soft, so sensitive. He felt her arch against him and heard her gasp as his knuckles deliberately brushed against the swirling dark curls between her thighs. He loved the sexy sound she made when he touched her so intimately.

He made love to her, telling her without words how he adored her.

Laurant had never experienced bliss like this. Such exquisite sensations coursed through her. She arched up against him again, far more demanding now.

"Now, Nick...please. Oh, God, now..."

He thrust into her forcefully, unable to quell the groan of sheer satisfaction as he became part of her, and when she wrapped her legs around him, he groaned again. Reality was much better than fantasy. She was better than anything he could have ever imagined.

Fully imbedded inside her, his head dropped to the crook of her neck, and he took a deep, calming breath and tried to slow the pace. Nick was determined to make their lovemaking unforgettable.

He began to move slowly within her. "Do you like that?"

"Yes," she cried out.

"And this?" he whispered as his hand slid down between their joined bodies to stroke her. Her cry of ecstasy was all the encouragement he needed. Her arm curled around his neck, and she dragged him down for a long, hot kiss.

"Don't ever stop," she whispered.

He drove deep once again. She lifted her hips, straining against him to take as much of him inside her warmth as possible. She wanted to please him, but in the web of passion that he had created, there wasn't room for worry or for the fear of disappointing him.

Neither one of them could slow the pace, both frantic now to find release.

She came before he did and began to sob with the beauty of her surrender and the love she felt for him. Nick felt her tremble in his arms as every part of her body tightened around him, and with a near shout of pleasure, he climaxed deep inside of her. The orgasm was unlike any he had ever experienced in the past. He neither questioned the difference nor understood it. He merely accepted that this was unique and so special he would never be able to settle for anything less again.

He stayed inside of her a long time, but when

he finally rolled to his side and tenderly took her into his arms to hold her close, she trustingly curled up against him, her hand splayed across the curly mat of hair on his chest.

Laurant was too overwhelmed to speak. She could barely form a coherent thought. When she was finally able to breathe again, she leaned up to look at his face.

She stared into those deep blue eyes, so intense now with the residue of raw passion, and smiled as she arched against him like a well-fed cat. She loved the feel of his hard body against hers. The hair on his legs tickled her toes, and she loved that feeling too.

She loved him. Now and always, she admitted. Then she saw the worry creep into his gaze, and she tried to think of a way to ward off the regret she knew he would be feeling soon. She gave him a long, lingering kiss, and then she smiled at him again. "You know what I think?"

"What's that?" he asked on a yawn, still too exhausted and content to move.

"I could get really good at this."

He groaned, but then she felt the low rumble building in his chest, and he suddenly was laughing. "You'll kill me if you get any better."

"You liked it too?"

"How can you ask me such a question?"

She traced the corded muscle along his shoulder, noticed the faded jagged scar on his upper arm, and leaned up to kiss it.

"How did this happen?"

"Football."

"And this?" she asked as she touched the faint scar on his hip. "Was it a bullet?"

"Football," he said again. She didn't look like she believed him. "Honest," he said. "It's a football cleat."

"Have you ever been shot?" Her voice trembled when she asked.

"No," he answered. "Stabbed, punched, kicked, scratched, and spit on, yes, but shot, no." Not yet anyway, he silently qualified. A scar from a knife wound—an ice pick actually—was on his back, down low by his left kidney. A couple of inches higher and he wouldn't have lived. Maybe Laurant wouldn't notice that scar, but if she did, he decided he wouldn't lie to her.

"Most of the scars are from football," he said.

She threaded her fingers through his hair. "Except for the ones you carry inside."

He pulled her hand away. "Don't get sentimental on me. Everybody carries around a little baggage."

He was trying to close up on her, to pull away emotionally, but she wouldn't let him take the coward's path. When he rolled onto his back and curtly told her it was time they got a little sleep, she ignored the suggestion.

She rolled over on top of him. Stacking her hands under her chin, she stared down into his eyes.

His hands were already on her hips. He wanted to make her get off him and go to sleep before he gave in to his desire and made love to her again, but he couldn't make himself let go of her.

"Promise me something, and I'll let you sleep," she said.

"What?" He sounded suspicious.

"No matter what happens..."

"Yes?"

"No regrets. All right, Nick?"

He nodded. "What about you."

"No regrets," she vowed.

"Agreed," he said.

"Say it."

He sighed. "No regrets."

And both of them were lying.

CHAPTER

29

Heartbreaker didn't like surprises, unless, of course, he was the one doling them out. Tonight was chock full of unpleasant surprises. He had already heard that the mule was ridiculing him, and he had taken it all in stride. He expected stupidity from mules, so he was only mildly bothered to hear some of the names he was being called. Sticks and stones...words couldn't hurt him. Until tonight, when he heard that Laurant was also spreading vile lies. She had called him impotent. He could barely stand the thought of her lips forming the hideous word. How dare she betray him? How dare she?

He had to get even, and he was driven to act quickly. The need to punish her overrode caution. How long had he stood in the back lot looking up at her window? At least an hour, maybe two. He didn't know. When the need grabbed hold of him, time wasn't important.

And then he'd seen Lonnie. The stupid boy was climbing up the tree, the very same tree Heartbreaker had used countless times to get inside her house and watch her during the night.

He watched Lonnie crawl across the roof and slip onto the overhang outside the bathroom window. Just the way he had done. *Clever boy,* he thought. *Following in my footsteps.*

While waiting to see what Lonnie was going to do, his attention was distracted by another man. Good old Steve Brenner was creeping around to Laurant's back door. Now what was he up to?

The neighbor's dog couldn't tell on him. Heartbreaker had killed the animal so that he could move freely about the yard during the night. He had seen to the yapping dog, and now Lonnie Boy and Steve Brenner were taking advantage of his work.

The surprises kept coming, escalating until the house was in flames and Brenner was surrounded by mules.

He could walk away now and no one would

be the wiser. They thought they had their man. After he'd taken a little stroll down the streets of Holy Oaks and found what he was looking for, he'd made a little deposit and gone happily on his way. The opportunity had fallen into his lap. Yes, he could walk away, but would he? Now that was a question haunting him.

What a quandary. Yes, sirree. Could he? Would he?

His obsession was turning him into a cold-blooded murderer. No, that wasn't true, he forced himself to admit. He was already a killer. A perfect killer, he qualified. His ego insisted that he give himself his due. A part of him was quite analytical about it all, and he was able to recognize what was happening to him, but he couldn't make himself mourn the loss of what others would call his sanity. He wasn't crazy. No, of course, he wasn't. But he was vengeful. No doubt about that. It was his sacred duty to give back what had been given to him.

He paced about the little room, planning and fuming. That sleazy little Lonnie boy had messed things up good, and he couldn't let him get away with it, could he? Because of him, the perfect plan had been ruined, and what was he prepared to do about it?

The stupid ingrate was forcing him to move up his timetable. What an inconvenience that was, and Lonnie should have to pay, shouldn't he? Why, yes, indeed he should. Fair was fair, after all, and besides, he'd noticed Laurant didn't like the young slug. But then who would? Maybe it was time he showed her how much he cared for her. He decided to give her a gift, something special...like Lonnie's spleen or liver, maybe. Certainly not his heart. He wanted to please her, not insult her, and he wouldn't have her thinking Lonnie was a heartbreaker. No, sirree.

He glanced at the clock on the nightstand. My oh my, where does the time go? So much to do, so little time left to do it, thanks to Lonnie boy. Oh, he'll pay all right, with his spleen and his liver and maybe even a kidney or two. But first things first, he cautioned. There was work to be finished.

Preparation, after all, was everything. The party had to be perfect.

She loved sleeping with him, tucked safely in his arms with her legs trapped under one of his thighs. She awakened before he did but was feeling too content to move. Nick looked so peaceful. She didn't want to disturb his rest, and so she stayed perfectly still while she studied his face with the critical eye of an artist. He had the most wonderful profile. The chiseled line of his jaw, the straight nose, the perfectly sculptured mouth. She wanted to paint him, to capture the strength she saw in his eyes. She wondered if he knew how beautiful he was or if he cared. He was such a practical man. He didn't have time for such thoughts or vanities.

She wanted him to wake up and make love to her, but she knew that wouldn't happen. He'd turned to her again and again during the night, but now it was morning and everything was different. She had asked him for one night, and the cost, she knew, had been dear. She couldn't and wouldn't ask for more.

How was she ever going to go back to the ways things were? She was a strong woman. She could do anything she set her mind to, and she was a master at hiding her feelings. She could pretend that it had been a glorious night of recreational sex, that was all, a simple way to release pent-up frustrations and tensions...but oh, God, how was she ever going to pull that off? She wished she could be more worldly. She had plenty of friends at school in Europe and at work in Chicago who believed it was perfectly all right to take a man they had only just met home with them for the night and then never see him again. Women had needs, after all. What was wrong with a one-night interlude? Everything, Laurant thought. Because the heart had to be involved. She could never have given herself to Nick so completely if she hadn't already made a commitment and acknowledged that she loved him.

Memories...she would have the memories of their night together, and that would be enough. She squeezed her eyes shut. She wanted more than memories. She wanted to wake up next to Nick every morning for the rest of her life.

She hated feeling this vulnerable and wished to God there was a way to harden herself. Throwing the sheet back, she nudged Nick's thigh away and got out of bed.

No regrets.

Both of them were in a hurry to leave the motel. He wanted to get out of the room before he grabbed her, threw her on the bed, and made love to her again. She wanted to leave as quickly as possible before she started crying again...like the stupid, small-town girl that she was.

The silence between them was strained and horribly uncomfortable. She stared out the window while he drove. She wondered what he was thinking but didn't ask.

Nick was silently cursing himself for being such a bastard. What kind of man was he to take advantage of his best friend's sister? A sick, perverted bastard. That's what he was, all right, and Tommy was never, ever going to understand.

Regrets? Hell yes, he had regrets, yet he knew

that if they had stayed in that motel room another five minutes, he would have made love to her again.

They stopped at a superstore off the main highway and spent a quick half hour shopping. At a filling station, Laurant changed while Nick got a couple of Diet Cokes out of the machine. When she came out, she was wearing a seven-dollar pink-and-white checked blouse tucked into a fifteen-dollar pair of stonewashed blue jeans, but the inexpensive clothes looked like designer labels on her. The fabric hugged the curves of her luscious body, and he had to look away until he got his heartbeat regulated. *Scum,* he thought. *I'm lower than scum.* Then he looked again and noticed that her hair shone with copper highlights in the sun. He remembered how the soft curls felt when she was leaning over him. Realizing what he was doing, he cursed himself again. He had the discipline of a pig.

She walked to the car, gliding over the pavement with her sexy, long-legged stride. He handed her the can of Coke, frowning as though she'd done something offensive, then got behind the wheel and didn't say another word to her for a good twenty miles. As much as he tried to keep his mind on the road and other pressing matters, he couldn't keep himself from glancing over at her every few minutes. She had the sexiest mouth, and when he thought about the things she'd done with it, a tightness settled in his chest.

He couldn't block the images. "Hell."

"Excuse me?"

"Never mind."

"Has Pete called you back yet?"

"What?"

He was as grouchy as a hungry bobcat. She calmly repeated the question.

"No," he answered curtly. "I told you he was on his way to Houston. His plane won't land for another hour."

"No, you didn't tell me."

He shrugged. "I thought I did."

The road curved to the east, the sun blinding. Nick put on his sunglasses and then took a long swallow from the can.

"Are you always this grumpy in the morning?" she asked.

"We've been living together long enough for you to know the answer to that question. What do you think?"

"You're in a mood," she said. "That's what I think."

"In a mood?" He glanced at her with a quick scowl. "What the hell is that supposed to mean?"

"It means you're acting like a jerk," she calmly explained. "What do you think is causing it?"

Gee, I don't know, he thought. *Maybe it's due to the fact that I spent most of the night screwing my best friend's sister.*

He thought it prudent to keep silent. He finished his Coke and dropped the can in the cup holder.

"Are you still thirsty?" she asked, offering him her drink.

"You don't want it?"

"You can have it."

And that was the end of their conversation for the next ten minutes. Laurant waited for him to get past whatever was bothering him, and when she couldn't stand the silence another minute, she said, "I imagine Noah's told Tommy by now."

"Good God, I hope not. It's my job to tell your brother. Not Noah's."

"He's going to know," she began.

"I'll tell him," he insisted.

It occurred to her then that they might not be talking about the same thing. "The fire, Nick, I was asking you if you thought Noah had told Tommy about the fire yet," she explained. "And about Steve Brenner being arrested."

"Oh. Yeah, I'm sure he's told him by now. At least I hope he did before Tommy read about it in the paper."

"What were you talking about?"

"Never mind."

"I want to know. Tell me."

"Us," he said, gripping the steering wheel. "I thought you were asking me if Noah told Tommy about us."

Her head snapped up. "And you said you should be the one to tell him. You did say that, didn't you?" She sounded incredulous.

"Yeah, that's exactly what I said."

"You're joking though, aren't you?"

"No, I'm not."

"You are not going to tell my brother about last night." She was vehement.

"I think I should," he argued, and he suddenly sounded quite calm and reasonable.

She thought he was out of his mind. "Absolutely not. What happened between us stays between us."

"Normally that would be true," he agreed. "But you're...different. I should tell him."

"I'm not different."

"Yes, you are, sweetheart. Your brother's my best friend, and he also just happens to be a priest. Yeah, I've got to tell him. It's the decent thing to do. Besides, he's gonna figure it out. He'll know."

"He isn't clairvoyant."

"I've never been able to pull anything over on him, not since second grade. He's always known what's going on inside my head. He's bailed me out of a lot of trouble. For a while, when we were at Penn State, he was like my conscience. No, I'm not going to lie to him."

She could feel a headache coming on. "You don't have to lie. You don't have to say anything."

"I'm telling you he's going to know. I've got to tell him."

"Have you lost your mind?"

"No."

"You are not telling him. I know you feel as though you've betrayed him, but—"

He wouldn't let her finish. "Of course I feel like I've betrayed him. He trusted me, damn it."

The road was deserted and so he pulled the car over on the shoulder.

"I know it's going to be a little awkward for you, but you'll get past it," he said.

She couldn't believe they were having this conversation. "Nick, my brother trusted you to keep me safe. You've done that. You don't need to tell him about last night."

Astonishment had given way to anger and embarrassment, and she was so upset tears came to her eyes. She vowed she'd die before she cried in front of him again.

"I haven't done anything I'm ashamed of," she insisted. "And you promised me you wouldn't have any regrets."

"Yeah, well, I lied."

She jabbed him in the shoulder. "If you feel so guilty, then go to confession."

She was glaring at him now, and all he could think about was how pretty she was when she was angry. He wouldn't have been surprised if sparks flew out of her eyes.

"I thought about going to confession," he admitted. "And then I pictured Tommy's fist coming through that grille, and I thought, no, that wouldn't be right. I can't tell him that way. It should be face-to-face."

She put her hand to her brow to try to stop the pounding. "I didn't mean for you to go to confession to Tommy," she said. "Go to another priest."

"Don't get into a lather."

"You have nothing to feel guilty about," she cried out. "I seduced you."

"No, you didn't."

"I most certainly did."

"All right," he said. "Then tell me, how'd you do it?"

"I made you feel sorry for me. I cried."

He rolled his eyes. "I see," he drawled. "So I made love to you out of pity? Is that the way you see it?"

She seriously contemplated getting out of the car and walking back to town.

"Let me ask you something," she said then, trying to make him realize how unreasonable and stubborn he was being. "You have slept with other women, haven't you?"

"Yes, I have," he agreed. "You want the number?"

"No," she countered. "I want to know what happened after you had sex with them. Did you feel compelled to tell their mothers?"

He laughed. "No, I didn't."

"Well then?"

"Like I said before, honey. You're different."

She folded her arms across her chest and stared straight ahead. "I'm not talking about this any longer."

"Laurant, look at me. How about if I promise you something?"

"Why bother? You don't keep your promises."

"Making me promise I wouldn't have any regrets was just plain stupid, so I don't think that should count. I'll keep this promise," he assured her. "If he doesn't ask, I won't tell. I won't say anything to your brother for a couple of days. That should give you enough time to calm down."

"Not good enough," she countered. "Since you're compelled to be a blabbermouth, you have to wait until you're back in Boston."

"I should tell him face-to-face so, if he wants to punch me, he can."

"Boston," she gritted out between clenched teeth.

He finally relented. They got back on the road and headed for home again.

"Nick?"

"Yes?"

He sounded downright cheerful now. He was the most exasperating man.

"Any other bombshells you want to drop on me before we get home?"

"Yeah, come to think of it, there is one more thing I should probably mention."

She mentally braced herself. "What is it? No, let me guess. You want to put it in the paper."

He laughed. "No."

"Then what?" Now *she* sounded cranky.

"When I go back to Boston..."

"Yes?"

"You're going with me."

"Why?"

"Because I'm not letting you out of my sight until I'm convinced we've got the right guy under lock and key."

"For how long?"

"As long as it takes. Until I'm satisfied."

"I can't do that."

"You're going to," he countered.

"I'll go with you to Boston while the anniversary is going on here, but then I have to come

440

back. I have to find a place to live, open my store, make some decisions about what I'm going to do with the rest of my life. I need some time to sort things out."

"I want to talk to you about something else while I'm thinking of it."

"Yes?"

"You aren't in love with me."

She blinked. "I'm not?"

"No," he said emphatically. "You just think you are. You're confused," he explained. "You've been under a hell of a lot of stress, and we've been tied together."

She knew where he was headed. "I see."

"Transference."

"I'm sorry?"

"It's called transference. It's kind of like a patient falling in love with her doctor. It's not real," he stressed.

"That's what I'm suffering from?"

"Not suffering, honey," he said. "But I do think you've confused gratitude with love."

She pretended to ponder the possibility for a long minute and then said, "I believe you might be right."

She swore that if he looked the least bit relieved, she would do him bodily harm.

"You do?" He sounded a little stunned.

"Yes, I do," she said more forcefully.

He wanted confirmation. "So you realize you don't love me."

No, she thought. *I realize that telling you I love you terrifies you because it means commitment and taking a chance.*

441

"That's exactly what I realize," she told him. "It's that transference thing all right. I was confused, but I'm not any longer. Thank you for clearing it up for me."

He shot her a hasty glance. "That was pretty damn quick, wasn't it?"

"When you're right, you're right."

"That's it?" He was suddenly furious with her and didn't care that it showed. Damn it, she had told him she loved him, and after a one-minute argument, she caved. What the hell kind of love was that? "That's all you have to say?"

"No, actually there is just one more thing I'd like to mention."

"Yeah? What's that?"

"You're an idiot."

CHAPTER

31

Laurant used Nick's phone to call Michelle and give her the bad news about the bridesmaid's dress.

Michelle answered on the first ring. "Where are you? Are you all right? I heard about the fire, and Bessie Jean told Mother you left

442

with Nick, but no one knew where you went. My God, can you believe Steve Brenner turned out to be such a pervert? Did you know he'd hidden a camera in your house?"

Laurant patiently answered her questions and then told her about the dress. Michelle took the news surprisingly well. "If only you'd left the dress with Rosemary," she said, referring to the dressmaker who had fitted the gown for her.

"You told me to pick it up, remember?"

"Yes, but when have you ever listened to me?"

"Michelle, what are we going to do? Should I just bow out?"

"No way," Michelle cried. "You can wear something of mine."

"You've got to be joking. You're tiny. Nothing of yours would fit me."

"Listen, Laurant. I'm stuck with Christopher's two insipid cousins in my wedding, but I'm not letting either one of them be my maid of honor. Are you or are you not my best friend?"

"Of course I am," she said. "But—"

"Then improvise. I don't care what you wear. Come naked if you want. No, you better not do that. You'd cause a riot," she said. "Christopher wouldn't remember his vows," she added with a laugh.

"I'll find something," she promised, wondering how in God's name she was going to have time to shop.

"You'll still be here at four?"

"Give me at least until five."

"Was the dress destroyed by the fire? Maybe the dry cleaners could repair it if it wasn't burned up."

"No," she answered. "It's gone."

"The town's in an uproar over Brenner," she said then. "How stupid was he to torch his own house? Did you know he'd browbeaten poor Mrs. Talbot into selling it to him. He didn't have any insurance either. Did you know that? The pervert paid cash."

"How did you find all that out?" she asked.

"Mother's nosy friends. Little Lorna's called Mother three times in the past hour to give more information."

"Steve didn't start the fire," Laurant said. "Lonnie did. I guess he didn't know Steve had bought the house."

"That wasn't in the paper," Michelle exclaimed. "The sheriff's son was in on it?"

"Yes," Laurant answered. "There's a lot more too, Michelle, but I can't go into it now."

"You can tell me everything while we get dressed," she said. "And I mean everything. I've got to hang up now. I'm getting my nails done. I'll see you at five, and please, stop worrying. It's going to be fine. Nothing can ruin this day for me, and do you know why?"

"Because you're marrying the man of your dreams?"

"That too."

"What were you going to say?"

"That no matter what, I'm going to have hot incredible sex tonight. Uh-oh, Mom's glaring at me. Got to go."

444

Laurant handed the phone back to Nick. "Let's go by the house first," she said. "If the fire didn't reach the second floor, maybe I can find something suitable to wear in the wedding."

"Your clothes are going to smell like smoke," he said. "But the dry cleaners could probably clean the dress before five."

She mentally went through her wardrobe of once-upon-a-time clothes. That's what she called them, the beautiful designer dresses and suits that the head of the European modeling agency had given to her, trying to entice her to work for them. The ice blue Versace might do, or the peach Armani. Both of the formal dresses were long, and her high-heeled sandals would work with either one. If the clothes had been destroyed in the fire, she didn't know what she could wear. The local ladies' dress shop didn't carry formal attire.

"What else do you have to do before the wedding?" Nick asked.

"Find a place to stay tonight," she said. "I'll wait until tomorrow to pack up whatever I can salvage from the house. It's too overwhelming to think about today. We have to get a suit for you to wear to the wedding," she added. "Did you bring one with you?"

"Just my navy blazer and a couple of pairs of dress pants."

"That will work. We'll drop them at the cleaners too."

She sounded weary.

"Cheer up, honey. It's going to get better."

She tried to think of something optimistic. "It's a nice day for a wedding, isn't it?"

"Was your friend upset about the dress?"

"No," Laurant replied. She smiled then. "Michelle doesn't get upset about things like that. She told me nothing could ruin today for her."

The phone rang, but it wasn't Morganstern, as Nick had hoped. Noah was on the line, wanting to know when he and Laurant would be coming to the abbey.

"Is Tommy worried?"

"No," Noah answered. "He just wants to know if we should hang around or not."

"We'll be there in about an hour. Make him stay put."

Laurant was getting hungry, but she didn't want to take time to eat. There was so much to get accomplished before tonight, and it was already going on noon.

They reached Holy Oaks and wound their way down the quiet streets to her house.

"You know what Michelle told me? Lonnie didn't make the newspaper. She thought Steve Brenner set the fire."

"Farley told me he would pick him up and take him to Nugent," Nick said. "He and Brenner can share a cell."

"You wish you were there, don't you?"

He glanced at her as he admitted, "Yeah, I do. I'd love to sit in on the interrogation. Look Brenner in the eyes. Then I'd know for sure."

"That he's the unsub."

"No, that he *isn't*."

"I want you to be wrong."

"I know you do." He sounded sympathetic.

"Until last night, I never would have believed that Steve could be a Peeping Tom," she said.

"That's because you hadn't seen the dark side of good old Steve."

"I certainly saw it last night. His face was contorted with hate, and the venom spewing out of his mouth shocked me. I think he is capable of anything, even murder. You know what strikes me as odd though?"

"What's that?"

"Steve's always been very uptight, around me anyway. He's very controlling, or organized, as you would call him. Always planning," she added with a nod. "He was pretty smooth the way he manipulated the shop owners into selling. He'd purchased five stores before the town found out what he was up to. He was sneaky and very clever, wouldn't you agree?"

"So?"

"He had to have known from reputation alone how volatile and unpredictable Lonnie was. Why would he involve him?"

"Maybe he thought he could use him as his scapegoat."

"Maybe," she agreed. "How did Steve get in the house?"

"He came in through the back door. He broke the glass, reached in, and unlocked the dead bolt. It was sloppy," he added.

"I think Lonnie was looking for a way in through a window."

"You told me he was on the roof."

"I heard him outside the bathroom window."

"But you didn't see him, did you?"

"No," she answered. "He could have been checking to make sure no one was home. He didn't see me. I dropped to the floor the second I saw the light."

Nick pulled up to a stop sign and waited while two little boys, about seven or eight years old, rode their bikes across the intersection. What were their parents thinking to let them out of their sight? Hell, anyone could grab them. Anything could happen, and they wouldn't know about it until it was too late.

His attention returned to Laurant. "Lonnie had a flashlight?"

"No, it was more like a penlight, a red one."

"A red penlight...you mean, a laser beam, maybe?"

"Yes, exactly."

"Why didn't you tell me this last night?" he demanded impatiently.

"I told you Lonnie was on the roof."

"The son of a bitch could have had you in his sights." His face was tight with anger. "Where in God's name would he get his hands on that kind of equipment?"

"From his father's cabinet," she answered. "The sheriff prides himself on his gun collection, and Lonnie would have easy access."

Nick picked up his phone and started dialing. "And that's why you came out of the bathroom."

"Yes," she answered. "Who are you calling?"

"Farley," he answered. "He can find out if Lonnie was on that roof or not."

"Who else could it have been?"

Nick didn't answer her.

Agent Farley was just about to step onto a plane in Des Moines when his phone rang. When he heard Nick's voice, he moved away from the crowd filing on board.

"You just caught me," he said. "Another minute and I would have turned my phone off."

"Did you pick up Lonnie?"

"No," he answered. "He's gone to ground, and I've been reassigned. Wesson's letting the Nugent sheriff and his deputies go after Lonnie and bring him in."

"Is Feinberg still around, or did Wesson send him packing?"

"I'm not sure," Farley answered. "They both went to Nugent with Brenner," he said. "And they could still be there. This isn't sitting right with you, is it, Nick? You don't think Brenner's our man."

"No, I don't," he said. "But I don't have anything to prove it yet."

"This could be an easy case, and you've just never had one of those before."

"Yeah, maybe."

"Are you going to stay in Holy Oaks?"

"Yes."

"Sorry I had to bail on you, but I didn't have a choice. As soon as Wesson E-mailed headquarters and let them know I was ready for reassignment, they pounced."

"Where are you headed?"

"Detroit. There's a situation brewing there, and it's a messy one. Be thankful you're on vacation."

"You be careful," Nick said. "And Joe, thanks for helping."

"A lot of damn good I did. I'll tell you this. I've worked with Wesson a couple of times in the past, and he was always a pain in the ass, but he was never this difficult. I think it's you," he added. "You bring out the worst in him. He's gone too far this time though. I'm never going to work with that egomaniac again, even if means handing in my badge. By the book, my ass. Wesson doesn't know what teamwork is, and that's what's going in my report," Joe paused a second. "Nick, you know what's worrying me?"

"Getting on that plane?"

"No, that's your hang-up, not mine. It's that gut feeling of yours."

"What about it?"

"If you're right, and Brenner isn't the unsub, then you and Noah are out there all alone. God help you."

aurant found a couple of gowns that would work for the wedding, and after they dropped off the clothes at the cleaners, they drove to the abbey. Noah was in the kitchen eating cold fried chicken with all the trimmings. Nick pulled out a chair for Laurant as he grabbed a chicken leg.

"You should eat something, honey."

Noah's right eyebrow shot up, and his gaze bounced between Laurant's flushed face and Nick's pained expression. Then he burst into laughter. "It took you long enough."

"Don't start," Nick warned.

"Don't start what?" Noah asked innocently.

"Nick calls everyone honey," Laurant blurted, feeling like a fool.

"Sure he does," Noah agreed. "He's been calling Tommy and me honey every chance he gets."

"Let it alone," Nick insisted. "Where is Tommy?"

"He's in one of the conference rooms with that editor woman."

"What does she want?" Laurant asked.

Noah shrugged. "Beats me."

Nick heard a door close behind him and

crossed the kitchen to look out the window. He saw Lorna hurry down the stairs.

"Where did this feast come from?" Laurant asked Noah.

"Noah's fan club," Tommy answered from the doorway.

Noah grinned. "The ladies like me. What can I say?"

"He's been doing a little counseling." Tommy shook his head in exasperation.

"Hey, I'm good at it."

Laurant was having trouble looking at her brother. It was Nick's fault, she knew, because he had planted the ridiculous notion that Tommy would know what happened last night if he looked in her eyes.

"Laurant, I want a word in private with you," Tommy said.

Nick gave her an I-told-you-he'd-know look and turned around. "Tommy, you and I have to talk."

"No," Laurant all but shouted as she pushed the chair back and stood. "What do you want to talk to me about?"

"Lorna was just here."

"What did she want?" Laurant asked. "She has enough news to keep her busy for the next month, what with the fire and Steve Brenner. Is she trying to figure out a way to blame me for all that too?"

"She is writing another article about you, but it doesn't have anything to do with the fire or Brenner. She wanted confirmation from me. It seems she ran into the banker's wife, who

452

mentioned the money you borrowed for your store, and one bit of gossip led to another. Damn it, Laurant," he said, his voice shaking with anger, "why didn't you tell me the trust was gone? All this time, I thought you were fine and I wouldn't have to worry about you."

Laurant was stunned by Lorna's audacity. "I had to fill out a financial statement, and I had to explain about the trust in order to get the loan," she cried. "But the banker had no right to tell anyone, not even his wife. That was confidential information. And how dare Lorna poke her nose in my affairs." She took a step toward her brother. "Did you hear what you just said to me? All this time you thought I was fine and you wouldn't have to worry about me? I'm not ten years old, Tommy, but you can't seem to get that through your head. The money was gone before I turned twenty-one and could do anything about it. The lawyers took it. Every cent. I didn't tell you because I knew you'd get upset, and there wasn't anything you could do."

"Millions of dollars...our grandfather's hard-earned money gone? When I signed my trust over to them to put with yours, I thought..."

Her brother's expression made her want to cry. He looked devastated. And horribly disappointed in her. He made her feel as though she had squandered the money.

"It wasn't your sister's fault," Nick said quietly.

"I know that."

"You're not acting like you do."

Tommy's shoulders slumped. "When exactly did you find out the money was gone?" His face was red with the anger he was trying to contain.

"On my twenty-first birthday."

"You should have told your family then. Maybe something could have been done."

Noah knew it wasn't his place to interfere, but he couldn't stop himself. He looked Tommy in the eye and said, "What family? From what I've gathered, Laurant didn't have one of those when she was growing up. Who exactly was she supposed to tell?"

"I'm her family," Tommy railed.

"Try to see it her way," Noah insisted. "When you were growing up, you had Nick's family to help you, and when you joined the priesthood, the church became your new family."

"My sister will always be part of my family."

"She was in Europe, and you were here. You can't change the way things were. The guilt is making you angry because she was left out in the cold."

Tommy looked tormented. Laurant slowly shook her head and went to him. "That isn't true. I wasn't out in the cold. I always knew you were there for me. I knew you were fighting to get me to the United States. Tommy, I always knew you loved me. Please don't be angry."

He put his arms around her and hugged her. "It just came as a shock, that's all. Don't

454

keep things from me, Laurant. Big brothers are supposed to look out for their little sisters, no matter how old they are. Look, let's make a pact, okay? From now on, we don't hide anything from each other. If I have to have chemo, I tell you, and if you have a problem, you tell me."

"I don't expect you to solve my problems for me."

"No, I know you don't, but you should be able to talk to me about them."

She nodded. "Yes, okay."

"When's the article going to run?" Nick asked. He was trying to figure out if there was time to stop it.

"It isn't going to be in the paper. Lorna and I had a little talk."

Noah grinned. "Did you threaten her with the fires of hell?"

Tommy wasn't amused. "No, I didn't, but I did talk to her about being jealous of Laurant. She didn't want to hear my opinions, but she agreed not to run the article. She's afraid other people will think she's jealous because she's gone after Laurant so many times."

"I need a glass of milk," Laurant said. Her stomach was upset, thanks to Lorna, and she hoped the milk would settle it.

"I'll get it. You go sit down," Tommy offered.

Noah pushed her plate in front of her. "Eat," he suggested.

"Isn't there anything you can do about those lawyers?" Nick asked her.

"I am doing something."

Tommy poked his head out of the pantry. "What?" he asked.

"I'm suing them."

Her brother grabbed a glass and hurried back into the kitchen. "You're suing?"

"Yes," she said. "The day after I found out, I started searching. It took a year to find an attorney who was willing to take on the giants."

"David against Goliath, huh?" Noah said.

"You know, Noah, you're starting to think like a priest. Maybe you ought to consider joining up," Nick teased.

Noah grimaced. "That isn't going to happen."

Tommy got the gallon of milk out of the refrigerator and poured some into Laurant's glass. "But about the suit? What's happening?"

She took a drink before she answered. "I won the first round, and then I won again. They've been dragging it out with motions to delay, but my attorney told me that this next round is the last appeal. I should hear something soon. Win or lose, it will be final."

"So, there's a good possibility you could get the money back."

"It could go either way," she said. "I'm prepared for either outcome."

"No wonder you drive that junky old car," Nick said. "You've been living on a shoestring."

He was smiling at her, as though he thought she had done something remarkable.

"I budget like most people do," she said. "And I happen to like my car."

The conversation came to an abrupt end when the sheriff came storming into the kitchen.

"Where the hell is my boy?" he demanded in a snarl. He had his gun half drawn as he shouted, "What have you done with him?"

Nick's back was to the door, but Noah sat facing the stampeding sheriff. In a heartbeat, his hand reached inside his black robe and pointed the gun under the table at Lloyd. "You pull that weapon out, and you're a dead man."

Lloyd stopped, frozen in his tracks. He was stunned by this priest who dared to threaten him.

Laurant hadn't even had time to turn in her chair before Nick had whirled around and drawn his weapon. He was standing now, shielding her, and the barrel of his gun was pressed against Lloyd's temple.

Tommy came up behind the sheriff and took the gun away from him. Then he calmly suggested that Lloyd sit down and discuss the problem in a reasonable manner.

"I'm the authority here," he bellowed.

"No, you're not," Nick informed him. He put his gun back in the holster and told the sheriff to do as Tommy had said and sit down.

Lloyd chose the chair at the far end of the table. "Give me my gun back."

Tommy handed Nick the weapon, and he quickly unloaded the magazine before he slid the gun toward the sheriff.

"What seems to be the problem?" Tommy asked.

"My boy," Lloyd muttered. "He's gone missing. That's what the problem is."

"He's hiding," Nick told him. "He started that fire, and now he's hiding."

Lloyd shook his head. "I ain't gonna get into all that fire business 'cause you and I see it different from each other. My boy knows he's got me for his alibi. He wouldn't think he had to hide. He was in bed, sleeping sound, when I got home from Nugent. I was dead tired," he added. "Up most of the night, and I was just getting myself in bed when the low-life sheriff from Nugent knocked on my door. He said he was gonna take Lonnie and book him on arson. We argued a bit, but then I decided to let the lawyers handle it, and I let him on in. Lonnie weren't in his bed though, and his window was wide open."

Nick glanced at Noah, who promptly shook his head to let him know he hadn't done anything with Lonnie.

Nick said then, "Maybe Wesson decided to pick him up."

"That ain't what happened." The sheriff was whining now. "He's still with the others cooped up with Brenner in a two-by-four room, questioning him. They wouldn't let me listen in, didn't want me to know nothing that was going on. I finally gave up and was heading out the door when I heard they were accusing him of murder. One of the sheriff's deputies told me they had the goods on him." He took his hat off and rubbed his brow. "It's all going in the toilet."

"Do you really care what happens to Lonnie?" Noah asked bluntly.

The question flustered the sheriff. Seeing the turmoil in Lloyd's face, Tommy took over. He dragged a chair to the end of the table and sat down next to Lloyd.

"Your son's given you a lot of heartache over the years, hasn't he, Lloyd?"

The sheriff's voice dropped to a whisper. "He ain't never been right in the head. Never. He's got a real mean temper."

Tommy coaxed Lloyd to talk, urging him to let go of all the anger and disappointment he'd kept inside for so long, and within minutes, the sheriff was spilling his guts, telling him all the problems he'd had to clean up for his son. The list was appallingly lengthy.

"He's done some terrible things. I know he has, but he's my son, and I had to protect him. I'm so sick of it. I know I'm supposed to care about the boy, but I can't, not anymore. I've still got to find him because if I don't and he comes home, he'll be...upset with me, and I don't want that to happen. He can forget himself and get violent." He wiped at his eyes as he confessed, "I'm ashamed to admit it, but I'm afraid of my own boy. He's going to kill me one of these days. He's come damn close a couple of times already."

"Maybe it's time Lonnie learned the consequences of his actions," Noah suggested.

"He'll come after me. I know he will."

"You need time to think about your options," Tommy said. "Why don't you get in your car and leave Holy Oaks for a week or two, just until things calm down and Lonnie's behind bars."

The sheriff leapt at the idea. "What will folks say? I don't want them thinking I'm running away."

"They won't think that," Tommy said. "You're entitled to take some time off, aren't you?"

"Sure, I am," he agreed. "And maybe...just maybe, I won't never come back. I'll leave it all here, won't pack a thing, so my boy won't think I'm gone for good. Then he won't come looking for me."

"They'll catch him and put him behind bars," Noah said. "You be sure to let Father Tom know where you are."

The sheriff was suddenly in a hurry to get out of town. He was walking out the door when he stopped and turned to Laurant.

"He's been skimming money from the very beginning," he said.

"Who?" Laurant asked. "Brenner?"

Lloyd nodded. "He'd tell his backers at Griffen it was gonna cost a hundred grand to buy a store, then offer half that amount to the owner and pocket the difference. He's got himself an account, but I don't know where it is. You might want to look into that before the town meeting."

"Yes, I will," she said.

The sheriff turned to leave again, but Nick stopped him.

"How deep are you in all of this, Lloyd?"

Lloyd turned away. "I helped him some. I'll

testify against him. Maybe if I help make this right, I won't have to serve time." He gave Nick a hopeful glance, and then spoke to Tommy. "I'll let you know where I am. I'll come back when you call me." He shuffled back like a broken-down old man and placed his gun and badge on the table, then walked out the door.

They watched him leave.

"You sure you want to let him go?" Noah asked Nick.

"Yeah, he won't go far," Nick answered.

Nick tried to get Wesson on his cell phone, but he didn't answer. Then he tried Feinberg and got his voice mail. His frustration mounted. He kept glancing at his watch. Morganstern should have landed in Houston by now. Why the hell hadn't he returned his call?

Tommy had gone back into the pantry in search of potato chips, and Nick followed him. Laurant heard him tell her brother that he shouldn't let his guard down until Nick was convinced Brenner was the unsub.

The two stood in the pantry and talked. It appeared that Tommy was doing most of the talking. Laurant was so busy watching the two of them, she didn't notice that Noah was watching her.

"Stop worrying," he said.

She turned her attention to her food. "I'm not worrying."

"Sure you are. You think Nick's going to tell Tommy that he slept with you."

461

She didn't even think about trying to deny it. She looked into those devilish blue eyes and asked, "Are you always this blunt?"

"Yeah, I am."

"How did you know?"

"The way both of you are avoiding looking at each other. I've known Nick a long time," he added. "But I've never seen him this uptight. I figure you're the reason."

She picked up a chicken wing and then put it down. "Nick might tell Tommy."

"You think so?"

"Yes, I do, and Tommy's going to be upset, being a priest and all."

"Maybe," he shrugged. "But you're a big girl now, and it really isn't any of his business."

"He won't see it that way."

"So how long have you been in love with Nick?"

"How do you know I am?"

He laughed. "I know women."

"Meaning?"

"Meaning I know you're not the kind of woman who would go to bed with a man unless you loved him. Nick knows that too. You must be scaring the hell out of him now."

"I do scare him. He doesn't want any of the things I want, but he doesn't want to hurt me. Last night was a mistake," she whispered. "And now it's over," she added. She tried to sound as though she'd already moved on, but she knew she'd failed when Noah patted her hand.

"Did it feel like a mistake last night?"

She shook her head. "No, but like you just said, I'm a big girl. I can get on with my life. I'm not so easily shattered."

"No, of course you aren't."

"You're humoring me, aren't you?"

"Uh-huh."

"Let's talk about something else," she suggested. "Could I ask you something?"

"Sure. What do you want to know."

"How come Wesson dislikes Nick so much?"

"It goes way back," he said.

"But what started the antagonism?" she asked with another quick glance at Nick.

"I guess you could say it was a cat that started the rivalry, although now that I think about it, Nick's attitude also played a part. He was new to the section, and he thought he knew it all. Morganstern had only just gotten the okay to run the Apostles, and Nick was his second recruit."

"Who was the first recruit?" she asked.

"I was," he answered with an arrogant grin. "Pete was handpicking his agents, getting them from outside and putting them through his own special training program. Wesson was dying to be a part of it. Actually, I think from the very beginning he wanted to run the program, but that wasn't going to happen."

"Did Wesson become one of Morganstern's recruits?"

"No. Morganstern didn't take him in, and that really chafed."

"So that's what started it?"

"No, it was a cat," he patiently repeated.

"There was this particular case. A three-year-old girl was missing, and the FBI was called in. Wesson was on the rotation schedule, and there was no way he was going to let one of Morganstern's hotshots come in and take over. Wesson wanted to solve the case and solve it quick."

"Did he?"

"No, but Nick did. Here's what happened. The little girl was with her mother in a department store. The building was real old, with wooden floors that squeaked and groaned when you walked on them, and high plastered ceilings, and big old vents along the baseboards. It was drafty and cold inside. The building was located near the warehouse district and the city market right next to the river. It was a nice little shopping area, all the buildings had been buffed and restored, but there was a problem with rats, and so the owner of this particular family-owned department store kept a cat there."

"Go on," she urged, wanting Noah to finish before Nick and Tommy returned.

"It was around noon on the Saturday before Christmas, and the store was crowded with last-minute shoppers. It was real chaotic and loud, with Christmas music blaring, but one salesclerk happened to notice a man in his midthirties wandering around the store. She thought he might be a shoplifter. He was wearing beat-up old clothes and a long gray raincoat. She said it was dirty and torn. She couldn't give a great description other than to say he was thin and had a scraggily beard. She told us she was going to call security, but then she saw him heading for the front door, and she thought he was leaving. She was being pulled in twenty different directions by impatient customers.

"A customer in line remembered seeing the man squat down next to the little girl and talk to her. She said the mother had elbowed her way to the counter and was digging through her purse, looking for her charge card, and she didn't notice her daughter was talking to the stranger. Then the customer said the man got up and walked away."

"Did he take the little girl?"

Noah didn't answer the question. "Another customer said she almost tripped over the child when she darted out in front of her. The little girl was chasing the cat," he added. "About five or ten minutes later, the mother was frantically searching for her daughter. Everyone was helping, of course, and then the clerk remembered the man in the raincoat, and the customer remembered she'd seen him talking to the child. The security officer called the police while the owner called the FBI. To his credit, Wesson got there fast," he added. "Morganstern got the call from Wesson's superior and wanted Nick and me to get a little experience, and so he sent us in, but neither one of us could get there until late that night. I came in from Chicago, and Nick caught a plane out of Dallas. He got in about fifteen minutes before I did, rented a car, got a map, and picked me up."

"Wesson wasn't happy to see you, was he?"

"That's putting it mildly. It didn't matter to us though. He didn't have any authority over us. We reported to Morganstern and no one else. Wesson was extremely reluctant to share what he had with us, and that really pissed...I mean, angered Nick. When he gets mad, his temper's worse than mine," Noah said with admiration in his voice.

"What did he do?"

"He let Wesson know what he thought of him. Nick could have been more diplomatic, but, anyway, he backed Wesson into a corner, and Wesson told him he had a suspect, and that the situation was under control, which, of course, wasn't the case. Wesson also went on record as saying that Morganstern's team was a waste of time and money, and that Nick and I should go home and find real jobs."

"In other words, butt out."

"Yes," Noah said. "Of course, we didn't care what Wesson thought or wanted. We had a job to do, and we were going to do it with or without his approval. While Nick was looking around, I got one of the other field agents aside and read his notes."

"Was the little girl all right? Just tell me, please. Did you find her in time?"

"Yeah, we did, thanks to Nick," he said. "It was one of those too few happy endings."

"How did he find her?"

"I'm getting to that," Noah said. "Everyone

left the store. It was around two in the morning, and it was freezing inside that building. Wesson had set up a command post at the police station a couple of blocks away, and every available man was out on the streets searching for the man in the raincoat. Nick and I were standing on the curb outside the store, trying to figure out what we were supposed to do. The security officer was locking the doors to go home when Nick told him he wanted to go back inside. He convinced the old man to turn the alarm off and give us the keys.

"Both of us went through the building from top to bottom again. We found nothing, so we left. I was driving," he said. "I wasn't sure where I was headed. I was just trying to clear my mind the way Morganstern taught us, and I remember I had just driven past a hospital when I asked Nick what the hell we were going to do, being squeezed out by Wesson the way we were."

Noah paused to smile and then added, "Nick didn't say anything. He popped a piece of gum in his mouth, and I figured he was doing the same thing I was trying to do. You know, trying to clear his mind. And all of a sudden, he turned to me and said, 'So, where's the cat?'

"We started doing what Morganstern would probably call a little free-associating then. Kids love animals, most do anyway, and a customer had reported she'd seen the little girl chasing after the cat. We both figured out what might have happened then. I was driving like a bat out of hell, trying to get back to the department store as fast as I could, but then

I saw the hospital emergency entrance, and I pulled in. Nick and I went running into the emergency room, flashed our badges, and grabbed a doctor who was just going on break. Nick told him he was going with us and to bring his stethoscope with him."

"The little girl was still in the store, wasn't she?"

"Sure she was," he said. "She went in one of those big old vents after the cat," he explained. "Crawling around on the floor by the walls, no one would have noticed her, as busy and crowded as the store was. The vent didn't hold her, and she went down two and a half floors and got trapped on a ledge above the basement. The fall should have killed her," he added. "She had hit her head and was unconscious when we finally got to her. The cat stayed with her. We could hear the faint meowing through the stethoscope."

"But she was all right."

He smiled again. "Yeah, she was okay."

"You and Nick must have been jubilant."

"Yeah, we were, but we were also frustrated with ourselves at the same time. Both of us had missed the obvious. We let the guy in the raincoat get in our way," he said. "We should have noticed the vent the girl crawled into was a little bit off-kilter from the others, but we missed it. And we shouldn't have taken so long to notice the cat was missing."

"You found her within hours of your arrival," she pointed out.

"But if we had been more observant, we could

have cut the time in half. We were damn lucky she was still alive. She could have been bleeding down there, and if that had been the case, we would have been too late."

Laurant knew that nothing she could say would change his opinion of his performance.

"Normally, Wesson would have been just as happy and relieved as everyone else," he said.

"He wasn't?" she asked, surprised.

"He isn't a monster, or at least he wasn't back then," he qualified. "But jealousy was eating him up. Sure he was happy the little girl was all right..."

"But?"

"Nick deliberately left him out. He should have told Wesson what he suspected and let him run with the ball." Noah paused for a moment. "Yeah, that's what he should have done, but I'm glad he didn't. Tit for tat, as childish as that was. And in his defense, and mine because I backed him, we were young and stupid back then, and neither one of us gave a damn about career politics. We still don't. Nick had to be sure the kid was there, and so did I. Anyway, Wesson found out about the girl after the fact, from Morganstern. Nick and I were already on our way to the airport. Nick had wanted to prove a point, but he had humiliated Wesson, and ever since then, the mere mention of his name or mine gets the same kind of reaction as pouring salt on an open wound. Neither one of us have had to work with him since, until this case."

Laurant propped her elbow on the table,

resting her chin in the palm of her hand. She stared at Noah, but didn't really see him. She was thinking about the story he had just told her.

Until this moment, there had been a tiny little hope in the back of her mind that Nick would quit his job. And, oh God, how selfish and wrong she had been to want such a thing.

"Life doesn't have any guarantees, does it?" she said.

"No, you've got to grab what you can while you can. Nick's good at what he does, but he's burning out. I can see it in his eyes. The stress is going to kill him if he doesn't get some balance in his life. He needs someone like you to come home to at night."

"He doesn't want that."

"He may not want it, but he needs it."

"What about you?"

"We aren't talking about me," he said. "You and Nick are something else, you know that? Being on the outside, observing, it's really easy to see what's going on. Want me to enlighten you? I'll warn you in advance. You won't like what I have to say."

"Go ahead," she said. "Enlighten me. I can take it."

"Okay," he agreed. "Here's the way I see it. You and Nick are both trying to alter reality. You're both running away from life. Don't argue with me until I'm finished," he told her when he saw she was about to interrupt. "Nick's trying to close himself up, to distance himself from everyone, even his family, and that's a big mistake in his line of work. He needs to *feel*, because that's the only way he's going to stay sharp and focused. I can see he's getting to the point where he doesn't want to take a chance on feeling anything at all because that would make him too damned vulnerable. If he keeps going this way, he's going to become hard and cynical. And he sure as hell won't be any good at his job. Now as for you..."

"Yes?" She straightened in the chair, tense now as she waited to hear his verdict about her.

"You're doing the same thing, just in a different way. You're hiding out here in this little town. I know you don't see it that way, but that's what you're doing. You're more afraid of taking a chance than Nick is. If you don't put yourself out there, you can't get hurt. That's how you view life, isn't it? And if you keep going this way, you're going to turn into a bitter, old, dried-up prune, and a coward to boot."

She knew Noah wasn't deliberately trying to be cruel, but what he had just said devastated her. Was that how he saw her? Laurant shrank back and gripped her hands together. A coward? How could he think she would ever become a coward?

"I don't believe you understand—"

"I'm not finished. There's more. Want to hear it?"

She braced herself. "Yes, go ahead."

"I saw one of your paintings."

Her gaze flew to his. "Where?" she asked, astonished. Why did she feel the sudden pang of fear?

471

"It's hanging in Tom's bedroom," he told her. "And it's one of the most powerful paintings I've ever seen. You should be damned proud of it. I'm not the only person who thought it was incredible. The abbot wanted to hang it in the church. Tom told me he stole the painting from you. He also told me that you keep all your paintings wrapped up tight and hidden away in your storage closet so no one can see them. That's one sure way to beat rejection, isn't it? It's safe. Like the kind of life you're building here. Well, guess what, babe. There's no such thing as a safe life. Bad things happen, like your brother getting cancer, and there isn't a damned thing you can do about it. You're sure trying though, aren't you? Maybe thirty years from now you'll have convinced yourself that you're content with your perfect, safe life, but I assure you, it's going to be lonely. And by then, the amazing talent you have will probably have dried up."

Laurant shuddered under the weight of the future Noah had just described. He was forcing her to open her eyes and take a hard look at herself.

"You don't know what you're talking about."

"Yeah, I do. You just don't want to hear it."

She bowed her head as she mentally argued against his bleak prophecy. Perhaps when she'd first moved to Holy Oaks, she had been running away from life. But it wasn't like that now. She'd fallen in love with the town and the people, and she had become involved with the community. She hadn't just sat back and let the world revolve around her.

Noah was right about her painting. She had always considered it too personal to share with anyone else. It was a part of her, and if others saw her work and rejected it, she felt that they would be rejecting her.

She had been a coward. And she would lose what little talent she had if she kept on this path. If she didn't experience life, how could she possibly translate it onto canvas?

"I don't throw them away," she admitted hesitantly. "I keep the paintings."

Noah grinned. "So maybe you might want to think about unwrapping them one of these days and letting other people see them."

"Maybe," she said. After a moment's reflection she looked at him and smiled. "Yes, maybe I should do that."

Noah took his plate to the sink and rolled up his sleeves as he prepared to do the dishes. He was complaining about the fact that the abbot wouldn't spend the money for a dishwasher while he worked.

Laurant wasn't paying any attention. She was still lost in thought. Noah had just given her a wake-up call. He'd opened a door for her, and she had the choice of going outside or pulling the door closed again.

When Tommy came back into the kitchen, Noah said, "I told Laurant you took one of her paintings."

Tommy immediately took a defensive stance.

"I stole it, and I'm not sorry. You want it back now, don't you?"

"Which one was it?" she asked. Suddenly, she was very hungry. She took a bite of the chicken and reached for a cold biscuit.

"The only one I could get my hands on," he said. "It was in front of the others in the closet. I didn't even know what I was taking until I got it home and unwrapped it. And do you know what's a crying shame, Laurant. It's the only painting you've done that I've ever seen. You keep them hidden away, like you're ashamed of them."

"But which one was it?"

"The kids in the wheat field with all that light shining down on them. I love it, Laurant, and I want to keep it. You know why? Because there's such joy and hope in it. When I look at it, I see heaven smiling on the children. It's as though the streams of light are actually God's fingers reaching down to touch them."

Emotion welled up inside her. She knew that he meant every word he'd said. Joy and hope. What a glorious compliment. "Okay, Tommy. You can keep it."

Her brother looked shocked. "Really?"

"Yes," she answered. "I'm so happy you like it."

Nick wasn't about to be left out. "Damn it, I want to see it," he said.

"All right," she agreed.

Noah winked at her, and she suddenly felt like laughing. "Yes, I mean it, but I'll warn you, it's not one of my best efforts. I can do much better."

Nick's phone rang, interrupting the conversation. Smiles vanished in a heartbeat, and the atmosphere in the kitchen became tense with anticipation. Nick answered as he walked into the pantry for privacy.

Pete was on the line, and he had stunning news. Tiffany Tara Tyler's phone had been found in Steve Brenner's white van, neatly tucked under the front seat. This new evidence put a lock on the case. They had their man.

"Did they find any prints?"

"He wiped it down, but he was a little sloppy," Pete said. "He missed a spot on the bottom of the phone. The tech found what looks like a partial thumbprint next to the metal charger. He thinks it's going to be enough for a solid match. It looks like they're about to wrap this one up, Nick."

Nick was shaking his head. "It doesn't feel right," he said. He paused and then added, "So that's it. Case closed. Right?"

"Just about," Pete agreed. "There's other evidence, of course," he said. "But as I understand the situation, Agent Wesson didn't share what he had collected against Brenner with you."

"How did you know that?"

"I spoke briefly with Agent Farley."

"So Wesson has enough to convict?"

"With the woman's phone in his car? Yes, he has quite enough."

"That could have been planted."

"We don't believe that's the case," he said. "Had you been given information as it was being collected, I think you'd be feeling more confident that Brenner's our man. You were kept out of the investigation," he added. "And I plan to address that problem with Agent Wesson's supervisor first thing Monday morning. This will not happen again," he added emphatically. "As for you, I suggest you take Father Tom fishing. Relax a little. God knows, you've earned it."

Nick rubbed the back of his neck, trying to ease the knots of tension. He was weary and frustrated. "I don't know, Pete. My instincts are telling me that this is all wrong. I think maybe I'm losing it."

"Your objectivity?" Pete asked.

"Yeah, I guess. I really did figure it all wrong. Tell me something. They're running a voice match from the confessional tape and Brenner's interrogation, aren't they?"

"Yes, of course they are."

"Brenner hasn't confessed, has he?"

"No, not yet."

Nick was filled with self-doubt. Maybe he just didn't want to believe what was staring him in the face. From the very beginning, Wesson had put him in the position of trying to work the case blindfolded. Tiffany's phone was found in Brenner's van. That should have clinched it. And yet he still wasn't convinced.

"Why are you fighting this?" Pete asked. "We've had a good result here."

476

Nick sighed. "Yes, sir, I know. I guess I do need to take some time off. You were right," he finally admitted. "I got too personally involved."

"With Laurant?"

"You saw that coming?"

"Oh, yes."

"Yeah, well, I'll deal with it. You'll let me know what the lab results are?"

"Yes," Pete promised. "Give my best to Father Tom and Laurant."

Nick disconnected the call and stood in the pantry for a long minute staring into space. He was trying to work it out in his mind, to go with it, to believe that it was over. He told himself he was trying to make the case more complicated than it was. Some cases were easy. Like this one. Yeah, it was finished. Case closed. They had their man.

And still the nagging doubt wouldn't go away.

The nightmare was finally over. Tommy and Laurant were astounded to learn that Tiffany's phone had been found in Brenner's car. Nevertheless, both brother and sister were overjoyed that the killer was now behind bars. When Noah suggested they celebrate, Tommy nixed the idea. He reminded him that two women had been murdered and said that he was going to go into the church to say a prayer for the souls of Tiffany Tyler and a young woman named Millicent.

"He sure was good at masquerading his voice when he was whispering to me in the confessional," Tommy said. "He fooled me all right," he added with a shake of his head.

"He fooled all of us," Laurant said. She felt weak with relief. She decided to join her brother in the church for a prayer.

She stood and looked directly at Nick when she asked, "So you and Noah will be leaving soon, won't you?"

"Yes," Nick answered without a second's hesitation.

"No reason to hang around, is there?" Noah looked at Nick as he asked the question.

"No," he answered curtly. "No reason."

Laurant turned away so he wouldn't see how his words had hurt her. She knew she was overreacting. From the beginning, she had known he would leave when his job was finished. His life was in Boston. He had stopped everything to help his friend, but now he would, of course, need to get back home.

"Places to go, people to see...," she said.

"Right," he agreed.

Tommy was holding the door for her. "Come on, Laurant. Quit dragging your feet."

She put her napkin down on the table and hurried after her brother. Nick and Noah followed. When they reached the back of the church, Nick pulled Noah aside while Laurant and Tommy went on ahead to one of the pews and knelt down together.

There were at least a dozen workmen rushing around trying to get the church ready in time for the wedding. Five of them were dismantling the scaffolding from the center aisle while a couple of others were folding up the tarps and carrying paint cans outside. The people from the local flower shop were standing up front, holding vases of lilies, impatiently waiting for Willie and Mark to finish wet mopping the steps and marble floor in front of the altar.

Nick and Noah moved under the balcony to get out of the way when the double doors opened behind them and two strapping men rolled in a baby grand piano on a dolly.

"Where do you want this, Father?" one of the men asked Noah.

"I don't know," Noah replied.

"Geez, Father. This thing's heavy. Could you find out for us?"

Justin hurried down the aisle toward them. He was carrying a video camera and had a long, red extension cord looped over his shoulder. He slowed to say hello.

"Do you know where the piano's supposed to go?" Noah asked him.

"Sure I do," he answered. "They're putting the choir on the south side of the church in that little alcove."

He backed out of the way so the men could roll the piano around to the side aisle.

"How come they don't just use the organ?" Noah asked.

Justin turned to answer. "They have to get those pipes cleaned first. The abbot says all the dust in the air will mess up the chords if it isn't cleaned before it's used again."

"What are you doing with the video camera?" Nick asked.

"I've been roped into filming the ceremony from the balcony," he explained. "Michelle's father asked me. He's already got a professional guy filming downstairs, but he wants all the angles covered I guess. I don't mind doing it," he added, grinning. "He's paying me a hundred dollars, and I can use the money. Besides that, he's invited Mark and Willie and me to the reception, and we'll get free food and beer. You coming to the wedding?" he asked Nick.

"Wouldn't miss it," he answered.

"See you later then," Justin said as he raced on. "I just hope the church is ready. We've got a heck of a lot of work to get done before seven."

They moved out of the way again so Justin could open the wrought iron gate and go up the stairs to the balcony.

"Okay, what were you going to tell me?" Noah asked as he followed Nick to the back pew.

"It doesn't feel right."

"Brenner?"

Nick nodded. "Maybe I'll be convinced when I hear the reports. They've got a thumbprint, a partial anyway, and they're working on a voice match with the confessional tape. When the results are in confirming Brenner's the unsub, then I'll relax. Until then..."

"You want me to stay."

"Yes. I know Pete's going to be calling you with another assignment—"

"I'll try to fend him off. Besides, we're going to hear what the techs have concluded by tonight. Tomorrow at the latest."

"I really appreciate this, Noah."

"If it doesn't feel right to you, then of course I'm staying. Do I have to keep wearing this dress?"

Nick smiled. "You probably should keep wearing it until you leave Holy Oaks. Too many people know you as a priest. Let's leave it that way."

He looked Noah up and down and then

asked, "Where are you hiding your gun? Ankle strap?" he guessed as he glanced down at Noah's feet. The tips of his black tennis shoes were protruding from the hem of the long robe.

"Too hard to get to," Noah answered. He lifted the full sleeve covering his left arm. The holster holding the gun was strapped just below his elbow. "Thank God for Velcro."

"Nice," Nick said.

"Tell me something. Don't you think you should tell Tom and Laurant you still have reservations?"

"What am I going to tell them? The evidence is pretty conclusive, and God only knows what else Wesson has on Brenner. Besides, Laurant and Tommy have been living under a tremendous strain, and Laurant's been looking forward to her friend's wedding. I want her to be able to enjoy herself tonight. You keep your eye on Tommy, and I'll watch out for her."

"No, I'm not going to work that way. You do what you want with Laurant, but I'm telling Tom to stay sharp. I don't want him to relax until you're convinced."

Nick nodded. "Yeah, okay."

"Did you tell Pete how you're feeling about this?"

"Yes."

"And?"

Nick shoved his hands in his pockets. "I'm not being objective because I'm too personally involved."

"He could be right."

"When the reports are in, I'll stop worrying."

"Then what?"

"We go home," Nick said. "Another day,
another case."

"You're just going to walk away from her,
aren't you?" Noah sounded incredulous.
"She's the best thing that ever happened to
you, but you're too chicken to take the chance.
You're nuts. You know that?"

Nick responded to the question by turning
around and walking away from his friend.

CHAPTER

30

Michelle's father returned from the abbey at
a quarter of six to report that the scaffolding had been removed, and the red
carpet had been rolled down the center aisle.
The florist and her assistant were frantically
working to tie the bouquets to the ends of each
pew. It would be close, he told his wife, but
he was sure the church would be ready when
the wedding march began.

Michelle's mother, a vision in blue chiffon,
continued to worry, but the bride took all

the last-minute wrinkles in stride. She sat on the bed with her back against the headboard and watched Laurant dress while she caught her friend up on the latest gossip she'd heard.

"They've got an APB or a ABP—whatever it is—out on Lonnie now. They're going to charge him with arson and hopefully lock him away for the rest of his life. He's gotten away with so much in the past couple of years. He deserves to rot in prison." She paused to take a sip of lemonade. "And everyone is still in shock about Steve. Don't pin your hair up, Laurant. Leave it down."

"Okay," Laurant agreed. She picked up the peach silk dress she'd draped over the chair and slipped it on. She had her back to Michelle as she zipped the dress up and adjusted the bodice. Then she turned around, the full skirt floating about her ankles. "What do you think? Does this work or not? I could wear the blue Versace, but I thought this color would blend better with the dark pink dresses the other bridesmaids are wearing."

Mrs. Brockman walked into the bedroom to try once again to hurry her daughter along. She came to an abrupt stop when she saw Laurant.

Both mother and daughter appeared to be speechless. Laurant felt self-conscious under their close scrutiny. "Say something, Michelle," she demanded. "Do you like the dress or not?"

"You look like a princess in a fairy tale," Michelle whispered. "Doesn't she, Mother?"

"Oh yes," she agreed. "My dear, you look exquisite."

Michelle awkwardly scooted off the bed and held on to the post as she stood. Her mother noticed her grimace. "Is the new brace still bothering you?"

"A little," Michelle admitted. Her gaze was locked on Laurant. "If I could look like that... Turn around and look in the mirror. Mother, Laurant doesn't have any idea how beautiful she is. She doesn't see herself the way the rest of the world does. I should make her wear a grocery sack over her head because every eye in the church is going to be on her."

"No, they'll be staring at the beautiful bride." Laurant laughed then. "Well, you *will* be beautiful as soon as you get your hair out of those ridiculous jumbo rollers and put some clothes on. Or were you planning to wear that old robe down the aisle?"

"Yes, that's it, Laurant. Hurry her along. She won't listen to me, and she's going to be late for her own wedding," Mrs. Brockman said as she turned Michelle around and gave her a gentle nudge. "I'm too old for this stress," she added. "I was already old when I had Michelle," she reminded them.

Michelle grinned. "Yes, Mother. I was your change of life baby, and I changed your life."

Her mother smiled. "You've been a blessing. Now get dressed, or I'm going to send your father in here."

Michelle tightened the belt on her robe and began to pull the Velcro rollers out of her hair.

"Laurant, your bra's showing," she said. "Just below the straps."

485

Laurant tugged on the bodice, but the white lace continued to show. "I don't have any other bras with me."

"Then don't wear one," Michelle suggested.

Her mother gasped. "Laurant will not go bra-less into the house of God."

"Mother, I'm not suggesting she go topless. No one will know if she's wearing a bra or not. The dress is lined."

"God will know," her mother announced. "I'll get the safety pins."

As soon as the door closed, Michelle said, "She's a nervous wreck, and so is Daddy. He got all teary-eyed this morning. He told me he was losing his little girl. Isn't that sweet?"

Laurant pulled out the chair for Michelle so she could sit at the vanity table.

"Yes, it is sweet," she said. "Did you remind him that you and Christopher will be living two blocks away?"

"It's not the same," she said. "He's going to cry when he walks me down the aisle, and I'll be crying too if the church isn't ready."

Laurant picked up the brush and handed it to her friend. "Do you realize how lucky you are? You have such wonderful, loving parents, and you're about to marry the most won-derful man. I envy you," she added in a sigh.

Michelle looked at her friend in the mirror. "It won't be long before I'm helping you get ready for your wedding."

Laurant could have told her the truth then, that it had all been a lie and that she and Nick weren't getting married, but she kept silent. Today was Michelle's day, and Laurant didn't want her friend to waste a minute thinking about anything else.

"Don't you get all emotional on me," Michelle said. "Or mother will put you to work too. That's how she deals with tears," she explained. "She had poor Dad running all over town. She's already made him make two trips up to the abbey. First, she made him go see for himself that the scaffolding was down. Then, she made him go back to make sure the flowers had arrived. And before he drives us to the church, he has to drive over to the Vandermans and pick up Bessie Jean and Viola."

"Bessie Jean has a car."

"Have you ever seen her drive it?"

"No, but I've seen the car parked in her garage."

"She doesn't want to drive. She wants to be chauffeured. She told mother, with so much traffic these days, it's too dangerous."

"Traffic in Holy Oaks?"

They burst into laughter. "And get this," Michelle said. "She blames the Catholics. Says we drive like maniacs."

They laughed again, but Michelle's mother put an end to the conversation when she came rushing into the bedroom once more. "Michelle, I'm begging you now. Get dressed." She headed for Laurant, brandishing two giant safety pins. "These were all I could find," she said apologetically as she pinned Laurant's bra to the lining of her dress.

Michelle was finally ready to leave for the church at twenty minutes to seven. Her beaded ivory wedding gown was a replica of a Vera Wang design she had seen in a magazine and had fallen in love with. It fit her petite hourglass frame perfectly. When she finally turned to face her mother and Laurant, they both grabbed Kleenex to dab at their eyes and wipe their noses.

"Oh, Michelle, you look beautiful," Laurant whispered. "Absolutely beautiful."

"Your daddy's going to cry when he sees you," her mother announced, sniffling.

Michelle adjusted her veil, then squeezed Laurant's hand. "Okay, I'm ready. Let's go."

As she was walking to the door, she called over her shoulder, "Don't forget to wear the necklace I gave you."

Laurant would have forgotten it if she hadn't been reminded. At the rehearsal dinner Michelle had given to all the bridesmaids a delicate gold chain as a gift.

It took her several tries to get the necklace fastened. Then she stood in front of the full-length mirror and put on her diamond-studded earrings. The only other piece of jewelry she had on was the engagement ring. She held her hand out in front of her and stared down at the shimmering diamond for a long moment. Tears blurred her vision. Her heart felt as though it were breaking. She thought about taking the ring off and giving it back to Nick right away, but then she changed her mind. She would wait until after the reception.

Then she would give him the ring and say good-bye.

Dear God, how was she ever going to get through that? Oh, how she loved him. He had come into her life and changed it forever, for he'd made her open her eyes and her heart to the world around her, and to all the possibilities.

How was she ever going to live the rest of her life without him? Laurant stared at herself in the mirror and slowly straightened her shoulders. Her heart would be broken, yes, but she would survive.

Alone, once again.

CHAPTER
35

The church was packed. Everyone who lived in Holy Oaks must have been invited to the wedding, Nick decided as he stood in the back of the church, watching the people stream in. Several families tried to go upstairs, but the iron gate that led to the balcony was locked, and there was a hand-printed sign above simply stating, DO NOT ENTER. Some of them tried to jiggle the lock loose and go

489

upstairs, but then they gave up and went searching for a seat inside the main church.

Two ushers were urging guests to move closer together so that more people could squeeze into the pews even as the mother of the bride was being escorted down to the front row.

Nick was trying to stay out of the way. Laurant was with the bridal party in the vestibule below the balcony. The door was open, but the bride couldn't be seen. Nick watched Laurant open the closet door and put her purse on the shelf inside. She caught his eye as she was turning around, gave him a hesitant smile, and then walked out of sight.

Michelle's father had partially closed the double doors leading into the church so that the wedding party could line up and not be seen. He stood with his hand on the doorknob, peeking inside as he waited for Father Tom to come out of the sacristy and take his place in front of the altar. Worried and flustered that he would forget what he was supposed to do or that he would trip on his daughter's dress and send her flying, he began to pant with anxiety. In a few minutes, he was going to be giving his only daughter away. He reached into the vest pocket of his rented tux and pulled out his handkerchief. It was while he was mopping his brow that he remembered the Vanderman sisters.

"Oh, good Lord," he whispered loudly.

His daughter heard him. She saw the panic on her father's face. "What's wrong, Daddy? Did someone faint?"

"I forgot the Vanderman sisters," he told her.

"Daddy, you can't go get them now. The wedding's starting."

Her father frantically looked around for help, spotted Nick, and grabbed him. "Could you please go and get Bessie Jean and Viola? They're probably waiting on the curb, and I'll never hear the end of it if they miss this wedding."

Nick didn't want to leave Laurant, but he was the only available man or woman in the vestibule who wasn't in the wedding. He knew it would only take him a couple of minutes to drive down the hill and back, yet he still resisted.

Laurant saw his hesitation. She got out of line and hurried over to him, her silk skirt rustling about her ankles. "You won't miss anything," she said loud enough for Michelle's father to hear. Then she leaned closer and whispered, "It's over, remember? You don't have to worry about me anymore."

"Yeah, okay," he agreed reluctantly. "I'll go in just a minute, after you walk down the aisle."

"But if you hurry—"

"I want to watch you walk down that aisle," he said a bit more abruptly than he'd intended. In truth, what he wanted was to make sure she was in Noah's capable hands before he left the church.

He didn't give her time to argue further, had that been her inclination. He slipped inside the church and hurriedly walked along the back wall to the south corner so that he was directly in line with the sacristy. He was waiting for Tommy and Noah to come out so that he could get Noah's attention.

A hush of expectancy fell over the crowd. Then Tommy walked out, and with a noisy clatter, the guests got to their feet. Tommy was wearing his ceremonial white and gold robes, and he was smiling as he slowly made his way around the altar to take his place at the top of the three steps in front of the main aisle. Once he was in position, he folded his hands, then glanced at the pianist and nodded.

The second the music started, the crowd turned in unison to the double doors, craning their necks and shifting for the best view when the bride appeared at the entrance.

Noah had followed Tommy out onto the altar, but he stayed in the background by the sacristy door with his arms folded across his chest. His hands were hidden inside the sleeves of his black cassock, his right hand curled around the butt of his Glock as he slowly scanned the audience.

Nick raised his hand and motioned to Noah. The first bridesmaid had just started walking toward Tommy when Noah went down the side steps and crossed to the side aisle heading for Nick.

By the time he reached the corner where Nick was waiting, the second bridesmaid had just stepped into the main aisle.

"I got stuck doing an errand," Nick said.

"Once Laurant's down at the altar, I'll leave. I'll only be gone a couple of minutes, but I need you to cover her and Tommy until I get back."

"No problem," he assured him. "I won't let either one of them out of my sight."

Nick looked relieved. "I know I'm being stubborn about this..."

"Hey, you've got to go with your gut," Noah said. "I'd trust your instinct over Wesson's hard evidence any day of the week."

"Like I said, I'm only going to be gone five, ten minutes tops."

Noah nodded toward the back doors. "There's Laurant. Lord, she's hot."

"You're in church, Noah."

"Right, but man oh man, does she look...good."

Nick barely glanced at her. While Noah slowly made his way back to the altar—getting waylaid by young women who grabbed hold of his hand to say hello as he passed their pews—Nick searched the faces in the crowd.

Nick spotted Willie and Mark near the front. Neither one of the men had shaved, but they had changed their clothes to short-sleeved shirts and ties. They, too, focused their complete attention on Laurant.

As soon as she reached Tommy and turned to join the other bridesmaids at the bottom of the steps, Nick went out the side door. He ran to his car, cursing loudly when he saw that the parking lot was crammed with cars blocking his exit. He got inside, started the motor, and then drove over the curb, and down the manicured lawn, trying to avoid the flower beds brimming with impatiens and rosebushes.

He went at a snail's pace until he reached the main driveway. Then he floored it and sped down the street. He was fighting the instinct to turn around and go back to the church. He tried to reason away the panicky feeling. Laurant and Tommy were safe with Noah. He wasn't going to let anything happen to them. As long as they were in church, they were okay. The ceremony and the mass would take about an hour, depending on how long Tommy's sermon ran. Even if Nick was delayed, everything would be fine.

He wouldn't be so tense if he had the results of the damned reports. What was taking so long? Nick thought about calling Pete now to find out if he knew anything more, but then he changed his mind. He knew Pete would call him the second he had the information.

He was going sixty by the time he reached the Vandermans' street and had to brake hard to come to a screeching stop in front of their driveway. The car was still rocking as Nick shoved the gear into park. Bessie Jean and Viola were waiting on the sidewalk. He left the motor running as he jumped out and ran around to the other side to open the back door for them. He noticed Viola was holding a large plastic container but didn't want to waste time asking her what it was. Besides, Bessie Jean was lacing into him, irritated that she was missing the wedding.

"I just hate to be tardy. I don't like to be late for anything, not even—"

"Couldn't be helped," Nick said, cutting into her complaints. "Let's go, ladies."

"We might as well take our time now," Viola said. "We've missed the bride walking down to meet the groom, haven't we?"

"Well, of course we have, Sister. The wedding was set to start at seven o'clock, and it's after that now."

"Let's get in the car, ladies," Nick urged, trying to hold on to his patience.

Viola wasn't going to be rushed. "Nicholas, will you be a dear and run this cake across the street? Put it in the kitchen, please. The boys aren't home."

"They're at the wedding," Bessie Jean said. "They probably got there in plenty of time too."

"I baked the cake for Justin," Viola said, "because he helped with the flower bed."

"Couldn't you take it over tomorrow?" Nick asked, his frustration near the boiling point.

"No, dear, it will go stale," Viola said. "I would carry it over, but I'm wearing my brand-new patent leather shoes, and they're pinching my toes. It won't take you but a minute," she added as she held the cake out to him.

It was quicker to do what she asked than stand on the curb arguing with her. Nick grabbed the cake out of her hands and ran across the street.

"I told you to wear sensible shoes, but you

never listen to me," Bessie Jean chided Viola.

Nick crossed the yard and ran up the stone steps. He wanted to leave the cake at the front door, but he knew Viola was watching, and if he didn't follow her instructions, she might nag him into going back.

What a pain in the ass, he thought as he shoved the door open. It was dark inside, and cool, the only sound the gentle hum of the central air conditioner kicking on. He crossed the cluttered living room, stepping on old newspapers and discarded pizza boxes and empty beer cans littering the floor. Out of the corner of his eye he saw a cockroach scurry into one of the boxes. He noticed the beer cans and bottles on all the tables and on the carpet by the coffee table, that also was piled high with old newspapers and empty beer cans. On top of the stack of papers was a large pink and yellow seashell, obviously meant to be decorative, but instead being used as an ashtray. The shell was overflowing with cigarette and cigar butts, and the air in the room was rank and stale.

The place was a pigsty. The dining room table was covered with an old, torn, paint-splattered tarp, and on top were several unopened cans of house paint and a couple of big plastic sacks from the local hardware store with paintbrushes sticking out. A swinging door connected the dining room to the kitchen, exactly like the one in Laurant's house. Nick pushed the door open and then stepped into the kitchen.

The first thing that struck him was the pungent smell. It was strong, acrid...familiar. Whatever the stringent combination was, it made his eyes tear and his throat burn. Unlike the other rooms, the kitchen wasn't cluttered. No, it was immaculate. The counters were bare, spotless, shining...like another kitchen he'd been in. Recognition was sudden. He remembered the odor...vinegar and ammonia...and he remembered exactly where he'd smelled it before. His gaze frantically searched the kitchen. Truth slammed into him like a wrecking ball. Everything clicked into place. He dropped the cake and instinctively reached for his gun as he whirled around toward the table, guessing before he looked what he was going to find. There in the center of the table, placed neatly between the salt and pepper shakers, was an extra large, clear plastic, quart-size jar of antacid tablets. Pink. The tablets were pink, just like he remembered. And right beside the jar sat a tall, narrow-necked bottle of red hot sauce. The only thing missing was the cocker spaniel trembling in the corner.

"Laurant!" He lunged through the doorway. He had to get back to the abbey before it was too late. As he ran through the living room, he crashed into the coffee table, overturning it. He leapt over the legs and ripped the front door open. The church. The bastard was going to grab her when she left the church. Shoving the gun back into his holster, he raced to get to the phone in his car.

He couldn't waste valuable time trying to reach the closest authorities. Pete could sound the alarm and get him help while Nick and Noah protected Tommy and Laurant—the pawns in Heartbreaker's deadly game.

He reached the street, shouted to Bessie Jean, "Go inside and call the Nugent sheriff. Tell him to get every available man to the abbey."

He dove into the car, leaving the door open as he reached over to pull a Glock and another magazine out of the glove compartment. He grabbed the phone and continued to shout at the stunned ladies watching him. "Go," he screamed. "And tell them to come armed."

He jerked the gear into drive and slammed his foot down on the gas pedal. The momentum shut the door as the car shot forward. He punched the speed dial for Pete's cell phone. He knew he always carried it and that the only time the power was turned off was when he was home or in the air.

He got his voice mail on the first ring. Shouting a blasphemy, Nick disconnected, then hit the speed dial for Pete's home number. As he raced up the hill, going seventy miles an hour now, he chanted into the phone, "Come on, come on, come on."

One ring. Two rings. Then on the third ring, Pete answered the phone.

Nick shouted, "It isn't Brenner. It's Stark. He's using Laurant to get to me. It was a setup from the very beginning. He's going to kill her and Tommy. Get some help, Pete. We're all targets."

Donald Stark, known to the residents of Holy Oaks as that nice, polite farmer, Justin Brady, was crouched down below the railing of the choir loft, waiting and watching for his opportunity. Oh, how he had planned for this day. The celebration was finally at hand. It was going to be his moment of glory, and Nicholas Buchanan's day of reckoning.

His good mood was being sorely tested now, though, by Nicholas. The mule was, in fact, making Stark quite frantic. Trying to ruin all of his wonderful plans by making him waste time worrying.

Once again he slowly inched up over the wall and searched the crowd below. He could feel the rage building inside and fought to contain it. All in good time, he promised himself. And then he looked again. Where had the mule disappeared to? After searching through the crowd a third time, Stark concluded he wasn't in the church. Where oh where could he have gone? And then the thought occurred to him that perhaps the mule was standing in the back, under the balcony.

Stark had to be sure. He decided he would have to risk it and sneak downstairs to look for himself. He had to be certain. Had to, had to, had to. It was imperative that the mule attend the celebration. He was the guest of honor, after all.

Keeping his head down, Stark crawled back to the bench where he'd put the key to the iron gate. He was reaching up to grab it when he heard the screech of tires. Scrambling over to the window, he peered out just as the mule's green Explorer came barreling up the driveway.

Stark grinned. "Good things come to those who wait," he whispered. Then he sighed. Everything was back on schedule. The guest of honor would be strolling into the church any minute now.

He picked up the rifle, adjusted the scope, and then got into position, hunched down on his knees beside the tripod.

The video camera was focused on the altar, and he reached up and pushed the button to start the tape. Timing was everything, of course. What good was killing Father Tom and Laurant if the mule wasn't there to watch? No good at all, Stark reasoned. He was determined to get both the murders on film too—how could he boast that he had bested the FBI if he didn't have the goods to prove it? Stark knew he was smarter than all the mules put together, and soon now, very soon, the world would know it too. The tape would mock them, prove their incompetence, humiliate them in the same way that Nicholas had humiliated him.

"You messed with the wrong man," he

whispered, his voice shimmering with hate. His fingers curled around the smooth barrel. He could feel the power under his fingertips growing stronger, more potent with each caress.

And still he waited for the pretty boy priest to finish the wedding ceremony and go up the steps and get back behind the altar table to start mass. Stark had done his homework. He knew exactly where everyone in the wedding party would be sitting. He'd been pretending to be working in the balcony while the rehearsal was going on, and he knew that the bride and groom, the best man, and the maid of honor were going to follow the priest up on the altar and sit in chairs, like royalty, slightly behind the altar table and to the right, against the north wall. Both brother and sister would be center stage in the camera's lens.

It was going to be perfect. He would kill Tommy boy first—one shot through the center of his forehead that would look absolutely marvelous on film. And while Nicholas was still reeling from the shock— who wouldn't, after witnessing his best friend's death—Stark would swing the rifle to the right and kill Laurant. The camera would be capturing her reaction to her brother's death. Stark pictured the look of horror in her eyes the scant second before he killed her, and he smiled again. It was going to be delicious. Bam, bam, thank you, ma'am. He'd get the brother and sister before the crowd had time to react. Stark was counting on the guests to panic and stampede their way like cows to the doors. He needed the pandemonium to give him time to get downstairs through the trapdoor he'd built in the floor behind the organ. He'd land in the closet off the vestibule, get outside through the front window, and blend in with all the hysterical men and women. He might even decide to have a little more fun and do some screaming too.

"So much to do, so little time," he whispered. For, in those precious two or three seconds, maybe even as many as four, before the crowd swelled from their seats, he was going to try to kill Willie and Mark. They were seated next to the main aisle, six rows from the front. Stark knew he was being greedy, but he didn't care. He had to get rid of them. He'd been fantasizing about it for as long as he'd had to endure living with them. His housemates were pigs. Vile, filthy pigs. He couldn't abide the thought of letting such garbage continue to pollute the world. No, that wasn't an option. They had to die, and if he couldn't kill them today, then he would come back and get them later. He wouldn't bother to film their deaths, however, for like the whore, Tiffany, Willie and Mark weren't worthy enough to be remembered.

He stifled a girlish giggle as he thought about the garage door opener he'd made such clever adjustments to. It was clipped to the visor in his van. No one would notice it or give it a second thought. It wasn't going to open any garage doors. No, sirree. One push of the button, and wham, bam. News at eleven.

Are we having fun yet? Oh, yes, yes indeed.

Because of Michelle's metal leg brace, she wasn't able to kneel, and for that reason Tommy married the couple at the beginning of the ceremony instead of waiting until the middle of the mass, as was the usual custom. He had great hopes for this couple. Christopher was a good, decent man and very level-headed. He believed in marriage and commitment, as did his lovely bride. Both of them had endured hardships in the past and had survived with grace and dignity, and Tommy knew that they would fight to keep their vows to each other when they hit those inevitable rocky patches.

It was a joy to marry them. He smiled as Christopher put the wedding ring on Michelle's finger. Her hand was trembling so, it took the groom two tries. Christopher was as steady as an old oak.

Tommy gave the blessing and then turned to go up the stairs. The choir began to sing "O Precious Love." While the other members of the wedding party quietly filed into the front pews, the bride and groom, flanked by the best man and the maid of honor, followed Tommy up to the altar. Crossing behind him, they walked to the chairs against the wall and took their seats. Laurant straightened the long train on Michelle's wedding dress and then sat down next to her. None of them would get up again until communion was served.

The two altar boys, cousins on Michelle's side of the family, sat on the opposite side of the altar by the sacristy door. Noah stood beside them. As Tommy was coming around the altar, he noticed Noah slouching against the wall. He frowned at him and, cupping his hand at his side, motioned for him to stand tall. Noah immediately complied.

Tommy turned to the congregation then. He bowed his head, braced his hands on the cool marble top, and then slowly genuflected.

And that was when he noticed the flowers. There, tucked under the altar was a beautiful crystal vase filled with white lilies. Tommy assumed the flowers had been placed there by the florist to get them out of the way while the altar was being prepared for the wedding ceremony. Whoever had put the white linen cloth across the marble top had simply forgotten to put the flowers back. Tommy bent down and leaned in to pick up the vase, but as he was lifting it, he saw the tiny, pin-size, red light blinking at him.

Puzzled, he leaned in to get a closer look. Then he saw the oblong block attached underneath the altar top. It was about the size of a brick covered in a mass of gray duct tape. There were red and white and blue wires protruding from the tape, and in the center was a red light.

He knew exactly what he was looking at now. It was a bomb. And from the size of it,

Tommy thought there was enough there to blow the church apart. The blinking red light indicated the bomb had already been activated.

"My God," he whispered, so stunned he couldn't move. His heart felt as though it had just stopped. His immediate reaction was to jump up and shout a warning, but he was able to stop himself in time. Stay calm. Yes, he had to stay calm. The last thing he wanted to do was cause a panic. He let go of the vase, then grabbed it before it toppled over. His hands were shaking violently now, and he could feel the sweat beading on his forehead.

What in God's name should he do? Still down on one knee, he half turned toward Noah and motioned for him to come to him.

Noah saw Tommy's stricken expression and immediately hurried toward him. He thought Tommy was sick. His complexion was as gray as the marble.

Tommy had to grip the edge of the altar to get to his feet. All he could think about was getting the congregation outside. His mind raced. He hadn't been down on his knee for more than four, five seconds at the most, but it was still long enough for the crowd to wonder what he was doing. He held on to the altar top with one hand, grabbed the vase with the other, and stood up just as Noah reached him. Tommy forced a smile on his face, put the flowers on the altar, next to the microphone, and then stepped back. He didn't want the microphone to pick up his whisper when he told Noah what he had found.

Noah moved to stand in front of Tommy with his back to the congregation. "What's wrong?" he whispered.

Tommy leaned close and whispered into his hear, "There's a bomb under the altar."

Noah's expression didn't change. He simply nodded as he whispered, "Let me have a look."

Then he turned toward the crowd, made a hasty sign of the cross the way Tommy had taught him, and knelt down. He wanted the congregation to think he was participating in the ceremony. Bowing his head, he ducked lower and leaned in. "Lord," he whispered. He'd wanted to see what he was dealing with, his hope that it was a simple, homemade device that could easily be dismantled. No such luck. One glance told him the explosive was damned complex, too complex for him to deal with. It would take an expert to figure out which wires to clip, and where in God's name were they going to find an explosives expert in a town the size of Holy Oaks?

Noah pulled back and looked up at Tommy. "Can't undo it."

As he raised to his feet, Tommy whispered. "Okay, we've got to get them all out of here. I'll get Christopher to help. You get the altar boys moving."

Tommy hurried toward the groom. He was halfway there when he stopped and motioned for Christopher to get up and come to him. He didn't want Michelle to hear what he was going to say. She was watching him closely, a puzzled look on her face, and then she

506

leaned toward Laurant and whispered to her. Laurant shook her head slightly, indicating she didn't know what Tommy was doing.

In a low, urgent whisper, Tommy said, "We've got a problem here, and I need your help getting everyone outside. There's a bomb under the altar. We don't want a panic," he added when he heard Christopher's drawn-in breath. "We can do this. They'll follow you and Michelle. Now go," he ordered.

"The grotto," Christopher whispered. "Tell everyone to follow us to the grotto, like I've got a surprise for Michelle."

"Yes, good," Tommy whispered. He quickly turned around and headed back to the altar. Adjusting the microphone, he took a breath and said, "Ladies and Gentlemen, Christopher has a surprise for Michelle. Please follow the bride and groom to the grotto at the bottom of the hill."

Christopher had already reached Michelle before Tommy began his announcement. She looked quite stunned when he pulled her to her feet, then swept her up into his arms.

"Christopher, what are you doing?" she whispered.

"Just smile, honey. We have to get out of here."

Michelle wrapped her arms around his shoulders and smiled as he had instructed. She whispered, "Am I going to like this surprise?"

Christopher didn't answer her. He strode across the altar, down the steps, and up the center aisle.

His enthusiasm made Laurant smile. Christopher was practically running. She and David, the best man, waited until Tommy had finished his announcement. Then they stood. Laurant slipped her arm through David's and followed the bride and groom, but at a much more sedate pace.

A murmur rolled through the crowd, and it became quite noisy as the wedding guests gathered up their possessions, kicked the kneelers back, and stood up to file out of the church.

Stark couldn't believe what he was seeing. They were leaving. No, his mind screamed. This was not acceptable. No one could leave. What surprise was the priest babbling about? Leaving early wasn't part of the rehearsal. The grotto? Why were they going to the grotto? What had he missed? His mind was speeding now, his thoughts getting jumbled together in his mind. Not acceptable. Laurant. She was leaving too. No, No, No. She's walking across the altar now. Tom first, then Laurant. Like he planned. But the mule, the mule had to see it happen.

The priest was speaking into the microphone again. "Those of you who are close to the side doors should go out that way. It will save time," he added.

Stark, shaking with fury, could feel his control slipping away, disintegrating, but then, just as he was about to leap to his feet and start shooting, he saw the side door open, and there he was, the mule himself, trying to get inside as the crowd was pushing out. Nicholas had finally arrived. "There now, there now, it's all right now," he whispered. He felt like shouting with joy. He was so thrilled to see the mule, he wanted to wave to him. Good to see you, Nicholas. Yes, sirree.

There was still time...show time...if he acted quickly. Swinging his rifle up, he went for his first target. "Don't laugh. Don't laugh," he whispered, but the thrill was so exquisite, he didn't know if he could stop himself. He looked through the scope as he slipped his finger on the trigger. Gentle now. Gentle now. Wait for it.

Noah had just nudged the altar boys toward the side door and was turning to intercept Laurant before she reached the center aisle. He wasn't about to let her out of his sight. She would leave with Tommy and him.

He was about twelve feet away from Tommy when he saw the beam of light bouncing across the wall. He instantly reacted. "Gun!" he shouted as he pulled his own weapon from his sleeve and raced toward Tommy. His attention was focused on the choir loft as he fired at the source of the light.

Nick had seen the laser beam skipping across the altar toward Tommy just as Noah shouted the warning. "Get down!" he yelled as he shoved his way through the startled crowd.

Tommy didn't have time to react. He heard a spitting sound, and a chunk of the altar splintered into the air. One second Noah and

Nick were shouting, and the next, Noah was firing his gun at the balcony as he made a diving leap at Tommy and knocked him to the floor. Noah's head struck the edge of the marble top as they went down, and then he fell like a dead weight on top of him. Tommy pushed himself free and scrambled to get the unconscious Noah behind cover. As he struggled to pull him back, Tommy saw the blood pouring from Noah's left shoulder.

The screams from the crowd, frantic to get out of the church, pierced the air. The aisles were crammed with hysterical men and women. Nick had his Sig Sauer in his right hand, and as he pushed forward, knocking people out of his way, he reached behind him under his jacket and pulled out the loaded Glock from his waistband. He leapt onto a pew and opened fire. Running along the tops of the benches, he fired the guns in succession, trying to keep the bastard pinned down.

Stark ducked behind the railing. What was happening? The blond-headed priest had pulled out a gun and started shooting at him, and he'd been able to get off only a few shots. He'd seen Father Tom go down, then the other priest, and he was sure he'd hit both of them.

Now he had to get Laurant. Stark inched the gun up and got her in his sights. She was down on her knees at the bottom of the altar steps. She was struggling to get up when he fired. She went down again, but he couldn't tell where the bullet had struck her. Gunshots were blazing away at him. He dropped the rifle and scrambled on his belly to get to the trapdoor. The videotape. He had to get the tape. The air around him sizzled with bullets. One nearly got him in his hand as he reached for the video camera. Couldn't get it, but he couldn't leave without it. Stark crawled to the outlet next to the organ, then jerked the cord. Gunfire and screams ricocheted around him. The camera crashed to the floor, shattering, and he reeled it toward him. A second later, he had the tape. He shoved it into the pocket of his windbreaker, zipped it closed, and then scrambled behind the organ and lifted the trapdoor. Swinging his feet in first, he slid down onto the ledge he'd built in the ceiling below. Then he reached up, pulled the trapdoor closed, and slipped the bolt in place.

There was so much noise he didn't worry about anyone hearing him kick through the ceiling. He landed in the closet, opened the door, and peeked out. No one was inside the vestibule, but he could see the swarm of people pushing and shoving to get out the front doors. Stark decided to blend in with the mob. He ran through the vestibule and then elbowed his way into the crowd. An old woman grabbed his arm to keep from being pitched forward, and gentleman that he was, he wrapped his arm around her and helped her outside.

He glanced back once and had to fight the laughter. Nicholas was probably still fighting the crowd, trying to get to the iron gate.

Eventually, he'd make it up the stairs, but would he find the trapdoor? Stark didn't think so. It had been so cleverly designed. He could just picture the mule standing there, scratching his head in puzzlement. Where oh where had Justin Brady gone? Yes, that's who the mule would be looking for, but when Nicholas next saw him, Stark was sure the FBI agent wouldn't recognize him. The beard would be gone, the farmer's haircut would be longer, styled, and dyed a different color. He'd also change the color of his eyes, maybe green or blue. He had such a nice collection of contacts to choose from, every color of the rainbow at his disposal.

Stark believed he was the master of disguises. Subtle changes, that was the ticket. Nothing dramatic, just a little of this and a little of that to make a world of difference. Why, his own mother wouldn't have recognized him today if he'd walked up to her and tapped her on her shoulder. Of course, Mother Millicent wasn't seeing much of anything these days, rotting as she was in her backyard under the petunias she was so partial to. Still, if she could see him in his farmer's getup, Stark was sure she'd get a kick out of it.

He didn't let go of the old woman on his arm but dragged her along with him as he turned the corner. He kept close to the building so that when the mule got up to the loft, he wouldn't see him if he looked out the window.

The hag was crying. He reached the side door where the crowd was spilling out of the church, and she started to resist. "Let me go. I have to find my husband. Help me find him."

He shoved her away from him and watched her fall into the bushes. Then he moved on, pushing his way through the throng of people and turning again to make sure the mule wasn't hot on his trail.

He let out a low squeal. Father Tom was rushing outside, and the crowd was parting for him. He was carrying the other priest. Tom's white vestments were bloody, but Tom didn't look any the worse for wear. And Laurant. God Almighty, she was coming out of the door with him.

He was so shocked to see that both of them were still alive and kicking, he almost shouted at them. He recoiled against the wall, his shoulders pressing into the cold stone. What to do? What to do? No time to plan, no time at all, but he had to do something before the opportunity slipped away.

A crowd surrounded Tom now. Stark watched as he slowly lowered the other priest to the grass, then knelt over him and whispered into the dying priest's ear. Praying for him, no doubt, as if that would do any good.

Only, the priest he'd shot wasn't a priest, was he? He had a gun. He was a mule, a pretender. How dare they trick him? How dare they? He was a mule all right. But now he was dying.

Stark desperately wanted to kill Tom, yet he knew he couldn't get a clear shot at him— too many people running around like chickens with their heads cut off.

He turned his attention to Laurant. Easy pickings, he thought. She was standing by the door, against the wall, trying to stay out of the way, but every couple of seconds she turned to try to look inside. She wasn't more than thirty feet away from him. He slowly crept forward. She looked dazed, and that gave him an added advantage.

He pulled the gun out of his pocket and hid it inside his jacket.

"Laurant," he shouted her name and tried to sound pitiful. He doubled over, his head down, but he peeked up at her as he called out to her again.

"Laurant, I've been shot. Please help me." He staggered closer. "Please."

Laurant heard Justin Brady call her name, and without a second's hesitation, she started toward him.

He pretended to stumble. Then he groaned loudly. An Academy Award. He should get an award for his flawless performance.

Laurant took a step in Justin's direction and a sting pinched the calf of her right leg. Most likely she'd cut herself when she'd been thrown to the floor by one of the bridesmaids trying to push ahead of her into the aisle. She could feel blood trickling down into her shoe.

She was limping but moved as fast as she could. When she was about fifteen feet away from him, she suddenly stopped. Something wasn't quite right. She heard Nick's voice inside her head. Don't believe anything anyone tells you. And that's when she glanced down and saw what was wrong.

Justin watched her take a step back, away from him. He had his right hand inside his jacket, holding his gun flush against his side. He kept stumbling toward her, half doubled over, trying to look as though he were in terrible pain.

She wasn't buying it. What was she staring at? His hand. She was staring at his hand. He looked down and then he saw it. The surgical glove. He had forgotten to remove the surgical gloves. Jolted by his own carelessness, he ran at her like a charging bull. She was turning to run away, shouting for Nicholas, when he slammed the butt of his gun against the base of her skull, silencing her scream.

Hurry, his mind told him. Get her, get her, get her. She was unconscious, falling, but he caught her around the waist before she hit the ground and dragged her back, and around the corner of the building. People were still pouring out of the church, and there were clusters of men and women and children in the parking lot, but no one tried to stop him. Did they see what he was doing? Did they see the gun pressed against Laurant's chest? The barrel was pointed upward, the muzzle under her chin. If anyone dared interfere, Stark knew exactly what he would do. He would blow her pretty little head off.

He didn't want her to die, not yet anyway. He might have to make a few adjustments, but he still had such grand plans for her. After he locked her in the trunk of his other car—the old souped-up Buick that none of the mules knew belonged to him—he'd drive somewhere safe and tie her up. There were lots of abandoned cabins up in this neck of the woods. He knew he'd find the perfect spot easily. He'd leave her there trussed up like a turkey with a gag in her mouth, and then he'd go shopping. Yes sir, that's what he was going to do. He'd buy another video camera—high quality, of course, only the best would do—and he'd purchase at lease a dozen videotapes as well. Sony if they had them, because the resolution was oh, so much better. And then he would return to his sweet Laurant and film her death. He'd try to keep her alive for as long as he could, but when the inevitable occurred and the light went out of her eyes—and it would—he would rewind the tape and relive the glorious execution. Stark knew from past experience that he would spend hours and hours watching and rewatching the tape until he had every twitch, every scream, every plea memorized. Only when he was completely satisfied would he be able to rest.

Once he had disposed of her body in the woods, he would go home. He would make copies of the tapes and send them to everyone he wanted to impress. Nicholas would get one for a keepsake, a reminder of how impotent he had been, daring to go up against the master. Another tape would be sent to the head of the FBI. The director might want to use the gift as a training tape for future mules. Stark would, of course, keep several for his own personal library—even the best tapes eventually wore out after all—and the last tape he would make would be auctioned on the Internet. Although he wasn't driven by the almighty dollar, a nice nest egg would give him the freedom to go searching for another perfect partner, and this tape would bring a fortune. There was a large following out there surfing the Internet with similar tastes in voyeurism.

Laurant lay slumped on the ground next to the van while Stark got his keys out. No one could see them, tucked in as they were between two other cars. He unlocked the door, slid the panel back, and then lifted Laurant and threw her inside. As he pulled the door closed, her long skirt got caught, but he was in too much of a hurry now to open the door again. He knew he was being sloppy, but that couldn't be helped. Things were changing so quickly—and then there was also his own forgetfulness with the gloves. He ran around to the driver's side, saw the ambulance threading its way up the drive, trying to get through the crowd and the cars. The siren was blasting away.

Stark knew he couldn't get down the driveway, which was the only exit. "Not to worry," he whispered. He started the motor and slowly edged the van over the curb. Then he gunned the engine. The van lurched forward and crashed into the rosebushes. A thorny branch flew up against the window, and Stark instinctively ducked, as though it were going to slice through the windshield and strike him. He was all but standing on the gas petal now, pushing down with all of his weight. The van raced down the grassy slope, bouncing and rocking along. Stark felt like he was flying.

He glanced in the rearview mirror and then began to laugh. No one was following him. He was as safe as a bug in a rug.

Should he do it now? Blow them all to kingdom come? The detonator was just above his forehead, clipped like a real garage door opener to the visor.

No, he wanted Laurant to watch the fireworks. He decided to stick with his original plan then. He'd blow up the abbey on his way out of town. He'd already picked the spot. Best seat in the house, at the top of the hill outside of town. He'd be able to see every brick explode. And oh, what a sight that was going to be. My God, he ought to film that too. Send it to all the television stations. News at eleven. Yes, sirree...

"Green-eyed girl, won't you wake up and play. Wake up and play...Laurant, it's time to wake up."

He glanced down at his watch and was shocked at how little time had passed. Then he heard the screech of tires, and his head snapped up. He looked in the rearview mirror and saw the green Explorer at the top of the hill. The SUV was soaring through the air, the front tires coming down as Stark watched in disbelief. His rage was uncontrollable. "Not acceptable," he screamed as he pounded his fist against the steering wheel.

The van careened onto the main street, sideswiped a parked car, and slid into a spin sideways. Stark slammed his foot down on the gas pedal, sped forward, and fishtailed around the next corner. He was going eighty now as he raced toward the park. The van almost turned over as he took another corner on two wheels, but it righted itself as he swung the wheel hard to the left. He turned yet another corner and there it was, the back entrance to the park through the preserve.

The mule wasn't behind him now, and Stark was certain he'd lost him. Giggling, he slowed down and entered through the joggers' path. The van bounced along the black tarred surface, the left wheels gliding on smooth surface and the right wheels grinding over rocks at the edge of the path.

He thought he heard Laurant groan. He had to stop himself from leaping over the seat and tearing her skin to shreds with his bare hands. The rage was getting stronger, and the thoughts were coming so fast now, he was having trouble concentrating. He reached up to adjust the mirror so he could watch her. She was huddled in a ball on her side with her back to him, and she wasn't moving. His mind was playing tricks on him, convinced now that she hadn't groaned. He'd only imagined it.

He was so busy watching her, he almost drove the van into the lake. He swerved back onto the road, then adjusted the mirror again so he could see behind him. Because of the angle the path took, he had to slow the van down even more. He couldn't slow his mind though. He glanced over his shoulder to look at Laurant again, but it wasn't Laurant that he saw. It was the whore, Tiffany. He shook his head. Then, just as suddenly, it was Laurant again.

He wanted to stop and close his eyes. He wanted time to clear his mind and get organized again. He had to be organized. He was a planner, meticulous down to the very last detail. He didn't like surprises. That's why he was so rattled, he decided.

The surprise of seeing the blond priest leap in front of Tommy boy. The priest with the gun, shooting at him. The priest who wasn't a priest at all. Stark couldn't get over the fact that the mules, as stupid as they were, had actually tricked him. He'd never considered, not for one second, that Tommy's friend was a mule in disguise.

Oh yes, that was why he was so rattled now. They had tricked him into making a mistake. He sighed then. He could feel himself becoming centered again. The thoughts weren't bombarding him. Control, that was the ticket. He was getting his control back.

"Almost there," he sang out to Laurant. He slowed the van so he could edge through the pines when he reached the main road that wound around the lake. Then he increased the speed again. The Buick was about two hundred yards away, parked between the trees behind the abandoned shack. He couldn't see it yet, but he knew it was where he'd left it, ready and waiting.

"Almost there," he repeated. All he had to do was drive around the entrance to the park, then along the curve, and hide the van among the trees.

He had just reached the road to a cabin when he saw the green Explorer again. The SUV shot through the entrance of the park and then slowed to take the turn.

"No." Stark slammed on the brakes. There wasn't time to back the van, turn it around, and try to outrun the mule. He couldn't go forward either. Nicholas would see him and block him. What to do? What to do? "No, no, no, no," he chanted.

He threw the gear into park, grabbed his gun, and jumped out of the van. Because he'd removed the door handles on the inside so that his lady friends couldn't escape while he was busy driving, he had to run around and open the door from outside.

He shoved the gun in his jacket and then reached with both hands to lift her. A new plan. Yes, a new plan. He could do it. He'd get her inside, where it was nice and dark, and he'd work on her there, with the doors locked. The mule would be outside, trying to get in, listening to Laurant's screams. The mule would make mistakes then. Yes, he would. And then Stark would kill him.

Laurant didn't come awake slowly or in a foggy daze. It was instantaneous. One second she was unconscious, and the next she was struggling to keep from screaming. She could feel the bile burning the back of her throat.

She was inside his van. She didn't move for fear he would see her in the mirror or hear her groping around the floor for something to use as a weapon. She dared a quick look, saw the toolbox, but she'd have to move to get it. It was against the back door. Could she get out that way? Swing the door open and jump? Where, where was the latch? She squinted in the darkness, and then she saw the gaping hole in the back door. The madman had taken the handles off. Why would he do that? Her feet were pressed against the side door, but she couldn't see if that handle had been removed as well unless she moved, and she didn't dare.

She was shaking now and tried to stop, terrified that he would notice and know she was awake. The van hit something in the road. She was lifted and then thrown into the back of the front seat. A second later, she was thrown back again when the van lurched forward. She felt cold metal against her chest. The safety pin was pressing into her skin. She fumbled to get it open. Her hands were trembling, so she almost dropped it, and she caught the whimper before it escaped. She unhooked it and then bent it until it was straight. She didn't know what she was going to do with it, but it was the only weapon she had. Maybe she could drive the pin through his throat. Tears stung her eyes. Her head hurt so much, it was an effort to think at all. Was he watching her now? Did he have a gun in his hand? Maybe she could jump him from behind, surprise him.

Ever so slowly she moved her legs up, thinking she could turn and spring upward, grab him by the neck, and then slam his head into the steering wheel. But something was holding her. Her skirt was caught. She was afraid to turn her head and look for fear that he would see.

The van suddenly came to a jarring stop. She did drop the safety pin then, but she grabbed it from the floor before she heard the door open. Where was he going? What was he going to do?

Oh God, he's coming for me.

She had to be ready. When he tried to get her out of the van, she would have to be ready. Frantic, her hands violently shaking now, she hooked the pin around her middle fingers, just above the knuckles. The metal fastener dug into her skin, tearing it as she hooked it there, anchored so that the long needle was sticking straight out. She cupped her left hand around it, trying to hide it.

Don't let him have his gun in his hand. Please, God, don't let him have the gun. She couldn't spring up and get him if he was holding the gun. He'd kill her before she touched him. *If he does, I'll wait. Make him carry me. He'll put the gun down if he has to carry me.*

The van moved when the side door was slid open. Her eyes were tightly closed, and she was trying not to cry as she silently prayed.

Help me, God, please help me...

She could hear his harsh breathing. He grabbed her by her hair and jerked her toward him. When he bent down to pull her out of the van, she opened her eyes and saw the gun. His fingers dug into her sides as he lifted her over his shoulder.

He was strong, terribly strong. He ran with her draped over his left shoulder as though she weighed no more than a speck of dandruff on his collar. Laurant's eyes were wide open now, but she didn't dare lift her head for fear that he'd feel the movement. As long as he thought she was unconscious, he wouldn't focus on her. She recognized the abbot's cabin up ahead.

She heard a car coming toward them, then the madman's obscenity. He ran up the steps and then suddenly stopped.

She heard him jiggling the doorknob, but it was locked. A second later, a gunshot went off next to her ear. She flinched, and she was sure he felt it.

Stark was in such a state to get inside, he kicked the door and tore it from its hinges. He hit the wall switch, and two lamps, one on a credenza by the door and another on a table upstairs on the balcony, lit the cabin. Still holding her on his shoulder, he ran across the front room and into the kitchen. He put the gun down on the countertop and ripped the drawers open, throwing them to the floor.

"There we are," he cried out gleefully when he found the drawer of knives. He grabbed the biggest one there. A butcher knife. It looked old and dull, but he didn't care if it was sharp or not. The work he intended to do wasn't going to be meticulous. There simply wasn't time. This one would do nicely. Yes, sirree.

He grabbed his gun, then turned around and ran back into the living room, kicking drawers and utensils out of his path. When he reached the center of the room, he stopped and shrugged her off of him. She crashed into the coffee table, then hit the floor, her left side taking the brunt of the impact.

He waited until she was down, then grabbed her by her hair again and jerked her up to her knees.

"Open your eyes, bitch. I want you to look out the door. Look at the mule when he comes running in here to save you."

As he was speaking, Stark realized he had the butcher knife and the gun in the same hand. He let got of Laurant and switched the knife into his left hand. "There now," he said. "What was I thinking? Can't shoot and cut with the same hand, now can I? Look at me, Laurant. See what I have for you?"

She was still up on her knees, and he squatted down behind her. Her body would shield him from Nicholas's gun. He held the knife out in front of her face. "Now what do you think I'm going to do with this?"

Although he hadn't expected an answer, he was still disappointed she didn't cry out when she saw the knife. She would though, once he started working on her. Oh yes, he knew how to get what he wanted. He was still the master.

He jabbed her left arm with the knife and then chuckled with delight when she screamed. Blood spurted down her arm, thrilling him. Then he stabbed her again. "That's my girl. Keep screaming," he encouraged, his voice eerily high-pitched, manic with excitement. "We want Nicholas to hear you."

He squatted and waited. He braced her shoulders against his with his arm as he pointed the barrel of the gun at the open doorway. He kept his head down behind hers, but he peeked around her toward the door. He jabbed her again, just for fun, but she didn't cry out this time. He put the tip of the bloody knife against the side of her neck.

"Trying to be brave, Laurant? When I want you to scream, by God, you will."

He heard her whimper and smiled. "Don't you fret. I won't shoot the mule right away. I want him to watch me kill you. Tit for tat," he sang. "What's taking Nicholas so long? What's that boy up to? Maybe he's trying to sneak in through the kitchen door. Oops, there isn't one. He can't do that, can he?"

Had he not been talking, he would have heard the faint creak above him. Nick had come in through the bedroom window. The tree branch had given way just as he grabbed hold of the window ledge, but the crashing noise he heard from inside covered the sounds he made.

The bedroom door was open, and Nick crept forward. He could see Laurant and Stark below the balcony, halfway across the room, facing the front door. Nick had his gun in his hand, and the Glock tucked into the back of his waistband.

He couldn't get a clear shot at the bastard. If the bullet went through his body it would hit Laurant. He couldn't risk it. He couldn't go down the stairs either. Stark would see him. What the hell was he going to do?

Laurant looked up and saw the shadow on the ceiling. It moved ever so slightly, and she knew that Nicholas was upstairs. It was only a matter of time before the man behind her saw the shadow too.

"Why are you doing this, Justin?"

"Shut up. I have to listen for the car. I have to hear the mule coming."

"You were too quick for him. He must not have seen your van, and he turned north instead of south. He's on the other side of the lake."

Stark strained to hear footsteps on the gravel outside, but he was smiling. "Yes, I was quick, wasn't I? A mule can't outsmart me."

"Are the mules the FBI?"

"Yes," he answered. "You're a very clever girl, aren't you?"

She had to keep him talking. Keep him focused on what she was saying so he wouldn't look up. "Not as clever as you. Why did you choose me? Why do you hate me?"

He drew his thumb down the side of her face. The rubber glove was cold. "Hush that talk. I don't hate you. I love you," he crooned. "But I'm a heartbreaker. I break hearts."

"But why me?" she persisted. Her head was down, but her eyes were looking up, watching the shadow slowly creep forward.

"It wasn't you at all," he said. "The mule killed my wife, and then he bragged about it in the newspapers. Oh yes, that's what he did. All that time and energy training her was wasted. She was almost worthy. I sought perfection, and she was getting there. Yes, she was almost perfect. Then Nicholas killed her. They called him a hero. He ruined my life, and they called him a hero. They said he was oh so smart. I couldn't have that, now could I? I had to prove to the world that I was the master."

She cringed at the hate in his voice. She didn't have to ask him another question. He seemed to want to explain himself to her. The words were coming faster now. He wanted to tell her everything, to brag about how he had fooled the mules.

"When I read the newspaper article and knew who had killed my wife, I had to retaliate. Don't you see? I was forced into it. Your brother was mentioned in that article, and I wanted to know more about good old Father Tom. I read that he and Nicholas had been best friends since they were little boys. At first, I thought I'd kill Tom and then go after the mule's family, but then I thought, why give Nicholas the home advantage? Holy Oaks was the perfect town for what I had in mind. It's so nicely isolated. I did my research, found out everything I could about Tommy boy, and imagine my joy when I found out about you.

"It was Nicholas I was after all along," he said, snickering. "Until I met you. Then I wanted you too. When I met my wife, there was something about her that reminded me of my mother. You remind me of her too. There's a bit of perfection in you, Laurant. Had the circumstances been different, I would have trained you.

"Mother's gone now. There wasn't any reason to keep her alive. She had reached perfection, and I knew I had to act quickly."

The second he stopped, she blurted, "Who was Millicent? Did she exist?"

"Ah, so you listened to the confession tape, did you?"

Laurant felt him nod against her. She could smell the sweetness of the Calvin Klein cologne mixed with the sourness of his breath.

"Did Millicent exist?" he repeated. "Maybe."

"How many did you kill?"

"None," he answered. "Mother doesn't count. You can't kill perfection, and whores don't count either. No, of course not. So you see? You'll be the first."

He saw the shadow. He swung Laurant around and shouted, "I'll kill her. I'll kill her. Drop the gun, Nicholas. Do it now, now, now, now."

Nick had reached the center of the balcony. He put his hands up, but he didn't drop the gun. The dining room table was directly below him. If he could just get over the railing...

Stark was still crouched behind Laurant,

trying to turn her with him so he could face the steps and be fully protected by the wall behind him.

"Drop the gun," he shouted again. "And come on down and join the party."

"You aren't going to be able to sneak away this time," Nick said. He could see the terror and pain in Laurant's eyes. If he could just get Stark to move away from her, just a fraction, he could get a shot before he got hit.

"Of course, I'm going to get away. I'm going to kill Laurant and you, and I'm going to get away. The stupid mules will be looking for the hick farmer, Justin Brady. I'll cut her throat if you don't drop the gun."

Nick let go of the weapon. It barely made a sound as it dropped onto the carpet at his feet.

"Kick it out of reach," Stark screamed, waving his gun as he gave the order.

Nick did as he was told but slowly lowered his hands until they were level with his shoulders. Every second would count. He wanted his hands close to the railing so he could spring when the time came.

"I've got you now, don't I, mule?" Stark shouted. "Who's the master? Who's the hero? They'll never find me, no sirree," he gloated. "They don't even know who I am."

"Sure they do," Nick called out. "We've always known. You're Donald Stark, and we know all about you. You're a sleazy film-maker. You use prostitutes to simulate amateur death scenes. S and M crap," he added.

"And not at all believable. Homemade stuff. You barely make a living selling the junk on the Internet, and you've got a lot of dissatisfied customers."

"Dissatisfied?" he roared.

Nick deliberately shrugged. "You aren't any good, Stark. You ought to get in another line of work. Maybe you can learn a new trade in prison."

Stark's full attention was riveted on the balcony. He wasn't aware that he'd lessened his grip on Laurant or that the butcher knife was now pointed at the doorway and not her throat.

"No, no, you're lying. No one knows who I am. You heard me talking to Laurant, and that's how you knew—"

"No, we've always known who you are, Stark. The article we planted in the papers was just a way to draw you out. Everyone was in on it, even Tommy. We planned it down to the last detail."

Nick could tell that his lies were working. The bastard's face was red and blotchy, and his eyes bulged out of his head. He hoped that Stark's anger would push him into making a mistake. Nick only needed a second.

Come on. Come and get me. Forget about her. Come after me.

Laurant saw the barrel of the gun coming up, felt the madman tense against her. He was trying to lift her up with him as he shot Nicholas. Then she heard the screech of tires on the gravel outside the door. Was it Tommy?

Oh, God, no. Whoever came through the doorway was going to get killed.

"No," she screamed as she twisted in his arms and threw herself backward. Her shoulder knocked the hand grasping the gun. Stark fired wild, hitting the glass picture window, shattering it. The blast was so close to her face she could feel the burning heat. She kept fighting and pushing as she turned, but he was too strong. He wouldn't let go of her and he wouldn't be budged.

Stark's gun was swinging upward again just as Jules Wesson appeared in the doorway. Crouched down in a shooter's stance, his arms straight out, both hands on his gun, he waited for a clear shot.

Laurant jerked back, twisted again, fighting with all her might until she faced Stark. Then she attacked. Her left hand gripped his wrist, her nails digging into his skin to keep him from aiming his gun. He tried to reach around her to stab her hand with the knife, and that's when she swung her right hand up and rammed the needle into his eye.

Stark screamed in agony. He dropped the knife and reached for his eye, howling like a crazed animal.

The second Laurant struck Stark, Nick grabbed hold of the railing and swung over. Shouting for her to get down, he reached behind him, grabbed the Glock and started firing.

Stark leapt to his feet, uncontrollably firing

his gun. Wesson dove for the floor, narrowly missing a bullet, and then he too fired.

Nick fired in midair, landed on the table and fired again. The first bullet struck Stark in the chest. Wesson blew the gun out of Stark's hand, and Nick's second shot got him in the head as he was turning to run. The third shot struck his leg.

Stark was on his back, one leg twisted under him, his eyes wide open. Nick stood over him, his chest heaving as he tried to calm his rage.

He heard a sob and whirled around. Laurant was on the floor, her head in her hands. As Wesson rushed forward, Nick dropped to his knees beside her and put his hand out to touch her. Then he stopped. He was afraid that he would only make her pain worse.

"I'm so sorry," he whispered. "God, I'm sorry. I brought this to you and Tommy. It's all my fault."

She threw herself into his arms. "Is he dead? Is it over?"

He wrapped his arms around her and held her tight. Then he closed his eyes. "Yes, love. It's over."

By the time Nick got Laurant to the hospital, Noah was already in surgery. Tommy, still wearing his bloody vestments, came running down to the emergency room when he heard from one of the nurses that his sister had been brought in.

He was in a panic until he saw Laurant. She looked like she'd been through hell, but she was breathing and even managed a smile for him. Nick was sitting on the exam table beside her with an arm around her waist. Tommy thought he looked worse than she did, which was pretty awful. Nick's face was gray and his eyes had a haunted look.

"What about Noah?" Nick asked. "How's he doing?"

"They're working on him now," Tommy said. "The doctor told me the bullet didn't hit anything major, but he's lost a lot of blood. He's going to be all right," he assured them. "It's just going to take him time to get his strength back."

"How long has he been in surgery?" Nick asked.

"About twenty minutes. He's going to be

534

okay," he said again. "You know Noah. He's as tough as nails."

Laurant sagged against Nick and put her head down on his shoulder. Her hand was in his lap and he was holding tight. She hurt everywhere. She couldn't make up her mind which was worse, her head, her arm, or her leg. Every inch of her body seemed to be throbbing in pain. She wanted to rest, but when she closed her eyes, the room began to spin, and that made her queasy.

"Where the hell is the doctor?" Nick demanded.

"They just paged him," Tommy said. He went to his sister and gently brushed her hair away from her face. "You're going to be all right." He tried to sound certain, confident, but it came out all wrong, and it sounded like he was asking her a question.

"Yes, I'll be fine. I'm just tired."

"Can you tell me what happened? You were right behind me when I carried Noah outside."

"He was there, and he called to me. He asked me to help him. I think he told me he'd been shot."

"Who called to you?"

"Justin Brady," she answered. "Only he wasn't really Justin." She looked up at Nick. "I started to go to him, but then all of a sudden I could hear your voice in my head."

"What was I saying?"

"Don't believe anything anyone tells you. I knew something wasn't right about him, and then I saw the glove on his hand. It was a surgical glove, I think." She looked at Tommy when she added, "I tried to run, but he came after me, and the next thing I remember was waking up inside the van. He took all the door handles off, and I couldn't get out. Tommy, he showed me a photo of his wife. It was at the picnic, and he showed me a photo. He must have stolen it from someone."

"Let's talk about this later," Tommy suggested when he saw how upset she was. "Don't think about it now."

"Tommy, go hurry up the damned doctor," Nick barked.

The physician, a cranky, middle-aged man named Benchley, pulled the curtain back just as Tommy was leaving to go search for him. The doctor took one look at Laurant and then ordered Nick and Tommy to leave.

He had the bedside manner of a Doberman. Shouting for a nurse to assist him, he glared at Nick when he didn't move from the table, and once again he demanded that he get out.

Nick refused to leave Laurant's side. He wasn't diplomatic in his refusal either. Fear made him hostile and belligerent, but he didn't realize he was up against someone just as belligerent. Dr. Benchley had worked in Los Angeles for over twelve years in a rough inner-city emergency room. He had seen and heard it all. Nothing intimidated him, not even an armed FBI agent with a crazed look in his eyes.

Tommy stepped in and dragged Nick out of the cubicle before he lost his temper.

"Let him examine her," he said. "He's a good doctor. Come and sit down in the waiting room. If you sit near the door you can see the curtain from there."

"Yeah, all right," Nick said, but he couldn't sit down. He paced instead.

"Why don't you go upstairs and wait," Nick suggested. "Have the nurse page me when Noah comes out of surgery. I want to talk to the doctor."

"I'll go up in a minute," Tommy said. "But I want to stay here until Benchley finishes with Laurant. She's gonna be okay," he added, more of an assurance for Nick. "She looks bad, but she'll be all right."

"What if she isn't? Tommy, I damn near got her killed. He had her. The bastard had her pinned up against him with a knife at her throat. I've never been so scared in my life. One second. That's all it would have taken to cut an artery. And it's all my fault. I should have known."

"Known what?"

Nick didn't immediately answer. He was reliving those terrifying moments when he'd crept out onto the balcony and had seen Laurant down below.

"I should have figured it out before he had a chance to grab her. And he never should have gotten that chance. Because of my incompetence, Laurant almost lost her life, and Noah got hit."

Tommy had never seen Nick so shaken. "Stop beating yourself up, and tell me what happened. What should you have known?"

537

Nick rubbed his brow and leaned back against the wall. His gaze was glued to the curtain. He told Tommy everything, and when he was finished, Tommy needed to sit down.

"My God, you both could have been killed." He expelled a long breath and then stood. "You know I'd tell you if I thought you screwed up."

"Maybe."

"You didn't screw up," Tommy insisted. "Pete didn't figure it out either," he pointed out. "You did your job. You protected my sister, and you saved her life."

"No, she pretty much saved herself. There I was, armed to the hilt, and she nailed the son of a bitch with a safety pin. Drove it right through his eye."

Tommy flinched. "She's going to have nightmares."

A nurse came to get Nick. There was a phone call from Agent Wesson. Tommy stayed in the waiting area. He happened to look down and only then realized he was still wearing his white robes and that Noah's blood had saturated the garment.

"Wesson found the detonator. It was inside a garage door opener," Nick said when he returned.

"What about the bomb?"

"The abbey's blocked off, and the bomb squad is coming in by helicopter."

"You know, Nick, we're fortunate that no one else was hurt." He was trying to keep his friend occupied because he knew Nick had about had it with waiting. He didn't want him to go charging into the exam room.

"Why is the doctor taking so long?"

"He's being thorough."

"You're awfully damn calm."

"One of us has to be."

"You're her brother, and you saw what she looked like. If I were you and it was my sister in there, I'd be going nuts."

"Laurant's a strong woman."

"Yeah, she's strong, but a body can only take so much."

The curtain parted, and the nurse who had been assisting the doctor came out. She went to the desk and picked up the phone.

The doctor stayed with Laurant. One-on-one with his patient, his bedside manner had vastly improved. He was kind, soft-spoken, and gentle. He numbed the arm and cleaned the wound. Then he wrapped it in gauze to keep it protected until the plastic surgeon arrived to stitch it. He probed the area around her left eye but stopped when she winced. "You're going to have a doozy of a shiner."

The doctor told her he was sending her to radiology. The swelling at the base of her skull worried him, and he wanted to make sure she didn't have a concussion.

"We're going to keep you overnight for observation."

He put another strip of tape on the gauze to hold it in place as he remarked, "I heard what happened at the church. Bits and pieces anyway. You're lucky to be alive."

Laurant felt numb and a little disoriented. She was finding it difficult to concentrate. She thought the doctor had asked her a question, but she wasn't certain, and she was too weary to ask him to repeat it.

"The nurse will help you get into a hospital gown."

Where was Nick? Was he out there with her brother, or had he left? She wanted him to take her in his arms and hold her. She moved her leg and bit her lip to keep from crying out. It felt like it was on fire.

The doctor was turning to leave when he heard her whisper, "I think it's bleeding again. Could I have a Band-Aid, please?"

Benchley turned around. "You need stitches in your arm. Remember I told you that the plastic surgeon was on his way?"

He was talking to her as though she were a child. He held up two fingers and asked her how many she saw.

"Two," she answered, squinting against the penlight he was shining in her eyes. "I was talking about my leg," she explained. "I fell down, and it's bleeding."

The queasiness was getting worse, and deep breaths didn't seem to be helping.

Benchley lifted her skirt and saw the blood on her slip. "What have we got here?" he asked as he gently pushed the slip up over her knee and then lifted her leg. He examined the bloody wound.

She couldn't see the injury. The skirt was

in her way. "I just need a Band-Aid," she insisted.

"You sure do," he agreed. "But first we're going to need to remove the bullet."

The surgeon had a busy evening. Pulling his cap off, he walked into the waiting room to report that Noah was in recovery. He assured Nick and Tommy that there hadn't been any surprises or complications and that the agent was going to be fine. Then he turned around to scrub again and operate on Laurant. While he worked on her leg, the plastic surgeon stitched her arm.

A nurse gave Tommy his sister's watch and engagement ring. Without a thought, he handed them to Nick.

Laurant wasn't in the operating room long, and for a short while she and Noah were in recovery together. She was still unconscious when she was wheeled into a private room.

After checking on Noah, Nick went to Laurant's room and stayed with her all night. As soon as Noah was taken to ICU so that he could be closely monitored, Tommy went back to the abbey to change clothes. Then he returned to the hospital and sat with Noah.

Pete Morganstern arrived around two in the morning. He went to see Noah first. Tommy had fallen asleep in a chair, but he woke up as Pete was reading Noah's chart. They went out into the hall to talk, and then Tommy told him where he could find Laurant and Nick.

Laurant slept fitfully. In those random moments of consciousness she called out to Nick. The anesthetic was slow to wear off. She couldn't quite manage to open her eyes, but she felt him taking hold of her hand, and she would fall asleep again comforted by his soothing voice.

"Nick?"

"I'm right here."

"I think I threw up on Dr. Benchley."

"That's my girl."

Another hour passed. "Nick?"

"I'm still here, Laurant."

She felt him squeeze her hand. "Did you tell Tommy we slept together?"

She heard a cough, and then Nick answered, "No, but you just did. He's standing right here."

She fell asleep, but this time she didn't have any dreams or nightmares.

When Pete walked into the room, he saw Nick bending over Laurant. He stood there and watched him slip the engagement ring on her finger and then clasp the watch around her wrist.

"How's she doing?" he asked, his voice low so he wouldn't disturb her.

"She's okay."

"What about you?"

"Not a scratch on me."

"That isn't what I was asking."

They walked into the hallway to talk. Pete suggested they go down to the cafeteria, but

542

Nick didn't want to leave Laurant. He wanted to be there in case she called out to him again.

And so they sat together in the hallway in chairs Pete carried over from the nurses' station.

"I came here for two reasons," he began. "First was to see Noah, of course."

"And the other reason?"

Pete sighed. "To talk to you and to apologize."

"I'm the one who messed up."

"No, that's not true," he said emphatically. "I messed up, not you. I should have listened to you. When Brenner was arrested, you told me it didn't feel right to you, and how did I respond? By ignoring everything I trained you to do. I was so certain you couldn't see the forest for the trees because of your personal involvement in this case. I ignored your instincts, and that was a mistake I won't ever repeat. Do you realize how close to disaster we came this time?"

Nick nodded. He leaned back against the wall and stretched his legs out. "A lot of people would have been killed if that bomb had gone off."

Pete began to question Nick then and didn't stop until he had heard every detail and was satisfied.

"Reading the article in the paper...yes, that's what set him off," Pete said.

"I guess so."

"His wife was almost perfect. That's what you heard him tell Laurant?"

"Yes," Nick said. "Stark's wife had to have known what was coming. Once Stark decided she couldn't get any better, that she was as perfect as she could be, he was going to kill her, just like he killed his mother. Knowing all the facts now, I think maybe her mind did snap, and that's why she took the little boy."

"We'll never know what her motive was," Pete said. "If I were to speculate, I would suggest that perhaps she thought a family would change things."

"Turn him into a doting father?"

"Something like that."

"I think maybe she wanted to end it...let us get her instead of him."

Pete nodded. "You could be right. What about Laurant?" he asked then.

"The doctors say she'll be okay."

"Are you going to be staying around?"

Nick knew what Pete was asking. "I'll stay long enough to tell her how sorry I am I got her into all of this."

"And then?"

"I'm leaving." His mind was made up.

"I see."

He glanced over at Pete. "Damn. I really hate it when you say that. You sound like a shrink."

"You can't shield your heart, Nick. Running away won't solve your problem."

"And you're going to tell me what my problem is, aren't you?"

"Of course I am," he agreed smoothly. "Loving Laurant makes you human, and that's what's frightening you. It's that simple."

"I'm not running away. I'm going back to work. What kind of a life could I offer her? She deserves to be happy and safe, damn it, and I can't guarantee that. Stark used her and Tommy to get to me. It could happen again. God knows, I've made enemies since I started working for you. What if another creep comes after her? No, I can't let that happen. I won't take that chance."

"So, you'll isolate yourself even more than you already have? Is that it?"

Nick shrugged.

"You've made your mind up?" Pete pressed.

"Damn right."

Pete knew he wasn't going to win this argument, but he felt compelled to interfere a little more. "Psychiatrists are trained to notice little things. We observe."

"So?"

"When I walked into Laurant's room, I noticed you were putting the engagement ring on her finger. I found that very curious."

Nick couldn't explain his actions. "I didn't want her to wake up and think she'd lost it. She can take it back to the store and get a refund. That's all there was to it. Now let it go."

"Just one more comment, and then I'll stop hounding you. I promise. Actually, it's a question."

"What?" he asked. He sounded miserable.

"Where are you going to find the strength to leave her?"

A week had passed since Noah was shot. The agent was recuperating at the abbey, but he was getting very little rest, what with the anniversary celebration and the constant stream of visitors, most of whom were women bearing gifts. The abbot was thrilled. They had enough home-cooked food to last a month.

Tommy had just walked one of the parishioners to the door, thanked her for the casserole, and returned to the den where Noah was sprawled out on the sofa. Tommy dropped down in the easy chair and put his feet on the ottoman. He was catching Noah up on the latest developments, but he kept getting interrupted.

"Okay, where was I?"

"You were telling me what happened with Laurant at the hospital."

"Yeah, that's right. Neither Nick nor I knew Laurant had a bullet lodged in her leg. So, the doctor comes out and tells us she's been shot. Nick goes crazy then."

"Love will do that to a man."

"I guess so," Tommy agreed. "He was already acting nuts, but this news pushed him right over the edge."

"Yeah?" Noah asked, smiling. "I wish I could have seen it. He's always so cool and calm. What'd he do?"

"He starts shouting, 'What the hell do you mean she was shot? What kind of a place are you running here?'"

Noah laughed. "Who was he yelling at?"

"Dr. Benchley. You met him, didn't you?"

"Yes. He's a real charmer."

"He's shouting back at Nick, 'Hey, Buddy, I didn't shoot her,' but Nick's out of his mind now, and I start to worry he's going to shoot Benchley."

"So, then what happened?"

"Nick wouldn't leave her side. He stayed with her all night, but he told Pete and me that, as soon as she woke up, he was going to say good-bye. He did too. He shook her hand."

Noah burst into laughter. "What'd she do?"

"She called him an idiot and went back to sleep."

"I do love your sister, Tommy."

"Nick was real determined. He had a lot of follow-up work to do, and that kept him in Nugent a few days. They found Lonnie holed up in a motel outside of Omaha. He's been charged with arson."

"What about Brenner? Did they find the bank account the sheriff told Laurant about?"

"Yeah, they did. Brenner was altering the books and stealing from Griffen, the developers. Steve's going to be going away for a long time. Hey, did I tell you what Christopher did?"

"The groom?"

Tommy nodded. "While he and Michelle were in Hawaii on their honeymoon, he spent a lot of time on the phone putting together a deal. He convinced Griffen to buy another parcel of land the city owns and leave the town square alone. The way he worked it out, some of the profits will go to renovating the square and bringing in new businesses. Christopher's done a very good thing for this town. As soon as he gets settled, he's going to hang his shingle two doors down from Laurant's store. When the store opens, Michelle's going to manage it."

"What will Laurant be doing?"

"Painting."

Noah smiled. "That's good."

"It's time for you to take another antibiotic."

"I'll wash it down with a beer."

"It's ten o'clock in the morning. You can't have a beer."

"You priests are too damned strict."

Tommy got him a Pepsi and sat down again. "I heard that Wesson is thinking about resigning."

The smile left Noah's eyes. "He should be encouraged to quit."

"You should cut the guy a little slack," Tommy said. "Nick told me he made himself a target in the cabin, trying to divert Stark and help Nick get a clear shot."

"It was too little, too late. I don't want to talk about Wesson. Pete already filled me in on what went down. So, tell me," he continued, "did Nick leave her or not?"

"She left him."

"No kidding. Where'd she go?"

"To Paris." Tommy was beaming when he added, "She won the lawsuit. She got every penny of Grandfather's money back, plus a heck of a lot of interest. She had to fly over to sign some papers."

"All's well that ends well."

"I didn't tell Nick why she went."

Noah raised an eyebrow. "What did you tell him."

Tommy shrugged. "That she went to Paris."

"Implying it was permanent?"

"I might have."

"There's no way in hell he went after her. Getting on a transatlantic flight. He'd never do that, not in a million years."

Tommy looked at his watch. "He should be landing in Paris any minute now."

Noah laughed again. "He is nuts. It was okay for him to leave her, but he couldn't stomach the notion of her leaving him?"

"Actually, he got to Des Moines before he turned around and drove back. Then I had to tell him she was gone."

"Forever."

Tommy nodded. "Tough love," he explained. "I love Nick like a brother, but I had to get tough."

"You mean you lied to him."

"Yes."

"Well, I'll be damned. I think you just committed a sin. Want me to hear your confession?"

Laurant was exhausted. She cried most of the way to Paris, and when she wasn't weeping, she was fuming because she had fallen in love with an idiot. She didn't get any sleep at all, and as soon as the plane landed, she had to go directly to the law firm's offices to sign the papers.

They wanted to celebrate. She wanted to go to Boston and find Nick, but couldn't make up her mind what she would do once she found him. One minute she thought she would kiss him, and the next she thought she would give him a piece of her mind, but then, she didn't know her mind anymore. She used to be such a practical, down-to-earth sort of woman, but Nick had changed her. She couldn't sleep, she couldn't eat, she couldn't do anything but cry.

She checked into the hotel and took a long, hot shower. She had packed a pretty nightgown, but she put on the red T-shirt with the open-mouthed bass on the front instead.

How could he leave her? The tears started flowing again, and that made her angry. She remembered his reaction when she'd told him she loved him. He'd looked horrified. She thought it was because she was complicating his life, but now she stopped fooling herself and accepted the truth. He didn't love her. It was that simple.

Laurant grabbed a Kleenex, got into bed, and called Michelle to cry on her shoulder.

Michelle answered on the first ring. She sounded sleepy. "If you're calling to tell me how sorry you are about the wedding, I forgive you, just like I did the last three times you called me in Hawaii. None of it was your fault. Okay? Mother forgives you, Daddy forgives you, and so do Christopher and I."

"He left me, Michelle."

Her friend was suddenly wide awake. "What do you mean, he left you? Nick? Where are you anyway?"

"Paris," she answered, sniffling.

"You're crying, aren't you? You lost the lawsuit. Laurant, I'm so sorry."

"I didn't lose."

"You mean you're rich again?"

"I suppose so."

"You don't sound very happy about it."

"Did you hear what I said? Nick left me. I didn't tell you the last time I called, but he left me the day after the wedding. He shook my hand, Michelle, and then he left. He doesn't love me."

"He shook your hand?" Michelle burst into laughter.

"It isn't funny. This phone call is costing money, so be sympathetic and be fast."

"Okay," Michelle said. "There, there. It will be all right."

"Now you're being sarcastic."

"Sorry," she said. "What are you going to do about him?"

"Nothing. He doesn't love me."

"I saw the way he was looking at you while

you were dancing at the picnic. It's the same way Christopher looks at me when he wants...you know."

"That's lust, not love. I scared him."

"Oh, dear. You do have a knack for doing that. There's only one thing left to do," she advised. "You're going to have to go after him. Hunt him down."

Laurant sighed. "You aren't helping. I'm feeling miserable. I hate being in love."

"Go after him," she repeated.

"And then what? I can't make him love me. I hate feeling like this. If this is what love is all about, you can have it. You know what I'm going to do? I'm going to get on with my life and forget him. Yes, that's what I'm going to do."

"Okay," Michelle agreed, and Laurant could hear the smile in her voice. "Just one question. How are you going to forget him?"

"I fell in love with him almost overnight, so it probably isn't the real thing. That makes sense, doesn't it?"

"Oh, please. Do you hear yourself? In your heart you know this isn't an infatuation. I fell in love with Christopher after our first date. Sometimes it happens that way. I just knew I wanted to spend the rest of my life with him. Go after Nick, Laurant. Don't let pride mess this up."

"Pride doesn't have anything to do with it. If he loved me, he wouldn't have left me. It's over, and I have to accept it."

Laurant felt like her heart was shattering.

Michelle was talking now, but she wasn't listening. She interrupted her friend to say good-bye. She wanted to go home, but she didn't know where that was anymore.

She called room service and ordered hot tea. Coping. That's what Nick had told her she was doing when she fixed herself tea.

She was suddenly anxious to get out of Paris. She called the airline and moved her flight up. She could sleep on the plane, she thought. She got out of bed and started packing her bags again. She had just closed her overnight bag when there was a knock on her door. Tea had arrived. She grabbed a tissue on her way across the room and then opened the door.

"Just put—"

Nick was standing in the corridor, glaring at her. She was so stunned to see him, she couldn't speak, couldn't move.

He looked awful. His hair was down in his face, his clothes looked like he'd slept in them, and his eyes looked haggard. She thought he was beautiful.

"Did you even have the chain on? What were you thinking opening the door like that? I didn't hear the dead bolt. Was the door locked?"

She didn't answer him. She just stood there staring up at him with a stunned expression on her face. He could see she'd been crying. Her eyes were red and swollen. He had to nudge her back inside before he could shut the door.

"This is how you lock a door," he said as he turned the bolt.

He had her now. He leaned against the door so she couldn't get past him. He took a deep breath, and the panicky feeling he'd been carrying around vanished. She was just a foot away from him, and the world was suddenly making sense again.

"How did you find me?"

"I'm FBI. It's what we do. We find people who try to run. Damn it, Laurant, how could you leave me like that? Without a word, you pack up and move to Paris? What the hell's the matter with you? Don't you know what you put me through? What were you thinking?" he railed. "You can't tell someone you love him and then run away. That's just damn cruel."

Laurant was trying to follow along, but Nick was talking so fast and furiously, it was difficult. Why did he think she had moved to Paris? And what made him think she was running away from him?

She was going to demand he explain as soon as she got over the fact that he was there, acting like a complete, adorable idiot.

"I'll quit," he said. He nodded to let her know he meant it. "If that's what it will take to get you to marry me, then by God, I'll quit."

He only then noticed she was wearing the T-shirt he'd bought her, and that conjured up all sorts of hot memories. He smiled that wonderful, melting smile of his, and then he pointed at her and said, "You love me."

He tried to take her into his arms, but she backed away. "You can't quit."

"Yes, I can," he said. "I'll do whatever it takes

to make you feel safe, but you've got to stop running. No matter where you go, I'll follow you. Damn it, Laurant, I'm never going to let you leave me again."

She put her hand out to fend him off when he tried to grab her. "I wasn't running away. You left me, remember?"

"Yeah, well, I came back and you were gone. You sure didn't waste any time pining away for me. Tommy didn't even want to tell me where you'd gone, but I made him."

She was starting to catch on. Her brother had become a matchmaker. "And what did he tell you?"

"That you moved to Paris. It made me crazy knowing you were so far away," he admitted. "I have to have you in my life. I want to come home to you every night. I want to grow old with you. I need you, Laurant."

She started crying again. He wouldn't let her back away from him this time. He pulled her into his arms and held her tight. He kissed her forehead as he whispered, "Will you marry me?"

"I won't marry a man who can't hold a job."

"Then I'll take the coordinator position they've offered me."

"No, what you do is too important. You have to promise me you won't stop."

"You mean it?"

"I love you, Nicholas."

"I won't quit."

He nudged her chin up and leaned down. He kissed her passionately, letting her know how much he loved her.

"Marry me, Laurant. Put me out of my misery."

Her head snapped back. She was suddenly looking stunned again.

"How did you get here?"

He wouldn't let her dodge his question. "Marry me," he repeated.

She smiled. "I want babies."

"So do I," he said. "With you, I want everything. I'll be a neurotic father, worrying about them, but with you as their mother, they'll turn out all right. We'll be a good balance for them. As long as I have you by my side, anything is possible. I love you, sweetheart."

She was fervently kissing his neck. "I already know you love me."

"Yeah? When did you figure that out?"

She hoped their babies would have his blue eyes. They were so beautiful. "When I saw you at my door. That's when I knew you loved me. You got on a plane and flew across an ocean for me."

He laughed. "Losing you was more terrifying. Besides, it wasn't all that bad."

"Are you telling me you're over your phobia?"

"Sure I am," he choked.

She smiled, kissed him gently, and whispered. "We'll go home by boat."